TH   STS

Robert W Kirby

ACKNOWLEDGEMENTS

Many thanks to my wife, Emma, for putting up with the endless hours of being ignored, whilst I wrote this novel (and for suggesting that I get started on the book in the first place). Thanks to my sister-in-law, Linda, who undertook the first read-through of the manuscript, which was very much appreciated. Thanks to my publishing team at KINDLE BOOK PUBLISHING who designed the cover and helped with the entire publication process.

CONTENTS

One

The boy stood still and silent in the undergrowth, amongst high stinging nettles and bracken, and spied on the group as they trudged up the steep hillside. Their bulging backpacks swayed, and some of them moaned and grumbled as they struggled with the incline. The boy wore full camouflage gear, though he had no genuine fear of the others spotting him. He was too good at this game. Not that he needed to be, because they were so busy bickering, they wouldn't have seen him if he'd launched a firework straight out of his arsehole. After watching the film American Ninja again last night, he was more than ready for an afternoon of stealth. He spotted a kestrel hovering on top of the hill, awaiting its chance to strike its prey. Behind the kestrel, the clouds began moving fast, and the sun flashed as it disappeared and reappeared in quick succession. He gazed back in the distance, noticing that a darker sky now blanketed the town below. The boy considered his options. How should he play this? Maybe pick them off one by one. He envisaged himself appearing behind the straggler, ghost-like, stifling their pitiful cry with one hand – a swift blade across their throat with the other. Silently dragging the victim away into the trees, before the other idiots even acknowledged what was happening. Then he smiled; he only came here for *one* of them. Being patient and waiting for the right opportunity to present itself was essential. The boy felt indestructible – like John Matrix in the film Commando. He peered up again, seeing that the idyllic summer's day was well and truly disappearing. Heavy black clouds loomed all around the hilltops. And was that… a rumble of thunder? He smiled and shivered, as he sensed the adrenaline surging through his veins at a thousand miles per hour. A storm. How perfect was this? Soon it would be time to put his skills to the test.

Two

Edinburgh, Autumn 2019

Alex stepped into the darkened bathroom, switched on the small overhead light, and stared at his reflection as he rubbed the sleep from his heavy eyes. He decided he didn't look half as awful as he felt, although if he didn't know better, he'd swear someone had removed his eyeballs whilst he slept, coated them in grit, and stuck them back in his head. He considered that he'd lost some weight, as his cheeks looked somewhat bony, but then he'd had no real appetite for a while now. Alex prodded his cheekbone, grunted and ran the cold tap, splashing handfuls over his face and head. The water cascaded over his short, brown hair, as he gripped the sink with both hands and tried to remember the last time he'd slept the entire night through. It was still dark outside, and the rain was hammering against the window. He thought he could also hear distant music, a radio perhaps, but his damned tinnitus had returned, as it always did after a bad dream, so it was difficult to tell. It rang and fuzzed, muffling his hearing. Still, on occasions, it sounded like a miniature dentist's drill inside his mind, so at least it wasn't quite to that extent today.

Alex peered into the kitchen. She hadn't seen him yet, as he stood in the unlit hallway, watching her fill the coffee machine. She was wearing her short kimono robe, with the blue floral pattern, and her pert bottom was peeking out from under it.

Alex had a sudden fleeting vision — a flash of last night's dream. Those two trees on the high hillside in the heavy wind.

Alex stepped into the room, flinching from the ceiling spotlights, which seemed as bright as a lorry hurtling towards him with its full beams on.

Natalie was scraping butter onto toast, the awful noise making him grind his teeth, and it seemed amplified, more like fingernails on a chalkboard. Then the coffee machine boiled – sounding like a bomb exploding in his brain.

Natalie yawned as she poured a black coffee. She noticed Alex, but ignored him. The radio was playing a song that was only just audible, but it sounded like a child's piercing scream in Alex's head. He hoped he hadn't lashed out in his sleep, though that seemed unlikely; at least, he thought it did.

His sleep issues started around six or seven weeks ago and had got progressively worse. His night would start with him wiggling and tossing about, and then he'd fight with his pillows as he fidgeted into the endless night. The restless leg syndrome would kick in and, for some bizarre reason, he'd get hot, itchy feet that drove him bonkers. Some nights, with medication, he drifted off, but he despised the ominous places his mind roamed during his slumber. Natalie was, in the beginning, sympathetic, and she would check he was alright when he'd awoken, disorientated and jittery, sometimes even passing him a glass of water and stroking the back of his head. He wondered if sleep deprivation had kicked in.

Natalie picked up her toast and coffee and went past him without a word. He flinched as the bedroom door thudded shut. She'd never been much of a morning person.

In recent days he was spending way too much time Googling the term *reoccurring memory dreams*. He would scout for new links, trying to find material that he hadn't already read, and he'd also purchased a handful of books from various online stores that he found of little help and now gathered dust in his office. Nothing seemed to help, though. If he was honest with himself, he didn't expect to find a miracle cure that easily.

Alex gazed at the ceiling, the spotlights blurring his vision, though he didn't bother to move from the sofa to switch them off. He heard Natalie coming through the front door, just as an image flashed in his mind – the silhouette of a boy digging between those two trees. The rain was beating down as another figure held a bright torchlight over the muddy hole. Others were watching. And Alex was with them.

Alex snapped out of his daydream and gazed at his wife. She was wearing a light-grey, pinstriped suit.

'Hey,' said Alex.

Natalie gave him a faint, sleepy smile, which made the tiny dimples on her cheeks more noticeable. Her warm blonde, shoulder-length hair was wet and windswept, her almond-shaped eyes lacked the vitality and energy they normally possessed, and the best cosmetics in the world would do little to disguise those puffy eyes. But even dog-tired and miserable, he thought Natalie looked stunning.

'Did your meeting go OK?' she asked.

'The editor cancelled on me. Wants me to email my portfolio,' he lied, 'sounds like a time-waster.'

Alex was the one who pulled the plug on the meet because he could scarcely function today. A trip to the bathroom was like running a marathon. He ached from head to toe, and his brain felt like it had been through a blender.

Natalie let out a dramatic sigh. 'Did you take them?'

Alex nodded. 'Why?'

'Because you slept. And you called for her again, Alex.'

Alex got up. It took some effort to drag himself from the sofa. He gazed out of one of the tall apartment windows and considered his reply. His wife had already quizzed him about his sleep rants, though Alex just blamed the ten milligrams of Temazepam he'd taken and changed the subject. Though suspicious, she hadn't pressed him further on the matter. He'd have to explain now, and he would have to stop taking those pills.

'Do I need to worry about her?' she asked.

Another image flashed through Alex's mind and he saw himself digging in that sludgy hole. It had all been so clear… so realistic. Just like they always were.

'Is she important to you?' she asked, frustration now creeping into her voice.

'A friend, from my past. That's all,' he said, palms against the pane of glass as he peered outside; but saw nothing but the thudding rain.

'OK, so you're dreaming about a previous girlfriend. Well, that's not weird then, Alex.'

'No, she—'

'You were shouting for that lass,' she interrupted.

'I was?'

'Ah-huh. You sounded upset. No, more, I dunno, frightened.'

'That's odd.'

'Odd,' she snorted, 'it's not odd. It's freaky. Screams of passion would be less disconcerting.'

'Come on, are you serious? You wouldn't be a tiny bit jealous? I don't believe that, Nat.'

'It was scary.'

It was rare for Alex to fall out with his wife. In their eleven years of marriage, he'd guesstimate they'd quarrelled four times. Proper arguments that resulted in a day or so of some major eggshell walking, and those toe-curling moments of awkwardness. They were best friends, and they both hated fighting, believing life was too short for all that nonsense.

'She helped me. Around the time my mum died,' said Alex, still gazing outside. The rain was getting heavier.

Natalie slumped down onto the sofa and rubbed her puffy eyelids. 'I see.'

'I'm sorry, Nat.'

'What, sorry that I resemble a pooped panda bear?' she said, flashing him a teasing smile.

Alex sat down next to her. 'I'm sure I read somewhere that pandas eat for about sixteen hours a day.'

Natalie clobbered him on the shoulder with a scatter cushion. 'Rude.'

Alex chuckled. 'But I think we're all out of bamboo today.'

'That still leaves a good eight hours to sleep,' said Natalie.

Alex patted the sofa. 'I'll crash out here tonight.'

'So, what's happening in these dreams, Alex?'

'Did I ever tell you about the time my mum died?'

'Um, you said you moved in with your gran.'

'I did… but that year, a lot of… *stuff* happened. It was all a bit crazy.'

Natalie picked up a plump cushion and hugged it. 'OK. What stuff? Does this have anything to do with why you don't ever talk about your parents, Alex?'

'I have spoken about them plenty.'

'Right, I must have forgotten those long chats. You'll have to jog my memory.'

'Yeah, but it's not like you've told me much about yours either, Nat.'

'Oh, come on, that's total shite and you know—' Natalie stopped, noticing Alex's wry grin. 'Ha bloody ha, Alex.'

'I always love hearing about your childhood,' said Alex.

'Aye, sure you do,' said Natalie, narrowing her eyes in mock annoyance. 'So, come on then, tell me what happened when your ma passed.'

Three

Kent, Summer 1988

The school gates were swarming with students trying to leave. The summer holidays were here, and the unrelenting mob made for the gates. Monitoring the exit stood a gangly teacher with a wispy beard who was doing his best to herd the elated and rowdy youngsters through. Alex glanced at the teacher, just as he scolded a mouthy lad for swearing. The teacher's focus moved to Alex as he tried to skulk past. The teacher frowned and gave him a sympathetic smile. Alex knew he felt sorry for him; all the teachers did. They treated him differently from the other kids, and it drove him crazy and just made the bullying worse. Alex was a lonely soul with no *real* friends, and a handful of wretched pupils ridiculed him daily. Sometimes they'd call him the munchkin-fucker, bird-nest hair, or the usual stuff; spastic, freak, nerd, saddo, dick-face or dip-shit. Several excited kids shoved past Alex, and he probably appeared to be the only pupil who was in no hurry to make a getaway. But he couldn't wait to leave, wishing it was forever, not just the summer. Alex heard a kid behind him cackle and say something about his trousers, which forced him to trudge along faster. He was loath to get chased home and have dog poo lobbed at him again, so he upped his pace. A lad called Brad Jenner and been the culprit, he'd flung the gungy dog turd at him using a stick and Alex had to ditch his best school jumper in a skip to avoid receiving a stern telling off from his dad for being such a pansy. One of Jenner's mates also gobbed on him last week, and he hadn't even realised until he got home and took off his shirt and found it covered in thick, frothy spit.

Alex knew his white socks were displaying with every step he took. His old grey trousers were far too short for him, but he'd not been able to find a pair that fitted properly; with his mum not currently at home, nothing was getting organised, and life was total chaos without her there to manage the house.

Just as the crowd started thinning, Alex spotted the white Ford Escort hatchback. Surely that wasn't him, thought Alex as he scrutinised the car's journey. To his dismay, the Escort stopped alongside him and the dirty window rolled down with that familiar-sounding annoying screech. Alex forced a polite grin, but his dad, as expected, looked his normal, miserable self. Alex tried to think of a reason for his dad to bother to drive over and collect him. He'd call him a lazy shit-stain if he ever dared to request a lift.

Ian was in his late thirties, and his expression seemed eternally grave and hostile. Alex tried to recall ever seeing him laugh, but the picture didn't seem to materialise. He was wearing his grey baseball cap, which was faded and frayed across the peak.

'Get in, scruff-bag,' said Ian.

Alex got in. God, the cloying stench in there. It hit him like a hard smack in the face; fags and stale sweat. And something else. Perfume. Awful, cheap perfume.

'Can I have a mint?' asked Alex, already picking them up and doing his best to avoid the filthy, overflowing ashtray.

'Yeah,' said Ian, scratching at his five o'clock shadow, as he lit a Marlboro cigarette, blowing smoke through his large nostrils as he drove away.

It was after about ten minutes of driving, in which neither father nor son uttered a word, when Ian spoke again. 'Your mum's dead.'

Ian squashed the cigarette butt into the fag heap with his thumb. Ian had relayed that news to Alex with as much heartfelt sentiment as confirming the time or asking if he wanted a cuppa. There hadn't been a shred of tenderness in those words.

Alex, mouth gaping, stared at his dad in utter disbelief. He just sat in stunned silence as his dad lit up again, sending a long plume of smoke through his lips. Ian didn't stare back at Alex, and instead just focussed on the road. Alex went numb and his world crumbled. How was he going to survive without her?

The day after receiving the bombshell news, which had blown his world apart,

Alex sat on the concrete steps outside his house. He'd been up all night crying. He examined the lavender he planted with his mum last summer. There was no life in them; they were wilting away. Alex had never known genuine loss until this point in his life. He felt so empty. Felt just like the flagging lavender in front of him. He had no purpose.

Alex walked barefoot along the path and gazed back at his home. Was it his home? It didn't seem like it anymore. The red-bricked house was a semi-detached, two-bedroom council property. It wasn't the nicest looking street around, but it had been a peaceful enough area to live in. And the neighbours were ever friendly, with a proper sense of community spirit. Some would consider the Brookacre estate, located on the outskirts of Maidstone, to be a bit on the rough side. Alex didn't think that. He'd always considered it to be a safe place to live. Until now.

It wasn't until he spotted the two girls that Alex remembered he was still wearing his damn pyjamas. His cheeks felt hot as they approached. The pair stared at him for a while, but it was Sheryl Denton, the girl in a faded jean skirt and black Bon Jovi t-shirt that spoke first. 'I'm so sorry, Alex.'

Sheryl had blonde hair and a splash of freckles on her nose and cheeks, but it was her pale-green eyes that mesmerised Alex. She looked genuinely upset as she rubbed his shoulder and stared at him with a sad smile. Alex had always considered Sheryl to be pretty, but those eyes – why hadn't he acknowledged those fascinating eyes before? He'd known her from the estate for years, and they'd played together when they'd been younger, but they'd barely spoken since going to secondary school.

'Yeah, sorry, Alex,' said the other girl, though with far less sincerity. It seemed almost a struggle for her. Janette Portland, who, like Sheryl, was fifteen, a year older than Alex, was a tall girl with light brown hair that hung naturally about her shoulders. She was undeniably pretty too, but her permanently sullen expression did somewhat mask it. Her nose was a tad hooked, Alex noticed, and together with her grey, beady eyes, gave her witch-like menace. It was common knowledge that Janette carried a notorious mean streak, so most kids were far too wise to tangle with her. Alex struggled to pair these two girls. They seemed so different. Sheryl kind with a gentle nature, whilst Janette was mistrustful, cold and spiteful.

'We should let him get dressed,' said Janette, eyeing the faded image on the chest of his pyjamas.

'Take care, Alex. Let us know if you need anything,' said Sheryl, as Janette dragged her away.

Alex saw Janette whispering in her ear as they went, and he assumed she was taking the piss out of his pyjamas. She should look in the mirror, he thought. That polka-dot dress she was wearing was hideous. And way too short. Although, in fairness, perhaps he'd outgrown He-Man and the Masters of the Universe. Sheryl turned and, to Alex's astonishment, winked at him. *So, this is what it takes to get a girl's attention,* Alex considered. *You need to lose a parent.*

Alex could smell that pungent, chemical odour that choked the back of his throat. After entering the dining room, the stench was so overpowering it made him gag. Did the woman bathe in the stuff? He wouldn't be surprised if the dense cow was mixing up her tart spray with toilet freshener. He found her eating dinner with his dad, sitting in his mum's chair and sipping red wine. Kay Barton – plastered in makeup, wearing tacky jewellery and skinny as a rake. Her nose was so thin; it looked as though she'd be able to cut a thick crusty loaf with it.

She gave Alex a sympathetic smile. 'Aw, there he is, poor little pickle.'

Alex looked past her and glared at his dad. 'We haven't even had Mum's funeral and you have already replaced her.'

'Alex, no one is being replaced, sweetheart,' said Kay. Her voice was gentle, and not the same tone she'd used earlier. It had been about ten o'clock that morning when Alex started spying on her in the main bedroom. He watched in horror as she rummaged through his mum's belongings, with the help of her equally vile sister, Tia, who had permed hair, so bleached, it appeared a piss-yellow colour. The pair laughed as they disrespectfully tossed garments to one side and joked about the huge bonfire they'd make with them. Then Tia found the jewellery box with the two curved horses. Alex gaped in outrage when she emptied it and sifted through its contents with an oily, eager grin.

'Kay, check this out. Jackpot.'

'Debatable, Tia.'

They failed to spot the piece fall from the bed and bounce towards the door. But they both noticed Alex, on his hands and knees, grabbing it. The pair glared at him.

'That's *her* boy!' said Kay.

Clambering to his feet, Alex had gripped his mum's brooch so tightly, even Hulk Hogan wouldn't have been able to prise it from his hand at that moment. 'Why are you in my mum's room?'

'It's my room. So just piss off, you annoying weirdo,' said Kay as she booted the door so hard a picture plummeted from the hallway wall. Later, when Alex studied the photo in the fallen frame, he found a crack down the middle, which separated his parents on their wedding day.

Now, here sat Kay, sipping her wine, whilst his dad slammed down his cutlery, with a brooding look slapped on his face. 'Me and Kay are good friends, Alex. We have history. You wouldn't understand.'

Alex understood all too well as he eyed their steak and chips. His stomach grumbled as Kay devoured a huge red chunk, its juices spilling down her chin.

'Did you make me some, Dad?' asked Alex, smiling hopefully.

Ian curled his lips and swore under his breath, then said, 'I'll make you a sandwich later.'

Alex guessed it would be pointless to request his usual bedtime hot chocolate and biscuits. Those days were gone forever. Sensing his presence was unwanted, Alex slipped out of the room, though not before he noticed the apologetic smile his dad gave the two-faced cow as he topped up her wine, and the sneering, wine-stained grin on her pinched, ugly face. His blood boiled, and he dashed upstairs, stomping with each step.

Alex stood in the lounge. His eyes stung and his nose wouldn't stop running. He had never cried so much as he had today. The pain he had felt as he watched his mother's casket pass into the crematorium's furnace was unbearable. He wanted to follow her into the flames just to make it stop. Luckily his nan, Penny, had been there and held him, cooing that everything would all be alright, that his mother would always be with him, watching over him.

Alex was wearing a black, crumpled suit that was way too large for him. The sleeves hung so far down; he knew he looked ridiculous.

Ian strolled in, smoking. He was wearing a shoddy dark-grey suit, with the jacket and shirt open, so his wiry chest hair poked from the top. 'Go pack some stuff, Alex,' he said.

'Where am I going?'

'I'm taking you to Penny's. To stay for a while. She said that's OK.'

'But what about all my stuff? And all my friends?'

'Right, yeah, what friends, Alex?' said Ian. 'I bet you still think Harry's your best mate.'

'You've never liked my friends. And admit it, you want me gone,' said Alex, 'so you can start a new life with that… bitch.'

'You speak about her like that again, I swear I'll throw you out now and you'll leave through the window!'

'Sorry,' sniffed Alex.

'And you need to stop blubbering every five minutes, boy.'

'OK, I'll try,' said Alex, sobbing.

'Fuck a duck, are you listening or what? It's time to get out of this house.' Ian waved his cigarette around. 'Time to get away from the memories. You won't be happy here. You know it, and I know it. Fact.'

Alex nodded. He wasn't happy here, and if he had to listen to those horrendous noises coming from his dad's bedroom one more time, he'd end up clogging his ears with superglue, sticking his head in the oven, and turning it on full heat.

Four

From the Brookacre estate, it was only a ten-minute walk to reach, what he liked to call, his rural sanctuary. Alex loved the countryside, and unlike most people in the area, he appreciated the escapism offered in the surrounding woodland areas, vast orchards, and open fields. He'd hate to live in a bustling city surrounded by tall concrete towers and suffocated by swarms of people hurrying around the busy streets.

He stood at the edge of a huge rapeseed field that stretched for miles. The sun blazed and there was a fantastic blue sky with not a single cloud in sight. Alex crouched down in the bright yellow crop as the voices approached. He watched as Sheryl and Janette strolled right past him. They were unaware of his presence and chatted quietly to themselves as Alex peeked through the crops, observing them. As they headed away, Sheryl ran her palm across the crops.

There were eight missing posters stuck to the newsagent's notice board and the reward prices varied, though one, Alex noticed, offered twenty pounds for the safe return of a mean-looking Siamese kitten. He could do with twenty quid.

Alex mooched about the shop front, waiting patiently.

'Hey,' said a girl's voice.

'Hi,' said Alex, feigning surprise at seeing Sheryl leave the shop.

'Want one?' she asked, offering him up a white bag crammed with aniseed twists.

He gingerly took one from the bag and popped the sweet in his mouth. He wasn't keen on them. 'These are my favourite,' he lied.

'Same,' she said, with her hand in the bag, rustling as she stared wide-eyed at the posters. 'Thinking about becoming the town's first cat detective?'

Alex shrugged. 'I might keep an eye out.'

'My mum reckons it is the local Chinese takeaway.'

'What?'

'Yeah, she thinks the dogs will be next.'

'Really?'

Sheryl nodded sombrely, then burst into laughter. 'Of course not, Alex. Well, I hope not. We eat from there once a month. The food is amazing.'

They both laughed.

'It's weird though, because it was the same last year. About eight or nine cats vanished. They were never found,' said Sheryl.

Once Alex and Sheryl left the newsagent's, they took a stroll together. Alex learnt some things on that short walk. Like Alex, Sheryl was an only child, and she also only had one parent, because her father walked out of the family home when she was twelve. He packed a suitcase, left for work one morning, and hadn't been seen since. It was alleged that he'd left Sheryl's mum to be with his younger, Scottish girlfriend, but this was merely a theory; no one knew for certain where Adrian Denton currently was.

So, they did at least have something in common, Alex mused. Although Sheryl worshipped the ground her mum, Eileen, walked on. Whereas Alex wasn't sure what he felt for his dad. He felt little love for the man, but he didn't hate him either. It was just an empty feeling.

Sheryl popped a Juicy Fruit chewing gum in her mouth, offering Alex one. He took a stick and smiled his thanks.

Sheryl gave him a bubbly smile, and her eyes seemed to sparkle as she did.

With Sheryl constantly on his mind, Alex could find zero enthusiasm during puzzle afternoon with his nan.

'That's four pieces to your one,' said Penny. She gave him a perky grin, slotting in yet another jigsaw piece.

Penny Dove was in her late fifties, she had a ruddy complexion, short, dishevelled, steel-grey hair and a kind smile that always made Alex think of his mum.

'You look tired, love,' she said.

Alex sighed and studied the puzzle's box. The finished picture was a large lakeside house with swans on the water. They'd barely made a dent, and there were puzzle pieces strewn everywhere.

'Smokey bacon and chips for tea?' she said, offering Alex a custard cream.

Alex gave her an unenthusiastic nod, popped a biscuit in his mouth and chewed it mechanically. His nan was always so good to him, and he kept selfishly forgetting that he hadn't just lost his mum – Penny had lost her youngest daughter. He knew he was lucky to have his nan in his life. She was always so patient with him and saw the positive in every situation.

'Chin up. We have all summer to have fun. How about we blow the dust off the Monopoly? Not played for ages, have we? All your old toys are still in the shed, Alex.'

'Thanks, Nan,' said Alex, as he smiled and found a correct piece. But Alex's mind was busy trying to solve another, more important, puzzle. How could he spend this summer with the green-eyed girl who was constantly in his thoughts?

When the group saw Alex emerge from the trees, an awkward silence engulfed them as they regarded him with odd, distant expressions. Alex panicked. What was he thinking coming out here? He searched for Sheryl and saw her sitting on a tree stump, looking at him with a quizzical expression.

'Hey, Sheryl,' said Alex, as he caught Janette's stony glare from the corner of his eye. She was leaning against a tree, sipping on a can of Fanta.

'Hi, Alex,' said Sheryl.

'What the fuck are you doing here, Clayton?' said the shortest boy. This was Gavin Gouch, a weaselly faced boy with a pointy nose, and ears that were too large for his peanut-shaped head.

'Heard Mummy died,' said Gavin. He dropped his lower lip and pretended to wipe a tear from his eye.

Ben, the bulkiest boy, who wore square-framed glasses, flicked Gavin on the ear.

'Ouch, piss off, Ben,' said Gavin.

'How'd she die, Clayton?' asked Ben.

'Cancer,' said Alex.

'That's… so shit,' replied Ben.

Ben Napier had broad shoulders, a chunky face, and a gut that hung from his tight black Fila t-shirt. Alex considered Ben was almost twice as wide as most boys he knew.

Alex knew Gavin and Ben from the Brookacre estate, though he wouldn't say they were friends. He'd known them ever since he could remember. Gavin had been invisible at secondary school until he'd hooked up with Ben, but now the lad was the school's class clown and general pain in the arse. He was notorious for his jet-black sense of humour, stupid pranks, and was a thief. It was rumoured he'd lifted personal items from a cleaner's handbag, who felt so violated, that she quit her job after twenty-five years of service to the school. This, among various other claims, circulated the school, and all of them were no doubt true, thought Alex.

Alex also knew the tallest boy with the sandy coloured hair, tied back in a ponytail, who was in his year at school. This was Mark Corker, or Corkscrew, as most kids called him. Unlike the other two, Mark had a trusting aura, and his smile seemed gentle and sincere. He was also exceptionally pale, and his small nose looked sore, with a peel of pink sunburn on its ridge. Mark wasn't a known troublemaker, but he was quick-witted and it was commonplace for Mark to have entire classrooms in stitches with his witty one-liners. Alex noticed a deep scar under Mark's right eye and considered there was perhaps a darker side to this boy that he just wasn't familiar with.

Alex looked at Sheryl again – was she embarrassed?

'So, what are you doing in Colt Woods?' said Ben. 'We don't normally see you hanging about in here. Not without your mu—' He stopped himself.

'I'm staying with my nan, she lives quite close,' said Alex. 'I can cut through this way.'

'Did Granny knit you that lovely jumper?' said Gavin, speaking in a childish voice. 'Bit warm for that today.'

Alex saw Janette sniggering at this. *I bet the silly cow went and told them about my pyjamas too,* he thought.

Gavin scooped up a plastic bottle and Alex read the label: *Killner's Triple Vision Kentish Cider. Four Litres.*

'Can I try some?' asked Alex. He wished to God he wasn't wearing his blue jumper with the stupid gaming aliens across the front. He was now boiling and knew his cheeks would be glowing.

'Can you have some—' Gavin looked at Ben and cackled. 'Is he taking the piss or what?'

Gavin unbuttoned his shorts and whipped them down together with his pants, giving Alex the full moon.

Janette let out a long sigh. 'Here we go again.'

'You think I'd get this,' shouted Gavin, slapping at his white, pimple-covered bum, 'so you, Alex cheesy-cock Clayton, can drink my lovely cider?'

There was a purple welt on his right bum cheek, with a brown edge to it.

Alex wasn't sure how to respond, so said nothing. The rest of the group were hissing with laughter, and when Ben slapped Gavin's arse, the shriek of pain that Gavin let out, made them all burst out into hysterics.

'Why is he always getting his arse out?' spluttered Mark.

'Napier, you spastic, you hit me on my pellet wound!' screeched Gavin, now sprawled on the floor and trying to pull up his pants, whilst in fits of painful laughter; his tiny penis and gonads on show for everyone to see.

Alex caught Sheryl's eye, and she raised her eyebrows, giving him a reassuring grin.

'Aw, man, put ya gherkin away. Ew!' said Janette, covering her eyes.

'Gherkin? More like a raisin,' sniggered Ben.

Janette laughed. 'Yeah, a much better description.'

Gavin pulled up his shorts, opened the cider and started necking the booze.

Only Gavin Gouch would be stupid enough to steal from Freddy, mused Alex. Freddy Killner owned a large area of farmland and for a time, ran an unlicensed cider shop from a ramshackle hut on his property. The cider was legendary and meant to be so strong, it could kill you if you drank too much; or at the very least, blind you, rot your brain or give you serious amnesia – or all of the above. It gave no alcohol content on the label, so the percentage was unknown. Freddy would drink this potent stuff daily from his personal vat in the farm shop. Alex could remember his dad talking about buying some and saying that local police officers were regulars at Killner's cider hut. Some people believed it contained a special ingredient that made it addictive. Some even said that he mixed in magic mushrooms. With all this taken into serious consideration, Alex wasn't sure why he even wanted to sample it. But he did.

Nowadays, Freddy was a local folk legend, with disturbing stories surrounding him, and since the horrific incident with his family back in the mid-80s, Freddy was a total outcast and a loner. Alex thought that a salt pellet in the bum would have been a lucky escape. The man was a total fruitcake.

'So,' said Ben, 'you best get going, Clayton.'

'Yeah, Nanny-plops will worry sick about her little poppet playing in the woods with all the normal kids,' said Gavin.

Mark grinned. 'Normal?'

'What are you saying, pal? We're normal, Corkscrew,' said Ben.

'Yeah, about as normal as ET's shrivelled wanger,' said Mark.

Alex, blinking, just stood there.

'Well, bye-bye then, Clayton,' said Gavin.

'OK. See you about,' said Alex. He gave Sheryl a sullen glance, but she didn't return his look.

'We doubt we will, Clayton,' said Gavin, 'you little Fraggle-faced faggot.'

Then Sheryl waved at Alex. 'Take care, Alex.'

Alex couldn't face the long walk back to his nan's just yet, so he sat on the stream's edge and gazed into the fast-moving water. Colt Woods was a ten-minute walk from the estate where he lived. Well, previously lived. It was a tranquil place, populated with tall elms, silver birch trees, and blankets of lush bluebells. In the sun-drenched clearings grew rosebay willow-herb, thick blackberry brambles, and stinging nettles that grew wild and tall. Throughout the summer, kids would attempt to jump across the wider stream sections, or they'd make crazy rope swings that would send them spinning across. The stream eventually expanded out into a crescent-shaped lake that was edged with crooked, ancient oaks, and thick tree roots sprouted through the banks, making it the ideal place to climb and leap from. He'd often see kids swim and play in the water, but Alex was told he must never go in, otherwise, he'd catch Weil's disease. Alex came here for walks with his mum, but she wasn't keen to let him get near the stream or lake. 'I don't want you playing on those dodgy swings. They can't be safe, Alex,' she'd say. 'You can drown in a puddle, don't you know, Alex?'

He would explain that he could swim OK, but it still made her nervous. She hated water. Alex pictured his mum's face and remembered the last time he'd seen her. He would never forget how waxy and colourless her face was. Even though she tried so hard to perk up for him, she just wasn't capable. She was so drained and frail. Alex just stood in the corner of that claustrophobic room and froze, and she said he was her special little man; and no matter what happened, she would love him for all eternity. He walked to her bedside and held her hand, and she was clammy and her hands felt so brittle, like he'd break her fingers if he held her too tightly. And he knew, somehow he just knew in his heart, that he would never see his mum again. He'd been right, because the next morning she left him forever. Whilst Alex finished his last day of school before the summer, she finally gave up her long and desperate fight with that dreadful illness.

Hands grabbed Alex, and someone shoved him forward.

'Saved you, Clayton.'

It was Ben, and he held a fistful of Alex's jumper and was stopping him from falling forward. Though he'd clearly pushed him in the first place. Alex pulled free and jumped to his feet.

'Don't shit your pants,' said Ben, 'just winding you up, stud.' Ben's face darkened as he glared at Alex. 'You know Sheryl's with us, right?' He lit up a bent cigarette he'd taken from behind his ear and eyeballed Alex.

Alex shrugged. 'So?'

'So, you're not.'

'And?'

'She was only nice to you because she felt sorry for you. Don't start getting a hard on for her, you little creep. She doesn't want to be your friend, so stop stalking her.'

'I'm not stalking her. Who is saying that?'

'I mean it, Clayton.'

'What if I take *the tests*?'

'You…' Ben sucked on the cigarette, eyes full of amusement, 'take the tests?'

'Yes, why not?'

'Not going to happen, Clayton.'

'Gavin took them,' snapped Alex.

'Yeah, Gavin might look like a shrimp that would break if you farted near him, but he's tough, and he's loyal. And he's a head-case. If I told him to drink a litre of petrol, I bet he'd do it.'

'I'll do them.'

'No, you won't.'

Chatter often drifted around the school about the notorious tests, though Alex had no real clue what they were or what they entailed. A cocky lad, called Jonathan Gambridge, was the last one to attempt Ben's initiation tests. What happened wasn't common knowledge, but Gambridge ended up with two broken wrists, one so severely damaged, the bone snapped and tore through the skin. The nurse told him he almost lost the use of his right arm. He never spoke about the actual test, and few stepped up to the challenges following that incident. Gambridge was a changed kid after this, subdued and sulky. The tests changed him.

'Guess you couldn't risk it, could you? Wouldn't look good,' said Alex. He smirked at Ben, doing his best to bait him.

Ben's eyes narrowed. 'What are you on about now?'

'If a little nobody like me could pass your tests.'

'I'd seriously shut up if I were you,' grumbled Ben, 'you'll get hurt... or worse. You can't join the Brookacre Pack... you're just... I dunno, a skinny geek.'

'So, when do I start?' asked Alex.

Where was this coming from? Alex considered he'd cracked and gone full-on crazy. It was always going to happen. He wondered why they called them the tests and not the trials. The former gave him the impression he would have to complete a written exam. He also thought their name was naff. The Brookacre Bunch had a much better ring to it.

Ben stared at Alex with a confused frown. He opened his mouth to speak but stopped upon noticing the two older lads approach on BMX bikes.

One of them was Shane Napier. He sat proudly upon what looked like a new gloss-black Mongoose BMX. Shane was sixteen, stocky, with a moon-shaped face, thin lips and a shaved head. He glared at Alex with open animosity.

Although, his skinny friend scared him far more. Patrick Lynch.

Patrick had a messy tangle of light brown hair, acne-scarred cheeks, and a rash of angry red spots on his forehead and nose. He slouched over the handlebars of his chrome BMX, and the frame to his bike looked as though he'd sprayed it himself – and made a rubbish job of it too. Though Alex knew it wouldn't be wise to bring this to his attention, because Patrick was strange, barely spoke and was quick to use his fists. Patrick became infamous at school, after an altercation with a PE teacher some two years ago. The teacher called Patrick a spotty-faced, useless pillock, and whacked him hard across the back of the head. After punching the teacher, Patrick grabbed the dazed man by his hair and scraped his face along a pebble-dash wall, shredding half the man's cheek and forehead to bits. One unfortunate witness fainted on some steps and smacked his head on a walkway railing, requiring fifteen stitches. To top it off, a chubby girl chuffed up all over the unconscious boy's face. Patrick got expelled, though somehow, no charges were brought against him for the offence; which Alex thought bizarre. The wounded teacher also left and never returned to work. Alex's morbid fascination had got the better of him, and he'd gone to the place of the altercation one afternoon. He ran his hand along that wall, touching the jagged stones on its surface. Some were as large as cinema popcorn. He wondered what poor bugger had landed the foul job of cleaning off those bits of face, but then he'd guessed it was the ancient school caretaker, cheerful Dodds. The image of the white-haired Dodds, happily whistling a tune as he hosed away skin and meticulously scrubbed away at the gore, haunted Alex for days. Alex wasn't sure if it had been true, but it was said the teacher needed skin grafts, and they'd applied skin from his bum cheek. The nicknames would have been unending.

'I have to go see my brother,' said Ben. He whacked Alex across the back, hard enough to wind him. 'Meet me here tomorrow at four o'clock. But don't say I didn't warn you, Clayton. And don't you dare back out.'

'I'll be here,' said Alex, jutting out his jaw to appear resolute and unperturbed.

'Alright then,' said Ben. Then he headed over to Shane and Patrick. He spoke to the pair in a hushed voice. Then the boys looked in Alex's direction, all three grinning in amusement.

Alex pulled off his jumper, leaving him in a tight white vest, and tossed the jumper in the water. He would show them. He'd show everyone. He was done with silly Alex Clayton – the stupid wimp who got bullied and had shit thrown at him. Because he'd do these tests. Even if it killed him.

Five

A terrible pang of guilt struck Natalie. In all their time together, Alex had doggedly avoided discussing his childhood, and he'd always been evasive about bringing his past into any conversation, but she'd never considered how distressing the situation must have been for him. She should have pushed him to open up. Natalie knew he had little to do with his father after his mother's untimely death, and Alex told her he *chose* to live with his late nan, but she didn't know the full story. Their childhoods and upbringings were a world apart, and she now felt privileged. Spoilt, even. She grew up in Haddington, a picturesque town twenty miles east of Edinburgh. The family home was a detached cottage, with an amazing riverside view. Her father, Thomas McCloud, was a charismatic man. Until he retired five years ago, he'd been a well-respected head teacher at a primary school in a neighbouring town, and there were no deranged pupils that stole, no brutal attacks on teachers or excrement tossed at other students. He was a fantastic parent and both Natalie and her older sister, Hannah, wanted for nothing. Perfect home, perfect garden, a bonkers Cairn Terrier, called Wee Tam, and best of all, a homely mother that doted on them, cooked for them and was always there when it mattered. Christ, she even got on with her sister; they were like best friends. Natalie always knew her folks had blessed her with a wonderful childhood, but hearing Alex speak about his past made her realise this even more.

'Wow,' she said. After a momentary pause, added, 'That must have been some mad crush you had on that wee lass. I bet she was a real stunner, hey?'

Alex smiled coyly. 'I'll make us a latte.'

'So, did they let you join their wee gang?' she asked.

'Well, I guess I kinda did.'

'So, you completed all their tests? What were they?'

'It was silly kids' stuff. Just a load of nonsense, really.'

Natalie nodded and watched him intently, trying hard to picture her fella as a wee little nerdy boy who so desperately needed to prove himself. Alex was a quiet, well-mannered man, handsome, and his job kept him fit and in good shape. A lot of guys in their mid-forties she knew had let themselves go, but Alex hadn't. He was rarely outspoken or argumentative. In fact, he avoided confrontation, and she'd never witnessed him lose his temper.

'You want sugar, Nat?'

'Aye, go on then,' she said. 'You never told me about your dad being such a total shite-bag. Jesus, why did you keep this quiet?'

Alex was stirring in the sugar and frowning. She considered he was perhaps regretting telling her so much, as he handed her the frothy latte in the tall coffee glass.

'I just don't think about him,' he said.

'When did you last see your dad?' she asked.

A smudge of froth appeared on Alex's lip as he sipped the drink. 'That same year.'

'Did he marry that woman?'

'No, I think she walked out on him.'

'But he could have re-married. You might have half brothers or sisters that you've never even met, Alex.'

'Stop looking at me like that, Nat.'

'Like what?'

'Like I was some sort of abused child. I wasn't,' said Alex jokingly.

'But he dumped you. Just like that. When you needed him the most.'

'I didn't want to stay.'

'Still, isnae right what he did.'

Alex shrugged. 'There was never any connection between us. I was just an inconvenience to him. I think there is a packet of almond Biscotti. Would you like some?'

'Um, sure.'

Alex went back to the kitchen, and Natalie sensed the shutters were well and truly down; it was obvious he no longer wanted to talk about this. But she craved to know more. More about these initiation tests. And she wished to know about Sheryl, and why her husband was yelling for this girl during his sleep. He had sounded so scared. It made her go cold inside, and she started to get a bad feeling that Alex had some skeletons locked away in the closet. Shit scary ones; and perhaps they were trying to break out. She was about to speak, about to ask him about Sheryl and demand answers when a mobile phone ringing jarred her thoughts. It was hers and it was Rhona.

Natalie sipped her drink and looked at Alex. 'I need to take this. We will continue this later.'

She left the room, phone to ear, but as her business partner waffled on about some important McAllen files that were missing from the storage cloud, Natalie wasn't really listening, because she couldn't stop trying to picture that girl, and it worried her to the very core. Did something terrible happen to her?

The engine of his gunmetal Jeep growled incessantly, and he wondered how long he'd been slumped at the steering wheel. His eyes were so heavy. He slept on the sofa last night. Well, he laid on the sofa all night, mucking about on his iPad; there had been no sleep. He decided against taking any pills, and he'd acted more tired than he was when Natalie tried to engage him in a conversation after their late dinner. He'd lied, saying he was too drowsy from the pills, so he didn't have to face a proper conversation. Then it was like a bubble burst in his mind. He heard birds chirping, smelt the lush grass, and saw Sheryl Denton. She was standing on a hillside, surrounded by oxeye daisies and cowslips, and those flowers were so bright and wild, just like her. She was wearing her favourite denim jean skirt and the sky-blue top with the white dye patterns. She smiled. A warm and natural smile. A gentle breeze fluttered against his face and he gazed at her amongst the endless sea of flowers. Her mum had called the oxeyes moon daisies, and she loved wildflowers, he'd remembered Sheryl telling him. And his mum had too. Something else they had in common. Sheryl started chuckling and those green eyes sparkled with happiness. Alex couldn't hear what she was saying… but her words were making her laugh, though. Alex wanted to laugh too, and he didn't have a clue why, but he felt happy and full of joy… then he saw that photo with that crack that separated his parents. Alex reached for it…

He jolted awake and gazed around his Jeep, eyes flickering in confusion. His

Jeep was parked in the office car park, though Alex couldn't even remember driving here this morning. He clambered out of his vehicle and took in a huge lungful of air. He could still picture her vividly and smell those flowers and the fruity chewing gum on her breath. Alex heard a distant car alarm going off. A low plane descended towards the nearby airport. A passing office worker waved at him, a balding man with a limp that Alex vaguely recognised. Alex nodded back and gazed to the three-storey office block ahead of him. Life carried on around him as normal, but Alex felt detached from everything. He needed to sort this mess in his head and clear the fog in his aching brain. There was only one way. He needed to go back, because he couldn't live like this anymore.

The office block was situated five miles from Edinburgh centre and was two miles east of the airport. The building itself was bright, modern, and always buzzing with activity. Alex's office was one of the smallest on the ground floor, but it was perfect for him, and he'd always been proud to invite clients into the naturally lit room. The walls were decorated with stunning images from his portfolio, and some of his best work was tastefully displayed in thin acrylic panels. Mountain bikers, snowboarders, trail runners, and his favourite shot, a free climber, hanging, one-handed on a ridge, that he'd taken at a magazine shoot in Applecross. The shot was both extraordinary and terrifying. Alex always watched in awe as those fearless climbers would risk it all for the sport they loved. One slip and it was game over. He was envious of them. Only once had he taken such a dangerous risk involving heights, and he wasn't keen to repeat it. Alex slumped at his desk, not acknowledging the other person in the room. He yawned and rubbed his eyes, but his vision was still hazy.

It took Alex around thirty-five minutes to drive here from his apartment in Edinburgh Old Town, though occasionally he'd use the tram-line that stopped in walking distance from the office. He'd wished he'd left the car at home today. The missing journey was disturbing him. He tried so hard to remember, but he just couldn't. There was just zero recollection. The last thing he pictured himself doing was making a strong coffee and drinking it whilst slouched at the kitchen breakfast bar.

'Look at the state of you. Been out on a bender?' asked the man.

Alex peered around his iMac. 'I didn't know you were here today.'

'I can see that. I thought an extra from The Walking Dead just ambled in, looking to eat my brain.'

'I'd have been a very disappointed zombie then, Baz.'

'And I was just about to praise your Snowdon Enduro pics.'

'You've seen them?'

'You got some decent shots here, man. Impressive work,' said Bassem.

Alex brought up the images Bassem was referring to on his screen and scrolled through image after image of professional mountain bikers captured mid-flight.

Though Alex always called him Baz, his actual name was Bassem Sharif. He was a wiry Asian man in his late thirties, with black curly hair that was thinning. He wore wire-framed glasses and a well-worn Corduroy suit. Bassem thought the attire made him resemble James Bond, and would often refer to his dress sense as distinguished. Alex wasn't convinced. They'd first met six years ago, not long after Alex's nan had passed away. Alex took a solo hiking trip to Loch Lomond, so he could take some time to process the loss of his beloved nan. He'd taken a lunch break on the edge of the loch, to take in the stunning view, when Bassem stopped next to him. They got chatting about the area and hit it off. Bassem was also a keen photographer and looking to quit his job in insurance to work in portrait photography. They hiked together that day, and Alex's solo soul-searching trip turned out an altogether different weekend. More trips followed, including walking adventures, wild camping, and sea fishing, and the pair toured the Outer Hebrides on a boating trip a while ago, a place Alex fell in love with. Alex didn't know how Bassem came to live in Scotland. He'd once spoken to Alex about his late parents being immigrants from the Sylhet region of Bangladesh. They took asylum in London in the late seventies, where they had lived and conceived Bassem, who was born in eighty-five. But Bassem never liked to discuss much else about his past, so Alex never pried. Alex confided in Bassem with almost everything, and he trusted him one hundred percent and considered him a true friend. Meeting him had been such a help in getting over his nan's death. She'd been clocking ninety when she passed. His nan had moved to a bungalow near York, where she lived in a retirement village, and Alex had visited as often as possible. Right until the end, she never appeared old and senile; she was always witty and bright. He was astonished to learn that she'd left him thirty thousand pounds in her will. So he had his amazing nan to thank for the apartment, as he'd put the entire sum towards the huge deposit required to secure the mortgage.

'Bad night's sleep?' asked Bassem. He was spinning on the swivel chair and licking a Cornetto ice cream.

'Yeah, you could say that. How can you eat ice cream this early?'

'It beats soggy bran flakes,' said Bassem, chewing the bottom of the cone. 'Besides, it boosts my mood.'

'Weirdo,' said Alex.

Bassem raised his eyebrows. 'Says you.'

'I told Natalie about Sheryl Denton,' said Alex.

Bassem stopped mid-chew. 'You did what? How did that go down?'

'No, I didn't tell her everything.'

'What *did* you tell her?' asked Bassem.

Alex scratched his neck and sighed, and ignoring the question said, 'I need to find some people.'

'Sounds interesting,' said Bassem, smiling wistfully.

'I'm gonna need lots of coffee,' said Alex, yawning as he turned back to his iMac. He'd start with Ben Napier.

He located Ben Napier easily. As a listed director of his own company, Napier Renovations Limited, Alex easily acquired his current home address from Companies House. He owned a large four-bedroom detached property, worth four hundred grand, and looking on Street View, he'd seen a black Range Rover Sport and red BMW X5 parked side by side. It appeared as though Ben was doing alright for himself, Alex surmised, not able to stop himself from feeling a slight stab of bitterness at his findings. He also happened upon a photograph of Ben and his wife on social media, both holding a champagne flute up to the camera. Ben, as he'd expected, was a hefty guy. He wore chinos and a tight, black t-shirt, which outlined his solid biceps, though he was packing some extra weight around the stomach. His hair had receded and was shaved short. He noticed Ben didn't have glasses on, but Alex recognised him straight away from his signature mischievous grin that hadn't changed over the decades. His skin looked bronzed and his face weathered with heavy frown lines etched on his forehead. His wife stood next to him in the photo, a curvy black woman wearing a sky-blue puff-sleeve dress. Alex thought she looked a few years younger than Ben. She had stunning, long brunette hair, tinged with burgundy and styled in corkscrew curls that almost reached her midriff. The photo captured Kayla Napier in a bout of hysterical laughter, her large ice-blue eyes shimmering with amusement.

Janette Portland had been easy to locate too, and like Ben, she hadn't moved far. Courtesy of Facebook, he'd established she was in a long-term relationship with a guy called Will Passmore, who looked like he'd walked straight out of a Hell's Angels biker's convention – the mature Chapter. Janette seemed obsessed with all things fitness. The maps on her Strava account gave him the precise location of her home address, and that account also gave him the information that she owned a dog called Peanuts, who was also her running companion. Alex didn't know the breed, but many of her activity photos were of Janette and Peanuts, taken during and after their woodland runs together. Janette was clearly athletic. In most of her photos, her hair was plaited in a ponytail that draped over her shoulder, and she wore sporting attire that accentuated her slender build. But Janette still had that flinty-eyed stare that had always unnerved Alex, and even in the photos where she grinned endearingly, with pinkish cheeks from her efforts, those cool-grey eyes seemed unfriendly. Alex didn't find a single photo of her that wasn't centred around running, cycling, or gym workouts. He struggled to envision Janette with this tubby, leather-clad, unshaven biker with the oiled, black hair. They seemed like a very odd pair.

Then the most interesting find. Mark Corker, or, more precisely, his profession. Mark was now a prolific DJ and music producer, and a renowned one too; especially in Germany, Belgium, and the Netherlands, where he often headlined major music events and clubs and maintained a huge following. Earlier, Alex watched a couple of Mark's sets on YouTube, one of them at a crowded beach event in Barcelona. Watching his old friend blast out booming Techno at events packed with bouncing revellers seemed unreal. Mark appeared much younger than his forty-five years and still had his long hair tied back in a ponytail. Alex got an email for Mark's manager through a DJ agency and sent him a message asking for a callback regarding a private, urgent matter. He planned to keep pestering with emails until he received a reply.

Alex drew a complete blank with Gavin Gouch. No social media, no electoral roll listings, and no director or business links, and he'd even checked bankruptcy listings, but still found no joy there. A ghost, thought Alex. Although Alex had stayed elusive himself. He'd never been one to broadcast his life on social media. He never saw the point. The accounts he used were mainly for work; he didn't use them as a source of glorifying his personal life or making himself feel important by showing others how great his achievements were. None of that seemed important to him. His online profile photo would always be a beautiful scenery setting or sunset, and he never posted a photo of himself, or Natalie, nor anything else personal or important to him.

'Gouch. Isn't that the area between your balls and your butt hole?' asked Bassem, peering around the screen, glasses perched on the end of his nose.

'Funny enough, I don't know,' said Alex.

'I think maybe it's spelt with two Os though.'

'I'm sure the correct term is the perineum.'

'Who on God's earth would name their boy Gavin with a surname like Gouch?' asked Bassem.

Alex didn't reply, he just visualised Gavin's smug, weaselly face. Just thinking about Gavin irritated him, even though he'd not seen the hateful bastard for over thirty years.

'Is this Gavin a childhood buddy or something?'

Alex smiled thinly. 'No, not exactly.'

Alex stared at another photo of Mark. He was grinning broadly, and Alex noticed that laughter lines were visible around his eyes. Mark's skin was still milky-white and his small, upturned nose looked just as Alex remembered. He clicked on another photo where Mark's arm was slung around another smiling DJ; a bald, black guy wearing shades. After some Googling, Alex established this guy was a superstar DJ, originally from Manchester. Mark was clearly frazzled in the photo, with polished eyes and a delirious smirk. Corkscrew had made it big, and Alex was happy for him. He'd always been fond of him. He wasn't like the others, and Alex would never forget how Mark had once helped him out of a desperate situation. Alex checked his emails for the third time. There was no reply from the manager.

Six

Mark took a long hit on his vape pen and plonked down on the huge hotel bed, plumping the thick, plush pillows and sinking back against them. This wasn't his usual stuff, and he screwed up his face at the odd, sour flavour. What was it, stale piss? He'd arrived in Mannheim less than an hour ago, and he'd decided he'd get a few hours' sleep before he headed out to the Quadrate for a spot of dinner. The city boasted some amazing restaurants, but he'd told his manager he was set on the Opus V today. They did the most unbelievable veal medallion – which he could practically taste now. One dry almond croissant had passed his lips all day. He needed to grab a few zeds first; he was pretty zapped. He wondered if Daan had remembered to book ahead and arranged for the seating with a city view, as he'd requested. Recently his manager had his head constantly up his arse. Some marital issues with his high-maintenance, young French wife, seemed to be at the centre of the chaos that complicated his manager's hectic life. Mark had a talented team of people behind him, but couldn't afford any dead wood. Daan needed to sort his head out or he'd be heading for the chop. Mark knew plenty of established managers in Europe that would snap him up; which he had been pointing out to Daan frequently. Still, Daan grew more incompetent and unpredictable by the day. He felt like *he* was the one managing Daan Van den Broeck. Mark guessed the Antwerp-born Daan was losing his grasp on the industry and his clients. He knew he'd have to decide soon, but with Daan being such a close friend, it was a massive problem. He'd helped Mark grow so much over the years, and in all honesty, Mark's tremendous success was all because of Daan's relentless commitment to his music empire. But things had changed because Daan's senseless conduct and perpetual mistakes were infuriating. Just last week, Daan got himself into a heated debate with a haughty club promoter in Berlin. Then he almost got himself removed from the event for threatening to trash the promoter's Mercedes with a fire extinguisher. This culminated in Daan throwing the extinguisher at the man, which missed him and spun into the road and subsequently caused a delivery driver on a moped to swerve off the road, and collide into a restaurant divider. A shocked waiter was then sent flying across a table, ruining a gay couple's romantic late-night dinner. It had all played out like a comedy sketch scene, and even the promoter found it hilarious. But Mark had struggled to find any humour in the situation, he'd just baulked at the unprofessional behaviour displayed. Nothing in this world was more important to Mark than his career and his reputation – that always came first. The argument and what followed had, of course, been filmed by some clown and made its way onto social media, with Daan screaming, purple-faced at the younger man in shrill, frenzied German – one of the four languages he was fluent in. Drink and drugs were taking a toll on the man and at forty-eight, he was pushing his luck. Mark guessed that Daan's wife was screwing around and constantly being away from his Parisian beauty, was driving Daan ever closer to insanity. Ridiculous really, considering the sleazy Belgian barely went a week without slipping his love-sausage into some young harlot, be it a call-girl, street hooker or drunk partygoer, or goers. And they weren't always female, as Daan was secretly bisexual. Although Mark was certain his wife was fully aware of her husband's sexuality, because she'd dropped plenty of sly comments during dinner parties and nights out. Two months ago the plonker had caught syphilis from a Romanian prostitute in Frankfurt, and freaked out frequently, after having drunk, unprotected sex and then convincing himself that he'd caught AIDS, gonorrhoea and everything in between. But he never learnt from his mistakes and kept repeating the process. The man could be insufferable.

Mark yawned and was glad he wasn't playing his next set until Friday night, well technically Saturday morning, so he had some leisure time. He was confident the set he'd prepared would be extremely well received, as it always was, by the uplifting German crowd. Just like the Dutch, Mark loved the German revellers and their love of good Techno. Proper banging Techno. After the event, he'd have a few hours' kip, if he made it back in time before his loyal roadie collected him after breakfast. Then he could enjoy a drive across the border and into Utrecht; ready for a midnight three-hour set Saturday. Trent was a well-muscled man in his early thirties from Bristol, and he detested being called *The Roadie*. He complained it made him sound like a sad wanker. *Events Technician* was his official position, and he'd put anyone firmly in their place if they dared to use the R-word. In his defence, it was very undermining, being as though he was a proficient DJ himself, sound technician, programming engineer and lighting expert. Although he was, on occasions, Mark's personal taxi driver and equipment carrier. Mark had never learnt how to drive and had no desire to get behind the wheel. Mark settled back on the soft pillows and closed his eyes, then sat up as he remembered he hadn't called his parents as he'd promised. He spoke to his mum and dad at least once a week. They'd retired now, and moved to Hampshire, near the beach at Milford on Sea, on the edge of the New Forest. His parents loved to hear from him and where his work was taking him, how his two sons were, and how his Swedish wife, Ida, was doing. They were pleased he enjoyed his work and got to travel around the globe doing what he was passionate about. Mark never forgot the support his parents gave him when he was in his late teens. He'd been so dead-set on a career in the music industry, and his dad was the one who purchased his first set of Technics turntables for him on his seventeenth birthday. They never once complained when he spent every waking hour in the loft banging out mixes, which most likely sounded like cats being violently strangled to their ears. He'd eventually repaid them, of course. A two-week cruise of a lifetime around the Caribbean islands, and a trip to New Zealand, visiting filming locations from The Lord of the Rings, their favourite movies. He picked up his mobile with the intent of calling them, but a text pinged through from Daan. Mark sighed and read it.

An urgent callback required. Mr Clayton. It's important!

What the hell was this about? Mark wondered as he sucked hard on his vape and scrolled his emails, coughing at the dire flavour. More messages from his publicist, his agent and a couple of promoters, but he dismissed them and dialled the mobile number provided, his curiosity now aroused. If it was some weirdo stalker, Daan would get a bollocking. He knew today was for chilling and that Mark needed to relax before the weekend madness. The phone answered with a polite voice on the third ring. 'Alex Clayton photography.'

'Yeah, hi, Mark Corker here. Apparently, you need to speak with me. Some sort of private matter. Who is this?' said Mark. He spoke discourteously, even though he sort of registered the name, but from where he wasn't sure.

'It's Alex Clayton. How's it going, Corkscrew?'

'Hey?' Mark bolted up off the bed. 'Clayton!' The name Corkscrew was all he needed to hear to clear the fog. A name he hadn't heard for a long time. A name that stirred a thousand memories and not all of them good. 'Wow, it has been a while. What's this about?' Mark sucked on his vape pen and his mind swam. His heart rate increased so much, the thump of blood became audible as it beat in his ears.

'I need to speak to you. But not over the phone. Needs to be face-to-face.'

'OK. But—'

'Are you free this Saturday?' asked Alex.

'I'm working in the Netherlands. So maybe not the best time, no.'

'I can come out to see you if you can spare me an hour? I'm free myself.'

'Sorry what? You want to come out to find me?'

'Yeah.'

'What's so urgent?'

'Just a drink and a quick chat. I gather you must be busy, but I'd appreciate it.'

Mark didn't answer for several moments as he considered what Alex could want. He knew it could only be about one thing.

'I'll meet you,' said Mark.

'Just say the place.'

'I can meet you in Utrecht. I'll have some time to spare in the afternoon. I'll text you a time and a place.'

'That's fantastic. I'll book a flight now,' said Alex.

Seven

Nottingham, Autumn 2019

Gavin felt done in. Four days' solid graft with the paving crew had all but destroyed him. The five a.m. starts were not great, and he hated having to go to bed before ten o'clock at night. Most of his work crew were younger, boisterous lads. But they were a good bunch, and friendly enough. They'd happily drink into the early hours and still rock up and graft like Trojans. Gavin wished to God he was twenty-odd again, as he pulled himself out of his blue Fiat Punto and stretched out his stiff back. The lads called him Gramps when he'd first started with them. Then Ned, a huge Jamaican guy, who was ironically two years older than Gavin, not that you'd know it, had taken to calling him Slash. This was due to him boasting that his guitar skills were far superior to the famous guitarist. Obviously, he was lying; he hadn't even played since his late twenties and wasn't fantastic back then. Stupid bullshit pub banter. Gavin liked a bit of beer talking; in fact, he excelled at it. Plus, once intoxicated, he had no qualms with urinating in public spaces, once getting a fine for relieving himself on a city-centre monument. So the name seemed fitting. Ever since he hit forty, he seemed to need a piss every five minutes once he'd had a couple of drinks.

He remembered the spliff young Sammy had given him, so he re-entered the motor and retrieved it from the glove box. Sammy had given it to him for medicinal purposes. He had said the strain was called Mike Tyson and it would melt away the pain within minutes of smoking it. Sammy advised Gavin to take it easy and to sample a couple of hits, to begin with, because as the name suggested, it packed a real punch. Gavin crushed the joint in his hand and threw it to the floor. He'd only taken it so he didn't look like a sad, boring loser. He didn't touch drugs anymore. Not after what happened last year. It smelled good though, he thought, as he rubbed his hand on his trousers. Another sharp pain hit his back and ran down his left leg, and he couldn't wait to get into a warm bath and sink a nice cold beer, or ten. After he shut the door, he saw Roland waving from the window of his ground-floor flat. Gavin always considered him a nice old fella – nosey as hell, but nice. Apart from Gavin, Roland was the only non-student resident in the block of flats, which was in Lenton, not too far from Nottingham's Jubilee University campus, and he'd got the place after the landlord evicted a bunch of lively students that trashed the place after several wild parties. It wasn't a palace, even after the lame clean-up job the landlord had undertaken; but he got a lower rate on his rent. Roland, a Nottinghamshire native, had white hair that was thinning, sticky-out ears and a nose that reminded Gavin of a veiny chicken drumstick. He was half smiling, but he looked irritable. Gavin squirmed. What had she been up to now?

The flat was a depressing sight to behold. The cramped lounge was a total mess. Zara was still zonked, sprawled out on the sofa, and still wearing the same stained, lilac pyjamas, with the white butterflies that she'd been living in for several days now. Her black hair was lank and unwashed, her cheeks sunken, and her skin was chalk white. On the smeared glass coffee table lay two spent syringes, amongst other drug paraphernalia. Gavin sighed and tidied up.

'Gav, is that you?' said Zara. 'I've not tidied up yet.' She gazed around groggily.

'No shit. You could toss a grenade in here and it wouldn't notice.'

'I'll sort it, Gav. Later, yeah.'

'Have you eaten? I'll make us some eggs on toast. Then I'm taking a bath.'

'I'll have a large vodka.'

'There isn't any.'

'What?'

'No voddy. Do you want eggs or not?' asked Gavin. When did she last eat? Gavin remembered how she looked not so long ago. Cheerier, curvier, with colour in those cheeks and no dark circles under her eyes. And those ringlets of chestnut coloured hair – hair that she obsessed over and spent hours to perfect. He couldn't recall the last time that poor hair had seen a shower, let alone celebrated the joy of a splash of fragrant shampoo and conditioner. God, he'd even noticed some flecks of grey hair too. The former Zara would have had an instant meltdown and dealt with those buggers tout suite. But that Zara no longer existed. The Gouchy curse. That was to blame. His dad and grandad always said, 'You'll never be happy, boy, just when you think you're sorted – it'll all turn to shit.'

Even if Gavin was holding gold, it would turn to dust in his hands.

'Did you go see the Bulgarian, Gav?' said Zara with a hopeful smile. She was sitting up now, gazing at him and blinking.

'Aw… crap,' said Gavin. He had forgotten.

'Gav, you promised,' she whined, 'why did you promise?' She was on the verge of crying, and a full-on breakdown was on the cards if swift action wasn't taken. Then more of his stuff would get smashed, and there would be screams to follow. It would be a disaster if the landlord dropped by to discover the place resembled a South Central crack den. They'd be out the door faster than those students.

Zara stood up and let out a derisive snort.

Five minutes later, Gavin was back in his car heading to St Ann's and wishing he was in that hot bath, soaking away his troubles and sipping on an ice-cold Heineken. Instead, he needed to go to that Godawful place. He shivered and a sharp pain stabbed his lower back.

Gavin rarely ventured to this side of the city. He'd taken at least two wrong turns and eventually used his iPhone as a sat nav to find the dead-end close he was searching for. It was dark, so the area seemed more menacing than on his last visit here when he'd first had the pleasure of visiting a couple of months ago with Zara. She seemed oblivious to the threatening aura of the area as she eagerly charged into the building, so intent of receiving what lay await inside. The painkiller for her mind and soul. Just one street light was working, and even that was flickering. Gavin zipped up his blue bomber jacket and wedged his phone into the back pocket of his jeans. He'd got changed out of his filthy work gear, but didn't feel clean having chucked on yesterday's clobber. Most of the lower floor to the drab four-storey block was derelict, and only one light was on. Most of the windows were shuttered up with metal council guards. Perhaps they were emptying the place, ready for refurbishments, he considered.

The scowling faces belonging to the teenage gang congregating by the entrance, all turned to focus on him. There were challenging glares and open hostility aplenty, but Gavin walked purposefully towards them, holding their stares, unperturbed. He gave a hard nod and a maniacal smile as he got closer, and they parted, just enough for Gavin to approach the entrance. The security door had been on the receiving end of several vigorous boots and strikes. The chequered security glass was also cracked, and the intercom system had an *out of service* notice across it. The place was a shit pit.

'Don't work, mate. Door's open,' muttered one of the gang members, a tall Asian lad with an eyebrow piercing. He looked at Gavin like he was weighing him up. His focus moved to his trainers.

'Cheers,' replied Gavin, observing the youth. *If you think these crappy trainers are worth a smashed jaw, you go right ahead,* thought Gavin. Then he entered.

As Gavin took the stairs, he spotted a girl, maybe six or seven, sitting on the top step. She was wearing a grubby pyjama t-shirt with a smiling unicorn on the front, and she chatted animatedly to a naked dolly. When she noticed Gavin, she gave him a beaming smile. As he passed her, she whispered in the doll's ear, and Gavin was certain he heard her say something about a drug fiend.

Gavin wondered why the door was ajar. It was possible that the gang of cock-heads out the front had signalled to alert of his arrival, or perhaps it just attested to the dealer's arrogance. He strolled in, a damn sight more casual and confident than he was. *In and out, with zero pissing about, you'll soon be necking that ice cold beverage in the bath,* he thought.

Eight

The place was, as he remembered, spruce, modern and a stark contrast to the exterior of the building. There were two chunky charcoal-coloured leather sofas. A forty-inch TV mounted on the wall, the screen sharp and deep-coloured. The current channel, a music station, played vibrant Dub-Reggae through a pair of giant Bose speakers, also wall mounted. The floor was genuine oak, not laminated as Gavin had first suspected, and at the centre lay a splendid, fluffy rug that twenty cats could lose themselves in. Gavin wasn't sure of the rug's colour – mocha would have been his guess. The place smelt of sweet, lemony weed, and there were a couple of tall glass bongs sitting on a stylish cube table. One looked like a peeled banana, the other decorated with painted cannabis leaves. The entire table glowed a brilliant neon blue. The one thing out of place was an enormous fish tank which sat in the corner, on top of a chunky wooden cabinet, its scratched doors locked with a heavy-looking steel padlock. Two young girls in their early twenties, both stoned out of their faces, occupied one sofa. Two lads, students he guessed, were on the other. Neither of the lads acknowledged him, their lifeless eyes too busy scanning phones. Gavin smiled at the girls. One girl, a fish-lipped, pouting, model wannabe, returned with a look that suggested he'd walked in there and farted straight in her face. Gavin shrugged, walked over to the tank and peered inside. The water was a disgusting lurid green and there was no chance of spotting whatever was living in the filth.

'Put ya hand in. I dare you!' said a man. It was Skender, the Bulgarian, as Zara called him, that spoke. Gavin reckoned he was Turkish, or Albanian. He was undoubtedly Arabic. Gavin speculated that Skender was on the run from someone back home, so that's why he lied about his nationality. Skender thought he was the mutt's nuts, though, and he swaggered about like he was Scarface, but he was no Tony Montana. Tony the Tiger was more intimidating than this utter cock-womble. He was a skinny man in his mid-thirties, with short-cropped hair and olive skin. He was a good-looking guy, but his face bore a constant, toothy, arrogant grin. Despite the late October weather, Skender was wearing a purple Nike sports vest, jogging shorts and white flip-flops.

'What's in there?' asked Gavin, tapping a finger on the side of the tank. 'I'd hazard a guess that your filters are knackered, mate.'

'Red-bellied piranhas,' said Skender.

'Right,' said Gavin, unable to hide his smirk.

'So, can I help you?' asked Skender.

Skender continued to smile broadly, but Gavin could see clear traces of anger in the man's eyes and guessed he should have knocked or shouted before waltzing in unannounced.

'Door was wide open,' said Gavin.

'So, it's OK to stroll on into my home?' said Skender, his smile finally waning.

Gavin heard the toilet flush – someone else was here.

'I'm Gav. Zara's partner. Sorry, but I've been here before. I assumed it would be OK,' said Gavin. 'I need to grab some gear and I'll be out of your hair.'

'Zara… oh, right, yes, the lovely Zara. The nurse who likes a bit of the old brown.'

'Ex-nurse,' corrected Gavin.

The other man was somewhere between twenty-five and thirty-five. He had a huge bushy beard, rugby player's shoulders and light-blond hair shaved at the sides, with the top tied in a short, high ponytail.

Skender turned to the hulking man and said, 'This is Gav, Zara's friend.'

The man stared at Gavin, his brow furrowed, and he looked as though he was trying hard to place him.

'You alright, pal?' asked Gavin. He grinned at the man and tried his best not to appear intimidated. Hard as it was. The big lump looked like he belonged on a Viking longboat. Gavin pictured him on the stern as it crashed through heavy waves. Snarling like a madman, axe raised as the boat slammed into the sand and he drove his crazed war-band towards some unfortunate village, to rape, murder and pillage some petrified peasants.

'I only sell to my regular clients,' said Skender, 'I don't open my door to any old stranger.'

'I came here before. With Zara,' Gavin reminded him. He remembered standing in the doorway and Skender nodding curtly at him, though he was far too engaged with chatting to Zara to pay him much heed. She had seemed so impressed by this slimy little worm-faced twat. But he guessed, well hoped, she merely wanted the escapism that he sold. Those little packets of *forget everything*. She had acted like a giddy teenager around him and laughed at his crappy jokes. All a pretence though. Wasn't it? Although, the Zara he'd fallen in love with wouldn't have even stepped foot in this sordid place, let alone befriend and support the illegitimate business of such a scuzzy, egotistic dick-head.

'I can't remember you, to be honest,' Skender said, 'so it's time for you to go.'

'Oh, come on. Zara will hit the roof if I don't get the stuff, mate,' said Gavin, with more irritation in his voice than intended.

'I'm getting the impression this one fancies himself as a bit of a tough guy,' said Skender, talking to his large companion now.

Yeah, and I'm getting the impression you're a total spaz that's going to get my boot up your skinny arse, thought Gavin. Instead, he said, 'OK fine, I'll go somewhere else.'

'Alright. Don't throw your toys out of the pram,' said Skender, 'if you can strip off all your gear first.'

'Sorry?' said Gavin.

'I don't know you. So—' Skender waved his hand, 'lose them, or leave.'

'You are joking, right?'

'Nope.'

Gavin gave him a confused grin. 'Right.' He undid his jacket and tossed it onto the floor. Yanked off his top, and pulled off his jeans, kicking them off. His temper was rising, but he kept it in check. Oh, great, of course – he just had to be wearing those Valentine's Day joke boxers. Zara had bought them. Before everything changed. The ones with the cartoon beaver across the front, with the slogan: chew on my wood. Revealing these got a few chuckles. Not from the Viking, though. His fixed, straight-faced expression was unchanged.

Skender gestured this wasn't far enough. Gavin sighed and grabbed the top of his boxers. There was no point backing out now; so he danced, shook his hips to the background music, slipped them off and launched the underwear in Skender's direction. They fell to his feet, and he smiled thinly as he nudged them away with his flip-flop. The two girls were in hysterics now, and one of them sounded like a pig snorting. Gavin knew he didn't have a tiny cock, but it was cold today and the anxiety of the situation was making his penis shrink back into his balls. But he didn't give a toss what these muppets thought. Especially the Tango-faced tarts with lips like a baboon's arsehole. He'd been in more embarrassing situations in the past.

'Are you sure you don't want to stick a cheeky finger up my ring piece?' said Gavin, in a mock, posh voice. Letting this idiot wear him down was not an option, so gave him a slanted grin and wink too. Let him play his games because his skin was as tough as a rhino's jacksy.

'No, you're good. So, you got the cash?' asked Skender. He appeared to be losing all interest now.

Gavin sensed he hadn't expected him to undress so readily and flop out his disco stick. Perhaps he had ruined the moment for him. He did hope so.

'Yeah, I have cash,' replied Gavin, pulling up his boxers, whilst smiling at fish-lips, who had stopped laughing and was now back to scowling at him. This wasn't how Gavin had envisioned his evening playing out. It got worse when Skender said, 'All three hundred and seventy quid, yes?'

'Sorry, what?' Gavin's head poked through his t-shirt. 'I know she owes a bit, but—'

'That's what she owes, and that's not including today's score,' said Skender. 'Quite the habit, your woman has got.'

'I wasn't aware it was so much. But I'll have it all next week. And I can sort you forty-five now.'

'Forty-five? Is that OK? I don't want you going hungry now.'

'Can I please grab the stuff? I need to get back.'

'OK, Gav. As it's you and we've had the chance to get properly acquainted now,' said Skender. His eyes drifted to Gavin's crutch, and he smirked. 'I'll sort you out.'

'Thanks,' said Gavin. He grinned pleasantly, though all he could picture was Skender's twisted expression, as he booted the skinny muppet hard in the testicles.

Skender fished a key out of his shorts and undid the padlock on the cupboard doors. Gavin watched Skender snatch up a bag of gear. He offered the packet to Gavin, but as he accepted, Skender's other hand came at him like a striking viper and snatched at his wrist. Before Gavin could react, the Viking grabbed his left arm and yanked it so hard behind his back, Gavin was certain his shoulder had dislocated. He yelled out and tried to break his right arm free, but the skinny Skender had quite a vice-like grip on him. Then panic set in when he saw the Stanley knife in Skender's free hand.

'Leave it—' squealed Gavin, as the Viking applied even more pressure, 'ouch, what are you doing? Ease off!'

Skender drew the blade across Gavin's knuckles – just enough to release a nice thick line of blood.

'Aww, fuck,' spluttered Gavin.

'You tell that slut girlfriend of yours,' said Skender, 'to stop ignoring my messages. She's been avoiding paying me for weeks now, the stupid skank! And in you walk, brazenly as you like, asking for more from me.'

'I'll get this sorted. Calm down, yeah,' said Gavin, staring wide-eyed at the water. He'd seen footage of piranhas eating chicken. The image of them stripping that meat to the bone was etched in his mind, as Skender forced his bloody hand into the murky water. He'd tried so hard to fight it, but with his arm wedged up behind his back, he felt so helpless. Time seemed to stand still. He could smell onions on Skender's breath; mixed with deodorant too, a nice expensive men's fragrance, something in the Hugo range perhaps, although he wasn't sure which one of them was wearing it, or why, in this compromised position, he was taking notice. His senses must be going into overdrive.

'You have proved your point,' said Gavin, gritting his teeth.

'Have I? I don't think I have,' said Skender.

Gavin fixed his eyes on that water. He felt movement – something brushed against his hand and he braced for the first bite.

'Are you trying to embarrass me in front of my friends?' asked Skender.

'What? No. I said I'd sort her debt. Just please—'

'Just please,' mocked Skender, 'are they nibbling yet?'

'I will pay.'

'I know,' said Skender.

Gavin shut his eyes and tried hard to switch off. But he'd now convinced himself that several fish were circling his hand. Didn't piranhas only eat dead things? He doubted that a hungry bastard fish would question what was on the menu.

'OK, Gav. The fun is over,' said Skender, yanking his hand out. The Viking released his firm grip and shoved Gavin away.

'What the hell?' shouted Gavin. He inspected his hand. The cut was bleeding but wasn't too deep.

'Calm down, it was a joke,' said Skender, chuckling like a loon.

Gavin looked around the room. Fish-lips and her mate were terrified. But the students didn't look in the least bit worried; just another day in Skender's crazy crib.

The Viking squared up to Gavin. 'Shall I see him out, Sken?' He spoke in a deep, Eastern European accent.

'No, Gav can see himself out, Tim,' said Skender, re-locking the padlock and grinning smugly at Gavin. 'Shut the door behind you.'

Gavin dried his hands on his work trousers. 'I will swing by with that cash soon.'

Gavin struggled to suppress a grin. The name Tim took the edge off his menace. Gavin strolled past the girls, who watched him with fearful, wide eyes. The cube table changed to a vivid purple. *Real smart touch, that,* Gavin decided.

Upon exiting, he took a quick gander around. The key hook snatched his attention, and he nabbed the single key hanging there and popped it deep inside his pocket. As an afterthought, he quickly took it out and gave it a test run in the lock.

Gavin parked up outside his flat just before ten. His eyes stung like hell he was so knackered. The cut on his knuckles had seeped blood down his hand and dripped over the steering wheel. It was bleeding heavily from what was essentially a minor scratch. After leaving Skender's, he'd remembered that the arsehole hadn't taken the forty-five quid, so he reluctantly phoned Sammy. He'd then had to drive to a pub in Gamston and ended up waiting another fifty minutes before he showed up.

Sammy didn't have much skin that wasn't covered with colourful tattoos.

The garish illustrations went right up to the top of his neck. His hair was styled in a short Mohican, dyed with blond highlights, which Gavin thought suited him well. OK, Sammy looked like an iffy sod, but he was a decent lad and he wasn't fond of dealing in smack.

When he'd arrived at the pub, he appeared rather put out. 'What do you want this crap for, Gav?' he asked in his strong Liverpudlian accent. 'I didn't have you down as a smack-head. The poppy is the devil's junk, man. Pure shite.'

'Nah, it's not mine, it's for a desperate friend,' said Gavin, as he snatched the drugs from his workmate. Of course, he hadn't wanted to call him. The last thing he needed was his work pals thinking he was a dirty junkie, but Sammy knew plenty of individuals in the right, or wrong, circles. There was no other option. It's not like he could Google 'drug pushers in my locality'.

Gavin dragged his weary self out of his car, and slammed the door, leaving a gooey, red handprint on the window. He stared hard at the blood and pictured Skender's disdainful mug. As he turned to leave, he spotted his neighbour trotting in his direction. Gavin muttered a curse under his breath.

'Hi Gavin,' said Roland, 'I don't like to moan, you know I don't, but that music… it's awful.'

'Sorry, she falls asleep sometimes and leaves it on. I'll have a word,' said Gavin, walking away and putting his thumb up.

'Falls asleep. With that racket? Look, I know what the poor lass has been through, but it's not acceptable.'

'I'll sort it. Goodnight, Roland.'

His neighbour spotted the bloody print and was gaping at it. 'Night, lad,' said Roland. 'You know you still have a taillight out? On the driver's side.'

'On my list of things to do. Cheers for the reminder, though,' replied Gavin as he made his escape. Though in theory, he wasn't escaping. He was dreading heading back in, but tonight she could just get on with it; he'd want no part. A hot bath and some kip were needed. And he just wanted his life back to how it had been not so long ago. *Fuck that Gouchy curse. Fuck it sideways up the arse,* he thought grimly, as he went back home to give the love of his life the horrible crap in his pocket.

Nine

Kent, Summer 1987

The boy had a polypropylene sack hung over his shoulder as he stood at the entrance to Gallows Hill Wood. He trekked in via the quarry where the byway traversed into a twisted tunnel of dense trees. This was a walking route, but he couldn't recall noticing anyone else use this pathway, and he'd never spotted another soul exploring the actual woodlands. Although discarded cans and crisp wrappers clung to bushes; evidence enough someone else had passed through at some point. The quarry entrance was sectioned off with a wide gate; the pea-green paint faded and blistered. A rusty chain, thicker than Popeye's biceps, secured them. He peeked through the gap between the gates, seeing the ruined remnants of the skateboarding jumps that lay inside the abandoned quarry proper. According to the tales, many years back, a ten-year-old kid played here. He'd sneak through that gap, ignoring the warnings of *Danger* and *Keep Out*, and he'd practice on his skateboard for hours. One day he ventured up here during strong winds and carried on regardless of the weather. A large piece of corrugated roofing blew straight off an outbuilding, spun through the air, crashed down and practically sliced the boy clean in half. He'd spent hours and hours in utter agony as he died up here alone, his guts dangling out of him and his screams of sheer pain going unheard. After this, several stories started floating around about ramblers hearing the distinctive sounds of a skateboard scraping across the ground. But when they checked inside the quarry, they'd find it empty. The odd person had indeed sworn blind that they'd heard a young child sobbing and calling for his mummy and pleading for help.

The boy chuckled to himself. He thought it was all a load of silly nonsense. Unpleasant stories told by parents to stop their stupid brats coming up here to play in such a dangerous environment. Gallows Hill Wood was a dingy, forbidding place though. Even on the sunniest of days, it was still damp and gloomy. It was full of twisted, fat oak trees and birds never sung here. It was always so quiet. Various unused and overgrown footpaths zigzagged through the trees, and the word labyrinth always sprung to mind when he thought about this place. Because once you found yourself deep inside the belly of the wood, trying to navigate the complex network of unkept tracks was both thrilling and daunting. He'd got himself lost here plenty of times, even though he was familiar with the entire area. It was weird because he'd always find a new, undiscovered spot, despite his many encounters here. He'd swear blind those pathways shifted around. The place was the polar opposite of Colt Wood, where the kids from his estate loved to congregate.

Earlier, the boy had been certain he'd felt a slight movement in the sack – like a feeble scratch. Surely it was just his mind playing tricks on him. He'd know soon enough. Once he reached the centre of the woods where the burial site lay. He so wanted to check the sack whilst he'd been heading down the lanes, but knew he daren't risk it, in case a car drove by or a walker noticed him. Once he got to the circle of dead trees, he'd check inside, and, if needed, finish the job. He would be stunned if any of the cats survived. He'd hit them all with brute force. The ginger Tom was definitely brown bread, as he'd watched in twisted awe when its head popped open. He'd slammed down that house brick so hard, its brains had spilt out all over the curb and sloshed over his trainers. Such glorious carnage, he remembered. The boy felled a mongrel dog several weeks ago, but that had been way too easy. The dog wilfully strolled over and accepted a chunk of chocolate, and it didn't even put up a fight when he started battering the shaggy animal with a lump of wood. It just cowered pitifully. Cats were far less trusting, and this added that extra challenging element. And this also added to the fun, because he liked to use both stealth and violence during his games. They would fight back too, hissing and scratching at him. He considered how he could take things to the next phase. Something often running through his mind these days. One thing was definite – it wouldn't be the last time he killed.

Ten

Alex hadn't slept last night, and he lay on the sofa under a wafer-thin sheet. It was five in the morning and he felt nauseous and so cold; it was like his body was pumping iced water through his veins. Even the slightest movement made him shiver. He wasn't certain if feeling rough was because of having zero sleep, or the nervousness of the current situation. Or both. After his brief conversation with Mark Corker, he immediately booked a flight for Amsterdam that was leaving early Saturday morning. And he hadn't told Natalie yet. He'd decided not to tell her about meeting Mark, knowing that things were complicated enough and it would just raise more questions. Natalie had gone to one of her gym workout classes with a friend last night, then out for dinner afterwards. So she'd been late back and hadn't pressed him for more answers about what they'd previously talked about. When they had spoken about Sheryl, Alex had been careful to omit her surname, in case Natalie tried searching for her. It would be unlikely she'd find anything, but he didn't want her to dig. He would of course explain everything to her. But in good time. She wasn't ready to know yet. She wouldn't understand without all the details and he knew how'd she'd react and what she'd think of him. Then he considered he didn't *possess* all details, even if he wanted to share them. There were pieces of the puzzle missing. And it was time to find them.

Mark woke up, gingerly slid out of bed and practically crawled to the fridge. He found a large bottle of chilled water and necked it greedily. Did he drink too much last night? The fragility of his head confirmed he had. Then it all started coming back to him.

After speaking to Clayton, Mark had headed straight to the hotel bar, turned off his phone and ordered a bottle of red wine, the first of several, and got shit-faced. Red wine hangovers were pure evil; he'd never face another glass again in this lifetime. He vaguely recalled a sour-faced Daan marching up to the bar area. 'You understand the purpose of a mobile phone, right?'

'You understand the purpose of a manager, right?' retorted Mark in a slurred voice.

'Hey just… kiss my Belgian buns!'

Mark remembered laughing hard at that, then spitting out a mouthful of wine and nearly choking on the vinegary plonk.

'You missed a delightful meal by the way,' grumbled Daan, 'and you could have had plenty of wine there. Decent wines.'

He recalled Daan glancing at the bottle next to Mark with a disdainful sneer. Mark wasn't too sure if Daan was more annoyed he'd missed their dinner date or the fact he was gulping a ten-euro bottle of red. Daan also said something about an amazing slot he'd bagged Mark at some top Romanian festival, but it was all quite hazy. Now he felt like a total mangled turd, as he lay back down on the bed and melted into the covers, his temples pounding. Alex getting in touch out of the blue was an almighty shock, so he'd just needed to take the edge off, but unfortunately, he'd got carried away on his solo booze-up. Why did he make that call? Surely nothing good could come from this.

Natalie sat on the bed and gazed at Alex's passport photo. 'Sex pest.'

'Thank you,' said Alex, snatching the passport and zipping it into his travel bag.

'The Netherlands isn't one of your usual destinations, Alex,' she said, sprawling herself on the bed. She was wearing her short pink bathrobe and nothing else.

'It's some PR charity event. A recommendation from a current client to cover a magazine article. So, I couldn't say no. Well, not without coming across as a total miserable arse.'

'What's the event?'

'Um, kite-surfing.'

'In Amsterdam?'

'No, on the coast. Scheveningen. The Hague.'

'That's nice. Why didn't I receive an invitation to this jolly excursion?'

Natalie observed Alex's expression intently as he answered, checking for any hint of deception in response to her little inquest.

'I can book you a ticket. It's no problem.'

'No, that's fine. You head off for a weekend of Dutch beer and wacky baccy on your own,' she said. 'I'll let you make it up to me.'

'I bet you will,' he said. 'Wacky baccy?'

'It used to help me conk out at uni.'

'Didn't have you down as a dope-smoker, Nat. But I'll bear that in mind.'

'Gotta be better than those pills, Alex.'

Not that you bloody take them often enough, she mused to herself. She'd even borrowed some of her father's sleeping tablets, that he assured her could topple an African elephant, yet still, her husband was reluctant to take them.

'Well, if you're ordering me… perhaps I'll sample some. But if it makes me puke and spin out, I'm blaming you, Nat.'

'Loads of US states legally use medicinal cannabis for insomnia.'

'Yes, I know, Doctor,' he said, giving her a silly grin.

Alex began tugging the cord to her dressing gown free and kissed her neck passionately. Then his hand slipped inside her dressing gown and snaked up her thigh. As their lips met and they kissed, Natalie just couldn't shake the sinking sensation that was gnawing at the pit of her stomach. Something just wasn't right with her husband and hadn't been since his strange dreams and nightmares started. He shied away from those pills because he didn't want to sleep. He was afraid of it. Wherever his mind journeyed to when he slept, frightened him senseless.

Mark was sitting in the green room sipping a bottle of cold water, awaiting his slot. Thumping music echoed through the enclosed room and Mark winced with every beat, his temples pulsating. Despite attempting to doze off the hangover, he still felt like utter crap. There was a slight waft of cigar smoke lingering, despite it being a no-smoking section, and the aroma wasn't helping. He grabbed a handful of multiple-coloured jellybeans from a large glass container and popped some in his mouth. Two brawny crewmen, wearing Hi-Vis jackets, ordered up vodkas at the bar, and the ice clinked as the bored barman piled it in their glasses. Mark eyed their drinks and considered that a sneaky hair of the dog could be worth a try, but quickly disregarded that notion as reckless. The crewmen spotted Mark and raised their glasses to him, and Mark gave them two thumbs up and forced a polite grin.

Daan strolled in and handed him a wrap of powder, with no attempt at concealing the action, and gave him a cheerful grin. 'Get that up your hooter, Marko.' His white teeth seemed to gleam.

'I don't want any,' said Mark.

Mark attempted to pass the wrap back, but Daan slapped his hand away with a moody tut. 'You need it. Trust me, you cannot go out there looking like a depressed ghoul. Wake the hell up, Marko man. You're on in thirty minutes. Plus, we have a private party with the promoter after your set.'

'Please tell me you're joking.' Mark studied the powder. 'Fine. Just a nip then.'

'It's ready to go. And it's good stuff,' said Daan, frantically rubbing his nose and sniffing like a lunatic.

Mark used a key to sniff up a hefty chunk of the powder and gulped back the water, tilting his head back. It had been over ten months since he'd touched cocaine. It had been during a three-day festival in Brussels. Daan wasn't able to get hold of his normal contacts – one was in Lisbon and the other in police custody, so Daan got a new contact through a Belgian-Moroccan fella, who worked on the events security team. Daan asked Trent to drive him to the north-east side of the city, to Rue De Brabant in the Schaerbeek region. Mark got dragged along too. Daan told him it was a minor detour when they'd been en route to a swanky restaurant in the city centre. They pulled into a desolate dead-end back street and stopped outside a food store with dirty windows that had signs and posters written in Arabic. Daan was happy to venture inside solo, but Trent, dubious about the situation, followed him in there. Mark, not wanting to be alone in the unfamiliar neighbourhood, cautiously followed the pair inside and what followed was the most nerve-racking moment of his adult life. Trent, ever a calm and collected guy, was a bag of nerves and adamant they should leave. And he'd been right. Within minutes of being in the shop, five stony-faced Moroccan men stormed into the store, brandishing machetes, and Mark and Trent were both forced to their knees with blades poised at their necks, whilst Daan negotiated with the headman. The dealer couldn't have been over twenty. Daan was a skinny guy, with bony cheeks and a sharp ski-slope nose, but the Moroccan was almost skeletal compared to him. His massive, dark eyes bulged out of his bony face and his twig-like arms waved frantically. God only knew what drugs he'd taken. Mark, convinced they were about to be hacked to ribbons and dumped in the Schelde River, almost soiled his pants. After a five minute discussion, in what Mark was sure was a fast, French dialect, the Moroccan gave a gap-toothed smile, and the men lowered their weapons. Daan departed that grim shop with enough drugs to supply a small army, but it turned out to be pretty subpar stuff. Well, that was an understatement – it was Godawful gear. Mark must have sniffed over two grams that weekend, and in the days that followed, he had hideous painful nosebleeds and terrible migraines. He dreaded to think what they'd cut the drug with. He'd decided it would be best not to know as he scooped up another nib on his key and blasted the powder up his other nostril. It turned out the Moroccan gang leader was an immense Techno fan, and he'd heard of DJ Corker, which helped to pacify the guy and stopped them from having their heads unceremoniously removed.

This gear was first rate, though. He felt like DJ Corker again and was ready to play. Ready to smash this venue.

Alex arrived at Schiphol Airport just after lunchtime, UK time. He'd barely had time to order a coffee before the next connecting train to Utrecht was due at the platform. Coffee in hand, he headed through the bustling crowds and down to the lower station, where he boarded the Intercity. Alex went onto the upper deck of the train and took a window seat. The train was soon rolling out of the cityscape areas and passing through the picturesque countryside of endless waterways and fields of livestock. Alex settled his head on his travel bag and his eyes became heavy. He tried to resist the urge to close them. Now was not the time for sleep. He thought about Natalie, laying with her back to him last night, sleeping soundly, whilst he lay awake, his mind racing. It was a shame sex didn't help him drift off, because he'd be jumping into bed like an amorous rabbit on Viagra if that were the case. Alex hadn't enjoyed lying to Natalie about this trip, but it was necessary. Lying came easily to him, but that didn't mean he enjoyed it.

Reaching Utrecht Centraal station, Alex grabbed another coffee and walked to his hotel, which took less than ten minutes. He'd been pleased when he'd realised that he'd booked a place that was next to the bar that Mark had asked him to meet him at. After checking in and dropping off his bag, he wandered around the pedestrianised canal area. It was a chilly, cloudless day, and the sun was high and bright. Alex was glad to be wearing his thick Crombie jacket as he explored the city. The canal paths bustled with people, and the waterway was active with boats and canoes. Golden leaves sprinkled the lower walkways and water.

After a ten-minute walk, Alex passed a coffee shop, which had a big queue snaking from the entrance to the counter. He'd smelt the strong, heady aroma way before reaching the shop. Alex wasn't certain if non-Dutch residents could just rock up and buy from cafés, so he would pop back later that evening. Hopefully it would be quieter. He didn't think they'd question him.

Alex made his way back towards his hotel, had a shower and charged up his mobile phone. He hadn't thought to bring a European plug adapter, but he had a slim charging block in his travel bag, that he always carried for work, so could get power to his phone. Alex wandered out of the hotel and strolled across a skinny canal bridge, where he had a decent view of the bar below. Although Alex had arrived early, Mark was already down there, slouched at a table on the edge of the canal, sipping on a glass of beer. He was wearing an expensive-looking tan leather jacket, blue jeans and wrap-around sunglasses. The bar was busy, but Alex didn't have any issues spotting him in the crowd of patrons. He headed down the steep steps and onto the lower walkway. The aroma of grilled meat wafted through the air and Alex noticed a steakhouse opposite.

Mark was gazing at a paddle boat trying to manoeuvre out of the way of a large sightseeing cruise boat, loaded with picture-taking tourists. The paddleboat, with its four young occupants, came out from under the bridge, where it collided clumsily into the wharf. Which they all found hilarious. Mark turned back to his beer, noticing he wasn't alone.

'Hey, Corkscrew,' said Alex.

Mark stood up, and the pair shook hands. 'Alright, Clayton.'

Alex took a seat, which was precariously close to the edge of the canal.

'You can call me Mark, that works for me,' he said. 'Beer?'

'Yeah, love one. Whatever you're having.'

'Gulpner. It's a nice drop,' said Mark as he waved over the server and ordered the drinks.

'Have you been here before?' asked Mark.

'No. But it's a cool place. Lots of character.'

'It's one of my favourite Dutch cities. Amsterdam is great, but you get fewer tourists from the UK here. It's tedious having to sit in a pleasant bar listening to pissed-up Essex wide-boys, boasting about their grubby sex exploits.' Mark sucked hard on his vape pen as two beers arrived in skinny half-pint glasses.

Alex sipped his drink appreciatively.

Mark knocked back half in one hit. 'So, a photography business. How's that going?'

'Yeah, good. I enjoy it. Keeps me out and about.'

'So, married? Kids?' asked Mark, checking his mobile as he spoke.

'Married, my wife Natalie is a partner in an accountancy firm. So no kids. Way too much going on. We have a place in Edinburgh. What about you?'

'Married with two boys. I live in Stockholm now.'

'I've watched some of your music sets, Mark. Impressive stuff. Must be quite the life, hey?'

Mark sipped his beer and checked his phone again. 'It has its moments.'

An awkward silence grew for a short while as they finished their first beer and Mark ordered two more.

'Can I buy weed here? Is that legal?' asked Alex, breaking the silence.

'Well, yeah, you can buy it,' replied Mark with an amused grin. 'You came all this way to get high? Don't they sell dope in Scotland?'

'I thought they might have something to help me sleep.'

'Yeah, they will. But don't take any back home with you… Jesus, Clayton… this is weird. You here like this, I mean, it's been over thirty years, we're practically strangers.'

'But you still came.'

'Yeah. I still came.'

Eleven

The pair consumed several beers and engaged in small talk for over an hour. They chatted about work, relationships, travelling, holidays and everything aside from why Alex wanted to meet Mark. The conversation became less stilted, and they were soon laughing and enjoying each other's company. Mark had ordered some ham and cheese sandwiches and two baskets of fries, accompanied by little glass jars of the creamiest and tastiest mayonnaise Alex had ever tasted.

As Mark tucked into the food, Alex decided to get to the point. 'So, are you in contact with Ben Napier?'

'I've not spoken to him in about fifteen years. I think he still follows my page on Facebook though.'

'Gavin?'

'God, no,' said Mark. 'Hey, I bet you didn't know Gavin and Janette dated back in the mid to late nineties.'

'Really?'

'They split a few times, then got back together. It was like that for yonks, before Jan finally saw sense and dumped the berk permanently. He left town years ago though.'

'So, where is he now?'

'Damned if I know, but he might be in touch with Ben. You must remember how close they were. That pair got into a ton of trouble as they grew up. They knocked about with Ben's dick-head brother, Shane, and some of his undesirable mates. I drifted away from them once I was in college. Found different friends. You know how it is?'

'I tried to find Gavin, but couldn't find any trace.'

'Why are you searching for that loser?'

'That's why am here, Mark. I want you to help me organise a meetup with them.'

'I'd guessed as much.'

'We all need to go back. All of us that were there.'

Mark sucked hard on his vape as he shook his head several times. 'I don't think so. You don't want to pick at that scab. It will open some painful wounds, Clayton.' He exhaled the smoke into the air.

'They'll listen to you, Mark.'

'Why now? Why wait all this time?' Mark sipped his beer. 'What's changed?'

'Six weeks ago, I did a photoshoot for a magazine. It was like a Tough Mudder type thing, but with your dog.'

'Sounds like chaos,' said Mark, suppressing a yawn.

'I was crouched down, capturing some shots of participants crawling through a tunnel. When I looked up, I saw a Doberman glaring down at me.'

'What did it say? "Hey, punk, I best make the front cover or your skinny ass is mine."'

'It was just staring at me as though it hated me. Then it started snarling and lunged.'

Alex was quite tipsy now, and the words had flowed out easily.

'Don't work with kids and animals,' said Mark.

Mark was texting now, and Alex was getting frustrated he was making light of the situation. The incident with the dog back in '88 had disturbed him, and he'd found it difficult to be around dogs ever since.

'The owner just grabbed her dog before it got me. The attack mortified her. The dog was usually placid and calm. It had never been aggressive,' said Alex.

'Yeah, or so she told you.'

Alex sipped his beer and shook his head. 'I could tell by her face, Mark. She was shocked.'

'And this evoked memories of Freddy Killner's farm?'

The pair locked eyes for a moment, and the events of that harrowing day flashed vividly in Alex's mind. He guessed Mark was remembering too. But Alex hardly needed reminding about that day. He carried the scars. Both physical and mental ones.

A young couple searched for a nearby table and Alex waited for them to pass before he continued. 'It all started after that day. That dog triggered something in my mind.'

'What started?'

'The dreams, or flashbacks, or whatever you want to call them,' said Alex, gazing out to the water as he spoke, almost trancelike.

'Yeah, it was all messed up. But it was a lifetime ago. We were just a bunch of errant kids.'

'I haven't slept properly since that day. Unless I take pills, and then I have dreams that are so intense, and so real, it's like I'm reliving the past. Reliving all the events of that summer.'

The pair sat in a stiff silence for a moment.

'It's as though my subconscious wants me to act,' said Alex.

Mark appeared as though he wanted to speak, but stopped himself, and he was swallowing so hard, Alex could see his Adam's apple teetering up and down.

'So there you go,' said Alex.

It felt fantastic to say everything out loud, even though it all sounded nuts. Of course it did.

Mark flashed him a nervous smirk. 'Yep, you are right... you definitely need a decent bit of ganja, Clayton.'

'Don't you want to know what happened, Mark?' said Alex in an angry whisper. 'Doesn't this matter to you anymore?'

Mark placed his vape pen on the table and breathed a long, heavy sigh as he tugged off his glasses. Mark looked lousy. His sagging eyes bore darkish rings and his pupils were bloodshot.

'Is that what you're saying?' asked Alex.

'I... I just think it's a bad idea—' Mark stopped and peered over Alex's shoulder, now looking puzzled. 'What's he doing here?'

Alex followed Mark's gaze to a slim man with tousled, sandy hair, wearing a semi-unbuttoned white shirt and humorously tight, bleach-washed jeans. The man swaggered towards them, flashing a scintillating smile at a couple of ladies on a neighbouring table.

'Hey, hey, Marko,' said the man in a loud, confident voice.

'Are you tracking my damn phone again, Daan?' asked Mark, with a suspicious and somewhat playful grin.

'Of course not. I remember all your favourite drinking dens. I bet I could track you down anywhere in Europe. Such a creature of habit.'

'I'm not so sure I am, Daan.'

'So, Marko, who's your friend?' asked Daan.

'This is Alex Clayton. A friend from my past. We've not seen each other in over thirty years.'

'Wow, and you've just bumped into each other? Small world,' said Daan as he patted Alex on the shoulder. 'Good to meet you, Alex. I'm Daan. I'm Mark's wonderful manager. I bet he's been telling you all about me.' The patting shifted to a clumsy rub, and Alex could see Mark shaking his head in embarrassment.

Alex grinned at Daan. The Belgian had clearly taken some sort of drug, as his pupils appeared dilated and his face was twitching.

'We arranged this, Daan. Alex wants to organise a reunion with some pals back in Kent,' said Mark.

'Whoa, that's great. Ah, wait… the urgent email. That was you, yes?'

'That was me,' confirmed Alex.

'I hope you've invited Alex to the event tonight. I bet he'd love to see you in all your noisy glory, Marko.'

'I'm not so sure it's my scene,' said Alex.

'Yeah, come along, Clayton,' said Mark.

'Marko, order me a large G&T. Lots of ice. I mean lots. I need to use the facilities,' said Daan.

Alex could smell coconut cream on Daan, which he thought was odd. It reminded Alex of his mum obsessively slathering sun cream on his shoulders at Camber Sands beach, despite his whinging protests.

Once Daan was out of sight, Alex stared hard at Mark. 'So, will you help me try to get them all together or not?'

Twelve

Kent, Summer 1988

He knew going to sleep would be impossible tonight. He heard the music from The Equalizer TV series coming from the lounge. His nan loved the show and the lead actor whom she had the major hots for. She'd recorded some episodes on the VHS player her sister had brought her last year, and the boxes were lined up on her walnut display cabinet that dominated the lounge, with handwritten scribbles on the sides, labelling each episode. She had suggested that they watch an episode tonight, but Alex had declined. Under normal circumstances, he'd have loved to join her. His mum had never let him watch any TV with action or violence in, as she said it would corrupt his young mind and etch violence into his subconscious. She didn't even like the A-Team, and the bad guys never even died in that, despite the endless crazy shoot-outs, mad fights and wild car chases. It was just silly entertainment, but even so, she hated anything with guns and aggression. She once let him watch Watership Down, and the pair had settled down together expecting a family adventure movie, but he never finished the entire film, as his mum had turned it off once she established the peril and graphic violence the film contained. He gazed up to the ceiling, contemplating his test tomorrow, and he couldn't shake the image of Jonathan Gambridge from his mind. He kept imagining his face contorting in agony as he gazed down at his twisted arms. The thought made him shudder. He didn't even see Gambridge until he was out of plaster, but that didn't stop those images of bones tearing through skin materialising, or of his bent, twisted limbs glistening with blood. His heart was racing, and he had to keep taking deep breaths to calm himself. Were all these sensations normal? Surely he was bound to be scared. Wouldn't anyone? He didn't have a clue what Ben had planned, or what dangers lay ahead. Alex was hot all over and started to think he might faint. He needed to relax and calm his nerves, so he climbed off the bed and paced the box-room, shaking his hands and taking in deep gulps of air. Would they all be there? Would Sheryl be there? Alex hoped she would be, as somehow he knew her presence would help him complete the task. Alex desperately wanted to spend time with Sheryl. Just the two of them, although he'd settle for anything right now. It seemed like the tests were his only option; his one way in. Whatever Ben expected of him, Alex would do it. He pulled out the brooch that hung on a shoe string around his neck and studied it. It was a gold piece with a diamond-encrusted silver twist coiled around it. He'd keep it safe forever, so he'd never forget his mum, and perhaps it would even be his lucky charm.

When Alex headed out of his nan's bungalow, he spotted a boy he'd never seen before exiting one of the neighbouring properties. The boy was olive-skinned, short, with a stocky build, and Alex gauged his age at sixteen. He was wearing baggy shorts, a tight white vest, and black slip-on shoes that looked like plimsoles or a type of martial arts footwear. His upper arms were tight nots of muscle and they bulged slightly under the weight of all his fishing equipment. Alex thought he looked like he came from the Mediterranean; Greece, perhaps. Either that or he had a cracking tan from a holiday abroad.

'Can I help you?' asked the boy, with an odd, almost American-sounding accent.

Alex realised he was staring openly at the boy. 'Where is your accent from?'

'I've been living in Alberta in Canada for three years. I sort of picked this up.'

'So… you're *not* Canadian?' asked Alex.

'Nah, I'm from South London.'

'Oh. So, what are you doing here?'

'Staying at my grandparents' place. I'm just visiting for the summer.'

'Just you? Are your parents staying too?'

'Nah, they are in Madrid. Gone to visit my dad's family,' then he added, 'yes, my dad is Spanish before you ask.'

'What's your name?'

'Jeez, are you always this nosey?' asked the boy.

'Sorry. I'm Alex. I'm staying with my nan. A couple of doors up.'

'Right, that's nice.'

Alex sensed that this lad, although he was being polite enough, didn't want to talk to him, and guessed he'd just seen him as an annoying little kid, but something about him intrigued Alex.

'I need to go. I've got to meet my friends,' said Alex.

Alex headed away, and the boy called over to him. 'I'm Eduardo. All my pals call me Ed.'

The group stood on a mound of dirt positioned on the outskirts of a sprawling building site. From here, they were given a panoramic view of the entire site. It wasn't obvious what was being constructed, but at the site's centre stood a vast skeletal structure, with scaffolding jutting out all around it. There were two JCB Backhoe Loaders parked on the site, and looming above the structure, was a yellow tower crane that stretched over two hundred feet into the blue summer's sky.

Gavin was wearing mirrored shades and had a rucksack slung over his shoulder.

Ben and Mark headed down towards the site, with Gavin tailing behind the pair.

Janette, sucking on a Drumstick lolly, shot Alex a contemptuous glare. 'You'd go back now, if you had any sense, Alex.' With that, she strolled after the boys, leaving Alex with Sheryl.

Alex smiled nervously at her, but to his dismay, Sheryl looked annoyed.

'Are you OK, Sheryl?' asked Alex.

He'd tried to sound and appear more confident than he was. His legs were turning to jelly, and he started to consider taking Janette's advice and turning back. He didn't want to upset Sheryl.

'Why are you doing this? What exactly are you trying to prove here, Alex?'

'I just—'

'Get your arse in gear,' shouted Ben.

The group made for the crane's base, and no one spoke as they gazed up at it.

Alex gasped as though a mythic creature stood before him, ready to devour him in one bite.

Gavin scooped up an orange builder's hat and donned it, despite it being too big for his head.

Alex peered down to Sheryl, and she avoided his gaze, as she sat on a stack of breeze blocks, arms folded, kicking away at some stray nails on the dusty floor.

Alex swallowed hard, his throat dry and sore. Yes, it was high, but he was an excellent climber and he'd climbed endless amounts of trees in the past. When his mum hadn't been around to stop him, that was.

'OK, Clayton, you ready?'

'Yes,' said Alex.

Alex headed for the crane, but Ben grabbed his arm and yanked him back.

'Whoa, hold up, half-pint. You are way too eager,' said Ben.

'Am I not climbing this?' asked Alex.

Gavin grinned psychotically. 'You are gonna shit your knickers, Clayton.'

Ben put his arm around Alex's shoulders. 'You climb to the top. Then you make your way onto the arm. Go right to the end—'

'Then you drop and hang. For ten seconds. We will be counting, Clayton. So don't cheat, you fucking little lemon,' said Gavin.

Ben's face screwed up, irked by Gavin's interruption.

Alex nodded. 'OK.'

To everyone's surprise, he set off again with no hesitation. But again, Ben pulled him back. 'Bloody hell, Clayton, I haven't finished yet!'

'Right,' said Alex.

Ben clicked his fingers at Gavin, who smiled, picked up his rucksack and opened it. 'Here it is. The good stuff,' said Gavin.

Alex regarded the container of Freddy Killner's cider, and his face dropped. He could even see his own mortified reflection in Gavin's shades as he passed him the drink.

'Glug, glug,' said Janette.

So, Alex would get to try some. He considered now was perhaps not the ideal time to experiment with alcohol. He'd not even tried a proper drink before. The odd stolen swig of beer at Christmas, but that was about it. What if he passed out mid-climb? He undid the lid and took a tiny sip. All eyes focused on him and the pressure was unbearable. He swallowed the liquid back, and it reminded him of a smooth and expensive apple juice, not too dissimilar to the stuff he tried in a hotel in Torquay years back. He took another sip and screwed the lid back on, licking his lips.

Gavin snatched the cider, took the lid off and tossed it over his shoulder. 'What the hell was that? You little pussy-faced princess!' He shoved the container back at Alex. 'Now take a proper drink.'

'Fine,' said Alex, lifting the cider to his lips. Gavin gave him a hand by tilting the container so Alex had no option but to guzzle the stuff until it practically exploded from his nostrils.

'Let me see,' said Ben, inspecting the container. He shook his head and handed it back. 'More.'

Gavin repeated the process until Alex was choking on the stuff.

'Hey, I want a slug this time,' grumbled Mark, grabbing the cider.

'What are you doing?' asked Gavin.

Mark gave Alex a quick, secret wink. 'I never got a drop of the last batch you nicked, Gav.'

'That's cos you're a total lightweight, Corkscrew. You talk enough twaddle when you're sober,' laughed Ben.

Mark smirked. 'Yeah, OK, Ben. Says you, who gets tanked up on Vimto.'

Ben puffed out his cheeks. 'No, it had Cinzano mixed in.'

Mark patted Ben on the shoulder. 'You keep telling yourself that, compadre.'

Ben seemed confused for a brief moment, then shrugged, unbothered.

'Um, can I start now?' muttered Alex.

'You're so keen. I like it. Go on, up you go then, you nutter,' said Ben.

Gavin curled his top lip and watched Alex furtively. Annoyance radiated from the boy, and it was obvious he didn't want Alex to conquer this; which made Alex even more determined. He guessed Gavin reckoned he would have bottled it by now, so he'd show that annoying peanut-head what he was all about.

Alex stepped up the metal steps towards the crane's concrete base and made his way through the lattice frame and onto the ladder. He started climbing and slipped off the third rung, then heard a nasty hiss of laughter from behind.

'Wicked start, Clayton. I'll get the shovel ready to scrape you off the floor, you stupid muppet,' bellowed Gavin.

Alex's mind swam. The alcohol must have gone to his head already. But strangely, his fear had faded away, and he felt intrepid and eager now. He craned his neck and looked up the ladder. Without a second thought, he climbed.

Thirteen

As Alex started his climb, Mark's mouth went dry and his temples pulsated so rapidly, he thought they might explode. This was too much, way too much. They knew this might end up like another Gambridge scenario. Although Alex would receive more than just broken bones if he slipped up today. He considered sharing the pun with the others but knew it was in bad taste, so kept his gob shut. Mark didn't know how he'd cope seeing Alex fall to his death. It would scar him for life, of that he was certain. It wasn't possible to undo images like that; once they entered the brain, you could never shift them. They stayed forever. Even some horror films he'd seen had left mental scars. That horrific Nightmare on Elm Street he'd watched stopped him from sleeping for weeks.

Alex was over halfway up the crane's mast now and was moving at quite an impressive rate. He climbed like an agile gibbon. Mark viewed his friends. Gavin, glasses now off, his eyes bright with excitement, was sticking out his tongue and biting it in nervous anticipation. Mark guessed he'd love to see Alex plunge from the top. It would make his year.

Janette, her arms crossed, was chewing her bottom lip as she gazed up, wide-eyed. OK, she didn't much like Alex, but surely she wasn't that callous that the prospect of seeing Alex splattered to smithereens excited her. She was protective of Sheryl and would find it difficult to accept any lad that fancied her best mate into the group. The girls had played together at nursery and grown up together. Same infant school, same secondary school and weekends and summers spent together always. They were inseparable, and Janette often said Sheryl was like the sister she'd never had.

Ben had also known both girls since a young age and was fiercely loyal to them. You upset them, you upset Ben. It was that simple. Gavin was no different.

Mark looked to Ben, who now gripped his dad's bird-watching binoculars and was eagerly scanning Alex's progress.

Mark gazed at Sheryl last. She fiddled with a piece of metal, making a point of not looking up as she sat in depressed silence. She knew Alex was only doing this to impress her. At this exact moment, Mark knew what was racing through Sheryl's mind – if Alex fell, it would be all her fault.

Alex reached as far up as the crane's control cabin and turntable. The arm was still a way up. He hadn't yet looked down, and his hands were sweating as he took the final ladder rungs and moved onto the rear part of the arm. The view surrounding him was stunning, however he tried to keep his focus on where he was placing each hand rather than soaking up the wonderful scenery. There was a thin platform that creaked underfoot as he gingerly stepped onto it and held onto the railing that was chest height on him. A concrete counterweight sat right at the end of the crane, along with the winch and motors. But he was going the other way. Across the main jib; the part with no safety railing. Inch by inch, he moved across onto it, all the while trying to imagine he was just playing on the huge dome-shaped climbing frame on the school field. It was at least the same colour. A voice played over and over in his head – *Don't look down – don't look down.* Alex wiped his palms across his t-shirt, rubbing off the sweat, though never letting both hands go as he moved along. His grip on that frame was so tight the metal squeaked as he eased along each gap, reaching for each bar that separated the sections on the jib. He tried not to lift his trainers, so he slid them sideways along the bottom bar. Alex guessed this must be a walkway bar for the workmen to access the crane's trolley, should it ever become stuck or require maintenance. Though they'd have specialist equipment, such as hooks and safety harnesses before they dared to venture along here. This thought made his legs wobble.

His body was at a slight angle as the jib was triangular, prism-shaped. It was like a giant Toblerone box, he considered, as a heavy breeze suddenly hit. It was a splendid, calm and breezeless day, but standing in the clouds, some two hundred feet high, the wind was bound to pick up. The urge to look down became immense, but he shook his head and squeezed his eyes shut, letting the urge pass over him, and knowing if he got a proper eyeful of the height, it would just cause him to panic. He needed to stay focussed and in control. He heard a faint shout of encouragement but wasn't certain who it came from. Ben, he guessed.

Alex opened his eyes and took a massive deep breath and started moving along, but his mouth started watering and sickness began rising in his stomach. He tried and failed to fight down the nausea, and the vomit violently expelled from his mouth and nose. His head started spinning as the rancid apple-flavoured liquid fell downwards. Then the inevitable happened. He glanced down. Then he gasped and retched again.

Ben and Gavin bickered over the binoculars; then Ben hammered his fist on the safety hat and Gavin winced and gave up. 'Arsehole,' mumbled Gavin, going over to the rucksack and removing a bag of Jelly Babies.

'What's he doing up there?' asked Janette, gazing up and shielding her eyes from the sun.

'I think he was puking. He's not moved for a while,' said Ben, peering through the binoculars. 'No, wait… he's off again, heading for the end.'

Janette crinkled her nose as she tried to focus on Alex. 'I bet he bottles it and doesn't hang.'

Mark assumed Janette must have been as nervous as he was. She must have been praying Alex would back out now. He certainly wanted him to. Mark visualised Alex silently falling in the distance as they all stared helplessly, their mouths hanging open. He wouldn't go over to bear witness to the aftermath. No way he would. Mark couldn't imagine the state of a body after falling from such a height, and he had no desire to find out either. No doubt Gavin would race over, eager to inspect the damage.

Ben's excited squeal snapped Mark from his morbid thoughts.

'He's there. He's at the end,' said Ben.

The moment of truth, thought Mark. Did this short, skinny lad have the guts to risk his life to prove himself? He realised both his hands were shaking at his sides and he thought he might piss himself at any given moment.

His belly was now cramping so badly it was painful, and he wasn't sure if he could move from the spot because his legs wouldn't work. It was like they'd been set in concrete. Plus, he was desperate for a poo now. Just nerves, of course. He needed to overcome them and swing over the side. He'd come this far, and there was no way he'd face Gavin's barrage of piss-taking. Not today. Alex thought about the bullying he received from those idiots at school. The belittling name-calling he'd just tolerated and accepted as part of his normal daily routine. That smelly, perfume-wearing cow, Kay, in his house, poisoning his dad against him. Janette's cruel smile as she whispered nasty comments in Sheryl's ear. Gavin's bitter little face. His mum. That cancer. That horrible cancer that had crashed into her life and ruined everything. That had crushed his world. He trembled all over as he crouched down, wiped the sweat from his palms using his t-shirt, found a decent grip on the middle bar, then turned and prepared to drop down.

Mark's stomach was in knots as he watched Alex preparing to hang.

Gavin offered the Jelly Babies around. Only Janette accepted one.

'Gav thinks he's at the movies,' said Janette. She giggled nervously as she popped the sweet in her mouth, but not chewing it, Mark noticed.

Gavin was chewing sweets like a madman. 'Better than the movies. A chance to see some real carnage.'

After one final, deep breath, Alex gripped the metal and let himself drop. He hung there, his legs dangling in the air, whilst he started counting in his head and focused on the hook block that hung a few feet from him.

'That's ten seconds… but he's still hanging,' said Ben, binoculars pressed hard against his face.

'He's gonna fall,' gasped Janette.

'Yeah, he's fucked,' said Gavin. He laughed, though it was a nervous laugh, and he looked worried.

'Where the hell is Sheryl?' asked Mark.

Sheryl was clambering up the crane's ladder.

'Oh my God, she's going up there,' shouted Janette.

'Corkscrew, go after her!' demanded Ben, still keeping his focus on Alex. But Gavin had already chased off after her.

He kicked his legs through the air and his trainer slipped off and plummeted. He cried out and bit his lip. His arms were burning and his hands began losing grip. Alex's fingers were slipping. He didn't have the energy to pull himself up; he just didn't have it in him.

Ben, Mark and Janette stood in stunned silence as Alex hung and swayed. Mark put his hands over his face, peeking through his fingers. He was certain Clayton was a goner. They were about to witness him die, and they were powerless to help. What would they say to the police and their parents? Would they all go to prison?

Sheryl shot up the ladder with Gavin not far behind. But it would be impossible for them to reach Alex, as he'd never stick it out that long.

He gritted his teeth so tightly his jaw locked and his muscles felt like they were on fire. Alex knew he must make a grab for the foot rail. And he needed to do it fast. He let his right hand go and grabbed onto the higher bar. His heart was racing as he started swinging his right leg, kicking his trainer-free foot onto the metal. He just got it up, but slipped straight off. Last chance. He wouldn't be able to hold on for much longer. Alex screamed in torment and swung his leg again, using every fibre of energy he could muster. He just about slung the leg over the foot rail and the pressure eased from his left arm. But he still didn't let go. He hooked the crook of his elbow over the bar and hung sideways, knowing the ordeal wasn't over.

Ben pumped his fist triumphantly. 'He's got his leg over!'

'He's not done yet,' said Mark. Though some hope was restored that Alex had averted death. Mark heard Gavin shouting for Sheryl to come down.

'He looks stuck. What's this div up to?' asked Janette.

Alex couldn't say how he mustered the energy, but he somehow found the strength to pull himself upright and he hugged that metal crane arm. His body shook all over and tears fell down his cheeks. He stared back along to the control cabin and tried to fight back the panic when he realised he still had to climb back. But he knew the sooner he did, the sooner his feet would be on solid ground; so he started the slow process of moving back along. When he saw Sheryl climbing onto the rear of the crane, he almost slipped off in shock. Then he saw Gavin.

'Are you OK, Alex?' shouted Sheryl.

'I'm fine. Go back down!' replied Alex. He was glad she'd attempted a rescue, but scared senseless she'd slip and fall.

'Stop titting about and hurry up, Clayton,' said Gavin.

Even from this distance, Alex could see Gavin was shooting him a baleful glare. For a brief moment, Alex thought Gavin was planning to wait and throw him off the crane himself; but then he muttered something and descended the ladder.

Alex was giddy with excitement and glowing with pride as he flopped onto a stack of polystyrene sheeting. He tried to fight back the impulse he felt to jump up, scream for joy and wave his fists in triumph. He hadn't been able to resist giving Gavin a smug smile when Ben had slapped him hard on the back and congratulated him as soon as he had reached the crane's base with Sheryl.

'You're a crazy little devil,' said Mark, offering him a couple of squares of Dairy Milk, 'I was so certain you would slip off there. Wasn't you scared?'

'Well, I—'

'I found it,' interrupted Sheryl. She was holding Alex's trainer by the lace. 'Next time you climb up a crane, tie your flipping laces, you silly moose.'

'Next time!' said Alex, arching his eyebrows.

Mark and Sheryl looked at each other. They both started laughing. Alex and Ben joined in.

'Nice one, Clayton,' said Ben.

Alex smiled at Ben, and couldn't help notice Gavin and Janette's resentful expressions, as they talked in hush voices away from the others.

Sheryl held out his trainer. 'That was the craziest thing I've ever seen, Alex.'

Alex knew he was blushing as he accepted the trainer and slipped it back on. Then his hand hunted for the brooch under his t-shirt. He wanted to check he hadn't lost it. He relaxed when his fingers touched it.

Fourteen

Alex was pretty plastered from the afternoon spent drinking with Corkscrew and his Belgian manager. It was early evening when he returned to the coffee shop, which still heaved with eager punters, so he joined the line, hands in pockets, and felt like a naughty schoolboy when he faced the weary man at the counter. The short, heavyset guy was in his late fifties, had a double chin and hooded eyelids, and didn't look very Dutch. Alex had envisioned chatting away with a young, hip bud-tender, discussing his options and being advised which strain would best serve his needs. In reality, he was under pressure and out of his comfort zone, so instead just asked for White Widow, which he'd seen on top of the menu board. He'd considered purchasing a space muffin, which was three euros, but decided against it.

'One gram... five?' asked the man, who appeared jaded.

'Uh, ready-made... please.' said Alex in a hushed tone.

The man grunted and rolled a clear plastic tube across the counter. It had a perfectly rolled joint encased inside.

'That's Amnesia,' muttered the man.

'Sounds perfect. I'll take two. And a latte, please.'

By now, Alex was way past caring what stuff he purchased, as the man rolled another tube towards him and Alex paid and waited for his drink. Once he received his change and coffee, he scanned for a free table. Locating the last empty table by the window, he took a seat, popped the lid on the tube and slipped out the joint. He chuckled to himself when he realised he had nothing to light the damn thing with. Total amateur. He guessed they sold novelty lighters here, but the queue was long and he couldn't be bothered to wait. Instead, he walked to the neighbouring table and asked to borrow the lighter from a couple of guys in their thirties, who were busy grinding weed and chatting in Dutch. One man handed him a plastic lighter and told him to keep it, and his companion said that he hoped Alex enjoyed his smoke and to have a great evening. Their English was flawless. Alex lit the joint and took a long drag, coughing as it hit the back of his throat. He took another two hits, before placing it down in a tin ashtray with the cafe's logo printed inside and sipping his latte. Alex didn't know if he was smoking neat weed, or if it had tobacco mixed in. He'd only ever tried smoking a cigarette once, and it made him throw up. Fags reminded him of his dad. Alex hoped this stuff was the answer to his sleep issues. Though if it was, he wouldn't know where to start searching for a supplier back home. Perhaps vaping would be more his thing? He'd ask Mark about that. He didn't want to keep taking those pills. Yes, they helped him fall asleep, but the dreams were so intense and so realistic, and it didn't seem to matter what he took. Temazepam, Zopiclone, Ambien, the results were the same and those memory dreams came. What he craved, more than anything, was to drift into a deep, dreamless sleep; a proper sleep where his mind emptied and his brain switched off. He couldn't remember the last time he'd slept like this. The Amnesia took effect fast. The high came on strong and he wondered if he should have tried one puff to begin with. He smiled to himself. Most people experimented with drugs in their early teens or twenties; not at forty-five. Had he missed out on the drug scene? The jam-packed raves, crazy parties, holidays to Ibiza and weekend-long festivals. He never had friends that took recreational drugs, nor did he mix in those types of circles. He was only trying cannabis now because Natalie had suggested it. Plus, it seemed normal to do it here. No different from ordering a glass of beer.

A strange, warm sensation washed over him as he sipped on a tall glass of beer that had a two-inch frothy head on it. It was like he'd taken heroin or ecstasy or something stronger. Weed was a real mind wreck. It was potent, and it didn't make you feel tired and dopey like he'd always imagined it would. He guessed he'd smoked too much for his first experience, or perhaps he'd picked the wrong strain for an inexperienced smoker. Not that he wasn't enjoying the sensations, but he was anything but tired, and his heart felt peculiar. Alex was sitting in the middle of a crowded, bustling bar, listening to music on his iPhone through his Ear-Pods. The place appeared dated and had a homely, relaxed atmosphere. He watched all the punters talking, drinking and laughing. Their mouths moved as they chatted away, but he could just hear the music as he enjoyed his beer. It was the finest beer ever to pass his lips, or at least it seemed that way at this moment. He'd found a two-hour set on Mark's SoundCloud profile and whacked up the volume to an ear-splitting level. Alex had always related dance and electronic music to that annoying distant thud, or doof, doof, that echoed from a passing teenager's car during the early hours of the morning, but never knew how engaging those sounds were when you listened keenly. He closed his eyes and sat back, drifting off into another dimension where he floated through a void. Here, there was no pain, no hurt and no uninviting thoughts about his past, as his mind became soothed by the mesmerising sounds of DJ Corker. His old friend, Corkscrew. The melodic beats built steadily, becoming deeper and deeper, then darker and faster; and then exploded like a train crashing through a window. The heavy bass boomed inside him, and he wondered why he'd not embraced music under the influence before. He'd go to the event and see DJ Corker in action. He wanted to ask Mark if he wouldn't mind if he used some of his music as a backing soundtrack for a fast-paced promotional YouTube film for Alex Clayton Photography. It would be epic. Unfortunately, the tap on his shoulder from the young barman snapped Alex from his reverie, and the room started spinning as soon as he opened his eyes. The bar was now less busy and five minutes later, Alex was outside being sick into the canal.

About a minute after emptying his stomach, he clambered to his feet and heard the ringing of a bell, before he even noticed the push-bike heading straight for him. It almost collided with him, though the female rider didn't seem fazed as she swerved around him and came alarmingly close to the canal's edge. Another bike zipped past; this one had a sidecar attached with two poodles seated inside it. The dogs regarded him with an aloof gaze as it passed by.

The area still appeared packed with people, and Alex had no clue what time it was, though guessed not past ten. He checked his Garmin watch, but his vision started to blur so he couldn't focus on the numbers. He shook his wrist to light up the screen, but that didn't help. Though his mind was hazy, he felt better after throwing up. Alex strolled along the canal and decided against the music event, as he conceded to the fact he was in no fit state to try to find the venue. He was sure Mark's manager had said the event was a fifteen-minute taxi ride. Was it Central Studios? He couldn't be certain without checking the ticket they'd emailed him. *Damn,* thought Alex, wondering where his mobile phone was. He frantically searched his pockets as anxiety washed over him and he panicked. His room keycard was also inside his phone case. Not finding it in his jacket or jeans, he raced back to where he'd been sick, dropped to his knees and scanned the floor. Relief washed over him when he located the phone face down on the ground. He scooped it up and put it in his back pocket, wiping a sheen of sweat from his brow. It had been a minor miracle no one had picked up the phone or unwittingly booted it into the water. Alex decided to call it a night and head for the hotel. He didn't know where he was, but he considered he could gauge which direction he needed to go by using the location of the Dom Tower cathedral, which he spotted towering above the buildings behind him. Alex remembered his hotel was close by there. Then he glimpsed the distinctive lights from another canal-side beerhouse, thinking it wouldn't hurt to get a quick nightcap.

Fifteen

Mark had gone back to his hotel, showered, shaved and had several coffees to sober up after the afternoon session with Clayton. He sat on the bed with wet hair and a towel wrapped around him, sucked on his vape, then slunk back and checked the time on his phone. It was nine-thirty, almost time for Trent to collect him. Mark could see the wrap of cocaine on the bedside cabinet and he sighed, disappointed in himself. He decided he'd finish the gear to get him through tonight's event, and that would be it. If Daan tried to ply him with anymore, he'd get a size nine boot up his rear end. Then he shook his head and grinned, knowing full well that was all bollocks. A bit of what you fancied now and again didn't hurt. It wasn't like he was shovelling the stuff up his nose every five minutes.

Mark massaged his aching temples. Clayton's words had echoed through his mind incessantly since their conversation. *Doesn't this matter to you anymore?* Of course it did. OK, if he was totally honest with himself, he didn't think about it regularly and he hadn't thought about it in a long while; but yes, the truth *did* still matter. And it would matter to Janette, Ben and Gavin. With an odd sensation in the pit of his stomach and the beginnings of a severe headache on the cards, he unlocked his phone and opened Google.

Ben finished up his fourth can of Thatcher's cider and opened a large bag of cheese-flavoured crisps, as he slouched back on the sofa to watch the television. They were settled in the back lounge, or the comfy lounge, slash viewing room, as his wife liked to refer to it. Kayla snuggled up next to him. She was wearing her thick pink onesie and reading something on her iPad. Kayla watched Ben out of the corner of her eye as he placed the empty can down on the table. She'd been counting, and he'd get it in the neck if he dared to sneak another can from the fridge. He fancied another one now, though. Kayla still nursed the same glass of wine he'd poured her an hour ago. He'd wait a bit and nab one more.

'I'm reading this story about a guy who had two families on the go,' she said, eyes focused on the device, 'he had five children between them. They even lived on the same estate. He got away with living a double life for almost ten years. Blimey, can you imagine?'

'What a twat. I bet he never gets five minutes' peace,' said Ben, licking crisp dust from his fingers.

'How could you live like that? The secrets people keep,' she said, shaking her head with her chin resting on her hand.

Ben yawned. 'Madness.'

He thought the guy deserved a medal for pulling that off. Then he grumbled, seeing his mobile phone vibrating and dancing.

'Ben, it's Saturday night! Turn that phone off.'

'It's withheld,' he said, wiping his hands on his t-shirt and snatching his phone from the marble coffee table.

'Well, let them leave a message, or tell them to call back Monday.'

Ben answered the phone. 'Ben Napier,' he said in a moody tone.

'Hi, Ben. It's Mark… Mark Corker,' said the caller.

Ben's face lit up in surprise. 'Corkscrew! How's it going, mate?'

Gavin pulled out the two bags of shopping and slammed the rear door shut with his bum. He'd popped up to the Tesco Express and grabbed some essentials, so he could at least rustle up sausage, egg and chips. He'd also got some milk for tea and cereals. He'd crashed out on the sofa at six o'clock this evening and didn't wake until gone nine. Some Saturday night this was. Zara used to thrive in the kitchen, enjoying nothing more than an afternoon of experimental cooking, but now she had zero interest in spending time in the kitchen and even less interest in eating food. He'd still make her a plate, though she'd just pick away at it and turn her nose up. Well, if she was conscious, that was. As he approached the main entrance, he saw Roland leaving the rubbish and recycling area. He trotted in Gavin's direction, waving to him. 'Hold up, Gavin.'

'You alright, Roland?'

'Hey, you had a visitor. He left a couple of minutes ago. You must have just missed each other.'

Gavin started scanning the area. He wasn't expecting anyone tonight.

'He said he knocked, but he didn't get a reply. I told him you'd popped out.'

'Did he say who he was?'

'Yes, Javon, nice polite black lad in his mid-twenties. He was wearing a blue sports jacket, with the tick label thing on the chest. And a baseball cap. A red one. Quite a dark red,' said Roland, tapping his chin, as though trying to recall any further details. 'Um, yes, he said it was about your car,' he continued eventually.

'Thanks. I know who it was,' said Gavin.

Roland loved to describe every visitor in fine detail. Sometimes he even did it with delivery drivers and cold callers. This was all Gavin needed. Javon was Ned's nephew, and he'd purchased the Fiat from him a few weeks back and only paid him half. He still owed him over five hundred quid. Ned had been the one who'd suggested Gavin buy the car, so he wouldn't have to rely on pickups from the other lads. Said it was a decent little runner with low mileage. He was surprised that he hadn't had it in his neck from his workmate yet, as the big Jamaican was very close to his nephew. He'd ignored Javon's calls and text messages, so a visit was on the cards. Gavin knew he'd need to bung him some wedge soon to placate the lad. Ned was well respected amongst the crew, so falling out with him would be a dangerous move, especially if he wanted to keep hold of his spot in the firm.

Gavin grinned at Roland. 'Night, Roland.'

'Turrah, Gav,' said Roland.

Zara sat on the sofa, cuddling her knees and watching a wildlife documentary. Well, staring at the screen at least. She wasn't taking much in. She gave Gavin a quick, sideways glance as he entered, then turned back to the screen.

'Hungry?' he asked, shaking the bags.

'No, I'm not,' she said, her voice deadpan.

He pulled off his bomber jacket and tossed it onto the back of the sofa, then took the shopping to the kitchen and slung it onto the side. An unfamiliar beep sounded from his phone, and when he checked it, found he'd received a message on the Facebook app. It was rare for anyone to contact him via social media. He opened the app and the name Ben Napier popped onto the screen. He grinned broadly and opened the message: *Hi Gav, hope all OK with you, mate. Just spoke to Corkscrew, and he said Alex Clayton wants to meet us all. Next week?? Will you come?*

Gavin took in a deep breath and read the message again. Although he was glad to hear from Ben, just seeing the name Alex Clayton made his entire body stiffen, and he had an impulse to launch his phone at the wall. Instead, he shoved it in his pocket, marched into the lounge and snatched up his jacket.

'Going out again?' asked Zara. 'Buy me some vodka.'

Gavin didn't reply. He shoved on his jacket and was heading for the door.

Sixteen

The line of cocaine he'd done on the way to the event had turned his stomach to jelly, and he'd spent fifteen minutes sitting on the toilet. He'd slipped off into the artist's bathroom, a hip area with walls that were covered in promotional posters, bold graffiti and flamboyant sketches. He felt hot, clammy and was keen to get his set done and dusted. Mark finished up, washed his hands and splashed water over his face. He heard the cubicle door thud and somehow knew it was Daan coming out before he gazed up.

'Hey, Marko. Ready to rock this place?' asked Daan, studying Mark with a serious expression.

'Yep,' replied Mark, turning off the taps and grabbing a paper hand towel.

'You OK? You look very odd. Grey, in fact.'

'I'm fine. Think I've been burning the candle at both ends.'

'Can I ask you something?'

'Yeah, what's up?'

'When your friend left the bar today, he called you Corkscrew. What's with that?'

'It's an old nickname. That's what everyone called me back in the day.' Mark tossed the paper towel in the bin. 'Nobody has called me that for years.'

'Why Corkscrew?'

'Well, my dad was a prison officer at Standford Hill, on Sheppey. And the kids called me the screw's kid for a time, until some genius thought, Corker and screw, and they started calling me Corkscrew. And it just stuck. It wasn't the worst nickname, I guess. It never bothered me. I mean, one lad, Steve Gibb, was called vadge-face throughout his school life, because of a very unusual birthmark.'

'You know, I thought perhaps you once had curly hair, like that Mick Hucknall,' said Daan.

'Definitely not, no.'

Daan started humming Simply Red's Pleasure at the Fairground.

Mark rolled his eyes and gave him a faint smile. Daan was referencing the story he'd told him about a few years back. He'd been having doggy-style sex with a stripper in a Hamburg club, and that song started playing on the radio in the background, which had, for reasons unknown, set Daan off, and he'd giggled like an insane loon. He'd subsequently been booted out of the seedy establishment. The security guys had tossed him out through a fire exit, leaving him in the cold and rain wearing just his pants. Plus his passport had been in his jacket, so he tried to sneak back in and a bouncer booted him a good one in the balls. He kicked up enough fuss to get his jacket back and ended up walking the streets with sore testicles, wearing just his leather jacket over his undies.

Daan stopped grinning and gazed at Mark. He looked concerned now, a characteristic his manager rarely showed. 'Is everything OK? What's happened?'

'I'm good, Daan,' said Mark, his voice breaking as he spoke. Then he turned away from Daan and gazed into the sink. This weekend had brought back some painful memories. His eyes filled with warm tears and his vision hazed.

'Whatever it is, you can tell me. You can trust me. With anything,' said Daan.

'I have a secret. It's messed up,' said Mark.

Ben opted for a can of Coke instead of cider as he stood in the glow of the American fridge light, absorbed in his thoughts. The fridge door alarm started beeping, but he didn't notice. He just held that can and stared forward, ruminating over that phone call.

'Will you shut that already?' said Kayla. 'What are you doing standing there with your head in the fridge?'

Ben sighed and shouldered the door shut.

'Coke? Come on, Ben. There are more calories in that sugary fizz than the cider,' she said, shaking her head with exaggerated disappointment.

'I just need a cold drink. I have a migraine coming,' said Ben.

'Then come up to bed already. It's late.'

'All right, Kayla, I'll be up in a while,' he snapped, instantly regretting his grumpy tone.

Kayla crossed her arms haughtily. 'Fine, goodnight then, moody-knickers.'

As his wife walked out, Ben leaned against the fridge door. Saturday, sexy-time was well and truly off the table. Though he was hardly in the mood now, of course. He grabbed a glass tumbler and hunted down the Jack Daniel's to accompany the Coke.

Gavin vowed to give up smoking about nine years ago, pretty much as soon as his old-man had dropped dead from a fatal heart attack. He'd been sixty-eight, and he smoked twenty a day. Gavin wanted to last longer than that. Unable to stop altogether, he'd cut down to a handful a day, and he kept some cigarettes knocking about in his car, in case of emergencies. He found a crumpled box that had two cigarettes and a disposable lighter wedged in the glove box. Gavin flicked the flame and lit up, as he leant back in the driver's seat, wondering what his old-fella would have made of his situation with Zara. He guessed he'd have unsympathetically told him to stop being a useless dick-head and take action. After three puffs, he tossed the cigarette out of the window. Luckily, he'd considered his actions on the journey here, and by the time he'd arrived, he decided he needed to stop, calm himself down and think about his next course of action. Skender's lounge light was on, but no movement had been spotted.

Then the light went off.

An hour passed and the gang loitering outside the flats started drifting away, leaving the entrance clear. He was about to make his move when he noticed Skender's lounge light come back on, so he paused and stayed put. Ten minutes later, he saw some movement up there and he was certain it was Tim, judging by the size and shape of the figure. Then the blind rolled down and Gavin swore under his breath. He'd have to wait until that huge lump had gone before venturing inside.

Ben checked his phone, letting out a disappointed sigh when he didn't see a reply from Gavin. He didn't have Gavin's mobile number and didn't have a clue where he was living these days. Last he'd heard, Gavin had moved to the Midlands somewhere. Facebook was the only method of contact Ben had for him, and the profile Gavin used was under the alias Grouchy Gouchy with his profile photo set as the Cookie Monster from Sesame Street. Gavin hadn't posted on there for well over a year, so Ben doubted he was even using it anymore. Would it be so terrible if Gavin was uncontactable? He hadn't seen his old friend for over a decade, and although he was intrigued to learn how the old reprobate was doing, did he really need Gouch back in his life? Trouble followed that man like a terrible stink. And Ben doubted that would ever change.

Gavin woke with a start and blearily gazed around the car. He let out a massive yawn and checked his watch. One thirty a.m. He'd drifted asleep and didn't have a clue if Tim had left during his snooze, but decided it was now or never, so exited the car. As he did, the entrance door flung open and Tim strolled outside. Gavin slid down behind his car as Tim walked past, hands stuffed in his pockets and eyes like slits. He headed away, spitting in the road, oblivious to the skulking presence right under his nose. Gavin gave it another ten minutes, then headed inside the flats. He took with him a crowbar and an empty North-Face rucksack.

As he ascended the stairs two at a time, he prayed the thick door chain he'd seen wasn't locked in place. It was game over if it was.

Gavin slotted the key in and winced as he pushed the door open and it squeaked loudly. He listened and waited for a few moments. Then he crept into the lounge, leaving the door ajar.

The coffee table was on, the light glowing neon blue, which lit up a semi-naked body on the far sofa. He stood still as he watched the figure, but it was soon obvious they were flaked out. He took several careful steps towards them for a better look and realised it was fish-lips, who had been here on his previous visit. She was wearing a pink thong and nothing else, unless you included the expensive-looking pair of studio-style, over-the-ear headphones. Music was thudding through them, and he guessed she was out of her nut.

A laptop balanced on the sofa's arm, and boxes, packages and parcels surrounded the sofa. He snatched up one of the smaller packages and read the label; it was addressed to a Mr B Wallace at a London address. Gavin opened it up, finding it contained another package, this one silver and vacuum sealed.

Written in black marker pen was 1G.

Gavin turned his attention to the laptop. The girl started snoring and a line of drool started rolling down her chin. He couldn't help but take a good gander at her tits, thinking those tiny pink nipples looked good enough to nibble on. Gavin pulled his gaze away, telling himself that now wasn't the time to get distracted, and instead, focussed on the laptop's screen. He touched the track pad, and the laptop flashed open on a shopping page. He scrolled through the page and soon established he was viewing a drugstore website. The page resembled an Amazon-style site, but this one had illegal substances up for sale. Ketamine, MDMA, weed, the lot. He even spotted an option to purchase Spice and a ton of listed drugs he'd never even come across before. All the prices were in Bitcoins and he guessed the page was on the deep-web or dark-net or whatever they called it these days. The lads at work had spoken about buying drugs online and having it posted straight to their door. They'd had no issues receiving their orders, and there was even a review system, so any dodgy sellers would be red-flagged and outed. So, Skender was branching out into online distribution and was no doubt making a decent wedge too. A sensible way to do business, he thought.

Gavin put the rucksack down and started methodically tearing through the outer packaging on each parcel, removing each silver packet and popping it in his bag. He was no expert, but he summarised that these online orders were worth a fair wedge. He'd estimate a gram of smack being worth between eighty and a hundred quid, and some of these were marked up three grams. Zara had never purchased H in such large amounts, mainly because she couldn't afford to, and Gavin tried to visualise the sort of clientele that could afford the luxury of bulk buying their illicit drugs. Probably upper-class junkies; pretentious business executives and aristocratic dopesters.

He shouldered his bag and scanned the floor, checking for any stray packets, but seeing only an assortment of clothes, including a bra that matched the girl's thong, and a couple of used condoms. He grimaced, stepped over the johnnies, and placed his trainer on a permanent marker pen that rolled underfoot. Although he knew he shouldn't waste time with any immature antics, the temptation was too much and he couldn't resist leaving a cheeky memento. So

Gavin snuck back to the sofa and drew two googly eyes and a smiling mouth on one of the girl's boobs. As an afterthought, he added a lolling tongue to the mouth. He didn't bother with a nose, as the nipple represented this nicely. Gavin stood back and grinned mischievously at his drawing. The girl didn't stir. God, how he'd love to be a crafty fly on the wall when Skender waltzed in to find the graffiti on Sleeping Busty and all his products missing. He'd go ape-shit.

He crept over to the fish tank and tugged at the padlock. It was heavy duty, but he was certain the door's brackets would give way easily enough. He stared down the hallway and listened. Part of him wanted to walk straight into the bedroom and batter Skender senseless. That was the original plan when he started driving here. That's exactly what this piece of shit deserved, but ripping him off would suffice. And that would hit him where it really hurt.

It took little effort to prise one door from its hinges, though it made more noise than he intended. He let the broken oak door hang as he rummaged inside the cabinet, locating the metal cash box, which was what he'd been focusing on just before they started trying to feed him to the piranhas. It was locked, of course, and it was heavy, too. Gavin put it in the rucksack and would worry about opening that up later. He also found some small packets of powder, perhaps ten or twenty-pound bags, which he just about managed to cram in the rucksack's top, before he zipped up.

Gavin headed back across the lounge, considering if it would be too much bother to carry that cool cube table under his arm. But a sudden, urgent urge to urinate made his mind up for him. The hallway light came on and the noise of footsteps broke the silence. Bare feet slapping on wood. He contemplated making a run for it, but instead stood by the hallway and waited. Skender marched in, eyes searching, though he didn't seem to acknowledge that one of the cabinet doors was hanging off. Skender wore nothing but a pair of tight boxers, and Gavin was quite envious at how well-toned he was in the flesh. The lad was in terrific shape, with a six-pack in the making.

So, Gavin became the proverbial fly on the wall. Albeit a large, conspicuous one, armed with a crowbar, and aching for a piss.

'Mel, are you ever coming—' Skender's voice trailed off as he gawped at the girl's defaced breast. Then he knelt and started tipping up boxes. 'What the fuck?' he said, in complete bewilderment at finding them empty. He stood up and whirled around to face Gavin.

Gavin assumed that, without his backup, Skender would be scared witless and would beg him not to attack. He massively misjudged him. Without a flicker of hesitation, Skender roared and charged straight at him. The pair crashed onto the floor, and before Gavin could use it, he dropped the crowbar and was wrestling and rolling around the lounge in a twisted heap. Skender was even trying to bite his shoulder and attempting to gouge his eyes.

Gavin somehow flung Skender off of him, climbed to his feet and searched the floor for the crowbar, but couldn't see it anywhere.

Skender sprung up and started running towards a small open kitchen area.

Gavin swept Skender's legs; he fell sideways and thumped onto the oak floor, cracking his head in the process. Gavin guessed he was going to get a knife, or something worse.

Skender scurried to his feet, and Gavin grabbed him from behind, slung an arm around his neck, and dragged him backwards. They collided into a wall and Gavin momentarily had the wind knocked from him. But he didn't let go. He kept him in a headlock and the pair danced around the room, grunting and cursing. One of them stood on the TV remote, and the screen came to life.

Skender slung wild punches, landing one solid blow on Gavin's ear, and another on the back of his head, causing a throbbing clang to soar through his skull.

Gavin felt a sudden pain and realised Skender was biting him under the armpit. They were near the fish tank now. Then the fight was frantic and everything became a total blur of fists and scratches. Gavin yanked Skender by the hair and shoved his head down… down into the grim water. Skender was flaying his arms and writhing about like crazy, causing water to splash everywhere. Gavin pushed down with all the force he could muster. Just seconds after hearing an almighty crack, the pair landed in a heap of water and broken glass.

Gavin scrambled to get up, slipped on some glass, or perhaps a fish, and pitched forward, rolling gracelessly away from the shattered tank.

Skender crawled away on all fours, glass crunching under him. Then he clambered to his feet. 'I'll rip out your fucking throat for this!'

Gavin got to his feet and tried to reply, but stumbled on his response once Skender spun to face him.

Sensing Gavin's obvious shock, Skender delicately reached up and pulled his hand away when he touched on the shard of glass that was protruding out of his cheek, dangerously close to his left eye. He swallowed hard and his face was a mask of pure terror. The skin flapped open on one side, and thick blood oozed from the awful gash. Skender's frightened eyes glanced down to see the jagged point of the glass, mere centimetres from his eyeball. The shard itself was a good five inches long.

'Aww, holy crap. State of that,' said Gavin, gazing at the injury. He imagined that the blood would jet out if he tugged the shard free. Not that Skender had a chance to remove it, because he took two steps forward, his legs wobbled and he passed out right in front of him.

Gavin stood statue-still, with his mouth gaping as he attempted to gather his thoughts. Then the girl's sharp scream jarred him into action.

Gavin snatched up the rucksack and scurried towards the door. Only then did he notice the piece of glass stuck in his forearm, and that he'd pissed his pants during the altercation.

Seventeen

He could hear two women talking in Dutch as he opened his eyes and assessed where he was. He'd fallen asleep in the bathroom, cuddling the toilet with his head on the seat.

The door opened, the light switched on and two cleaners peered in. They had a brief conversation in Dutch, sniggered, and left the bathroom. A moment later he heard them leave the room.

Alex shuffled to the sink and was about to run the tap but stopped, noticing his mobile phone was in there. His toothbrush lay there too, but judging by the funky taste in his mouth, he was positive he hadn't used the damn thing last night. More items from his wash kit were over the floor, and he picked up his soap and shaving kit and glimpsed at his naked body in the mirror. The multiple mirrors presented him with a view from every angle, and he could see them. The mass of zigzag scars spread across the top of his buttocks and lower back. They looked more vivid and noticeable than ever today, especially in this harsh lighting. He gazed at them in disgust for a while, convinced that they appeared more raised now, and then the phantom stinging racked his skin.

Seal's Crazy was playing, and he had no clue where he was.

'Rise and shine, bud,' said a familiar-sounding Bristolian accent. 'You were out for the count.'

Mark rubbed his face, yawned and scratched his stubbly chin, as he looked around and realised he was in the back of a moving car. 'Smells like a new motor this, Trent. What car is it?'

'Mercedes. Gotta take it back to the rental, once I've dropped you at the airport,' said Trent, turning the radio down a notch. 'It is the same car we've had all weekend.'

'Is it? I hadn't noticed,' said Mark, looking for his vape pen. He felt shattered, and he hoped he had packed everything from the hotel, as he was practically sleepwalking when he'd gone to the underground car-park this morning.

'I gave the room a quick once over and I collected everything,' said Trent, as if reading Mark's mind.

'Good, nice one,' said Mark, wondering how Trent looked so fresh. 'Are you in running gear?'

'Yeah, I nipped out for a jog around the city first thing. I didn't have time to change.'

'You're mental.'

Trent was a clean living guy; no drugs, no booze and always did some sort of daily exercise. Not that he ever frowned upon those that overindulged, and he had no problem enjoying himself, whilst those around him were off of their tiny minds. It could sometimes be quite irritating.

'Man, that set last night! Where on earth did that spring from, Mark?' said Trent. He was scarcely watching the road, as he kept turning around in his seat.

'So, you think it went OK?' asked Mark.

'Man, you destroyed that place. Zero build-up. You were straight for the jugular. Boom, boom, boom… and you didn't let up. It's the fastest, most relentless set you've ever done. Here, listen, it's on YouTube already.' Trent was scanning through his phone, his eyes flicking from the road to the device.

'I was there, Trent,' said Mark.

'Nah, man, that wasn't you in that booth. That was some crazy hyped up, Techno demon. Not DJ Corker. Not the one we all know. I thought punters were gonna start dropping from exhaustion. The set was so—'

'Relentless,' said Mark drily.

'Yeah, man.'

'I just wanted to play a darker, harder mix,' said Mark, shrugging his shoulders. He peered out of the window, seeing a sign for Amsterdam. Forty kilometres. He'd soon be at the airport and jetting back home. Then next week, he was going back to where he grew up. He thought about the Brookacre estate and an icy shiver ran down the nape of his neck and continued down his back. He never belonged there.

'Turn Seal up. I love that song,' said Mark, closing his eyes.

'Yep, no problem,' said Trent, cranking up the volume.

Eighteen

'Morning Foxy-Mister,' said Kayla, as she handed Ben a steaming cup of tea and a slice of jam on toast. He sat up in bed and accepted them with a grin. Kayla gave him a tight-lipped smile. She was wearing her lazy day, baggy blue tracksuit and her was hair tied up with a purple, velvet scrunchie.

'So, are you staying in bed and watching TV all day?'

'You know I hibernate on Sunday,' he said, sipping on the strong tea. 'Aw, nice brew, ta, Cupcake.'

'It's lunchtime and someone wants you to go downstairs and play with her new Peppa Pig house.'

'The little monkey keeps calling me Daddy Pig,' said Ben, taking a large bite of the toast.

'It might be that big tummy of yours.'

'Cheeky sod,' he said, then flashed her a playful smile as he pulled the quilt over his naked stomach.

'So, what did your old buddy want?' she asked.

'Um, he's in town next weekend. He wants to meet up, perhaps grab a beer and catchup.' Ben folded the rest of the toast in half and wedged it in his mouth.

'Just the two of you?'

'I'll tell Jan, she'd definitely like to see him,' he replied, his mouth full.

'Aw, a little reunion,' she said, sitting on the bed and switching the TV off with the remote.

'Yeah, be nice.'

'That phonecall from DJ Marky, seemed to darken your mood,' she said, brushing toast crumbs off the sheet.

'No, don't be silly, Kayla. I was pleased to hear from him. Migraine, that's all. Reckon that cider didn't agree with me.'

'As long as everything's OK,' said Kayla.

Ben nodded, and though she grinned back, Kayla's eyes locked on him with an almost accusatory gaze.

'I'll get up and find Molly,' he said, sliding out of bed, slipping on a pair of moccasin slippers and grabbing his dressing gown. 'Oh, and Shane is popping by later,' he added quickly, then rushed into the en-suite bathroom, still holding his tea.

'What? Seriously? Please don't tell me he's bringing his girlfriend,' she groaned.

Ben popped his head around the door. 'Um, he didn't say. It's just a quick visit. He wants to talk about a fishing trip.'

Kayla scowled. 'When did you last fish, Ben? You hate being outdoors after September.'

'I was thinking I'd ask Ryan to join us.'

'Will there be Wi-Fi and somewhere to plug in his beloved Xbox?'

'No, of course there won't.'

'Then no. I'm confident he'd rather stick pins in his hands, rather than get stuck out in the cold and wet with you two numpties.'

'I used to go with my dad,' said Ben glumly.

'They didn't have games consoles back then.'

'I would still have gone. And yes, they did.' Ben came out of the en-suite drying his hands. 'Perhaps I should just tell him he's going.'

'Well, best of luck with that. Now get yourself dressed and get your bum down to the playroom,' she ordered.

Gavin peered through the window again, knowing he was being super paranoid; Skender didn't know his address, and he would currently be too busy having his face stitched back together to be out tracking him down. Gavin also parked his car several streets away and walked back, just as an extra precautionary measure.

He shut the curtain and checked his bandaged arm, which he'd covered in Sudocrem before applying the dressing. The blood had stopped seeping through, though extracting the glass was a painful experience, but it seemed alright now it had been tightly wrapped. He could not say the same for the nasty bite wound under his armpit, which hurt every time he dared to move. There was also a lump the size of a walnut protruding from his noggin, and a giant, purple bruise across both shoulders.

He opened the bedroom door and saw that Zara was still napping. She would be in bed all day. He returned to the lounge where his packed bags lay. One large Adidas sports holdall, and his rucksack, loaded with all of Skender's product. He'd smashed open the cash box within five minutes and found it contained over seven hundred quid. Gavin was half tempted to ring Sammy's contact and see if he'd take the gear off his hands at a low rate, but decided not to risk dealing with anyone in the city. Dealers and criminals often knew each other; or mixed in the same circles, so he couldn't chance it. He didn't know who Skender had connections with, and Gavin wasn't exactly acquainted with the players who inhabited Nottingham's underbelly.

Gavin picked up his handwritten note from the table and scanned it. His writing wasn't great, but he'd taken his time to get it as readable as possible. Gavin considered sending it by text, but that would be too impersonal. Had he covered everything? He'd explained that under no circumstances, should Zara attempt to contact Skender. He'd left her the number for the contact that Sammy hooked him up with, telling her that this guy did a home delivery service, and to order via WhatsApp. Gavin also left her some money and some gear too. He told her he had urgent stuff that needed sorting out back in Kent. The last part was the hardest to write. He just wasn't sure if he'd worded it right, so he re-read it to himself:

I've tried to the right thing, but I can't carry on. You need to do this alone. I know if you truly wanted to, you could do it. I'm not sure you even want to anymore. But I will love you always and I want you to find some peace, happiness and closure – Gavin xx.

Gavin folded the note and grabbed his bags. He scanned the messy flat and tears rolled down his cheeks. He considered he was taking the first opportunity that had presented itself as a chance to leave. A chance to turn his back on the situation, like a complete coward. But surely that wasn't the case. What he was doing was, in fact, one of the bravest things he'd ever done.

He picked up his bags and left the flat. And he genuinely didn't know if he'd be returning.

Janette stepped off the treadmill and wiped her face on a towel. She'd decided against going out running today, as it was hammering down. Plus, she periodically enjoyed a good stint on the machine. She sipped on a bottle of tepid water and gazed around the garage. She'd padded out the floor with new interlocking foam squares, giving the place a gym-like appearance. As well as the treadmill that had set her back three grand, there was an exercise bike, a Concept rowing machine, an assortment of weights, and a tall rack containing medicine balls. Her two bikes, both Santa Cruz models, hung from the wall, and a heavy duty Everlast punch bag was suspended from a hook. The well-used bag needed re-filling, as it was looking a tad flat. When she was having a bad day, that bag got a severe walloping.

Janette tossed down the bottle and walked over to her medal display racks, rearranging a triathlon medal that had slipped down from its hook. The racks were all full and home to over eighty pieces gained from marathons, bike races, ultra runs and Ironman events. Partaking in these events was like an addiction to Janette. It's what she lived for. It was what motivated her. The training, the build-up, and the buzz of the event itself. Not to mention the competitive element and the sense of achievement when she crossed that line, completing something that she'd convinced herself was an impossible task. But that feeling was always short lived, and so she would fervently search for the next challenge. Sometimes during an event, she would curse herself. When her entire body hurt and it was like she was running through thick concrete. When she'd hit the halfway point and already felt like collapsing into a bawling mess. But those were the best ones. The harder the journey, the greater the reward. To most people, her medals were just bits of metal or show-off pieces. 'Oh, look how brilliant I am.' That wasn't the case. Not for her, anyway. They were memories, and each one held its own little story and its own epic adventure. One day, when she was elderly and unable to walk properly, she wanted to hold her medals in her wrinkled hands and reminisce. To fondly think back to the days when she could run fifty kilometres through dense forests and rugged cliff passes. Janette was fitter than ever before. Admittedly, she sometimes suffered from inflamed knee tendons, and on the odd occasion, it felt like a steel nail was being driven into her kneecap. And at times, her Achilles smarted like hell. But she'd endure a little pain for her passion to compete. After some events, she struggled to walk up the stairs and Will would carry her up, complaining that she wouldn't be happy until she crippled herself indefinitely.

Janette noticed Peanuts was curled up asleep on a foam square. Janette had even picked her pet based on its ability to run. German pointers were natural runners and could go for miles. She'd also considered other breeds, and Dalmatian and Springer Spaniel had been on the shortlist, but once she saw the Pointer pups on the internet, she fell for this one. It was the round brown patch on the predominantly white face that drew her to the dog. And she'd picked a winner, as Peanuts ran like a cheetah, although she snored like a pig.

Janette's mobile chimed, and she walked over and grabbed it from the treadmill's drinks holder. It was the Ring doorbell app, so she clicked the camera feed, seeing a guy with a stocky frame with his back to her. Then he turned, looking at the camera. Janette grinned, wondering what would bring Ben Napier to her door on a wet Sunday afternoon in October.

Ben smiled amiably. 'Hi Jan, how are you?'

'Surprised to see you. It's been a while.'

'You look good. Fit… I mean, you know, in the sporty sense. I'm not getting fruity.'

'You stopping for coffee?' she asked, thinking she should return the compliment, but let the moment pass.

'Um, yes please. If that's alright? Not disturbing you, am I? Being a Sunday and all.'

'Will's out. He has taken his bike to his mate's garage to tinker about and get all greasy,' she said, 'their idea of a fun and productive day, apparently.'

'That Willy loves his bikes,' said Ben, following Janette into the hallway.

'Come on in. Leave your shoes on, I don't have carpets.'

Peanuts came charging in, wagging her tail and barking excitedly at Ben.

'Hey, Peanuts,' said Ben, stroking the dog's ears.

'Coffee or would you prefer tea?' she asked, shooing the dog off to the kitchen. Janette and Ben followed.

'Tea, cheers, Jan. So, Corkscrew phoned me last night,' he said sheepishly.

Janette folded her arms. 'I see. How's he doing?'

'He's good. Alex Clayton has been in contact with him,' said Ben, swallowing hard. 'Clayton visited him, out in the Netherlands. They met for drinks and lunch.'

'Sugar?' asked Jan, turning her back on him and filling the kettle, using water from a Brita filter.

'No, thanks. Um, Jan… he wants Corkscrew to arrange a meetup. Next weekend. He wants us all together.'

Janette went numb all over. She wasn't sure how to respond to this news. She opened a container that was on the counter and gave Peanuts a couple of gravy bones.

'I've contacted Gav, but he hasn't replied yet,' said Ben.

'Well, you can count me in,' she said, trying her best to smile, whilst fighting down the urge to let the tears fall. She looked at Ben. It was obvious he was too.

After Ben left, Janette climbed the ladder into the loft. It took her about ten minutes to find the shoebox, but it was still there, buried amongst the endless amount of clutter. Most of it Will's crap from his previous house. She wiped the dust off the lid and popped it open. Inside were crumpled newspaper clippings, worn photos and a keyring. Janette hadn't rummaged through this stuff in years and struggled to bring herself to view the items. The keyring was a tatty Rupert the Bear; a gift from Sheryl. When they'd been tiny, the pair would watch Rupert and The Frog Song over and over, as they danced around Sheryl's lounge, singing along to the words. Janette picked up the keyring and smiled sadly. The lightbulb flickered, buzzed for a few seconds before turning off with a pop. Janette sat in the darkness and sobbed. Then she cried so hard her chest ached.

Nineteen

Kayla entertained Shane's girlfriend in the kitchen, whilst Ben spoke to his brother in the conservatory. It was evening and dark outside. Earlier, Ben switched on all his new garden spotlights he'd spent ages positioning along the gravel-filled borders. He was less than impressed that Shane hadn't commented on them, or taken any notice whatsoever.

Kayla flashed Ben a *please save me* expression. His wife hated girly talk – and it didn't come much girlier than the constant waffle that spewed from the bleach-blonde pouter, that was chewing her ears off at this very moment. Shane's partner was, well basically, a total sap. If his brother told her the world's core was filled with strawberry ice cream, she'd have smiled, doe-eyed, and said, 'Wow, Shane. I didn't know that!' Any joke or quip flew straight over that pretty head of hers. OK, he'd admit that she was an absolute stunner, but when intelligence was being dished out, Summer Reynolds was busy restyling her hair that day. Although she did, Ben considered, have the most amazing pair of pert tits he'd ever clapped eyes on. He recalled Kayla surreptitiously bollocking him during a barbecue last year when he'd given them one gawp too many, though, in his defence, her tiny bikini top made them impossible to miss. He often wondered what the air-head would make of her wonderful Shane's chequered past. The shameless things his brother got up to in his younger days. But he'd still talk her round. Shane was a model citizen now; albeit a grown man that acted like a teenager. He had two kids from his previous marriage, but they were both older and he rarely saw his sons. This meant he spent most of his time doing whatever he pleased, which was normally some sort of fleeting hobby which would require a ridiculously overpriced piece of equipment. The most recent being motocross, skiing and water-sports. And he often seemed to jet off to Ibiza, Corfu or the Algarve.

Perhaps Ben was jealous of his brother's fast-pace lifestyle – but just a bit.

He'd never swap his Kayla. Not for a million stunners. He'd never cope without her because she was his rock, love of his life, best friend and soulmate.

Shane waffled on for a while about his high-powered Yamaha Cruiser jet-ski and the fact he wasn't sure if he should have gone for a speed boat. He had the ridged inflatable, with the twenty-horse-powered outboard engine for fishing; but it wasn't fast enough for Shane. During the summer, Ben got dragged along on a lads' day out to Herne Bay, with Shane's sea buddies. He'd never met such a bunch of arrogant hooligans. Ben nicknamed them the Jet-Ski Pikies. One of them, a brute with no neck called Kev, nearly wiped out an unfortunate swimmer, then hurled abuse at the poor woman, swearing at her and telling her she shouldn't have been out there in *their* zone.

The conversation soon moved on to the new brand of sports drink the company he worked for had the impossible job of marketing, because it tasted like, in Shane's words, 'fermented cat piss.'

It wasn't until late into the evening, when Shane popped his fourth large bottle of Prava beer, that he said, 'So, what's he coming back for?'

Ben stared at his brother, wondering what Summer saw in this massive lump of a man. Shane's black hair was messy, and if his haircut had a name, it would be the just rolled out of bed style, and he was greying in several patches. He was always unshaven and wore glasses with expensive designer frames, but the square style he'd chosen just didn't seem to suit his round, chubby face. Plus, he was forty-seven, and she wasn't even thirty. Maybe it was his brother's wit and charm, though he very much doubted that in this case.

'I don't have a clue, Shane,' said Ben. He was about to speak further on the matter, but Summer's hyena-like laughter turned his attention back to the kitchen. Whatever Shane's girlfriend was finding so funny, his wife was not sharing in her amusement, and the glare Kayla gave him, spurred Ben to end his conversation and join the women.

'Turn off those lights, Ben. Why waste electricity when nobody is outside?' said Kayla, with a tight smile.

'Yep, right,' said Ben, picking up the remote from its cradle on the wall. He clicked the brightness button instead and checked to see if his brother took notice, as the warm glow in his vast garden intensified. Shane didn't, as he was too busy smiling like a fool at his mobile phone.

'Blimey, are you trying to land a plane out there?' asked Kayla.

Summer tiptoed and leant right over the granite counter, peering out of the kitchen window. It appeared as though she was actually searching the sky for aircraft, her expression a mask of concern.

Ben switched off the lights and shared a secret smile with Kayla.

Natalie hated Monday mornings. She was rushing about trying to slip on her black high-heel shoes, finish her coffee and find her office keys. Alex was in the shower, but she didn't bother to knock and say goodbye. They'd hardly spoken since he returned from his trip, and she wasn't impressed that he'd ignored most of her calls and messages over the weekend, and he was away again for a couple of days – a photo shoot in the Lake District. Her schedule was manic this week, but she was adamant she needed to spend time with Alex, so they could talk properly. Natalie planned to take him out for a meal on Saturday, where she would ply him with booze and ambush him; thus leaving him with no option but to talk everything through. She wanted proper answers about his disturbing night rants and everything else they'd discussed. Natalie headed for the door, heels clacking on the wooden floor. She wouldn't be fobbed off with his bullshit excuses any longer. Alex was hiding something, and she intended to determine what he was keeping from her.

What happened to Alex was heartbreaking, but now he was shutting her out, and it was impossible to comprehend why her husband was so reluctant to give her more details. He was treating her like a naïve idiot. She had news for him.

Ben was about to sip his tea when Kayla walked in, poking a finger at her iPad. 'There's been a strange car parked up at the end of the close since the early hours, Ben.' Kayla looked across the table where their three-year-old daughter, Molly, was munching away on a croissant, layered with Nutella. Molly beamed at her mother, and somehow there was more chocolate spread over her lips and cheeks than on the croissant itself. 'Ah, Ben, she's already eaten two of these,' she said, putting the lid on the Nutella jar.

'Whoops, sorry, the little sausage never told me,' he said, giving his daughter a naughty smile. 'What about the car?'

'It's all over the community forum. The neighbours reckon a bloke is sleeping in it!' said Kayla, as though a major crime was in progress.

'So?' said Ben, sipping his tea. 'Why's that a big drama?'

'You feel safe with some weird bloke out there? What if he's watching out for empty houses? Or waiting to spot a child to snatch?'

'They get their knickers in a twist on that group over everything. If somebody delivers a leaflet they don't like, they start a thread to whine about it. They need to get a life, Kayla.'

'Well, I've told them you're home today and you'll check it out. It's a blue Fiat.'

'What? Why do I have to go?'

'You expect Dean Peterson, the dork with goofy teeth and a limp, could deal with this? You're the only real man that lives on this close.'

'To be fair, Dean should go. With his halitosis, the geezer will bugger off as soon as Dean puts his head in the window,' said Ben.

'What's halitoe… sip?' said Molly, licking chocolate from her lips.

Ben laughed out loud, finished his tea and headed for the door.

'It's what you get when you don't brush your teeth every day. Poo-poo breath,' he heard Kayla say, as he slipped on his trainers and went outside.

He trudged along his driveway and into the close, spotting the old Fiat Punto straight away. It looked out of place. Houses here had driveways large enough to cater for several vehicles, so everyone deemed it unusual to see anything other than the odd workman's van parked on the road itself. The Fiat sat on a pristine grass verge next to a row of tall cordyline trees.

Ben approached the vehicle and peered inside the back. He considered knocking on the glass, but it didn't appear as though anyone was kipping in there. A bundle of bags and blankets lay on the back seats, and the windows were misted. He squinted for a better view, and when a figure sprung from the blankets and lunged at the window like a dog attacking a letterbox, Ben almost had a heart attack. The man's unshaven face pushed against the window and his skinny, pointy nose pressed up against the glass. His cheeks were sunken and his hair wild, but it was a face Ben recognised, and he smiled, despite his racing heartbeat.

Gavin slipped out of the car, smirking. 'Sorry, couldn't resist it, I spotted you coming down the driveway, so I hid.'

'You utter dick. Still the big prankster then,' said Ben, pulling Gavin in for a bear hug. 'You smell like stale pants. And you look… well, awful, if I'm honest.'

'You try sleeping in the back of a Punto. I ended up wrapping my legs around my head to get comfy.'

'Well, it's good to see you, mate. It really is. But why are you here already? We're not meeting until the weekend.'

'Gonna see my mum too.'

'That'll be nice,' said Ben. He scanned the close, feeling those suspicious eyes nosing out of the windows; though he couldn't see anyone, he knew there'd be gawping going on. 'Will you be staying with your mum?' asked Ben, praying he wouldn't ask to stay at his place. The idea of Gavin crashing at their house would be welcomed with about as much relish as finding a turd in your lunchbox.

'Perhaps. I wanted to catch you last night, but I started drifting off on the M1. So I stopped at the services for a coffee and a nap.'

Ben knew he'd had a lucky escape. Kayla would not have coped well with Shane, Summer and Gavin together. Kayla wasn't fond of Gavin. She just didn't trust him. It hadn't helped that Shane had told her plenty of stories from their past, that never painted a delightful picture of his old best friend. Ben had, in all honesty, thought Gavin should have been the best man at his wedding, but Kayla point-blank refused this request. She wasn't all that keen on the idea of Shane taking the role, but other than Ben's brother-in-law, Derrick the dick, Kayla's front-runner for the job, there was nobody else he could ask. In all fairness, Gavin would have been a total disaster. Anything he got involved in resulted in chaos. But it was OK because it was just the Gouchy curse. That always got the blame. He was never at fault. All the same, he still felt bad.

'So, do you want to join me for breakfast?' asked Gavin.

'I would love to, but I'm working from home today. Estimates, accounts and VAT—'

'Screw the VAT. Come on, my treat, it's been ages, Ben.'

Ben wanted to argue, but Gavin was gazing at him with imploring eyes.

'I'd like a good catchup. Just us, before we all meet up,' said Gavin, trying and failing to smooth his hair down.

'Alright. Let me grab my jacket then,' said Ben.

'I'm glad you came to keep me company, but please stop that, Baz,' said Alex.

Bassem looked bemused. 'Stop what?'

'That weird jaw clicking. You've been doing it for the last five miles.'

'Sorry. I do that sometimes. Don't know I'm doing it. Where are we now?'

'We just passed Penrith,' said Alex, 'we have a way to go yet.' Alex checked his sat-nav, they were heading right out into the middle of nowhere.

'So, this publisher, slash writer, will I have heard of his work?' asked Bassem, who was now peeling the lid from a cold frappuccino.

'His name is Martin Hawke Reeves. He writes adventure guides and travel books about hidden swimming locations, unknown biking and hiking trails and stuff like that.'

'Surely they won't stay a secret if he publishes them in a book.'

'Well, true enough.'

Alex watched Bassem from the corner of his eye, slurping at the drink and wondering why he'd asked him to tag along. Alex thought back to the last photo shoot Bassem accompanied Alex on; in the Yorkshire Dales. Bassem spent half the day moaning he was cold and complaining about waiting ages to get shots of the rear runners that had fallen behind.

'I like the way you capture the poor sods up here, breathless and beat,' said Bassem. The pair were nestled on a summit, waiting for the contenders to pass them. The participants looked like ants below, as they zig-zagged their way up the steep craggy hill, some four hundred metres above sea level. It was a stunning viewpoint though, and the moody backdrop with the broken clouds and verdant hills made for some fantastic photos.

'So they take part for fun?' asked Bassem.

'They do it for the achievement. Plus, the training helps them stay fit and in shape.'

'Rather them than me.'

'Yeah well, not everyone can stay as skinny as a twig like you, by luck alone.'

'I work out,' scoffed Bassem.

'Baz, you eat cake and ice cream for breakfast and it's doubtful that you have ever seen the inside of a gym.'

'I do a lot of walking.'

The pair had watched as a runner dragged himself up the hill, an old, bearded guy holding trekking poles. He had a yellow buff bandana wrapped around his forehead. As Alex pointed his camera, the old guy gave him a weak grin, which was probably all he could manage after the hideous climb he'd just made. He didn't stop though; off he ran as soon as he hit the top.

'Jesus, do any of these old farts ever croak it? That guy must have been ninety-odd,' said Bassem.

'Ninety! Mid-seventies,' whispered Alex, though evidently loud enough for the man to hear, because he glanced back to him and gave him a peculiar, narrowed eyed glare.

A chiming noise coming from the vehicle's dashboard grabbed Alex's attention back to the present.

'What's that blipping mean?' asked Bassem.

'Tyre pressure. I think we have a flat.'

Alex had removed the spare tyre, jack and tool kit from the Cherokee and was familiarising himself with how the jack mechanism worked. They were parked on a gritty lay-by on an area of vast moorland thick with russet-brown bracken. Bassem stood roadside, hands in the pockets of his trousers as he stared at an inky lake that appeared as still as ice in the distance.

'You know what you are doing?' asked Bassem, continuing to stare out into the wilderness. There were dark-coloured sheep dotted across the landscape and the eerie sound of crows cawing seemed to surround them.

'I haven't changed one in years,' said Alex, trying to loosen off the first wheel bolt. His hands were cold, but he wasn't prepared to ruin his expensive work gloves by getting them covered in grease. He was often using routes that took him off the beaten track, so it was surprising he'd never had a full-on flat before. He'd had a handful of slow punctures from screws and nails, but he'd always used his compressor to fill the tyre enough to drive temporarily and then get a repair. This rear tyre was toast though and had deflated as soon as he had started filling it with air. He was concerned that the uneven and rocky ground would make it dangerous to raise the Jeep, but he was losing time and didn't even have a signal on his mobile to text his client about the delay. He managed to loosen one bolt.

Bassem still looked at the lake.

'No, I'm fine, don't bother to help me,' grumbled Alex.

'What use would I be? It's not like I can actually help you,' said Bassem, flatly.

'Fine, see if you can get a phone signal then.'

'Are you still having those dreams, Alex?'

Alex had got all the bolts loose and had positioned the jack in what he hoped was the correct jacking point. He got the base as flat as possible and raised the vehicle an inch. Then he finally replied. 'If I do sleep, yes I have them.'

Alex removed the flat tyre and rolled it to the back of the vehicle.

Bassem was about to speak but was abruptly cut off by an articulated lorry that hurtled past them, causing them to jump back. The road shook and stones and earth flung from its huge tyres. The lorry had come close. Alex hadn't even heard it coming down the lane.

Aghast, the pair slowly gazed down at the jack, relieved the vehicle was still fixed on it.

'Close one,' said Bassem.

'Have you ever dreamt about drowning?' asked Alex, picking up the spare tyre.

Twenty

Alex followed Ben into a clearing in the woods and his heart sank as he scanned the area, confirming Sheryl wasn't present. Ben must have sensed his disappointment because he sneered at Alex and strutted off ahead of him. It had been three days since Alex had taken the first test, and he'd been thinking about her constantly. Pining for her, if he was honest. He wondered why the girls weren't here, though the bigger worry was why Patrick and Shane were waiting there. Shane was leaning over the handlebars of his Mongoose, eating a packet of cheese and onion crisps and glaring at Alex maliciously. Alex wondered what he'd ever done to Shane to receive such animosity from the boy, though Ben's brother was known to be a loathsome arsehole, so Alex wasn't special. Patrick was busy fixing his bike's chain. He fleetingly gazed up at Alex, gave him a blank stare, then resumed his tinkering. Patrick had a puffy, black eye, split bottom lip, and both his hands were cut and swollen across the knuckles. Alex guessed he'd been in a fight but wasn't about to question him about it, being as though Patrick scared the utter shit out of him.

Mark was sitting in an abandoned plastic garden chair and was using a twig to remove what looked like dog poo from the bottom of his trainer.

Gavin was urinating into what everyone called The Roman Bath. Alex didn't know if that's what it actually was, though he recalled his history teacher, Mr Bradshaw, once telling his class that historians found Roman coins in the grounds of a nearby church, back in the late nineteen sixties; so he guessed it was possible. But now, it was essentially a concrete pit, the size and shape of a large swimming pool, and filled with foul-smelling rainwater that had festered over the years. It also contained a mass of dumped garden and household waste, and around a gallon's worth of Gavin's reeking urine.

Ben was whispering to his brother, and Alex was sure he noticed an expression of disdain on Mark's face as he regarded the pair out of the corner of his eye.

Gavin strolled over to Mark and jabbed a finger at his chest. 'Corkscrew is only sitting in the wanker's chair.'

'What are you on about?' asked Mark, a look of twisted confusion on his face.

'Behind you,' said Gavin, nodding at the bushes.

'What are you—' Mark stopped mid-sentence and frowned as he spotted the scattered pages of pornographic magazines strewn about him. He sprung off the chair to the crackling of laughter from Gavin, Ben, and Shane.

'That is so grim,' spluttered Mark.

Ben walked over and pulled some crumpled pages from out of the bush.

'Aw, no, don't touch them,' said Mark, appalled, as he rubbed his hands along the ground with a twisted grimace, as if somehow the mud would clean his hands.

Ben opened up a page and held it up, revealing a photo of a naked woman spreading her legs. 'Here Gav, I bet you've never seen a real woman in this position.'

'Don't be a div, of course, I have,' said Gavin, crossing his arms defensively.

'Yeah, but your sister doesn't count, Gavin,' said Ben.

'Screw you, Napier, you spastic,' said Gavin.

Gavin's face reddened, though Alex couldn't tell if it was because of embarrassment or rage.

Ben and Shane were belly laughing, and even Patrick was grinning, though he hadn't bothered to look up from his bike.

'I bet this is really *your* chair, Gouchy boy,' said Shane, his shoulders bobbing up and down as he sniggered. 'You dirty little turd!' he added, in a nasty tone.

Ben bellowed with laughter.

Alex noticed that Ben's attitude seemed different today, and it was obvious he was showing off in front of his brother and his mate.

'Yeah, whatever, Shane. Are we doing this or what?' said Gavin.

'Clayton, follow me,' ordered Ben, walking towards the concrete pit.

Alex followed him. Ben hadn't said his second test was today. Surely he wouldn't drop this on him without some prior warning. How would he mentally prepare?

'So, was this really a Roman bath, Ben?' asked Alex. Even as the words left his mouth, he knew he wouldn't receive a sensible reply, but he needed to say something and it was all that popped in his head as they stepped to the edge of the pit. 'Because Mr Bradshaw said—'

'Fuck Mr Bradshaw,' said Gavin, 'he has a face like a flattened hedgehog and breath like a rotten gorilla's arse crack.'

More giddy laughter from the others.

'Who gives a shit what it is?' said Ben. 'It's just what we all call it.'

Alex gazed into the pit and, despite the day's humid weather, a shiver spiralled through his entire body. The water level was higher than it had been on his previous visit here, and that water was putrid, with a black, oily film floating on its surface. On the inner, shallower parts of the pit poked all sorts of debris – branches from fallen trees, a shopping trolley, a car door, and some roadwork cones. The middle must have been deeper, as Alex could see no rubbish, though he was sure that more surprises lurked down there in the filth.

'So, are you ready for round two, Clayton?' asked Ben.

Alex nodded. 'I guess.'

'Here,' said Gavin. His voice sounded strained as he struggled with a misshapen rock about the size of a large melon. He held it in both hands and his legs were buckling under the weight. He dropped it and it landed next to Alex with a thud. Alex gazed at the rock in confusion, then turned his attention to Ben, who was picking up something from the base of a nearby tree.

It was a piece of blue rope.

Ben strutted over to Alex with a cheery smile, crouched down, and bound the rope around his ankle. Alex watched, but didn't stop him.

'Shirt off,' said Gavin, pulling at Alex's white t-shirt.

'Get off!' protested Alex.

'Take it off,' said Ben.

Alex removed his t-shirt, huffing and puffing as he yanked it over his head.

'What is that gay thing?' asked Gavin, fingering the brooch hanging about Alex's neck.

Alex glared at Gavin. 'None of your business.'

Gavin grabbed the brooch. 'I want to look at it,' he said, gazing at the piece. 'Yeah, this will work,' he said, as he snatched the brooch, snapping the bootlace.

'Give that back now!' shouted Alex.

Gavin laughed and backed away from Alex, holding the brooch behind his back. 'Come and get it if you want it,' he said with a mocking grin.

Mark observed as the scene unfolded in front of him with a horrible sense of helplessness. He was in a foul mood anyway, as he was not a fan of Ben's dopey, arrogant brother, or his creepy friend, Patrick Lynch, with his dead-eyed stares and odd behaviour. Last summer, Shane had taken Mark's Sony Walkman from him and told him he wanted to listen to the rock compilation tape Mark had put together. Shane then sped away on his bike, taking the Walkman with him. When Mark had confronted him a week later, Shane denied everything and called him a total bullshitter. Mark had tried to argue his point, but Patrick strolled up behind him, and swept his legs right out from under him, using some sort of karate move. Shane had trodden on Mark's face and warned him if that if he ever spoke about the Walkman again, they'd stamp on his face until it resembled a pancake. Mark was furious, as the Walkman had been a birthday present from his uncle. He'd even seen Shane ride past him, wearing the distinctive orange earphones and smirking gleefully at him as he rode by. Mark hated the pair with a passion. They didn't always join the group, but now and then the pair would pop up like a foul smell. They had joined the local army cadet corps, so they were often busy with their new hobby or away on exercise weekends. Though Mark assumed it would only be a matter of time before they got booted out for inappropriate behaviour or violent conduct.

Gavin was dancing around Alex, who was getting so worked up now, Mark was sure he was going to burst into tears or scream.

'Oh, no, I think he's gonna slap me in a minute,' said Gavin, running circles around Alex.

Ben started coiling the rope around his forearm, and Mark knew what was coming. He felt awful that he didn't shout a warning, as Ben yanked the rope so hard, it pulled Alex's entire leg backwards and he plummeted into the grass with a heavy clump. A chorus of laughter echoed around the clearing. Even Patrick had stopped what he was doing to watch. Mark pretended to join in and wasn't proud of himself for doing so.

'Oopsy,' said Gavin, stepping over Alex and crouching down to the stone. He placed the brooch onto the rock and wrapped the other end of the rope around the rock. He went around it in every direction until he'd covered the rock, leaving a piece at the end to add a knot. 'That should hold.'

Alex scrambled up, darting at Gavin, but Ben grabbed him from behind and held him in a bear-hug. 'Stop being a naughty boy, Clayton,' said Ben, spitting the words vehemently. 'Here's what you need to do to pass the test,' he continued in an angry whisper.

'That was my mum's. Please don't throw it in the water,' pleaded Alex. 'I'll do whatever you ask, just don't.'

'Just don't,' mimicked Gavin.

Shane squatted and scooped up the rock. 'Right in the middle, yeah?' he asked Ben.

'Yep,' said Ben, then to Alex he said, 'you'll have five minutes to free yourself and get out of the water. Any longer, you fail. And you must decide if you have enough time to free your leg,' he paused and nodded to the rock, 'and retrieve Mummy's jewellery too.'

Shane hoisted up the rock and lifted it to his shoulder in a shot-putter's stance.

Ben let go of Alex and pushed him towards the pit.

'Now then! It's time to get ready,' said Ben. He spoke as though he was some sort of cheery game-show host. 'Go!' he boomed.

Shane let out a bellow as he hurled the rock. Everyone watched in awe as it flew some distance and landed right in the middle of the pit with a plop. All eyes turned to the pile of rope, which chased the rock's path.

Mark had expected, as they all had, that they'd witness Alex being dragged, leg first, into the pit. But to their complete surprise, he ran forward and jumped into the water, disappearing into the grimness.

Darkness enveloped Alex, and he tried to keep his mouth and eyes shut. As soon as he touched on the bottom, he swam upwards and something caught the side of his face, although there was no immediate pain, he was sure whatever it was, had sliced his skin.

Alex didn't think that opening his eyes would help down here. Plus, he feared this gunk might do some serious damage to his eyesight, so he tried to shake the grim thoughts that were crashing into his mind – the germs, rats, and diseases that would linger about such a dirty place. If his mum could see him now, she would have had a major breakdown. This would have been her worst nightmare.

He pushed up through the water and heard jeering, laughter, and howls. Then Alex panicked. He could barely get his face out of the water. He took some desperate gasps of air as the rope went taut and pulled against his ankle.

Alex tried to shout for help, but the water-filled his mouth, so he clamped it shut. He craned his neck and pushed his face above the water, but without having both legs free to tread water, he was pulled back under.

Alex knew he had to untie his leg, and he had to do it fast. He swam back under and pulled at the rope around his ankle, but the knot was so firmly bound, it didn't budge at all.

With a sense of dread washing over him, Alex swam up again, tilted his head for another rasping gulp of air, and plunged back under.

Half swimming, half pulling on the rope, Alex made his way down to the surface to locate the rock.

Gavin's knot came undone with little effort and he tugged hard at the rope. But it didn't come free. He groped all around it, yanking away at the loosened piece, and realised he was in serious trouble. The rock was sinking in the mud and taking the rope and the brooch with it.

Mark peered over the edge and tried to make out where Alex had gone. The rest of the group joined him. Patrick, still slouched on his BMX, had rolled the bike to the edge and was gazing down with bright-eyed wonder, and a cruel smile spread across his face.

'He's drowning,' said Shane, though he sounded unmoved by the statement.

'How did you know what length of rope to use, Ben?' asked Gavin.

Ben glanced at him, scrunched up his face, and turned back to the water. 'I didn't.'

There was a moment of silence, and then Gavin started sniggering. Within a few seconds, he was laughing hoarsely. Shane and Patrick joined in.

'Do you think we should get him out now?' asked Mark, addressing no one in particular.

'Piss off, you wouldn't get me in there for a thousand quid!' said Ben.

This statement caused another bout of silly, hooting laughter.

Mark had the sudden urge to push the lot of them in the shitty water and hurl rocks down onto their stupid heads.

Alex emerged, arms flapping and hands almost clawing at the water. The rope must have been pulling tight on his leg, as he was unable to keep his head out of the water to breathe properly. Mark considered that unbelievably lucky. For all Ben had known, there might not have been enough slack for him to surface at all.

Mark knew he must take action and the others wouldn't like him interfering. He saw Ben check his watch. Time was running out.

Alex was trying hard to lift the rock, but he didn't have the power to shift it out from the slushy mud. It felt like his lungs were going to explode as he swam back up for more air, though now he could scarcely get his face out. Undoing the knot hadn't given him any extra slack, and if the rock sunk any further, he was going to drown. His face stung badly. Then he knew what he had to do.

Mark stepped to the edge, wondering if he should remove his clothes first. The thought of his naked skin coming into contact with that foul sludge convinced him to keep them on.

Ben checked on the time again. 'Two minutes to go.'

Mark saw the worry etched on Ben's face, and it was clear he feared he'd gone too far. Once again. He wouldn't be happy until he got this boy killed. Mark stared at the water. He wanted to jump in and help Alex. He really did. But he was frozen to the spot.

Alex searched in the darkness for the culprit that injured his face. It had to be sharp. But where the hell was it? He ferreted around the floor and touched on what he thought felt like a shopping basket filled with bricks. His head felt strange, and he knew he was on the verge of unconsciousness. He frantically swam up – but tried to breathe too soon and swallowed back the foul water. His throat burned, and he thought his lungs were surely collapsing. Blood painfully pounded behind his eyes, and he was certain he was going to die down here.

'Don't,' growled Ben.

'We have to get him out,' said Mark, his voice sounding meek.

'When his time is up, you are welcome to be the hero.'

Mark knew that once the time was up, it would most likely be too late.

Alex's face burst through the water and he tried hard to gulp for air. They were all watching him drown, and some of them grinned as though they were savouring the moment.

His body ached all over and he was almost at the point of giving up. At the point he'd stop fighting and let the blackness take him. Alex wondered why the others weren't trying to save him. Would they watch him drown and do nothing? He couldn't even hear them any longer; with his ears submerged, all that was audible was the burble of water in his heavy head. It was like that water was crushing the life out of him, and the claustrophobic sensation that shrouded him was unbearable. He dropped back under, sinking towards the rock, and something sharp snagged his shorts. He grabbed at it. It was jagged-edged, like metal sheeting. Alex tugged the rope to him and begun dragging it along the metal's edge as frenziedly as possible. He desperately needed air, but daren't move away from this spot – if he did, he may not find it again. His lungs burnt and his mind spun as a searing pain stabbed at his brain, but he wouldn't stop until those rope strands parted.

Alex's mind was going dark now, and it was like his entire body was going into a convulsion. His head, throat, and chest felt like a million needles were piercing him.

Then the rope snapped, and Alex surged up, his mind whirling… and he burst through the water.

Alex took several short, deep rasping breaths, blinked away the dirty water, and viewed the hazy figures standing on the pit's edge. Everything around him looked blurry as he clumsily swam through the black, vulgar crud.

Twenty-one

There was no cheering, or hollering as Alex climbed from the pit. Just an ominous silence. Alex looked like death and the slice on his cheek looked painful.

'Close one, Clayton. Only ten seconds to spare,' said Ben sheepishly. He tried to laugh, but that just sounded nervy and feeble. Seeing how sickly Alex appeared had startled Ben more than he'd care to admit.

Mark stepped out of Alex's path as he walked past the group. Alex appeared distant, strange, and almost zombie-like.

'Bet you thought you'd be joining Mummy today,' said Gavin.

He got no reaction from Alex, and Gavin looked as though he regretted the words as soon as he'd uttered them.

Gavin chewed his lower lip, and surprisingly, appeared ashamed of his actions. What a momentous occasion, Mark mused in a stupefied lull.

Alex trudged away, head bowed.

Mark glared at Ben. The sneaky git had made sure Sheryl hadn't been here to witness today's events. She wouldn't have hesitated to jump in and rescue Alex, and that thought made Mark feel even more useless and racked with guilt. He went to follow Alex but stopped himself, deciding to let the boy be.

Alex felt no sense of achievement, no joy and no impulse to celebrate this time. He needed to go home and never wanted to see these boys ever again. In fact, he'd be happy to see them all dead and buried. Alex stopped in his tracks, trainers squelching when he heard shrieking breaks, and he gazed up to find Patrick staring blankly back at him. He held up Alex's t-shirt. 'You forgot this,' he said tonelessly.

Alex took it and nodded his thanks. Patrick stared at him for a moment, then rolled his bike back to let him continue. Alex trudged on. His heart raced and his head became dizzy, but he needed to get far away from this place as fast as possible. And he never wanted to return. Never.

Alex snuck along the back alley behind the bungalows, which the residents rarely used. With any luck, his nan would be perched in front of the TV and he could slip in via the kitchen and get himself cleaned up before she spotted him. He'd have to explain the cut, but he'd say he fell off a rope swing and caught himself on a branch. There was no way he could come clean. Otherwise, his summer would be over if she found out about the things he'd been up to.

Noises coming from a nearby garden caused Alex to stop and listen.

'Eeee-yah!' yelled a voice. He couldn't even tell if it was male or female. This was followed up with, 'Hiiii-yaaaa,' screamed in a brutal yell that made Alex jump backwards. Now he was positive that the voice belonged to a male.

As the shouts continued, Alex spied through a hole in the fence and gasped in awe at what he saw. A figure stood in the garden, dressed in a black ninja uniform. Just a pair of dark-blue eyes peered out from under a hooded cowl. The figure stood in a poised fighting stance, holding a sleek warrior sword, its blade glinting in the summer's sun. A set of nunchucks and some savage looking throwing knives were laid out on a beige canvas matt behind the figure.

A yellow target board, decorated with a red snarling dragon emblem, hung from the fence. It looked well worn and two throwing stars were embedded in its centre.

The ninja was statue still – fixed in a low fighting stance. Suddenly, the ninja swung the blade in a wide arc. 'Hyaaaahhhhhh,' he roared.

The entire fence seemed to shudder from the force of the move.

Alex continued to spy, marvelled as the ninja did several more fast slashes with the sword and ended with a fierce backward swipe that whooshed through the air. Then he slid the weapon into a sheath on his back. The figure gazed suspiciously around the garden, removed his cowl, and wiped the sweat from his brow. It was Eduardo. He spun on his heels and marched into the bungalow.

Before Alex even knew what he was doing, he'd opened the gate and started sneaking into the garden. It was identical to his nan's – a square lawn with a red slabbed path along the side of it; a concrete shed with a flat, felt roof and two hanging baskets on either side of the back door.

Alex moved to the practice board and touched the tip of a star. He instantly pulled his hand away when he established how razor-sharp it was.

'Whatcha, buddy,' said a voice.

Alex turned and was faced with a boy who stood at the gate. At first glance, he thought it was Eduardo and was astonished at how speedily he'd changed into shorts and a cameo army vest, and got himself positioned at the back gate. But as Alex looked closer at the boy, he concluded that this was not Eduardo. It looked very much like him, though his face seemed fatter and this boy's black hair was slicked back, with gel so thick, it glimmered. He had a wider build too, and though his accent sounded similar to Eduardo's, it came across heavier. The boy gazed at Alex for a while, then he showed his teeth and gums and smiled like some sort of demented chimpanzee, tilting his head sideways.

'Are you OK?' asked Alex, stepping back a few paces.

'Do you want to play with me?' the boy asked in a childish voice. 'I want to throw some knives,' he added. Then he began to slap his hands excitedly.

Alex wondered if the boy was retarded; though his bright and clever eyes did seem to betray this.

The boy giggled. 'I'm messing with you, buddy. Are you looking for my bro? Or are you stealing all his gear?'

'No. I was… are you Ed's brother?'

'Twin. We're not identical. Obviously, I'm the good-looking one,' he said.

'Whoa, your brother's a ninja.'

'My brother's a moody little bitch. If you speak to him, don't tell him you saw me, he's being a massive dick with me.'

'Um, OK.'

'So, you want to throw one of them?' asked the boy, nodding at the board.

'I don't know how to throw ninja stars,' said Alex.

'Shuriken. That's what they're called.'

'Can you show me?'

'Did you win the fight? Some scratch you've got. What did you battle, a tiger?'

'It wasn't a fight… it was—'

Leo interrupted him. 'You stink like manky old boots. Have you been playing in the sewers or something?'

'Not the sewers, I—'

Alex was cut off by loud singing coming from the bungalow. Well, to say it was singing, would be a stretch; the voice sounded cracked and squeaky.

The boy sniggered. 'Ed loves a bit of singing in the shower.'

Alex had heard the Phil Collins song, In The Air Tonight, many times, as his dad had played it often enough – but never sung quite like this.

The boy let out a deep laugh. 'Shit, man, if Ed knew we were listening to this, he would wrap those nunchucks around our heads.'

'Wow, I have never heard a ninja sing,' said Alex.

The boy looked at him seriously for a couple of seconds, before bursting out into maniacal laughter. 'Brilliant.'

'I'm Alex.'

'Leo.'

'Is that short for Leonardo?'

Leo walked into the garden and studied the knives. 'No, I'm Leonel. But only my mum calls me that. Use that name, I'll break your teeth.' Leo picked up a pouch that contained a shuriken and two empty slots. He passed the pouch to Alex. 'Go on then, try it. Be careful you don't slice your fingers though.'

Alex removed the star and examined it. 'It's amazing.'

'Go on,' said Leo, a crazy grin on his face, 'hard as you can. Bet you can do it.'

Alex raised the shuriken and took aim and hurled it hard. It thudded into the middle of the board, which wobbled on impact. 'Whoa!' shouted Alex, enthralled. 'Did you see that?'

'Fuck yeah, I did,' said Leo, nodding his head with a broad smile.

Twenty-two

Ben was getting ready to leave the pub when he noticed Gavin was at the bar ordering two more pints. He checked his mobile and saw the two missed calls and five text messages from Kayla. He had told her he was popping out for breakfast with Gavin and that he'd be two hours tops, but after indulging in a monster breakfast that could have fed a family of five, which the pair had consumed at a café in town, Gavin insisted Ben joined him for one quick pint. Now pint number four was being poured by the young barman. He couldn't deny that he'd enjoyed catching up with his old friend, though. They'd spent all morning chatting and reminiscing about their past escapades, school antics, and old times. Neither had yet spoken about the coming meeting with Janette, Corkscrew, and Clayton.

Gavin placed down the beers with an assortment of nuts. 'Drink up,' he said, taking a long pull on the drink. 'Cheers, dude.'

'I was talking about one of our old teachers the other day, Manky Mitchell,' said Ben.

Gavin crinkled his nose. 'Ew, his teeth were horrible. And you needed an umbrella every time he started speaking.'

'Do you remember when we glued all his stuff to the ceiling? His glasses, pens, and his diary,' said Ben.

Ben had told the story to his son, who'd been less than impressed. He'd not taken his eyes off his game whilst Ben had told him the anecdote.

Gavin spluttered with laughter. 'Do I remember? That lunatic threw a board rubber at me! Bounced off the wall right by my head.'

'He spent most of the lesson searching his desk, whilst the entire class was pissing themselves as they tried to hold in their laughter!' sniggered Ben.

'Naturally, I got the blame when he noticed.'

Ben smiled at the memory. He'd been a total nightmare at school, but Gavin had been something else. The trouble that boy got Ben into over the years. And when they joined the army cadets in their late teens, they soon gained a reputation for being a pair of unpredictable troublemakers at their local detachment. A rivalry started with the local sea cadets, whose base was almost next door to where their cadet centre was housed. Gavin had got things started by taking the piss out of one of their elite cadets, a loudmouth big-shot called Allen Rogers. This resulted in Rogers and his crew ambushing Gavin one night, and giving him a good pasting. In retaliation, Ben, Shane, and Gavin had returned the favour a week later. After they beat Rogers to the ground and booted him in the ribs, Gavin thought it would be a fabulous idea to push the lad into the River Medway. The trio had stood and watched in delight as Rogers had wailed and cried out that he couldn't swim. They'd all found the irony of this hilarious.

'Ready, aye ready,' Gavin had bellowed.

The trio belted away when a passing cyclist leapt from his bike and dived in to save Rogers from drowning.

That same year, during a two-week annual camp, Gavin fell out with a gaunt-faced boy called Stephen Bovey, or Bone-Face behind his back, over rowdy conduct in their billet. The rivalry came to a head when the boys tied Bovey, naked save a pair of white socks, to a Land Rover's roof-rack. Shane's mate, Cadet Corporal Haverstock, had borrowed the vehicle from a Staff Sergeant, and they took Bovey on a wild spin around the camp. Bovey had screamed like a baby and begged them to stop, whilst a massive mob of cadets cheered and bellowed insults at Bovey and some hurled rubbish at him.

The humiliation of the event was so much, Bovey later chased Gavin across the parade ground, brandishing a meat cleaver he'd stolen from the kitchens. Bovey ended up so crazed, he had to be subdued by several adults and was later removed from camp. They never laid eyes on him again. Ben heard a rumour that, back in the late nineties, Bovey got into a pub argument and punched a guy whilst gripping a set of keys and took the poor sod's eyeball out. If the rumours were to be believed, he got ten years for that.

As Ben, Shane and Gavin had become old enough to drink legally, they'd spent night after night out drinking themselves into a stupor. And Gavin, being

Gavin, couldn't see a night through without causing some sort of scene, argument or fracas, that usually led to violent confrontations in pubs, drunken brawls outside nightclubs, or scuffles with hard-faced bouncers when they attempted to remove Gavin from the establishment. Though it was normally Ben and Shane that would have to step in and sort out Gavin's mess or stop him from getting a major battering from a gang of drunken yobs. Luckily, their size was usually enough to deter most would-be aggressors.

Gavin headed off for yet another piss, and Ben gazed around the dreary pub. It looked worn, smelt of fusty sweat and probably hadn't been refurbished since the early seventies. It was busy too, especially for a drizzly Monday afternoon, though most of the clientele were drinking alone and were a sad-looking bunch of miserable, middle-aged guys. Ben decided this place was depressing. Gavin only liked it because it was cheap. The only redeeming thing was that the Guinness they served was cracking. Ben texted Kayla back, saying he was very sorry, and he'd be back within the hour. She'd have the hump with him, that was a certainty.

Gavin returned with two more pints. 'Thought I'd grab us a couple more on my way through.'

'I haven't finished this one, Gav,' said Ben.

'Drink up then and stop complaining,' said Gavin, tossing a handful of nuts in his mouth.

'I should get back, mate. You know how it is?' said Ben.

'No. Free spirit, me. I do what I like.'

'I thought you were with somebody now.'

'Nope.'

Ben noticed that Gavin's shoulders slumped as he spoke and was quite certain his old friend wasn't being truthful with him. 'Do you want to be alone? You're not exactly a youngster now, mate. No offence, but… surely it's a bit miserable, you know, having no one to go home to.'

Gavin pulled a face like he'd eaten something sour. 'I don't want some woman nagging me twenty-four-seven. Sod dealing with all that.'

'That's not what it's like, Gav,' said Ben, forcing a coarse laugh.

'Yeah, OK. Ever since we've been out today, your missus has been on your case.'

'I'm supposed to be working. It was just meant to be breakfast.'

'So sorry for wanting a chat and a pint with my best pal. And sorry for being such an inconvenience and ruining your day,' said Gavin.

'Behave, you silly tart,' said Ben.

To be fair, he'd not seen Gavin for years and it probably seemed like he couldn't wait to depart his company. Would it matter that he'd spent all day catching up? Surely Kayla would understand. Though he guessed she wouldn't. Because it was Gavin.

'So, your lad, what's he like fifteen now?' asked Gavin, clearly trying to divert the subject.

'Seventeen,' said Ben.

'Blimey. Bet he's a winner with the girls. Tall, dark and good looking. Lucky he takes after his mum, hey.'

'Well… he's not—'

'Aw, right, he bats for the other side?'

Ben moodily sipped his Guinness. 'No… I wouldn't know. He doesn't talk to me. He spends his life on screens and consoles.'

'He'll grow out of that. That's what kids are like now.'

'I just feel that sometimes he's missing out on a proper childhood. Doing fun and crazy stuff. Adventures like we had. That's not the real world, is it? Online gaming.'

'You'd prefer he was out burning down farmers' property or hanging off the side of cranes?' asked Gavin drily.

'Well, no… I dunno.'

'Things are not the same, Ben. We lived in different times.'

'But we lived… we—' Ben's voice trailed off. The booze hit him then.

'We were fearless,' said Gavin.

They both gulped away and nodded together.

Gavin stared seriously at Ben and said, 'Why's he coming back? Why's he crawling out from behind the rock he's been hiding under?'

'I don't know what he wants.'

'Yes, you do.'

Ben sighed and ran a hand over his head. 'Just don't do anything stupid, Gav.'

'We need to finish what we started.'

'If anything, we need to apologise.'

'Apologise! Are you taking the piss? There can only be one reason he's coming back. He wants to confess.'

'We don't know that.'

'I'll do it myself if you don't have the stomach for this anymore.'

'Oi, behave, Gavin. Stop talking nonsense. You're drunk.'

'No, I'm not.'

'What we did to him… it was cruel. We were nasty buggers, Gavin. We can't deny that. I mean, that day in Gallows—' Ben stopped and winced when he thought about that day.

What happened in Gallows Hill Woods was Shane and Patrick's idea, not his. The fourth and final test Ben had planned was for Alex to have a one-on-one scrap with a boy called Brad Jenner – one of Alex's tormentors at school. To pass, Alex had to beat Jenner in a fair fight, something he'd never have been able to achieve, even if Jenner had both his hands tied behind his back. It was similar to Gavin's final test when Ben set up a fight with a bully called Billy Davis. Ben was adamant Davis would deck Gavin, but Gavin sucker-punched Davis before the fight had officially started, and then jumped on his back and took a bite out of the boy's ear. Some older kids tried to break up the fight, but Patrick and Shane waded in and saw them off. It turned out Patrick had a score to settle with Davis himself, because after the fight was over, he finished Davis off by pounding the lad senseless whilst he lay curled up in a ball on the floor and broke the lad's nose and collarbone in the process.

Gavin snorted. 'I won't ever apologise.'

Ben knew the hatred his friend harboured for Alex Clayton. He'd hated him as a kid, and that hatred had festered for decades. As a father, Ben saw everything through a different set of eyes. Alex had been bullied and belittled for years; and what did they do? They put his life on the line for their entertainment, so they shouldn't have been surprised that things got out of hand and turned to shit. Back then Ben couldn't see it – but now it was all crystal clear. They had gone too far. Way too far.

Twenty-three

B en closed his eyes and sprayed his eyelids with his Optrex spray. When he opened them, Gavin was gazing at him with a questioning smile.

'Just concentrate on the road, Gav,' said Ben.

'Are you too vain for glasses these days?' asked Gavin with a smirk.

'My eyes get dry when I drink too much,' said Ben, 'and I still wear glasses.'

A mobile started ringing. Ben knew it was his phone, but couldn't deal with a scolding from Kayla.

'Wifey is calling and youse in trouble now, mister!' said Gavin in a raucous, hillbilly voice.

'She texted me ten angry faces. The red ones too.'

'Oh, gosh, no. Not the red ones.'

Gavin smirked as he changed gear, crunching the gear stick in the process. Ben gazed out of the window. It wasn't even six yet, and it was already dark outside. It was November at the end of the week. Ben hated this time of year. He liked barbecues and long evenings spent in the garden. A melancholy shroud fell over him.

'You shouldn't be driving,' said Ben. He knew he should have stopped Gavin from getting behind the wheel. He should have insisted they'd booked a taxi, but he thought letting him drive would be the quickest way to get back to Kayla. A selfish move, he now thought. He'd left just before ten-thirty this morning. Where had the day gone? It was amazing how fast the hours slipped by once you got drinking and chatting.

'Your missus sounds stricter than your mum,' said Gavin.

Ben glowered and was offended, but didn't bother to argue or even give a response. Instead, he gazed outside and wondered where they were going. It wasn't to his house.

Gavin noticed Ben's confusion. 'Scenic route.'

'Jesus, I need to get back already. Why come this way?'

'To be honest, I drove the wrong way. Isn't Colt Wood down here? Had some wicked laughs in there, didn't we?'

'Yes, Gav, but—'

Blue flashing lights illuminated the inside of the car. Gavin adjusted his mirror.

'Are they pulling us?' asked Ben. He swivelled in his seat for a better view. 'Gav… you best pull over, mate.'

Ben knew Gavin was screwed now. He'd guzzled about eight pints today. He turned back around, and to his astonishment, Gavin floored it. Then the sirens wailed and the police car took up pursuit.

Ben's phone started ringing again.

'My God! What are you doing?' yelled Ben.

'Are you ever gonna answer that phone?'

'No. Not right now!'

'Grab my bags from the back seats,' demanded Gavin.

'What? You need to pull over. You can't outrun them in this shit-heap! I watch Police Interceptors. They don't escape, Gavin.'

'Listen carefully… I need you to grab those bags—'

Gavin… whoa, road. Whooooa!' shouted Ben.

Gavin spun the wheel, sending the car screeching into a tight bend. Ben had no idea how he didn't lose control. Pure luck.

Gavin was slamming gears, grinding teeth, and had a look of utter determination on his face. But the sirens screamed behind them, and Ben was certain Gavin wouldn't lose the pursuers in a twenty-year-old Punto.

'Please get my bags. I'll ditch the car up here,' said Gavin. His stern eyes were fixed on the twisting lane ahead.

Ben obediently pulled both bags onto his lap. He felt queasy, and Gavin's erratic driving was churning the Guinness in his stomach. Then the car was shuddering and skidding, and Ben could see a metal barn gate looming ahead.

'Over that gate and run like mad!' said Gavin.

'What? …I can't—'

'Now! Go,' shouted Gavin. The car skidded to a complete stop and Gavin switched off the ignition and grabbed both bags. Before Ben had even unclipped his belt, Gavin was out of the car.

Ben emerged from the vehicle and the lane was flooded with blinding headlights and shimmering blue lights. Gavin was already over the metal barn gate, waving him to follow. Ben didn't even know why he was fleeing – what exactly had he done wrong? Nevertheless, he clambered over that gate and raced into the woods. Behind them, Ben heard the crackling police radios and shouts from the angry officers.

Gavin stopped and waited for Ben, who ambled along the muddy track behind him, looking as though he might collapse from exhaustion. Gavin's lower back and bruised shoulders were tender, and he was struggling for air, but Ben looked like he'd just run ten miles straight. They'd been running through the woods for about fifteen minutes. Ben had stacked it twice, and it had shocked Gavin that the police hadn't nabbed the idiot within twenty seconds. He concluded that they obviously couldn't be arsed to chase two idiots into a pitch-dark, muddy wood and made do with seizing the car. Unfortunately for them, the car was still registered to Javon's Nottingham address. Gavin would text him later and tell him the motor had been stolen. He'd still not replied to his previous messages about paying his debt off.

Gavin gazed around for somewhere to stash the rucksack. He had Skender's cash rolled up in a couple of pairs of socks in his holdall, but he didn't want to risk getting lifted with a load of smack. That would be fifteen years or more, especially as he carried previous convictions.

Ben was blinking and prodding his finger into his right eye, so Gavin nipped off into the trees to locate a spot. He found a reasonably deep hole, tossed the rucksack in, and kicked over a mass of leaves, mud, and twigs. He'd head back here tomorrow to retrieve it. Gavin scanned the area and tried to familiarise himself with the spot, though there were no distinguishing features to take stock of.

When he trudged back to the track, Ben had his head tilted back and was still blinking his eye.

'Are you having a seizure?' asked Gavin.

'My contact lens… aw, it's stuck in the top,' said Ben.

Gavin sighed as Ben continued to poke under his eyelid.

'Well, when you're ready… perhaps we should carry on escaping.'

'That's it, got the bugger,' said Ben. Then he flicked away the dislodged lens.

'You ready now?'

'Yep, let's go.'

'Are you sure you can see alright? Don't need me to hold your hand, princess?'

'Fuck off.'

The rain was hammering down as the pair huddled inside a hollowed-out tree stump and watched the drops thudding into the lake opposite them. Ben had his arms crossed and looked furious and just glared at the lake, refusing to look at Gavin, who had planted himself on his holdall.

'Easy fix, those screens, Ben. Eighty quid tops,' said Gavin. He wanted to point out that if he wasn't such a useless, clumsy twat, he might not have fallen over and cracked the shit out of his iPhone, although the sullen mood Ben was in, he'd have walloped him. Well, the old Ben might have, but this hen-pecked Ben was more likely to burst into tears or have a panic attack. Didn't the building industry keep you fit? Not in Ben's case. Too many lackeys to do his bidding, thought Gavin.

'You remember when we brought all those out-of-date Creme Eggs from the corner shop?' asked Gavin. 'Corkscrew ate like eight of them, then threw up in Janette's trainer. She chased him into the water and we spent the entire day here mucking around in there. That's the day we all taught Sheryl how to swim. Remember that, Ben?'

Ben crossed his arms and grunted. 'Course I do.'

The rain became much heavier and the tree stump was giving little respite from the relentless downpour.

'Sorry, it's not quite how I planned the day to pan out,' said Gavin.

'Just don't say it!' growled Ben.

'Say what?'

'It's the Gouchy curse.'

'Well, now you mention it.'

'One bloody day, Gavin,' said Ben irately.

'So, what do you fancy doing tomorrow?' asked Gavin.

Ben turned to him, his nostrils flaring. 'One bloody day,' he repeated. Then the pair started sniggering and were soon bursting into manic laughter.

'You had two bags. What did you do with your rucksack?' asked Ben. He'd stopped laughing and was giving Gavin a questioning stare.

'I stashed it.'

'And why would you do that?' asked Ben, wiping rain from his face.

'Do you really want to know?'

'I don't know. Do I?'

Gavin shrugged and thought about his reply. Then he told Ben all about what happened in Skender's flat.

Ben snuck into the house at just gone ten-thirty. He was soaking wet, covered in mud, had a twisted ankle, broken phone, and could only see out of one eye. To top it off, he had a beast of a migraine. He removed his mud-caked trainers and dripping wet socks and ventured upstairs, tiptoeing as he went. Ryan's door was ajar, and the room was alive with frantic lights flashing from his gaming screen. Ben peered in, but his son was way too engrossed with the on-screen killing to notice him standing there. He slouched in his bulky gaming chair, his back to him, wearing his absurdly large headset. Ryan's room was spacious, with modern furnishings and plenty of storage nooks, yet still, it was a chaotic mess. Why was he such a lazy slob? He hadn't inherited that from him, and certainly not from Kayla either.

Ben walked towards the bathroom and winced when he heard the bedroom door open. Kayla stomped out with two pillows, shoved them in his hands, snorted, and headed back into the bedroom, closing the door behind her.

Ben breathed a heavy sigh as he recalled what Gavin had told him earlier, and it felt like a dark cloud had just covered his world. There was no way he could have Gavin back in his life. Not if he wanted to keep his sanity.

Twenty-four

It was freezing when he opened his eyes and gazed around his gloomy surroundings. It smelt damp and oily, and for a moment he couldn't work out where he was until the previous day's events flooded back.

Gavin's first thought was that he should have listened to Roland and fixed that stupid light. It would be a pain in the arse being without wheels.

Gavin got up and bashed his head on a low shelf, sending tools cluttering. He flinched at the sound and at the pain that assaulted his head – he'd hit the exact spot where his lump was.

A streak of daylight streaked in via a gap in the shed's door.

Gavin's mobile phone was out of juice so he had no clue how early it was, but his mum always woke up at stupid o'clock, so he was confident she'd be up and pottering around in the kitchen. He'd wanted to buy her some flowers and turn up with handfuls of shopping and make them a nice breakfast, but unfortunately, that plan had gone to shit. Now he was turning up resembling Stig of the frigging dump. A coffee and a hot shower were all he craved now.

The shed was always his old man's domain and off-limits to Gavin. He thought about all the times his old man had embarrassed him in front of his mates. He was forever taking the piss out of him; calling him dumbo and dinlo-head. Sometimes he'd rub his disgusting armpits, rank with BO, over Gavin's face, until he gagged and retched. When Gavin was fourteen, as revenge for showing him up, Gavin pinched some vodka from this very shed. During the theft, Gavin decided it would be hysterical to replace the booze with water and then mixed in a nice big helping of salt. This turned out to be a terrible mistake, as when Gavin returned from school two days later and dragged his bike from the shed, the frame fell apart. His dad had used his angle grinder to cut the bike clean in half. He still remembered his old man's sneering face from the kitchen window, as Gavin stood mouth ajar in the back garden. You'd have thought that would have been the end of the matter, but oh, no. Around a week later, Gavin got another bike, conveniently left outside the newsagents, and not only did he cut that one in half too, but he welded the flipping frame back together – only the front part had been moulded on upside down. His dad strolled out into the garden, calm as you like, with an arrogant grin slapped on his face and said, 'New bike, Gav? I bet your mates will think you're super cool on that. Is that some sort of new design?'

Gavin left his booze well alone after that. There was always some serious, no-nonsense parenting in the Gouch household, but his dad never hit him; well, not in a spiteful way. But perhaps that's just how things were back in those days, and that's how kids became proper men. Not like now, where everyone seemed to be an entitled, prissy snowflake. His old fella could be a funny bugger though, and on a good day, he would have Gavin in fits of laughter with some of his antics. Strangely, he missed the silly tosser.

Gavin took off his jacket and his mum immediately focussed on the bandage. 'Work accident,' he blurted before she questioned him.

She gave Gavin a speculative scowl, then resumed making the coffee. His mum was skinnier than when he'd last seen her, but she wasn't looking too shabby. She had dyed dark brown hair, in a shaggy style, with a full fringe that almost covered her eyes. Those cold and suspicious eyes. He didn't know how old his mum was but guessed nearly seventy, though she didn't look it.

Gavin watched her as she sighed despondently whilst she stirred the sugar into a worn Tottenham Hotspur mug. The team his dad supported.

'I don't have any money to lend you,' she said.

'Nah, Mum, I don't want any. I've got some for you. That money I borrowed. Well, some of it.'

'What money are we talking about? Because I lost track.'

'I've got two hundred for you.'

She handed him the coffee. 'You can stay in the spare room, but I'm not cooking for you.'

'I saw Ben last night,' said Gavin, removing the cash from his bag. He'd already separated it from the rest, as he didn't want her to know there was a fair bit more, otherwise, he'd feel obliged to bung her extra.

'Ben's doing well for himself. He has a good business, employees, and a delightful house,' she said.

'Yeah,' said Gavin.

'Surprised he's giving you the time of day,' she said sourly.

Gavin sipped his coffee and stared at his mum over the cup. She always was a bit grumpy in the morning, and he could understand her bitterness. His dad was gone, he wasn't around himself, and his older sister, Kate, had emigrated to Australia over fifteen years ago and barely made contact. His mum, Rose Gouch, was a lonely lady.

Gavin placed the cash down on the table and tapped it, whilst giving his mum a cheerful smile.

'So, what happened to Zara? Did she dump you?' she asked.

Gavin shook his head. 'I decided to leave her actually, Mum. Things didn't work out.' He'd tried to keep the sadness from seeping into his voice. If he hadn't succeeded, she didn't appear to have picked up on it. For a moment he considered telling her what happened last year. He wanted to get it off his chest.

Rose snatched up the notes. 'Fake, are they?'

'Don't be silly, Mum, course not,' said Gavin, with a wave of concern washing over him. He hoped they weren't, anyway. He'd not considered that as a possibility.

'I'll put the bacon on,' she said, sighing through her nose. 'Still have your crusts off your bread like a big baby?'

'Ta, Mum,' said Gavin.

Rose tottered off and started clanking about in the pots and pans cupboard.

Gavin smiled and was, despite it all, pleased to be back in his old home.

There was so much crap stored in the bedroom, Gavin struggled to shove the door open. Why had his mum been hoarding all this useless clutter in his room? Boxes and plastic crates filled with all manner of junk had been stacked floor to ceiling and even on the bed itself. There was even a saxophone stashed in one corner. Who had ever played that damn thing? The rubbish people keep. He moved a box off the bed and the bottom flopped opened and a massive pile of

VHS tapes tumbled out. Gavin swore under his breath and started scooping them up. A surge of nostalgia hit him when he picked up the case for the Gremlins film. Gavin thought those little green buggers were badass. His old-man took the piss out of him every time he watched it. 'Load of silly old bollocks,' he'd always say. Which applied to any film that didn't have Arnie cast as the main role. His dad used to have a major hard-on for him. Gavin smiled when he found the Commando and Running Man videos in the pile, and assumed the entire Schwarzenegger collection would be here somewhere. He then found the Bruce Lee film Way of the Dragon and some ninja films he vaguely remembered someone lending him many years ago. Movies were epic in the eighties, but watching them now often spoilt the memories and it never carried the same impact as it did when you were fourteen or fifteen. He recalled watching his favourite movies over and over and enjoyed them more with each viewing, but these days he rarely came across a film he could be bothered to sit through even once, let alone give it a repeat viewing.

Gavin sat on the space he'd made on the bed and checked his phone. Several messages from Zara flashed up, and he considered replying. The promises were coming thick and fast. He'd heard them all before, of course, but that didn't stop him from wanting to believe her, though he knew he couldn't cave in. This needed to be a major reality check for her. Kill or cure. If Zara wished for them to have their previous life back, she alone could make that possible. It was a pure fantasy to think along those lines, though.

Gavin found what he'd come for – his old Paul Daniels' magic set. He popped the crumpled lid and rummaged inside.

Twenty-five

Natalie jolted awake from a fidgety, dreamless sleep and sat up and listened. She could have sworn that she'd heard a loud slam, but everything was silent now. She checked the digital clock on her bedside; it was 2.30 a.m. Alex was due home late last night, although she didn't recall hearing him come in, and he'd told her not to wait up and that he would crash on the sofa.

Natalie fell back against the pillows, still listening. The next noise was impossible to ignore, as it sounded like glass smashing. She sprang from the bed and slung on her dressing gown, eyes scanning the room for a weapon. She settled on wielding an upturned high-heel shoe.

Natalie pushed opened the door and peered into the hallway. The bathroom door was ajar and taps were running fast. As she slipped into the hallway, she heard someone let out a low moan, causing her to freeze and her blood went cold.

'Alex?' she said, hearing the croak in her voice as she spoke. She poised the shoe as she crept to the bathroom door.

'No! Please. Stop, please,' cried Alex.

Natalie knew it was her husband, but she still hesitated when she pushed the door open and reached for the light switch. 'Alex, what are you doing in here? Are you—' Her voice trailed away when the light came on and she noticed the blood. Splatters of the stuff over the sink and toilet seat. She took a step back, dropped the shoe and froze.

Alex, naked and muttering gibberish, hadn't acknowledged Natalie standing there. He looked pallid, and the blood running from his nose seemed bright as it glistened under the harsh ceiling lights. Steam poured from the sink, but she could not move to turn off the hot tap.

Alex shook his head. 'No… no, no, stop. You don't need to do this.'

'Alex, I'm here. Alex!' shouted Natalie.

There was no indication that Alex had heard her speak. He started muttering again. Blood dripped from his nostrils and pooled on the shiny white tiles by his knees.

'What's wrong with you?' she asked.

Alex was awake, but he seemed to be trapped in one of his nightmares.

He became silent. And that silence was eerie.

Natalie had no clue what to do. She considered splashing him with cold water, but then he slumped forward and his eyes flickered rapidly, and rolled upwards until only the whites of his eyeballs showed.

Alex started blinking and scanned the room, and his expression was that of a desperate man who'd awoken at a murder scene. Once he noticed the amount of blood at his knees, he recoiled, sliding himself backwards on his bottom, bare cheeks squeaking on the tiles, until he slammed up against the radiator. He trembled and shook, hugging his knees. Yet he still hadn't even noticed Natalie, and she still hadn't moved from the doorway. She stood fixed to the spot, wondering what she'd just borne witness to. Was it a severe night terror?

She grabbed some toilet roll and knelt next to him. Alex cowered away.

'It's me,' she whispered, pressing the wedge of tissue against his nostrils.

Alex's expression became one of sheer panic. 'Did I hurt you?'

'No, you didnae hurt me. You had a bad nosebleed in your sleep,' she said, speaking calmly, though her hands trembled.

'I... don't—'

Natalie wrapped a towel around his shoulders. 'Did you take anything last night? Any pills?'

Alex's entire body was shaking. 'I'm not sure. I can't remember.'

Natalie stepped to the sink, turned off that tap, and her jaw dropped. Their huge bathroom mirror had two massive cracks running down its centre. She gazed at her distorted reflection in the steam-filled bathroom and knew they could no longer live like this.

Alex and Natalie nibbled on some fruit and pancakes at the breakfast bar. They'd not spoken about the incident in the bathroom, neither had gone back to bed, and they both looked exhausted.

'We need to talk about what happened,' she said.

'I must have taken too many pills,' he said, in a matter-of-fact tone. 'Those pills I got from your dad are perhaps too strong. That's my theory, anyway.'

'No, don't you dare. Don't you make this out to be nothing, Alex. Whatever that was in there, it wisnae normal!'

Alex popped a strawberry in his mouth and avoided her gaze, looking at his phone instead.

Natalie's temper was rising. His placid demeanour wasn't helping to quell her mood.

'How do you expect me to help you when you keep shutting me out, Alex?'

Alex placed his hand on hers. She snatched it back.

'Why won't you talk to me? What's going on in that head of yours?'

Alex gazed at her and looked momentarily offended, then stood up and walked to the coffee machine. 'More coffee?'

'Tell me what's happening in these dreams. Don't be giving me all that utter shite about not remembering. You can remember. We both know that.'

Alex went to speak but hesitated, closed his eyes and rubbed his forehead.

'What did you mean, Alex? "You don't have to do this." Who were you speaking to? It sounded like you were pleading with them.'

Alex poured a black coffee. 'It was just—'

'If you say it was just a bad dream, I swear to Christ I'll ram these flipping berries up your nose. Stop treating me like some daft numpty!'

'Why are you getting so angry?' he asked.

'Because you keep shutting me out.'

Alex sipped his coffee, smiling sedately.

'Did you hurt that girl?' she asked, her voice filled with frustration. She shocked herself that those words had slipped out.

They stared at each other for several moments. Natalie broke the silence. 'That girl you told me about. Sheryl. Did something happen to her? Is that what you're dreaming about?'

'It wasn't about her.'

'Aye, sure. If you are not prepared to discuss this, what do you expect me to think?'

'And why would you think I hurt her?' yelled Alex, with a sudden vehemence that made Natalie jump and squash the berries in her hand.

Alex glared at her. It was a look that she'd never seen before. A hateful look. It unsettled her and tied her stomach into knots, and for the first time in their relationship, Natalie couldn't stand to be in the same room as her husband.

'What are you getting at?' he shouted, slamming his coffee glass down so hard, it cracked.

Natalie flinched, whilst stammering a reply that didn't leave her lips.

He backhanded the glass, sending it across the kitchen with a smash. 'Well?'

'I need to get ready for work,' said Natalie, annoyed at how panicky she sounded. She needed to get out of there. Who the hell was this stranger in their kitchen?

Alex snapped out of his hostile mood and stepped back, looking as shocked as Natalie felt. He put his hand over his open mouth. 'Jesus, I'm so sorry, Nat... I'm just so tired. I shouldn't take it out on you.'

'Since when did you act like a stroppy child, Alex?'

'I just lost—'

'I'll be late home tonight,' she said. She couldn't get out of the kitchen fast enough.

Natalie strode along, avoiding shoppers and sauntering tourists. She'd opted for flat shoes today, as cobbles, high-heels, and heavy rain weren't always a fabulous combination. Especially when she was running late and pissed off. She cursed herself for leaving her umbrella by the door. She'd left the apartment in a rush after the morning's events and left with a sadness in her heart that she'd never known.

The streets were already busy, despite the morning drizzle and the chill in the air. Every day she walked to work this way; along Victoria Street, down the hill onto West Bow and past the colourful shopfronts – the clothes stores, gift shops, and restaurants. Her Uncle Simon once lived in the area, and she'd visited here often as a child, and she always loved coming here to stay with him, because it was such a contrast to where she grew up. Edinburgh was always alive and buzzing with activity and the unique, stacked buildings, medieval architecture, and the winding alleys through the charcoal-coloured walkways had captivated her. She'd always dreamed of moving here as a girl. Now that dream was a reality, and she'd been so happy and content. She felt blessed they'd been able to afford to live in such a wonderful part of Edinburgh. Natalie had convinced Alex that their apartment would be the ideal location for them both, and although he'd taken a bit of persuading, he'd been glad of it. Despite his reservations, he'd settled into the city straight away. It suited them both perfectly.

An overwhelming sense of anger replaced Natalie's sadness. Everything seemed to be falling apart, and because of what? Because of a few stupid nightmares. It was insane. Alright, she didn't believe they were stupid, and Alex plainly didn't. If he'd just open up, then maybe she could help, but he just shut her out and blatantly pushed her away, which only made her believe more strongly that he was hiding something awful from her. She began walking fast, with sudden purpose and determination, as she weaved through the throng of people. If Alex wouldn't speak to her, then she'd find another way to unearth some answers.

Alex sat down on the bed with a heavy sigh. He felt terrible about how he'd treated Natalie. Where did that anger flare from? That wasn't him.

He suffered another memory blank again yesterday. He recalled the photo shoot in the Lakes. The weather hadn't been on their side and Reeves had been narked that the weather prediction had been wrong, and Alex's delay hadn't helped his crabby mood. But Alex couldn't remember leaving that remote place. Or the journey back. Or coming home. His mind was a jumbled mess. The dream hadn't been, though. That had been clear as day. It had been terrifying. He had relived that day on Freddy Killner's farm. The day he got those awful scars on his back. The day that changed everything.

Alex had always been embarrassed about those scars. He'd hated them. For most of his young life, he couldn't bear to look at them. Rarely would he take off his clothes, unless it was dark. In fact, it had been a long time into their relationship, before Natalie had got a proper glimpse of them. She sensed he'd been trying to hide them, and so they were outright ignored for a while. Until she'd been comfortable enough in his company to bring it up in conversation.

Credit to her, she had gone about it in such a tactful way, that it almost made him feel silly for being so ashamed of them. It had been on a long weekend trip in Valencia when he'd been practically forced to join her in the swimming pool, and then he was put into a position where there was no option but to discuss them. Afterwards, he was glad that he'd finally dealt with that issue. Happy that they were able to move on as a couple and he could stop obsessing over them.

Alex lied about how he'd obtained them, of course. He told her a story about falling backwards from a motorbike, whilst riding pillion with a friend. Saying that his trouser leg hooked onto part of the bike and he was dragged across the ground. Then added that he was flung into the bushes and sent hurtling down a rocky ditch. It had been all he could think of at the time, but she didn't question his story, and he didn't think he'd ever need to bring it up again. How could he tell her the truth now?

The phantom pain ran across his lower back again. Like it always did when he thought about those injuries. He decided that to save his relationship, he needed to distance himself from Natalie. He'd never lost it like that with her. She was his best friend, and he loved her more than life itself. His actions had scared him as much as they had her. Until he'd been back to sort out this mess, he wouldn't return home.

It was finally time to face the demons from his past. He would leave for Kent before Natalie got home.

Twenty-six

The boy had heard all about the incredible Black Widow catapult and popped into town with the sole purpose of finding one. Those bad boys could allegedly do some serious damage.

It smelt like wax jackets and armpit sweat in the shop he'd found. The shop was cramped, humid, and overstocked with army surplus stuff, such as tactical gloves, combat jackets, and desert boots. It also housed a music section, where you could pick up vinyl records, guitar chord books, and woven jacket patches and badges. The boy gazed at the patches that were slapped up on a display board: AC/DC, Def Leppard, and Iron Maiden to name a few bands up there. But it was the downstairs area the boy needed to go to. The sullen-faced young shop assistant peered up from his book, gazed at the boy fleetingly, then went back to his read.

The boy made his way down the treacherously steep steps and into the smaller shop area down below. It was a converted basement with a low ceiling. Behind a wooden counter sat a tubby, bearded bloke in his late fifties, with deep-set eyes and a triple chin. The shopkeeper gave the boy a suspicious scowl, crossed his arms, and eyeballed him as he dawdled around the display cabinets. Once the boy got a proper glimpse of what lay inside, his eyes bulged in total amazement. Inside the glass cabinets hung weapons of every description – knives, swords, throwing spikes and stars; a selection of pellet guns and an assortment of catapults – including the one he had come to purchase, or at least, attempt to purchase. He viewed another cabinet which sold ninja uniforms and his jaw dropped when he saw the ninja claws, a chain garrotte, and a hairbrush that contained a concealed blade. He pressed his nose against the glass and gazed in wonder. This place was something else. It was incredible. Another gleaming blade caught his attention, and he leered at the weapon. It was a stunning piece. He decided this place was an Aladdin's cave of brutal weapons.

'What are you after?' asked the shopkeeper in a monotone voice.

'I want to buy a Black Widow,' he said, trying to speak in an unwavering and mature tone. He looked into the shopkeeper's eyes as he spoke and was expecting the man to snigger and tell him to do one, but he didn't. Instead, he took the key from his pocket, shuffled to the cabinet, and unlocked it.

'Popular, these,' he said as he removed the item, 'this is the last one we have in stock.'

'That's lucky.'

It wasn't until he paid for the catapult and had it wrapped in a carrier bag that he truly believed he would leave the store with the weapon. The man hadn't even asked him his age, and to be fair, the man didn't seem to give a monkey's nut-sack. The boy fought down the urge to grin smugly, thinking he would return as soon as he had the money for more goodies.

The boy nodded his thanks and turned from the counter, clutching his new toy with both hands and pressing it tightly to his chest. Only then did he realise that someone else stood in the basement. A lad with unfriendly eyes. Eyes that were fixed on him with an unconcealed, scrutinising glare.

The boy eyeballed this lad and delivered his ultimate death-stare.

After what seemed an eternity, the boy caved in and averted his gaze.

The lad grinned. A nasty grin, full of malevolence and threat. He ran one finger across his neck in a slow and methodical movement.

But the boy wasn't afraid of him. A tad wary perhaps, but if anything he was more fascinated by him. There was something cranky and dangerous about him. He had a feeling this was just the start of things to come. The lad left, and the boy followed him outside, reaching in his pocket for something to load into his new weapon.

Twenty-seven

Gavin got out of the taxi and scanned his surroundings. He stood at the entrance of a compact industrial area a few miles north-west of Maidstone. It was a drizzly, miserable day, and the area seemed to be deserted. He headed past some neglected factory units and a tyre-fitting business that appeared to be shut down. There was a mountain of discarded tyres piled up outside and colourful graffiti covered the entrance shutter. Gavin was about to conclude the information he'd been given was incorrect, but then he spotted a caravan positioned next to the River Medway. He guessed its positioning was the reason as to why sandbags were stacked high on its far side. It was a vintage-looking caravan that wasn't in the best shape; the weather-worn fibreglass roof was covered in moss, and it appeared as though it hadn't moved for quite some time.

A mud-splashed black Toyota Hilux was parked nearby.

Gavin approached slowly, inspecting the vehicle as he went.

'Anybody about?' said Gavin, as he stepped towards the caravan's door. 'Hey,' he bellowed as he stepped over a mound of fag ends, crushed beer cans and bottle tops that were piled by the door. Gavin rapped his knuckles on the door, which immediately flung open and a man gazed out.

'How's it going, Patrick?' said Gavin.

'It's been a while, Gouchy boy,' said Patrick, his voice deep and gravelly. He scratched his chin, yawned, and waved Gavin inside.

Gavin entered and was assaulted with a pungent smell of fags, body odour, and grease. Gavin fought down the urge to gag. This crap hole made his flat look like a palace, and that was saying something.

'Want tea?' asked Patrick.

'Don't you fancy a pint, Pat?' asked Gavin, not wanting to spend a minute longer in this dump. He saw a messy bed at the far end. *Oh, Christ, he must kip here,* he thought grimly.

'I'm working security here at the moment. That's my job,' stated Patrick proudly. He sat at a chipped table and picked up a dusty brandy bottle. 'Fancy a nip of this instead?'

'Yeah, nice,' said Gavin, forcing a grin. He watched Patrick pull out two smeared glasses and pour the liquid in. Gavin studied his old friend. He was a weird-looking bloke – tall and wiry and his head was slightly lightbulb shaped. His eyes, as always, were dead and empty of emotion. Most noticeably was how badly his face was pockmarked and scarred. Gavin remembered when Patrick's face had been covered in severe, angry acne. There were days at school when he'd scratch his cheeks raw and bloody, and the kids would snigger and call him all the names under the sun. It hadn't been too long after that when Patrick became aggressive to the piss takers. By the time Patrick hit fourteen, few kids were brave enough, or stupid enough, to mock him. Not if they wanted to keep their teeth in their gob or the skin on their face. Patrick was a brutal bugger. Now, though, the bloke looked in a right state.

Gavin watched Patrick pick up the glass with his right hand and couldn't help but focus on his fingers, or lack of them. Patrick's three middle fingertips were missing. He had rounded stumps that were all the same length – the stumps were a fraction shorter than his pinky finger.

'It's still not my favourite wanking hand,' said Patrick with a wry grin. He'd clearly been well aware Gavin had been gawping at them.

'You always said you'd return the favour, if you ever got the chance, Pat,' said Gavin. 'Well, I decided it's only fair to inform you, that Alex Clayton is gonna be back in town soon.'

Patrick gave him a bitter smile. 'How did you find me?'

'I spoke to your cousin, Dennis.'

Patrick sipped the brandy and licked his thin lips.

Gavin sniffed his drink and took a tiny sip. 'Don't you want revenge anymore?'

'I'm past all that now, Gav. It was a lifetime ago. I don't care about that anymore.'

Gavin grinned. 'Yeah, right. Like fuck you don't.'

Alex had set off on the long drive down to Kent early Thursday morning and checked into the hotel a day earlier than planned. With an extra day to play with, he visited some of his old haunts.

Earlier, Alex passed through the Brookacre estate, which seemed serenely quiet, and he sauntered about outside his childhood home, briefly seeing a petulant-looking boy, with jet-black hair, staring out of his childhood bedroom window. The boy gave him a stony glare, then shut the curtains.

Afterwards, Alex drove by what was once the Brookacre school – now a housing estate, and then he checked out his nan's bungalow, which looked deteriorated; the back garden now resembling a jungle.

It was all part of the process, he told himself. There were more important places he needed to go, but he wasn't ready to visit those just yet.

Alex stepped towards the metal barrier and peered between the bars. The barrier was a seaweed green colour and was around three metres high, with curved pointed tops to ensure no one climbed over it. He could see the pit was mostly drained now, but it still contained rubbish sacks, tyres, and bricks. He envisaged his mum's brooch deep down in the centre, rusted and eroded. Just being here made him feel jittery, and he felt a heavy pressure on his chest.

He didn't stay for long.

Alex got back into his Jeep and checked his phone. Natalie had yet to reply to him, and they hadn't spoken since the incident on Wednesday. He'd received a text message from Mark though, saying he'd landed at Heathrow and would meet him at the hotel later. They'd agreed to stay in the same place so they could go to the pub meet-up together on Saturday. The thought of that meeting and seeing the others filled him with trepidation, but he knew the sooner he got that out of the way, the better.

'What was it Gran used to say? "You two lazy lassies need to stretch those skinny wee legs and get some fresh salty air." Or something along those lines,' she said jovially.

Natalie smiled at her sister. 'Yep, that's what she said.'

Natalie strolled alongside her sister as they headed through the grounds of St Mary's Parish Church in Haddington. They visited their late gran's plot every couple of months. It gave them a chance for a good catchup, or at least a good quiet catchup. Hannah's place was always lively. Having three boys and one girl, aged between five and fifteen, meant there was little peace in her house. Not that her sister complained. Hannah loved having a large family, and she was a fantastic mother and wife. She even managed to fit in a part-time job as a teaching assistant at one of the town's schools. Hannah was much more like their own mother than Natalie. Her sister even lived five minutes away from their parents' place. Natalie often wondered what her life would be like with children of her own, but her business commitments had always outweighed any maternal emotions that she felt. Well, that and the fact Alex could not father a child. Something he'd been honest about from the early stages of their relationship. Other options had been discussed, but never warranted a second debate. He just wasn't interested in being a father.

Natalie removed some withered flowers from a well-maintained graveyard plot, and Hannah placed down a fresh batch they'd purchased en route.

'OK, so, what's up then, hen?' asked Hannah.

'What makes you think there is anything wrong?' said Natalie, trying to sound upbeat.

'I'm ya big sister. I know a grumpy wee girl when I see one, you daft thing. You look pure done in too.'

Natalie looked at her sister and smiled despite her glum mood. People often said they looked nothing alike, and that was true, they didn't. Hannah was short and had a thickset build, her cheeks were always ruddy and her face rounded and pretty. She had a sweet and trusting smile, and her presence would always light a room. Everyone loved her sister, and Natalie knew Hannah would do anything for her, and anything for her family.

'We were talking about how Gran would take us on walks along the coast,' reminded Natalie.

'Aye, of course. Rain or shine, wind or snow, but I think we should talk about what's up with you.'

'You wisnae there that day at North Berwick. I think you were at one of your music clubs.'

'What's got you thinking about that day?' said Hannah.

'You remember I kept seeing that girl's face in my dreams. I didn't have nightmares before that day. Not awful ones. But—'

'Nat, it was a horrific thing to witness. You were only a wee lass.'

'My point is—' Natalie left that sentence unfinished. 'I know you have more important things to worry about.'

Natalie formed a mental image of the girl on the rocks near the old chain pier. The wind was gusty and the heavy waves were crashing against the rocks in a wild, foamy surge. The young girl had been waving to family members from those rocks when an enormous wave had wiped her out. When the girl recovered herself, she had stood up, laughed and smiled. The poor thing didn't comprehend the extent of her injuries. Not until she saw the mortified looks from her family. What stuck in Natalie's mind wasn't so much the injury, though that had been gruesome – but it was the girl's smile that had been in her nightmares. Her face had been badly dashed against the rocks and shiny bone, teeth and gums were on display – the rocks had obliterated her top lip and right cheek. Her goofy smile morphing into that horror-stricken expression haunted Natalie for a long time. That smile had caused her to wake in a cold sweat screaming for her mother, but she knew whatever was haunting Alex's dreams had to be far worse. That thought alone was a frightening one.

'This sounds pretty damn important to me,' said Hannah.

Natalie decided she would tell her sister everything. She would need her help after all.

Natalie's family had accepted Alex into the fold. Hannah occasionally joked that Natalie should have found herself a proper man, as in a Scotsman, but her settling down with an English guy hadn't been an issue with her family. Hannah and her husband, Evan, were pro-Scottish independence, but their parents were against it, which caused the odd dinner-time debate, and Alex always studiously avoided those discussions. Opting to say he didn't have an opinion or was neutral on the entire matter. Alex considered political matters to be a pointless argument. He liked to say, 'Voting aside, the average Joe couldn't do much to change the outcome of things. All these strong opinions do is divide people and cause unnecessary bickering.'

Natalie tended to agree with her husband on this one. Political bickering drove her bonkers.

'Is this about Alex?' asked Hannah.

'I think it's all falling apart,' said Natalie.

They left the church and walked onto the muddy footpath and along the River Tyne. They'd walked this river-bank route hundreds of times, and they never tired of it. The sisters hooked arms and Hannah said, 'So what's going on, hen?'

Alex and Mark ate breakfast at the hotel. Mark had complained about most things on his plate and had returned his egg, which was too runny, and bacon that was too crispy. He'd also caused a fuss at reception upon his arrival last night when he kicked off about his request for an orthopaedic mattress being ignored.

Alex laughed to himself at how high maintenance Mark was. He guessed he was so used to getting what he wanted these days. He had the money to be a fussy sod. Though that wouldn't stop the chef from mixing something unpleasant into his beans. Alex rarely complained about anything. He wasn't great with arguments and hated confrontations of any kind. He knew that was because when he lost his temper, which was extremely rare, the red mist descended and he felt he was losing control, so it was best not to put himself into that position.

'I'm not impressed with this place. For the money, it's a lame-arse service,' complained Mark.

'How long are you staying?' asked Alex, trying to divert the conversation.

'I'm going to Hampshire Monday. Thought I'd see the folks whilst I'm over. I need to be in Milan on Friday. Huge club night.'

'Sounds lovely. I love Italy. Beautiful country.'

'Yeah, I'll be in and out. I'll be lucky if I get a plate of pasta, let alone get the chance to indulge in any majestic, Italian culture. What was it you wanted to ask me, anyway?'

'Sunday morning, I'm going out to the farm. Fancy joining me?'

Mark almost choked on his orange juice. 'Farm? As in, Freddy Killner's farm? Why?'

'To speak with him. If he's still there. And still alive.'

'Like that crazy wanker will speak to us. He's far more likely to shoot us both in the balls!' said Mark, loud enough for the elderly couple on the neighbouring table to hear. Alex mouthed them an apology. They turned away in disgust.

'Only one way to find out,' said Alex.

'My God, Clayton, you do intend to stir up this wasp's nest, don't you?'

Alex shrugged and squeezed a dollop of mustard onto his plate. He'd go there, with or without Mark.

'Well, it's a ridiculously stupid idea. What time are we going?' said Mark sardonically.

Twenty-eight

Kent, Summer 1988

Alex had spent the last three days hanging out with Ben, Sheryl and Mark. Janette was away with her family for a short break, and Gavin, for reasons unknown, had got grounded. And as far as Alex was concerned, it had been marvellous without them present. Ben came across as quite a good-natured and easy-going character without Gavin about to egg him on, but most importantly, Alex could spend more time messing about with Sheryl. Without that moody mate of hers glued to her side, Sheryl acted differently in Alex's company. She also seemed to have more fun. The scratch on Alex's face had already started healing, and after he'd calmed down, he knew that sulking about what had happened, would get him nowhere. After all, it was his own choice to brave the tests. Ben had assured Alex there'd be a cooling-off period until his third challenge, although Alex considered Ben was only waiting for Gavin's parents to release him back into the wild again.

They were all sitting on a fallen oak tree, centred in a small clearing in Colt Wood.

Mark poked Sheryl in the shoulder. 'What's this rumour about you having a new boyfriend?'

Alex clenched his teeth. This was news to him.

'Piss off, Corkscrew,' said Sheryl, with an embarrassed grin.

'Hrm, Patrick Lynch,' teased Ben.

'You said he asked you to the cinema three times. I bet he wanted to take you for a pizza afterwards. Eh, that would have been awkward,' said Mark.

'Stop it. That's so nasty,' said Sheryl.

Mark spoke loud and imitated an Italian waiter. 'Ah, I see you already have your pizza. Aw, I am a sooo sorry, that is just your boyfriend's face.'

Ben laughed nervously and lit up a cigarette.

Alex knew mocking Patrick wasn't wise, but he couldn't help but snigger at the impression.

'His parents were drug addicts and were horrid to him,' said Sheryl, tersely.

'No wonder, having a kid that minging,' said Mark.

Ben whacked Mark on the back, desperate to bring his attention to something in the trees. Mark's amused expression shifted into one of red-faced panic, when Patrick rolled his bike into the clearing. If Patrick had heard any of the mickey-taking, he made no sign of showing it. He just looked at them all, one by one, with those dead eyes of his, and he stared at Mark last, keeping his eyes fixed on him for quite some time. Mark looked away, intimidated.

There was a tense silence, which Ben broke. 'Hey, you alright, Pat? Want a fag?'

'Where's Shane?' he asked, in a voice barely audible.

Alex followed Leo through a dense and overgrown woodland area. They headed off track and into the path of stinging nettles and some vicious blackberry bushes that attacked Alex's legs.

Leo used a machete to chop a track through the nettles.

'How's the Shuriken practice going?' asked Leo.

'I am getting better,' he replied, pulling a face at the pain he was receiving courtesy of the nettles.

'We'll work on your balance too. I'm not as well trained as my brother, but I can show you some stuff. Leg sweeps and defence blocks.'

'That's great. Um, where are you taking me?'

'The secret lake.'

A short while later, Leo and Alex approached a serene lake. The greenish water was surrounded by a low bank with lush, high grass, white water-lilies and encircled by tall beech and cedar trees. Insects and butterflies buzzed around, and Alex watched as a huge dragonfly glided right past his face. Alex thought it was like a little tropical oasis here. Calm, peaceful and hidden away. It wasn't an easy location to get to.

There was a rundown rowing boat floating amongst a long tangle of reeds. Leo made his way to it and unhooked the frayed rope from the rotten mooring post. Alex wondered how many years the boat had spent on the lake and who had brought the craft here. As he climbed inside, the wood creaked and moaned under his weight. Leo joined him and rowed them out.

They sat in the boat for hours, drifting around the water with sunshine on their faces. They ate crisps, drank Coke, and Leo smoked a couple of cigarettes.

'I've thought of a way you can pay them back,' said Leo, splashing his hand in the water as he spoke.

'Who?' asked Alex.

'Your dad and his silly tart. You said you wanted revenge. I'll help you.'

Alex nodded. He thought some payback was in order.

Leo laid back, and a cruel grin spread on his face. 'After that, we'll deal with your so-called friends. We will give *them* a little test. A little taste of their own medicine.'

'But… why do you want to help me?' asked Alex.

'Because I like you, buddy. I think you're gutsy. You have real energy and you are courageous. You have the heart of a lion!'

Alex felt his cheeks glow with pride.

'Plus I enjoy taking down total piss-fucks,' said Leo.

Alex crouched down behind a blueish-grey Ford Sierra. It belonged to a neighbour, Fat-Phil, as his dad liked to call him. They had been waiting here a while.

Leo tapped him on his shoulder. 'Get down!'

They watched as Ian's car jolted to a stop and he pulled himself from the car. He had a cigarette hanging from his lips and was wearing dark blue factory overalls and his baseball cap. He walked, at a lethargic pace, to his front door.

'Here we go,' whispered Leo, holding in his laughter.

Alex watched his dad put his key in the door, then knocked when he couldn't get it to open.

Kay appeared at the open bedroom window. She looked furious.

'I can't open this, love. Is the key in the door?'

'You dirty cheating manwhore!' she said.

'What on earth is going on?' asked Ian.

'I warned you, Ian! If you ever treated me like you treated *her*, I would make you pay. Didn't I say that?'

'Open this door, you mad bitch!' yelled Ian. 'You can't lock me out of my own house. Let me in right now.'

Kay spoke in a slow, sharp tone. 'You can do one, you lousy twat.'

'Don't wind me up, you dozy cow.'

Kay was wearing pink pyjamas. She also had on a pair of yellow marigolds. She held up a pair of skimpy red thongs, and with a twisted grimace, dropped them. They landed in the lavender plant and Ian gazed at them with a dumbfounded expression.

'What a piss-take. Down the side of the sofa. You dirty pig! Who is she? Cos I've been through all your stuff and I found her earring in your jeans too. And that condom stash you have been hiding in your sock drawer,' said Kay, narrowing her scorn-filled eyes.

'What?' said Ian.

'And three phone calls today. No one spoke. Suspicious.'

Ian could only stare at her in utter disbelief.

Kay gave him a smile oozing with spite. 'You pathetic rat. By the way, my brothers, Greg and Tyler, are on their way here. They want a word with you.'

Leo gestured they should go. Alex ran from the car and glimpsed his dad's confused face. He was certain that his dad had spotted him.

Alex joined Leo, who was leaning against a lamppost, laughing. 'Did you see his face?' screeched Leo.

Bewildered by what he'd witnessed, Alex wasn't sure what to say, and he wasn't finding it as hilarious as Leo.

A beaten-up red builder's van drove around the corner, tyres screeching. Alex only got a brief glimpse of the men inside, but they looked like big brutish louts with shaved heads. The Barton brothers carried a reputation on the Brookacre estate. No sane person ever crossed those violent thugs. Did he remember someone saying they were Patrick's cousins?

Leo stopped laughing and pulled a serious expression. 'Manwhore,' he said, before bursting into an uncontrollable belly laugh.

Later that day, Alex met up with Ben and Mark, but couldn't help feel guilty about his dad. Had Leo's retaliation idea been a step too far? There was little he could do now. He couldn't change the day's events.

'Move your arse, Corkscrew,' shouted Ben.

Mark was moving through the trees but seemed reluctant. Alex thought he appeared rather anxious, and this prompted him to ask, 'Where are we going, Ben?'

Ben gave him a crooked grin. 'The farm.'

Then Gavin emerged from the trees.

The four boys stood on the outskirts of Killner's farm. It was an unsettling place. A ten foot mesh fence ringed the property, with coils of razor wire twisted along the top. It seemed more like something that would secure a prison, not a farm. Bits of shredded tarpaulin dangled from parts of the fence, and a dead fox hung, tangled in the mesh. The animal had decomposed, the stench of rank decay lay heavy in the air, and hundreds of flies congregated around the carcass.

Alex gawped at the main farmhouse which was a charred ruin; the building had been destroyed, and the roof collapsed in on itself. Alex thought it looked like something out of a creepy horror movie. The whole place did. On the far side was a large, decrepit barn, its timber doors half hanging off. Around the barn lay discarded car parts, rusted farm machinery, oil drums, and a mini excavator, covered in weeds, ivy and vines.

Ben slung down his rucksack in the dust and wiped the sweat from his brow. The sun seemed huge in the sky and it was a scorching afternoon. Alex wondered what was in the bag. Whatever it was, it looked heavy.

Ben unzipped the front pouch and tugged out a set of wire-cutters. He winked at Alex and started cutting at the fence. They all watched him work, silent and alert.

It took Ben about two minutes to cut a hole large enough for them to crawl through. Gavin wiggled through first, followed by Mark and Alex. Ben came last, after one last scan of the area.

They ran over to some ramshackle store sheds and dusted themselves off.

Ben pointed to the farmhouse. 'We need to go around the back.'

Ben led the boys across the centre of the farm, to a large open gravelled area. From here, there was a wide driveway that led past the main farmhouse and down a narrow, twisty track to the entrance. The intimidating wooden entrance gate wouldn't have looked out of place in a Mad Max movie. It must have been eight metres in height, painted black, had thick chains wrapped around it, and was fixed on a roller system, and rolls of razor wire ran across the top. The boys watched that gate as if at any moment, it would slide open and the devil himself would charge through it, wielding a fiery sword.

It was so quiet here. An unnatural quiet.

The boys peered into the barn, but it was too dark to see anything inside.

Gavin approached a rusty chest freezer that stood by the barn's entrance. He popped open the lid, peered inside, sniffed and gagged. 'Ugh, smells like death in there.'

Gavin walked back to the group and opened his mouth to speak when a loud bark echoed from within the barn. The group spun to face the noise, just in time to see a dog race out, barking as it came. All four boys raced away from the animal, stumbling and slipping as it bolted for them.

They ran for a while, then Ben started laughing. 'Wait up! Stop. Stop running, boys. Look.'

Alex stopped and gazed back at the dog. It was growling, barking and wild with rage, but the chain attached to its collar meant it could only reach a few metres from the barn's entrance. They all started laughing in relief, which seemed to make the dog angrier. It was a Doberman, and it was a well-muscled animal, with cropped, pointy ears.

'It's a bitch,' confirmed Ben, 'lovely-looking dog.'

The dog had a shiny black coat, with a tan-coloured snout, legs and chest. She had stopped barking now and crouched low, snarling, with her teeth showing and the fur raised along her back.

'Come on, Dolly, be a good girl now,' said Gavin in a hushed tone.

'Don't name it, Gavin!' said Mark, edging further back. The Doberman seemed to focus her wrath on him.

'Will you stop winding her up, Corkscrew. She feels threatened,' said Gavin, seeming to enjoy the terror oozing from Mark.

'I'm not doing anything! What's her problem with me?'

'She can smell his fear,' said Ben, talking to Gavin.

Ben edged closer to the dog, holding out his hand, and run his tongue across his front teeth.

'She can probably smell the shit in his pants,' said Gavin.

'Can we please leave the dog be, and get out of here?' snapped Mark, who was again scanning the farm's entrance.

'Have you got any sweets to give her, Ben?' asked Gavin.

'I've got some Chewits,' said Ben, rustling in his pocket and pulling out two sweets. He unwrapped them and held out his hand. The dog's teeth were still showing, her growl almost a hiss now.

'It doesn't want to eat freaking sweets. It wants to eat us,' squealed Mark.

'It, is a *she*, and she just wants to eat you,' said Gavin.

Alex could sense what was going to happen and tried to warn Ben. 'Don't!'

The dog attacked. Her ferocious bark was harsh and horrible. Ben scrambled away and stumbled backwards in the gravel. He landed hard on his back, the rucksack breaking his fall, and his glasses flinging from his face. The dog had been inches from taking a bite out of him. She was now growling, insane and frustrated as she tugged and fought with her collar.

Gavin helped Ben to his feet, suppressing a smirk. 'You are so great with dogs, Napier.'

Ben glowered at the dog who was now occupied chomping a Chewit using one side of her mouth.

Alex scooped up the glasses and handed them to Ben. He snatched them from him, slid them onto his pinched face and wiggled them straight. He dusted himself down, whilst trying to appear unfazed by the situation. Lifting his chin high, Ben said, 'Time to get started, Clayton.'

They followed Ben past the side of the burnt-out farmhouse. Mark detested it here. Everything about the place was wrong; he'd bet a hundred quid it was haunted. If the rumours were true, it almost certainly was. As he gazed at the blackened ruin, he could picture the farmhouse searing with flames; hear the wood beams cracking; visualise Freddy standing outside, watching in silence as his family roasted alive.

Gavin grabbed him from behind. 'Corkscrew!'

Mark's heart thudded in his chest. 'Leave off, you dopey muppet.'

'How long do you think it took them to die inside there?' wondered Ben, aloud.

'Is it even true?' asked Mark.

Gavin nodded. 'My dad said Freddy's wife was gonna leave him. Cos he was a drunken, violent monster. So Freddy lit the place up and locked his two daughters in their bedroom.'

'Oooh, it must really be true if your dad said so,' said Mark.

'I heard the same,' confirmed Ben.

Mark felt a cold shudder and his stomach lurched. He somehow believed the rumours too, but he wasn't prepared to let these lads know how scared he was.

Alex appeared transfixed by the building. Unfortunately for Alex, Mark knew what was in the rucksack.

Ben threw down the rucksack with a thud. 'This is as far as we go. You're on your own from here, Clayton.'

They were on the far side of the farm now. Around two hundred feet ahead of them, set in the far corner, was a mobile home, positioned on concrete blocks and closed in by a low picket fence that was painted sky blue. An aluminium table and chairs sat outside with a large umbrella that looked like it had come from a pub garden. The charming little area looked as though it didn't belong here. It was way too neat and clean.

'You'll need this,' said Ben, tugging free a Jerry-can from the rucksack and placing it in front of Alex.

'Wait… what? Why do I need that?' asked Alex.

'If the door is locked, you can climb in using that window. Once inside, douse the place with petrol. Then light her up and meet us by the hole where we came in. We will wait there,' said Ben as he popped a zippo lighter into the pocket of Alex's shorts. 'Don't lose that. I sort of borrowed it from my dad.'

'But are we checking the cider shack first, Ben?' asked Gavin with a hopeful smile.

'Yeah, we can check on the way out. Let's go.'

'I can't do this,' whined Alex, 'I can't burn down his home!'

'Why? He deserves it. Think of it like you're dishing out some justice,' said Ben.

'But… I can't do that.'

'Fine, stay here if you like, because if you don't finish the test, you don't leave with us,' said Ben.

'Yeah, we'll block up *our* entrance. You can leave through the main gate. I guess Freddy will be back soon and he'll let you out,' said Gavin.

Alex looked at Mark. 'Corkscrew?' he pleaded.

Mark turned away and mumbled in a sheepish voice, 'Just get it done, Clayton, so we can all leave this awful place.'

The three boys turned and headed away. Alex gazed down at the can. Could he do this? He picked it up, hearing the slosh of fluid inside. The boys were heading off past the main house. Only Mark glanced back.

Twenty-nine

Taking caution with each step, Alex walked towards the mobile home. As he got closer, he saw a dirty chicken coop, the mud inside churned up and dotted with muck. Several skinny hens pecked at the ground in a desperate determination to find some food.

Alex slowed his pace as he got close to the low fence. He pushed open the gate and stepped into the garden. There were pink and red rose bushes growing in a small peat patch, next to a green water-barrel. A rusty watering-can and a pair of muddy wellies sat inside a dirty wheelbarrow. Alex swallowed hard and fixed his stare on those boots. They seemed massive. He'd never seen footwear so large and decided he had no desire to meet the owner.

Alex headed up three wooden steps and tried the door. It opened, and a sudden fear that someone was home struck him. 'Hello,' he called out, his tone sounding weak. Receiving no reply, he took a deep breath – and entered.

Gavin threw some garden shears, and they bounced against an oil drum. 'Bollocks.'

The cider shed was empty and Gavin was not happy.

Ben climbed a stepladder and peered into one of three tall cider vats. 'He's cleared the place out. Not a drop of booze. It's nothing but a store shed now. Gutted.' He climbed down from the ladder.

'Can we please sod off now?' said Mark. His nerves were shredded to bits and these two idiots were still searching for cider to steal. 'He's obviously had enough of you two breaking in and helping yourselves.'

'Let's go,' said Ben in a sulky tone.

Gavin picked up a claw hammer, studied it, then tossed that at the drum too, which hit with a loud clang.

Mark stepped outside, shading his eyes from the sun.

Ben followed him out. 'See any smoke yet, Corkscrew?'

Then they heard the dog bark.

'She's eaten Clayton,' said Ben.

Gavin came out with a garden fork, and with a playful grin, poked Ben's bottom with it. 'Get off my land, you God-damn varmints,' he said in a silly hillbilly voice.

Mark was about to tell Gavin to keep his voice down, but then he saw the Doberman. It was loose, and it was bolting across the gravel towards them.

'The dog is coming!' yelled Mark.

They all started running.

It was clean inside the dwelling. A single bed with a chipped wooden frame, made up, neat, with unwrinkled bed covers; a bench sofa with red leather upholstery and a handful of scatter cushions with black and white patterns. The kitchen area was tiny. On the slim counter were some crockery and cutlery, but only one of each item, every piece placed in a strategic line.

Alex picked up a silver box that was resting against a lamp on a tall table. The box was the size of a large box of matches, though much slimmer. The inscription on the front read: 'FJK' in a smart italic font. He tried to open it, but his trembling fingers couldn't get the tiny latch to unclip. Alex had no clue why, but he slid the box into his pocket, and his fingers touched on the lighter. He pulled it out and held it in his open palm. He glanced at the petrol he'd placed by the door.

Alex scanned the room. Could he really do this? Could he set fire to a stranger's property just to complete a test? What sort of person would that make him? He pictured Sheryl's face. He kept her image in his mind as he walked over, picked up the can and unscrewed the lid. The harsh smell of the fuel hit his nostrils, and his hands were shaking. If he wanted to keep seeing Sheryl, he had no choice. With zero enthusiasm, Alex splashed some petrol over the floor and felt a massive surge of guilt for just spilling the liquid onto the beige carpet. He threw the can to the floor, and the liquid seeped out with a sloshing sound. He watched it spill and soak into the carpet as he flicked open the lid on the lighter, thumbed the wheel and set the flame. But he couldn't do it. He couldn't set the fire.

Upon hearing the loud aggressive barking, Alex froze.

The howl of utter agony that followed was horrendous. He'd never heard anything so distressing in his entire life. The noise got louder and more intense and made his blood run cold.

'Clayton, get out. He's coming!' screamed Ben.

The lighter burnt his fingers and Alex dropped it in shock. After a sudden whoosh, his vision became blurred by an orange explosion, and before he could react, he found himself flat on his back and the fire was raging around him.

On his hands and knees, Alex scrambled for the exit. He reached up and opened the door, sprung to his feet and rushed for the outside. Disoriented, he fell down the entrance steps. Alex could still hear the dog, but an awful yelping sound had replaced her howl. Smoke poured from the building and the savage flames were already spewing from the door and window. The heat was unreal. Alex's face was hot, and he wondered if he was burnt. He got up and sprinted away, heading back towards the main farm.

When he reached the other side of the farmhouse, he skidded to a stop in the gravel and gazed down in disbelief. The now collarless Doberman lay on the floor a few paces ahead. He edged toward her. She was lying on her side, snout cut open, tongue lolling out of her blood-filled mouth. She whined in pain and Alex noticed the three puncture wounds on her side. Deep wounds pumping dark blood. Alex put his hand over his mouth and backed away. Then he noticed the vehicle. It was a limestone-coloured Land Rover Defender. Dust and grime covered it. The engine was running and the driver's door was open.

Alex sprinted back the way he came. He saw a bunch of weather-beaten wooden fence panels stacked high. He slid down behind the stack and pushed back against them. His breathing was erratic, and he tried to keep it under control as the surrounding sounds made him almost burst into tears. The cracking flames eating away at the building – the dog crying – the drone of the diesel engine. Then another noise – boots crunching on gravel. It sounded close. Alex breathed through his nose, clamped his mouth shut and closed his eyes.

Mark scrambled through the hole in the fence and helped pull Ben and Gavin through.

When Gavin got to his feet, he checked his arm. He had deep puncture wounds on his forearm. 'Bitch got me good and proper. Look at those teeth marks,' he cried.

Mark's mind spun, and he paced the fence. He bit his lower lip so hard he tasted blood.

Ben slapped Mark on the shoulder. 'Corkscrew, get with it. Can you see Alex?'

Mark stared through the mesh fence. 'No. We need to do something.'

Ben took off his glasses and cleaned off the dust using his t-shirt. 'We need to go. Now.'

Mark's entire body stiffened. 'No! We're not leaving him here.'

'Well, good luck with that, cos I'm out of here. The dog messed up my arm,' said Gavin, touching the wound and wincing as dark purple blood pumped out.

Alex dropped onto his stomach and wriggled across to a pile of rubble bags. Not able to see, he snaked back over to the fence panels and found a gap to spy through. Smoke was heavy in the air, the fire raged and thick smoke billowed into the sky. He spied an enormous shadow. Then a pair of scuffed rigger boots and blue jeans came into view. Alex didn't breathe. He didn't dare move an inch.

The bulk of a man loomed as he strolled towards the fire, his back to Alex. The man stopped and stood there, looking forward. Alex could honestly say that he'd never laid eyes on such a massive individual. He must have stood well over six foot five with the bulky frame of a rugby player. Alex knew it was Freddy Killner.

Freddy turned and rubbed his protruding chin, his eyes scanning the farm. And they were dark, unfriendly eyes, though he seemed unemotional and almost looked bored. Alex couldn't believe what he was witnessing. It seemed so surreal. The fire was wild behind him and he lit up a cigarette and blew smoke into the sky, as though it were just any other normal summer's day. He stood close now, so Alex was able to make out his features. His hair was black, shoulder-length, matted and messy. His cheeks were a reddish colour and his skin tanned and leather-like; apart from his right hand and arm, which were patched with scars, the skin discoloured and dipped in places, as if entire chunks of flesh were missing. Some parts of the limb looked bleached of colour. The tatty black vest he wore offered Alex a glance of just how thick and muscular Freddy's arms were. Alex did not know Freddy's age. Older than forty, but not as old as fifty.

Freddy coughed and started fast walking back towards the farmhouse. Alex shuffled on his stomach and changed position to gain a better view of where Freddy was heading. He watched as Freddy stopped by the Doberman, crouched down and checked her wounds. She let out a feeble whine, but still, he appeared apathetic. It was as though none of this fazed him in the slightest. He stood up and headed to the Defender. He switched off the engine and slammed the door shut. Then he opened the rear door and reached inside. Alex wondered if he should attempt to run, but stayed put.

Freddy kicked the rear door shut, and he was holding something. Alex squinted to see, and when he perceived what it was, he gasped. Freddy held a long whip, and he was heading back in his direction, taking massive strides as he came. At first, Alex thought Freddy was heading back to the dog, but he stepped over her and continued. The whip was brown, and it had what looked like barbed wire wound around it. Alex cried out in fear, clasping his hand over his mouth. Freddy snarled like a madman and raced in Alex's direction, his boots thundering across the ground.

Mark grabbed Ben's arm. 'We can't leave him.'

The pair stood in a woodland copse that edged Freddy's land, watching out for Alex.

'What are we supposed to do?' said Ben.

'Help him. Or get help. I don't know.' Mark watched the heavy smoke filling the sky. 'He'll kill him, Ben.'

Gavin jogged over to them. 'Hurry up, lads.'

Mark pointed with a frantic, stabbing finger. 'There he is!'

Alex was running across the farm in the distance. Freddy chased close behind him.

Alex's mind raced and for a moment he became so disoriented he couldn't work out where Ben had made the hole. He started to think he was running in the wrong direction. Even so, he sprinted faster than he'd ever done in his life. Boots thudded right behind him, and he knew if he missed that hole he would be in serious strive.

There was a glimmer of hope when he spotted the dead fox.

Mark picked up a chunk of rusted metal and tested its weight. It was some sort of rust-covered cog that he'd spotted half-buried in the earth. Perhaps a piece of a car's engine. He headed towards the fence and watched as Alex raced to it. Freddy was so close behind him, Mark didn't believe for a moment he'd make it through. He gazed back to the copse. Ben and Gavin had gone.

Alex spotted the hole off to his left and bolted for it. As he approached, he dived to the ground and scuttled through. The whip cracked and sent a searing pain across his back. He clawed at the mud but wasn't moving because his leg felt trapped. He felt more agonising pain as the whip slashed across his lower back.

Mark watched in horror as Freddy stood on Alex's ankle and bellowed in rage, as he repeatedly cracked the whip across Alex's back and buttocks. The whip shredded clothes and skin. Alex screamed as he fought to pull himself away from the attack.

Mark pulled back his arm and threw the metal. It plummeted down over the fence and smashed into Freddy's forehead, causing him to stagger back.

'You leave him alone! Or do you want some more? You ugly… camel-faced, bone-headed spanner!' spat Mark.

Freddy fixed him with an icy glare, and Mark didn't know which of them was more flabbergasted by his action and barrage of insults. Mark took the opportunity to grab Alex's arms and haul him through. Alex cried out and climbed to his feet.

The boys backed away as Freddy stared at the pair with utter contempt.

Blood trickled down his forehead and onto the tip of his nose.

Alex's lower lip dropped and trembled as he locked eyes with Freddy.

Mark pulled Alex's arm. 'Run!'

They both darted into the copse.

The pain was so intense Alex cried and snivelled, but Mark refused to let him stop running. They charged through the woods and made their way onto a narrow country lane.

When Alex noticed Sheryl heading towards them, he was sure he was hallucinating.

'What the hell is going on?' she said, frowning in confusion. 'Did you singe your eyebrows, Alex?'

'What… are you… doing out here?' said Mark, breathless.

'Gavin told Jan you guys were going to Freddy's. Please don't say—' Sheryl stopped and looked at Alex. 'What happened?' she said, shocked as she grasped the magnitude of Alex's injuries.

Alex tried not to sob, but tears of pain came.

Sheryl gasped. 'All that smoke, is it coming from the farm?'

Alex heard the distant hum of an engine. Before he even saw the vehicle, he knew it was his.

Killner's Land Rover came into view as it drove around the bend. The vehicle looked ominous and imposing as it slowed to a halt. The engine revved, and the vehicle jerked forward, then raced along the lane.

'In the woods!' shouted Mark.

Mark pulled Sheryl off of the lane and into the trees.

Alex chased after them.

Tyres screeched on the road. A door opened and slammed.

Alex braved a glimpse behind – lost his footing and fell into some nettles. He forced himself to get up, and the pain across his back became unreal. He hurt all over and didn't know if he could push himself on. And now he'd lost sight of the others. He panicked as he tried to spot them.

Sheryl and Mark yelled his name.

Then everything went black.

Alex drifted in and out of unconsciousness. He was aware he was travelling, and for a moment he wondered if he was in an ambulance, but that theory was short-lived. It smelt of diesel and damp. It was dark and humid, though, on occasions, the sun's rays flashed in.

The dog whimpered.

Alex opened his eyes, but his vision swam and he had a sickly, heavy feeling in his head. Was the dog here, or was the noise stuck inside his head?

The vehicle stopped. A handbrake crunched, and the door opened with a grinding sound. After a moment, sunlight blinded him as the back door creaked open. Alex held his hands over his eyes. The vehicle rocked, the dog whimpered again, and then everything became silent.

For a short while, Alex didn't move. He wasn't confident he even could. After about two minutes, he plucked up the courage to slide out of the vehicle. He struggled to stand and felt as though he'd spent an hour spinning on the waltzers at two hundred miles per hour.

Alex took in his surroundings. He stood on the outskirts of a woodland area by the side of a railway line. Huge, dirty hands grabbed him and Alex screamed in terror as Freddy carted him off towards the tracks.

'No! Please. Stop, please,' wailed Alex.

Freddy dragged him along like he was no more than a rag-doll.

'Don't kill me, please don't kill me,' he cried. 'Someone help me! Help! He's going to kill me. Awww.'

Freddy growled and forced Alex to his knees, on a verge near the line. Alex saw the Doberman and shrieked. The poor dog was dying, he was convinced of that. She viewed Alex with a vacant look that stabbed his heart. There was blood all over her. Freddy had placed the dog between the girders of the track.

'No... no, no, stop. You don't need to do this,' gabbled Alex, shaking his head.

Freddy put his forearm around Alex's neck. It felt like a huge steel chain choking him. He tried to fight, but it was a feeble attempt. He had no chance.

'We can take her to the vets, it's not too late,' sobbed Alex, 'we can save her. I'll pay to fix her. I'll get the money. I will. I swear, Mr Killner. I'll work off the debt. Anything.'

Freddy applied more pressure in response to this. Alex tried to turn away, but Freddy wrenched Alex's head, forcing it back.

The girders made a pinging noise, and the tracks vibrated. Alex saw the train in the distance. It appeared blurred in the fuzzy heat. The dog wailed and whimpered.

Alex sobbed and gasped for air and was sure he was suffocating. 'No. Don't. Please.'

The train was hurtling along at speed. It was too late to do anything. Alex tried to close his eyes, but Freddy clawed at his eyelids with his free hand, forcing Alex to watch.

Thirty

Alex could see the two trees on the hillside. They were well in the distance. He guessed about four miles away. Alex checked to see if Mark was paying any attention to them, but he was way too busy typing on his phone. Mark had on faded jeans and what looked like a new navy Canada Goose jacket, with a white-collar. A waft of expensive fragrance drifted over; it was pleasant and tasteful.

Alex hadn't seen the two trees from this distance since he was a boy. He had seen them plenty of times in his dreams, but he was always up there, on that hill, standing between them. Alex gripped his steering wheel. They were almost there.

'I would have driven myself. I'm not drinking a lot,' said Janette.

Will changed gear with a crunch and smiled. 'You might decide to have more than a couple. Now you can.'

'It's weird seeing you driving. I'm so used to seeing you on your bike.'

'Are you OK, Jan? I know this is a big deal for you.'

'I'm fine. All this has just brought back a lot of memories. It'll be the first time that all of us will be together since—' Janette's voice broke, 'well, that day.'

Will reached over and placed his hand on hers. 'Just call me if you need me to get you.'

Janette smiled at him and gazed out of the window. 'I'll be fine.'

Alex brought his Cherokee to a stop. 'This is the place.'

Mark looked up from his phone and gazed outside. 'Looks like a nice gaff. Are we eating?'

'Don't think we organised that.'

'Jeez mate, you look like you're about to go to a funeral.'

'I'm OK.'

'I checked this place on Trip Advisor, it's a well-rated little country establishment.'

'Go in ahead of me. I'm going to phone Natalie again.'

'Are you sure?'

Alex nodded. 'I won't be long.'

Mark grinned and got out. 'Don't you bail on me.'

Mark closed the door, and Alex phoned Natalie for the third time that day. As expected, she didn't answer. Plus, she'd ignored all of his texts. This wasn't like her. OK, he'd been a complete twat, and his tantrum was out of order, but she was acting like he had throttled her or something.

He got out of the car, straightened his Crombie and adjusted his jeans, as he stared at the venue. It was a charming eighteenth-century building, but for Alex, it was like he was preparing to enter the gates of hell. His palms were sweaty and his heart was racing. He felt like that fourteen-year-old boy again. All part of the process, he told himself. He stood ramrod straight, took a deep breath and prepared to enter, but then he had a sudden, strange sensation that he was being watched. He scanned the car park, and the Hilux caught his attention straight away. There was a ton of thick mud over it. It looked as though it had been off-road driving along woodland trails. Smoke poured out from the driver's window that was open a crack, but he couldn't see the driver. He smiled to himself. He was being paranoid.

Patrick drummed his stumps on the steering wheel of his Hilux. He'd seen that total prick Corkscrew get out of the Jeep Cherokee and stroll into the pub. He recognised him the moment he'd clapped eyes on him. Patrick wouldn't forget that bastard's pasty face in a million years. Nor would he forget Alex Clayton's. Patrick wasn't sure why he'd come or what he intended to do, but just felt he needed to see Alex in the flesh. Gavin hadn't even mentioned the DJ was coming to the party. He lit his roll-up and gazed at Alex. He looked apprehensive, and Patrick tried to think of a reason for him to return to town. What did he want? Alex seemed to stare right at him, but Patrick knew he wouldn't be able to see him through his tinted windows. Alex walked to the pub's entrance for the second time. He looked so nervous, and Patrick wondered if he'd even go inside. He took a drag on his roll-up. God, he was so tempted to start his engine and drive straight at the bloke. How he'd enjoy crushing that man's head under his tyres.

Mark walked into the bar area and nodded his approval. The bar was welcoming, rustic and cosy. There were hops wrapped around timber beams, photos of hop-workers on display, and delicious-smelling food filled the air. He glanced at a low table that had four silver milk churns for seats, which he thought was a pleasant touch. Though he didn't fancy sitting on one. Gavin waved at him from the bar. He was wearing a bomber jacket, black jeans and Faux Adidas trainers. Mark tried to hide his shock when he saw how old and haggard Gavin appeared. It was disconcerting. He gave Gavin two thumbs up.

'You alright, mate? What you drinking, Corkscrew?' called Gavin.

'Hey, man! I'll take whatever you're having, Gav,' said Mark.

'The DJ is in the house! Whoop, whoop,' boomed a voice from the corner of the room. Mark turned to see Ben waving a frantic hand from a table in the corner next to an open fire, piled with logs and kindling. It wasn't lit, which was a blessing, as it was toasty enough in here already.

Ben was wearing blue chinos and a well-ironed long-sleeve England rugby shirt. The man had put on a fair bit of chub around the stomach area. He bounded over and gave Mark a bear hug. 'Good to see you, Corkscrew. Been so long, man.'

'You too, Ben. But you can call me Mark,' he said with an amused grin.

'Wow, you smell so good. What is that?'

Mark grinned but ignored the question and walked over to the corner where Janette was sitting. She smiled at him. It almost seemed a shy smile. She was wearing skinny jeans, a cloud-grey baggy V-necked jumper, and wore her hair down over her shoulders. Janette didn't have an obvious prettiness, but Mark thought there was a certain something about her. A brooding, sultry something. Like a stern, but sexy school teacher, he considered.

'Looking well. And how are you doing, Jan?' asked Mark.

'I'm not too bad. I hear things are going well for you, Mark.'

'Well, I can't complain. Though I probably will,' said Mark.

'So, where is *he* then?' she asked with a thin-lipped smile.

'He's just coming. Think he's a tad nervous. Play nice, kids.'

'Think it's Gavin you need to tell,' said Janette.

Alex took a deep breath and entered the bar. The restaurant was busy, but the smaller bar area was quiet. He scanned the room. There were a couple of guys chatting at the bar, and the barmaid, a short-haired plump lady, gave him a friendly smile. Then he realised Mark was thumbing him over to a table in the corner.

And there they were. Ben, with a playful grin, his wide shoulders bobbing up and down as he spoke to Janette. She was smiling at whatever Ben had said, but stopped the moment she noticed Alex, and then seemed guarded. Then he spotted Gavin, who was handing out drinks from a tray. He hadn't seen Alex, but it was obvious he'd sensed the atmosphere at the table had changed.

Gavin whipped his head to face Alex, pursed his lips tight and gave him an icy glare.

Alex made his way to the table. His legs trembled as he walked. His cheeks were burning, and he hoped his face wasn't flushed. He needed to sit down.

Gavin stepped in front of him. 'Clayton.'

'Hi Gavin,' replied Alex.

Gavin had aged some and looked ten years older than the rest of them. He still had his sunken cheeks, big ears, and he was unshaven with a fuzz of stubble on his chin.

'What you drinking?' asked Gavin.

'Just a pint. Lager. Cheers.'

Gavin headed over to the bar, a sneer on his face, and Alex continued his journey to the table. As he arrived, Ben stood up and gave him a vigorous, but somewhat stiff, handshake.

Janette put her hand up and gave him a tiny wave. 'Hello Alex,' she said, her tone flat.

'Hi, Janette.'

Mark pulled up the seat next to him, Alex sat down opposite Janette.

So far so good, Alex considered.

After a while of forced, awkward conversation and a few mistrustful glances thrown here and there, the conversation at the table soon started flowing. Gavin aside, they had all spoken about their work commitments, general interests and marital statuses. Janette had been interested in Alex's business, and he had mentioned certain events he'd photographed on purpose, knowing it would spike Janette's interest. It was a good icebreaker, as she was soon chatting away about events she'd raced in and others she'd love to attend. She adored Scotland and the Lake District.

Ben had joked about Janette being a female Spartacus but had spent most of the time moaning about his son and winding Mark up about how electronic music was annoying, repetitive and only for drug addicts.

Alex noticed Gavin didn't seem keen to join the conversations. He was drinking fast, and he seemed distant from the group. It was like he had nothing to add. Like he didn't belong in the circle of friends. The rest of them had made Alex feel quite welcome, but Gavin was the odd one out; the dark cloud in the room.

'I'll get the drinks in,' said Gavin.

'Wait, my round,' said Mark. 'Cool, fair enough,' he shrugged as Gavin made his way to the bar. Mark made no further attempt to stop him.

'So, Corkscrew, you're a producer as well, you say?' said Ben.

'Yes, though I doubt I've produced much that you'd listen to, mate,' said Mark, 'I bet you like country and western don't you?'

'Yeah, I do a bit. But I'm more of an Andy Williams guy.'

'You should come along to a venue, Ben. You could even wear your cowboy hat if you wanted,' said Mark, sharing a secret grin with Janette.

Ben shook his head. 'All that whomp thump stuff would give me a headache. No offence, mate.'

'Loads taken,' said Mark, tugging on his vape and filling their corner with smoke.

'You can't smoke that smelly crap in here,' complained Ben, wafting his hands about.

'It's alright. It's only opium,' said Mark.

'Best pass it around then,' said Janette with a crooked grin.

Gavin soon arrived with several beers, a chardonnay and five shots that looked like pink mouthwash. He handed the drinks out.

Ben sniffed his pint. 'Is this one of the local ales?'

'Sheep shagger's scrotum or something like that,' said Gavin.

'Yeah, smashing, one of my favourites,' he said, gulping the drink.

Alex pushed the shot aside. 'Not for me, thanks. I need to drive.'

'Get a taxi,' said Gavin.

'Yeah, we'll get a taxi, Alex, you've already had too many,' Mark pointed out.

Alex studied the pink liquid that seemed to glow. 'What is it?'

'Poison,' said Gavin, with no humour in his voice.

'Well, in that case,' said Alex. And hit back the drink, whilst keeping his focus on Gavin.

Alex knew this would be a long night.

Thirty-one

Gavin strolled into the toilet. Ben was at a urinal, and Gavin unzipped and urinated next to him.

'You OK, Gav? You're quiet tonight,' said Ben, shaking himself and zipping up.

'Yeah, I'm fine. So the missus let you off the leash tonight?'

'Yes, Gavin. And my phone was unfixable, thanks,' said Ben.

'I need a favour, Ben.'

Ben washed his hands, whacking the dispenser that didn't seem to want to supply any soap. 'Do you?'

'I can't find my rucksack. I've been back twice and can't find the spot.'

'I couldn't care less, Gav. Perhaps a fox took it.'

'A fox? Right, yeah of course. I bet he's dealing out smack to all his woodland buddies. It must be like Wind in the Willows meets Trainspotting down in Colt Woods these days. Bad-boy badger jacking up on top of the ancient mossy hillock. Toad chilling on his lily toking on his miniature crack pipe.'

Ben sniggered. 'Wow, have you ever considered a career in children's books? I must remember that delightful tale for when Molly won't nap.'

'I can't get my bearings out there. It all looks the same.'

'That's just karma for dealing in that filth.'

'I hate drugs too. Trust me when I say that. But I need the cash.'

'I can't believe you ripped off an Albanian drug boss. You've put us all in danger, you know that, right?'

'Oh, rein it in Napier. I saw an opportunity, and I took it.'

'You're such an entrepreneur,' said Ben.

'Look, Patrick reckons his Uncle Jonah can shift the stuff. I just need to find it.'

Ben's eyes narrowed. 'You've seen Pat?'

'Only for a brief chat.'

'Christ, Gavin, please don't tell me he knows Clayton's in town?'

'What? No, of course not.'

Ben put his hands under the drier, eyeballing Gavin as he dried them. Gavin waited patiently for him to finish.

'So, you didn't mention it?' asked Ben.

'No. Why would I?'

'I bet you told him… I'm not having this bullshit in my life. Don't talk to me about it again. And stay away from Patrick and his family.'

Ben pushed the door open and stomped out.

Alex was waiting on an order at the bar as Ben strolled past.

'Need a hand?' asked Ben.

'Cheers,' said Alex. He thought Ben looked agitated, as though he wanted to say something to him.

'I drove to the Roman Bath today,' said Alex. God knows why he'd mentioned it, but he felt he needed to say something.

'You did?'

'It's got a massive fence around it now.'

'I read in the paper that some young kids messed around in there last year. One of them almost drowned,' said Ben.

The barmaid placed two beers down, sending beer slopping onto the counter.

'What sort of idiots would muck around in there?' said Alex, straight-faced.

'I know, right,' said Ben, hiding a grin behind his hand. 'Alex, about all the stuff that happened.'

'We were just kids, Ben.'

'That day… what happened in Gallows Hill Wood. I'm so ashamed about my part in that.'

'Just that?'

Ben grimaced. 'I'm trying to apologise here. I guess you shouldn't make it too easy for me.'

Alex looked into Ben's eyes and held his gaze. 'Emotions were running high. Everyone wanted someone to blame. And what happened on the Downs… it was my fault.'

Alex passed his debit card to the barmaid, who took it with a smile and handed him back the PIN reader.

Raucous laughter erupted from the corner. It was Mark and Janette. Mark laughed so hard, he had tears in his eyes.

Alex could see Gavin outside, pacing past the window and smoking.

'I have to hand it to you, Clayton, you were a determined little dude,' said Ben with a wry grin.

'Maybe I should thank you. I think those tests made me a stronger person... I'm serious, Ben.'

Ben was about to reply when Mark's voice cut him off. 'Oi, thirsty over here.'

Alex and Ben took the drinks over to the table.

'So, what work is it you do for the council, Jan?' asked Mark.

'I'm a health and safety operations manager,' said Janette.

'I see, right, well that sounds dreadfully unexciting,' joked Mark.

'Yeah, it is. Not nearly as fun as sitting in a booth, twiddling tiny knobs in front of sweaty teenagers all night,' she retorted with a wink.

'I'll have you know my followers are a diverse group. My eldest fan is eighty-nine.'

'Aw, cute. Is he deaf?' said Janette.

'I'd love to see that old codger cranked up on E's,' said Ben.

Mark crossed his arms. 'Some people only come for the music, Ben.'

Ben laughed. 'Yeah, of course they do.'

Mark pointed his vape pen at Ben. 'What's your idea of a good night out? Some dingy, tacky town-centre bar where loads of sad, middle-aged, over-the-hill wankers get excited and lose their shit when Cafe del Mar gets whacked on.'

'Nope. You can't beat a good karaoke night,' said Ben.

'Aw geez, I hate karaokes,' said Janette.

Mark raised his glass. 'Me too.'

'Boring gits,' said Ben.

Mark leaned to Janette, and said, 'I can picture the scene... panicked drinkers scramble to leave, crashing furniture from their path, as Ben eagerly steps up to begin his extended rendition of Can't Take My Eyes Off You.'

'Have you been chatting to my missus?' asked Ben.

'You better believe it, compadre.'

'Cock off, Corkscrew,' chuckled Ben.

As the evening drew on, the bar area packed out, Alex became aware they were receiving the odd stony-faced glare from three older men sitting next to them. The noise level at their table had risen a notch, and the more alcohol consumed, the louder and rowdier things got. Even Gavin had become more jovial, although he had not tried to converse with Alex, but he was now joking and chatting with the others.

'If we weren't all trashed enough, Jan only stole that champers from her mum's display cupboard. And we drank it in your cousin's garden, Corkscrew,' said Ben.

'They still, to this day, think my brother stole it. That was a special bottle being saved for their anniversary,' said Janette.

'Whoops,' said Ben, spraying his eyelids with Optrex.

'They mentioned this a few months back. I still haven't confessed,' she said with a playful grin.

Ben let out a loud belch. 'Eh, excuse me. To be fair, we did them a huge favour. If I remember, it tasted like utter garbage. They would have been very disappointed.'

Janette, her cheeks rosy, giggled and knocked back a shot. 'I'm still not convinced they'd see it that way.'

'Well, you're a bit too old to get grounded now, Jan. Besides, your folks are lovely. I imagine they'd forgive you,' said Ben.

'Yeah, I always thought that was weird. Were you adopted, do you think, Jan?' said Mark.

Janette sipped her chardonnay. 'It's quite possible. My dad used to say that I belonged to the milkman. Graham the grump, he called him.'

Mark and Ben chuckled.

Gavin sniggered. 'Well, all this reminiscing is wonderful, but I've got a question for Clayton.'

The mood at the table changed in an instant and the smiles faded fast.

'Sorry to bring the vibe down, but what the fuck are we actually doing here?' said Gavin. 'I know we've already waited over thirty years, so I guess there's no real rush.'

'Gavin, we're all just having a catch-up, no one here has forgotten,' said Ben in a pacifying tone.

'Go outside and get some air, Gavin,' said Janette.

'No. He's right,' said Alex, 'it's about time we spoke about this.' Alex's head was fuzzy from the drinking and he considered his words before speaking. He'd drunk way more than he intended to, but he felt less nervous about this now, so it wasn't a bad thing. 'Does anyone think they could lead us on the route we took that day? The exact route.'

'I can,' said Janette.

'I thought we could follow it. All of us here. Like a sort of—' Alex struggled to find the word.

'Reconstruction,' added Mark.

Alex raised his drink to Mark. 'Yes, a reconstruction. Perhaps we could take some candles and light them for her? We can all talk about what happened. Maybe we can try to make some sort of sense of things.'

'When?' asked Ben.

Alex glanced at Janette. She had tears in her eyes and wiped them away with the back of her hand.

'How about tomorrow afternoon?' suggested Alex.

Everyone nodded in agreement. Accept Gavin, who was just staring at Alex with a blank expression. Alex wondered if he should add the additional information about Leo, but decided against it. That could wait for when they all had clearer heads.

Gavin snorted. 'So that's it? You want to have a vigil? You've waited all this time and—'

'Gavin,' interrupted Ben, 'let's get another round in, yeah? That tight-arse round dodger Corkscrew is paying.'

Mark raised his eyebrows and gave them an indignant look. He removed his debit card from his wallet and slid it across the table to Ben. 'Get the receipt,' he said in a snippy tone. Mark then passed Janette a tissue and gave her a reassuring grin as he tugged on his vape pen. 'And the pin is my birth year backwards.'

Alex saw one of the older men muttering to his companions, before getting up and heading their way. The man targeted Mark. 'Can you please refrain from smoking that damn thing in here!' he nagged. 'And can you stop using such vulgar language? It is unnecessary and unacceptable. Families are eating in the restaurant,' he continued in a stiff tone. The stern-faced man was in his late sixties, with wiry, white hair and large, bushy eyebrows that were growing wild.

'I apologise for my friends' behaviour. Complete and utter riff-raff. You just cannot take them anywhere,' said Mark in an over-the-top, plummy accent. 'Total degenerates, the ruddy lot of them,' he went on.

Janette put her hand over her mouth to stifle a hissing laugh. Gavin and Ben had slipped away to the bar and watched with amused grins. Alex thought he heard the barmaid say something about ignoring the fun police.

The man straightened his posture and glowered indignantly at Mark. 'And I suppose you think you're clever, don't you?'

Mark shrugged and placed his vape pen in his mouth, but didn't suck on it.

'You silly moron of a man. And do you think the entire pub wants to hear your banal discussions?' said the man.

Mark put his finger on his trembling lip and feigned a hurt expression.

'Why don't you sod off back to your own table, Groucho Marx,' said Janette.

Alex considered that not everyone in the pub had been that interested in their table. They had everyone's attention now.

Mark held out his mobile phone and offered it to the man. 'Would you like to use the internet?'

'What on earth for?' said the man with a confused frown.

'I dunno, I guess I thought you could... *eyebrows* the net,' said Mark with a wide, mirthful smile.

Janette snorted with laughter.

Alex hid his grin behind his beer glass.

The man pulled an exasperated expression. 'I have never come across... such... such rude individuals!' he stammered, pulling at his collar as his ears started glowing red.

'And there was us just being polite too,' said Janette.

Chastised, the man returned to his table and even his companions looked like they were trying not to smile. The man was now self-conscious of all the gawping and rubbed at his eyebrows in embarrassment.

'Pompous prick,' muttered Janette.

'Groucho?' asked Mark.

'Yeah, your comeback was undeniably better,' she said.

Mark gave her a comical smile.

'You don't know who Groucho Marx is, do you?' said Janette.

'Yeah, course I do. He was in Sesame Street.'

Janette howled with laughter. 'That was Oscar the Grouch!'

The next hour flashed by.

Alex and Ben returned to the bar to retrieve the last drinks of the evening.

Ben, now quite drunk, whacked Alex on the shoulder. 'That's a marvellous idea, mate. You know… what you suggested.'

Alex watched as Mr Eyebrows walked past them, scowling as he went. One of his companions was ordering drinks at the bar and the third man was chatting to a group of people at another table.

Alex and Ben watched in open-mouthed disbelief, as Gavin brazenly walked up to the men's unattended table, unzipped his jeans and urinated into their half-finished pints; moving between the glasses and doing his best not to miss the targets.

The barmaid slapped her hand on the bar. 'Get that dirty sod out of here, right now!'

'Nice one, Gavin. Cocking things up comes so naturally to you,' said Janette, tugging on her burgundy parka jacket.

Gavin shrugged, staring at her with a blithe expression. 'Yep. But I didn't really care yesterday. I don't give a crap today. And I probably won't give a flying fuck tomorrow either.'

Janette let out an over-the-top laugh. 'Aw, is that your personal motto? I must get you a special t-shirt made up. So inspirational.'

'By the way, Corkscrew was sort of right, because Groucho did appear in Sesame Street. Well, a muppet version did,' said Gavin.

Janette zipped up her jacket. 'What a random and useless thing to know.'

Alex buttoned up his coat as Ben shepherded Mark across the carpark.

Mark, sloshed and slurring now, was giggling. 'Ben brought the cheery old fellows a round of beers and apologised for taking the piss tonight.'

'Hilarious. Anyway, here's my lift. I'll see you guys tomorrow. I'll message you all via the Snapchat group I setup,' said Janette. With that, she waved a hand and fast-walked over to a red Ford Fiesta. Then they heard a loud heaving noise, and all turned to see Ben throwing up in a bush.

'Want a bump?' asked Mark, holding out a key that had white powder on the nib. Alex glanced at the taxi driver, who was paying them no heed, then back to the key. Alex assumed it was cocaine, but didn't like to ask. He considered saying yes, but declined with a polite shake of the head. The last thing he needed was a substance that keeps you awake.

Mark shrugged and sniffed the powder himself.

'By the way, thanks, Mark… for what you did on Killner's farm. I don't think I ever thanked you back then.'

Mark smiled and gave him a quick salute.

Alex peered out of the window and mulled over how the evening had panned out. His childhood friends were a colourful bunch. Life wouldn't be dull with this lot around. Much the same as it had been thirty years ago.

Thirty-two

Mark opened the door and glowered at Alex. He was naked, save boxer shorts and white socks. His hair was also down and looked matted and bushy. 'I don't want breakfast.'

'I'm going out to the farm soon. You still coming?'

Mark rubbed his pasty face and blinked. 'What?'

'Killner?'

'Right. No… give me twenty minutes. Let me jump in the shower and I'll be ready. Oh, and grab me a black coffee.' With that, he slammed the door.

Alex made his way to the hotel restaurant where he devoured three eggs on brown toast and a large orange juice. Knowing that he needed to get some rest to tackle the day ahead, he necked two Diazepam when he'd got back to the hotel. After all the booze, the pills wiped him out and he was out within the hour. His dreams still came, but in hazy, jumbled fragments, and not the lucid visions he had become accustomed to and hated. He couldn't know if he'd ranted during his sleep, but the hotel room appeared to be intact. Alex felt good and considering the amount of alcohol he'd swilled, this surprised him. He often got grim hangovers when he drank. He guessed that the sleep, which he'd desperately needed, had helped. He'd also drunk two bottles of water before slipping into bed to keep him hydrated.

After spending over an hour waiting for Mark, they got a taxi back to the pub, collected Alex's Jeep, then drove to the farm. Mark didn't speak on either journey and spent the entire time tapping on his phone.

'I think this is it,' said Alex.

They pulled up to an electric gate. The gate rolled backwards on their arrival. On one of the tall, brick-made gate pillars was a house sign, carved in wood. It read: *Apple Barn House*.

As Alex drove into the grounds, Mark peeled his eyes from his phone. 'This can't be the place. Can it?'

'I'm certain it is,' said Alex.

Alex stopped his Jeep, and the pair got out.

Mark slipped on his shades as the pair admired the place. It couldn't have looked more different from what they'd expected. Where the burnt house once stood was a stunning farmhouse property. The building looked amazing and was both modern and rustic in style. The barn was now a stable block and horses were grazing lazily in several paddocks, and there was also a fenced-off training arena containing jumps. A second, open-fronted barn housed a white Mercedes-Benz A-Class, a red convertible Mini Cooper and a huge sit-on mower.

Mark took off his shades. 'There's something different about this place. I dunno, I just can't put my finger on it.' Then he froze as three muscular Weimaraners bounded over to them, barking as they came. The pair backed against the Jeep, watching the dogs.

'I knew this was a bad idea,' said Mark.

The grey dogs seemed more curious than aggressive; one sniffed at them, a tad wary, whilst the other two just seemed impassive and more interested in sniffing the wheels of Alex's Jeep. Then a shrill whistle cut through the air and the dogs all bounded away.

A lady strode from the house, wiping her hands on a tea towel. She was a tall, stocky woman with black-grey hair tied back in a long ponytail. She was wearing bright green Crocs, green high-waisted trousers, and a beige knitted cardigan.

'Can I help you?' she said in a friendly tone. 'I was expecting my cleaners.'

'Hi there. We were looking for Freddy Killner,' said Alex.

The lady stiffened. 'And why are you looking for him?'

Alex and Mark shared an uneasy glance.

'Um, to apologise, for one. And to talk to him about something that happened a long time ago. It is very important,' said Alex. 'We are sorry for the intrusion,' he added.

'Fred is my older brother,' she said. 'How about I make you a brew and we can have a quick chat? As long as you're not reporters.'

Mark scanned the farm. 'No… we're not.'

'Don't worry, the dogs are in the utility room. They are friendly and they only attack if I clap twice,' she said, giving Mark a devilish grin.

Alex couldn't tell if she was joking or not. Perhaps it was a subtle warning. The pair followed her towards the house, and Alex wondered that if willingly inviting two total strangers in meant she was fearless, or naïve, but then she was Freddy's sister, he reminded himself. He spotted two teenage girls mucking out the horse paddock, and they both waved at the woman.

'Fred sold the land to us over twenty years ago now. I'm Veronica by the way,' she said as she walked towards the front of the house.

'Alex Clayton.'

'Mark Corker.'

If their names rang any bells, she showed no sign of it. Alex couldn't think of a reason why they would.

She escorted them into the house, through the hallway and into the open kitchen. Alex couldn't believe the size of the kitchen's island, it was bigger than his entire apartment.

Mark ran his hand across the chunky, smokey-white granite work service. 'Oh, I like this. Is this Sensa granite?'

'I don't know, but it gets rather dusty. Tea or coffee?' she said.

'Tea please, thanks,' said Mark.

'Thanks, tea is good,' said Alex.

'I'll make a fresh pot. Please, go through to the lounge.'

They walked through the enormous kitchen. Everything was immaculate and the colour scheme a brilliant gloss white. The Aga, which had several hot plates, was almost as long as the average car. Mark pointed to the utility room where the three dogs sat behind a tall baby gate, their watchful eyes following them. Mark flashed Alex a playful smirk and pretended to clap twice as he passed.

They entered the double-height lounge and dining area. It was open plan and huge. Natural light streamed in through the ample glazing. On one side of the room were four massive window panels, floor to ceiling, giving a vast overview of the garden and beyond. The tall ceiling had a high V-shape structure, made up of thick timber beams.

'Wow, nice,' said Mark, running his hand across the lid of a grand piano.

'This is a Mason and Hamlin. Classy.'

'You can play?' asked Alex.

'Nope, but I shifted enough of them. Before the DJ stuff took off, I worked part-time for a removals company in Ashford who specialised in moving them.' Mark lifted the lid. 'My youngest son can play, though. He loves music. My eldest prefers playing football and being an obnoxious twat.'

Alex walked to the windows and peered outside. The garden appeared flawless and well maintained, with perfect bushes, contemporary ornaments and water features. The centrepiece was a large silver globe that had water gliding around it. He tried to visualise the mobile home, but everything seemed so different now. He then gazed past the garden, across the open farm fields to the hills in the distance. The North Downs. Alex could just about make them out, far off on the sloping hillside – those two trees. With some high-powered binoculars, Alex reckoned you could see up there from this window. He was able to see those trees from certain areas of the Brookacre estate, and as a kid, he'd gaze at them in awe, thinking how much he'd like to walk to them. And in '88 he did. Twice.

Alex visualised looking through binoculars and seeing his fourteen-year-old self up there, using that collapsible shovel he'd got from the camping store. Digging away in the late afternoon sunshine whilst Leo pointed and bellowed commands.

'Please take a seat,' said Veronica, making her way towards a pearl-grey corner sofa. She held a tea tray.

Mark sat down and crossed his legs. 'Stunning property, Veronica.'

Veronica placed the tray onto a large coffee table, also granite like the kitchen counters. She gave Mark a humble grin. 'Thank you. My husband designed everything. He's an architect.' She poured tea from a traditional bulbous silver teapot into three grey mugs.

'Sugar and milk?' she asked.

'Milk, please,' said Alex and Mark in unison.

Veronica poured the milk. 'So I assume this is about that girl. Was it… Shelly? You're definitely not journalists, are you?'

'We're not, no. We used to live on the Brookacre estate,' said Alex as he accepted his tea.

'Sheryl,' corrected Mark.

'That's the one,' she said, passing Mark his tea and adding sugar to her own.

'What happened to Freddy? Is he still alive?' asked Alex.

'Freddy.' She shook her head. 'No one that knows him, would ever call him that. Not that Fred has, or ever has had, many friends. My brother's name is Frederick James Killner, and yes, he is very much alive and living in a nice retirement community near Herne Bay.'

'Would we be able to visit him?' asked Alex.

Veronica sipped her tea and studied Alex for a moment. 'You could try, but I'm not sure you'll get a welcome response.'

'The kids on our estate feared Freddy... um, Frederick. There were lots of rumours about stuff that he'd done,' said Mark.

'Well, he didn't murder his family, if that's what you're talking about. His wife and two daughters died in a car crash, whilst visiting her family in France. An elderly man driving a motorhome suffered a stroke at the wheel and collided with them. They had only stopped in a lay-by to read a map. From what we learnt, the aftermath was... beyond horrific.'

Alex and Mark shared a surprised look as they both sipped on their tea.

Veronica shook her head and offered a sad smile. 'Fredrick should have been with them in France. That's why he blamed himself. After he lost them, he became a drunk and a recluse. He became lost to the world. Yes, he set that house on fire, though no one knows if it was deliberate or an accident. My personal belief is that he couldn't bear all the painful memories that house held.'

'That's awful,' said Alex.

'I've never been close to my brother, but we talked. I know he had a... a temper, should I say. At times he was an aggressive man. A frightful man,' said Veronica.

Alex noticed she was gazing at him as she'd spoken – he wondered if she knew what had gone on that day.

'So, why would you need to apologise? What did *you* do?' she asked, still looking at Alex, lips pursed.

Alex cleared his throat and wiggled about on the sofa. 'We... I did something awful to him. When I was fourteen. I burnt down his mobile home.'

'I see. Right. And are you also the one that killed his dog?' she asked, her posture going stiff.

'I… well—' stammered Alex.

Mark jumped in. 'No, that was another lad. The dog attacked him and he fended it off with a garden fork and—'

'He told me about that day. He was so upset about the loss of his dog,' she said, appearing cross for the first time since their arrival.

Alex wondered if Veronica's brother had told her the full story about that day, but knew it wouldn't be appropriate to ask.

'We shouldn't have been there. We know that,' said Alex.

Veronica stood up, so abruptly Mark almost spilt his tea.

'The things people said about my brother… some of it was true, he was a dangerous and unpredictable man. But one thing I know for certain.' Veronica spoke in a slow, stern voice now. 'He would never in a million years have touched that girl, and those appalling… those fictitious accusations, well they forced him deeper into a dark, desperate despair. And forced him to abandon his home. His land. And his hope at ever having a normal life again.'

Alex was about to speak, but Veronica cut him off and said, 'I think you two should go. Fredrick won't want to talk to you.'

Alex stood up and nodded. Veronica had given them more than enough information to find Killner's residential home.

Full of apprehension, he entered the snooker hall. The sounds of balls cracking filled the room, and the place smelt like stale sweat, cheap deodorant and fried food. He thought being Sunday lunchtime it might be quiet, but to his surprise, it was busy. Javon wondered if the place had a special offer allocated only to the unsavoury individuals of the city. Perhaps a free beer for every conviction you held. He'd only been here twice, but he was well aware the place had a notorious reputation. There had been two stabbings inside the hall this year alone, a fatal shooting in the rear carpark five months back, and just last week, three yobs set about a young Asian lad outside, using their motorcycle helmets to bludgeon him over the head so many times, they caved his head in and gave him a brain haemorrhage.

As he walked to the bar area, he gazed around. All the usual clientele were in. Nasty-looking thugs, underage drinkers and wannabe gangsters. There were several wall-mounted screens playing football and rugby, though one had a nasty crack in the corner, but this wasn't stopping a couple of hoody-wearing youths from gawping at it as they sipped bottles of lager. The man he was searching for was easy to spot. Javon found him slouched at the bar and stuffing fries into his mouth that were drenched in mayonnaise. He was without a doubt the largest guy in the hangout. A skinny, bald guy with close-set eyes, wearing a tatty, black leather jacket, sat next to him, reading something on his phone. Javon stood next to the huge man and felt dwarfed by him. He wasn't sure what to call him. His mate Dominic had told him his name was Timur, but most people called him Tim. He was Moldovan, staying in the UK on a Romanian passport, and that he was a face who had connections within Nottingham's serious criminal underbelly. Javon was no angel himself and on the odd occasion, dipped his toe into murky waters and had several friends that were dealers and thieves, but he wasn't exactly a career criminal.

'Timur?' asked Javon.

Timur didn't even look up from his food. 'Who are you?' he asked in a gruff tone, licking his fingers. His companion glanced up from his phone.

'I'm Javon Nicolls,' he said, 'I need to speak to you.'

Janette got out of the car and tightened the laces on her well-used Skarpa hiking boots. Will passed her running vest over, and she slipped it on and clipped the chest straps into place.

'How's the head now?' asked Will with a wry grin.

'Fine,' she lied. She felt rough. She had the beast of a headache and couldn't shift the pain in her temples. But she didn't have time for a wimpy hangover.

'Where are the rest of them, Jan?'

'Late,' she said. It riled her when people couldn't be punctual. She'd rushed around all afternoon to get organised and there was no sign of these idiots. They'd only have a couple of hours of daylight at this rate. She'd packed extra torches, knowing damn well one of them would have forgotten theirs.

'My brother will be on standby with the car. Ring him direct. Not the taxi firm.'

'Yes Will, you already said. I'm not deaf. Get going or you'll be late for your mother.'

Will kissed her on the forehead. 'Hope it… all goes OK.'

'See you tonight,' she said, walking off down the track towards an open, tall barn. The starting point for the walk. On the day they'd walked the route, hay bales had been stacked high inside the barn and the surrounding field lined with bright red poppies. Now, the barn looked unused and its four towering concrete pillars looked cracked and covered in moss. Several sections of its corrugated roof were missing, and the centre now overgrown with weeds and peppered with discarded rubbish. She heard a vehicle coming and gazed up to see Ben's Range Rover coming into view, followed by Alex's Jeep.

Janette walked to the field's edge and took in the scenery. Beyond the fields, the hills in the distance appeared patched with colours; a mix of dark green, russet and plum-red. Janette loved this time of year, the striking autumnal scenery, the cooler weather, and if she was honest, she felt the season had a certain romantic aspect to it. The chillier weather meant warm, cosy evenings, snuggled up on the sofa with a bottle of chardonnay and a decent movie. Peanuts loved it too, as she enjoyed diving and rolling about in the crunchy leaves. The downside was that those layers of leaves were ideal at hiding dog crap. It blended right in. Janette had thought about bringing her dog, but that didn't seem right. There was no dog with them on that late summer's afternoon. As silly as that sounded.

Gavin got out of the Range Rover and left Ben to mess about parking it in the correct spot, getting out twice to check he wasn't hanging too far out onto the lane.

Alex had parked his Jeep on the opposite side of the lane and was busy rifling through his gear in the back. Janette watched as Alex offered Mark a couple of jackets. Mark examined a wax jacket and tried it on for size, sniffing the material and scrunching up his nose as he did. She also saw Alex putting a head torch into his rucksack. At least someone else in the group seemed organised and prepared for the outing, she thought.

Ben stopped mucking about with his car and headed over to Janette. When she got a proper view of Ben's attire, she had to suppress a grin. She considered he looked like he was ready to join an American shooting range. He wore a grey New York Yankees baseball cap, a denim jacket with a thick fleece-lined collar, and Hunter's gilet over the top. He also had on well-ironed khaki cargo trousers, tucked into what looked like brand new yellow Timberland boots.

Ben adjusted his cap and slid on a pair of wraparound shades.

Janette turned away from him and stifled a laugh. 'All the wrong gear and definitely no idea,' she muttered.

Gavin was far more fourth coming with his insult. 'Say hello to Elmer Fudd's retarded cousin. Did you forget your rifle, Ben?'

'Right, and your gear looks perfect for a hike up the hills!' retorted Ben indignantly, as he scanned Gavin's Adidas trainers, worn jeans and a shabby jacket worn over a blue hoody.

Mark approached. 'Hey, buddy, we going shooting, partner?' he asked Ben in an American accent.

'You can sod off too,' said Ben.

'Come on then, let's get a shift on,' ordered Janette, heading towards a footpath that stretched through a vast cabbage field.

They all followed her. And the smiles faded, and the jokes stopped.

Janette knew, like her, the others were remembering the last time they'd all trodden this path together. Because on that day, six of them had left, but only five of them had returned.

Thirty-three

Kent, Summer 1988

Alex snuck around the back of the bungalows and stopped when he saw Eduardo and a short elderly man wearing a flat cap. They were carrying paint cans into the back garden. Alex assumed the man was Eduardo's grandad and recalled seeing him pottering about before.

The pair gazed suspiciously at Alex, so he waved and tried to appear normal. The searing pain he was feeling made that impossible, so his smile was more of a contorted wince.

Eduardo narrowed his eyes, and he looked cross.

Alex slipped in through the gate and closed it behind him. What had he done to upset Eduardo? Alex still had his ninja star, but Leo borrowed that and the other knives, not him. Leo said his brother wouldn't mind them using them, but he wasn't so sure now after seeing the incensed expression slapped on Eduardo's face.

Alex crept in via the back door and listened. He could hear the TV, so assumed his nan was in the lounge. He needed to act fast because her seeing him in this state was not an option. Not only would she have him rushed to the hospital, which he knew was where he should go, he'd also be spending the rest of his summer confined to the bungalow. She'd never let him out of her sight again. He rummaged through the cupboards, grabbing some Sellotape, carrier bags, kitchen roll and Cif cleaner. As an afterthought, he took some peas from the top freezer section in the fridge. Then he made his way past the lounge.

'Alex, is that you?' called Penny.

Alex waited until his hand gripped the bathroom door handle before responding. 'I need a bath, Nan, I fell in a muddy stream.' He rushed into the bathroom, locked the door and ran the bath taps. As he gingerly pulled off his clothes, he was forced to clench his lips together to prevent a scream of agony. At one point he even had to use his hand to clamp down over his mouth, the pain was so bad. It wasn't until he took off his socks that he even noticed the bruises on his ankle, where Freddy had stomped on him.

Alex bagged up the clothes and left them on the toilet seat. He'd hide them in the shed later and then bin them elsewhere. He located the Savlon and the bottle of TCP antiseptic liquid in the glass-fronted cabinet. His mum would always use this stuff on his scratches and cuts. It stung like a bugger. He knew the pain would be unreal, but he also knew it was necessary. He tested the water. It was lukewarm. Alex added some more cold and tipped the TCP into the swirling water and gave it a good mix. Turning off the taps, he stepped into the bath and stood naked in the coldness. Alex was shaking, he realised, as he took in a massive intake of air and slid down into the bath. He immersed himself in the water and the feeling was severe torture. Whilst under the water Alex cried out and had to fight the urge to jump out of the tub and shriek for his nan to help him. When he resurfaced, he heard a knocking on the door. 'Are you OK in there, love?' called Penny in a worried tone.

'I'm fine, I just… slipped in the bath.'

'OK, I'll make us something to eat after Blockbusters.'

'Great.'

Although sweat was running from his forehead, Alex shivered as he laid back and soaked his skin. As he sat in that pinky water, he sobbed. His nan would be mortified if she learnt what he'd done today. She couldn't find out.

Alex knew he'd never forget the day's events, and he didn't think he'd ever be able to forgive himself. He closed his eyes but could only see flashing images in his head. The destructive flames raging – the dog's pleading eyes – Freddy's baleful stare.

Alex bathed for fifteen minutes, though it seemed like hours. When he got out, he covered his lacerations with the Savlon cream and wrapped them with some kitchen roll, held in place with Sellotape. Then he used a large red towel to wrap right around himself, which hid everything. He used the Cif to clean the red stains from the bathtub and tossed all the evidence out of the bathroom window. He left the window wide open to allow the pungent smell of the cream and TCP to waft out. His nan would most likely still notice it, but he'd say he'd knocked the bottle out of the cupboard and spilt it. Then he took four paracetamol, washing them down with a handful of tap water. As he placed the peas onto the bump on his head, wondering what Freddy had clouted him with, he noticed the silver box laying on the floor. He'd forgotten it was stuffed in his shorts. After prising it open with a pair of scissors, Alex studied it in wonder. Inside was a photo of a pretty woman in her thirties with long dark hair. Two girls stood at her side – they looked like younger versions of the woman. Alex guessed they were around seven and eleven, both offering innocent smiles to the camera. And off to the side of them, stood Freddy, with a hint of a smile on his hard face. A cold chill ran through Alex's veins – he was looking at the family that, if those rumours were true, Freddy had killed.

They sat in the boat on the secret lake. Alex spent ages giving Leo the full rundown about the events on the farm four days earlier. Although, he omitted the last part.

Leo gazed at him for a full minute, his face blank, before he lit up a cigarette. 'Geez, dude, messed up or what. But you deserved everything you got, you know that, right?'

Alex wasn't expecting that response and frowned. 'I did?'

'If you'd have done that in Canada, they'd have shot you like vermin. Blasted you away like you were an annoying chipmunk. You trespassed, and you destroyed his property,' said Leo in a churlish tone.

'If that's what you think.'

'Aw, are you all sad because you got hurt? You won't get any sympathy from me.'

'I don't even want it,' said Alex, realising he sounded like an insolent child.

'So, what *do* you want?'

'I want… I want to teach Ben and Gavin a lesson.'

Leo shot him a wicked smile. 'And now you are talking my language.'

'What shall we do?'

'Don't you worry about that. I have a plan to deal with those halfwits. We'll see how they like having the tables turned on them.'

Alex could hear voices in the lounge so he shut the back door quietly. He crept in and moved along the hallway, peering into the room. His nan was sitting on the sofa with his Auntie Olivia.

'He's in a bad way,' said Olivia, 'they dislocated his jaw, plus he has two broken ribs and three broken fingers where the oafs stamped on him.'

Alex wasn't a massive fan of his aunt, she'd always seemed to look down her nose at him. If Olivia wasn't doing that, she was speaking to him as though he were a toddler. His dad wasn't keen on her either; one of the few things they shared in common. Olivia was a massive Princess Diana fan and always tried to style her hair and dress-sense on the famous royal. The similarities ended there. Olivia had a plump face, wide neck and bug-eyes. Alex always seemed to get a whiff of bleach from her, which he considered bizarre.

'Sounds like they did a number on him then,' said Penny.

Olivia dunked a Digestive biscuit into the tea and slid the entire thing into her mouth. 'Everyone warned him about that trollop Kay and her loathsome family. He just learned the hard way. The dirty sod should have kept it in his pants. My poor sister, putting up with that… perverse toad.'

'I haven't told Alex yet. Not sure how he'll take the news.'

'How has he been, Mum? Still having his… funny issues?'

Penny let out a long sigh. 'I think perhaps—' She trailed off and looked to the doorway as if sensing his presence. 'Alex? Are you home, love?'

Alex stepped into the doorway. 'Hello.'

'Alex, look at you,' gushed Olivia. 'How are you, sweetie?'

Alex knew Olivia was only being nice because she thought he might have been eavesdropping.

'Fine,' he said.

'Come and get a cuppa and biscuit then, love,' said Penny.

'I need to see my friends,' said Alex, giving them a stiff wave and dashing off.

Things were different after what had happened at Freddy's farm. In Ben's mind, Alex was a hero. He'd told Alex he should be proud that he'd had the bottle to face his fear, not to mention that he had also dished out some much-needed justice to such an evil person.

Alex didn't see it that way.

What happened with the dog had caused some major upset within the group, and it had affected the girls in a big way. Sheryl and Janette, both dog lovers, had scolded Gavin and given him a hard time about what he'd done, despite his protests that there had been no choice, and he'd only acted in self-defence. Alex didn't even mention what happened on the tracks. His story had been that Freddy had driven him out into the woods and thrown him from the vehicle onto a grassy verge, leaving him there, covered in blood. He hadn't told Leo that part either. He would take that to the grave.

Ben plucked a sizeable apple from one of the orchard trees. It had been his idea to come here, for a bit of cheeky scrumping, as he called it.

Sheryl and Janette said their goodbyes and started heading off through a long line of trees. They were off out with Janette's family, and the rest of them hadn't been invited.

Mark was standing on a tall stack of pallets, keeping watch. 'That's a cooking apple, Ben.'

Ben took a ravenous bite. 'And?'

'And, you'll get the trots.'

'It's an apple,' said Ben, spraying apple mulch as he spoke.

'That you're meant to cook. Before you eat. Hence the name,' said Mark sarcastically.

Ben lobbed the apple at Mark. 'Whatever.'

Ben hadn't mentioned the last test. Alex hoped that after the chaos they'd caused, his trials would be over. Maybe Ben felt he'd done more than enough to prove himself.

Alex hid a wry grin behind his hand. If everything went to plan, then the next test was for them. They'd know fear after the night *they* had planned. Now, it was time to get the ball rolling. An apple bouncing off his head distracted him from his thoughts.

Gavin was up in a tree sniggering. 'Your fat head best not have bruised my apple, Clayton.'

Alex rubbed his head. 'Ben, there's something I need to tell you. About Freddy.'

'Clayton wants to tell us how much he enjoyed his whipping,' said Gavin, 'fucking perverted little savage wants to go back for another spanking.'

'Shut up, Gouch,' snapped Mark.

Ben picked up a fallen apple and threw it hard at Gavin, who batted it away with his hand.

'What?' Ben asked Alex.

Alex swallowed, his throat scratchy and dry. 'If I show you something, you must all promise it goes no further than the four of us here now.'

Ben and Mark nodded.

'As long as it's not your tiny penis, Clayton, then I promise,' said Gavin. He jumped from the tree and strutted over to join the group.

Alex removed a diary from his shorts and held it in the palm of his hand. It looked old, burnt in places, with a corner missing. Ben grabbed it and scanned the pages.

Alex and Leo had spent a whole day creating the little book and making it appear as authentic as possible. Some tea staining, burning and scribbling, had done a grand job.

Ben smelt it. 'Freddy must have saved it from the house fire.'

'It was on his table, I'm not even sure why I took it,' said Alex.

Ben opened a crumpled page and unfolded it, tapping his chin deep in thought, as he viewed the crumpled map in front of him.

'I wonder where this leads. It's marked up with a route and there are two areas circled,' said Ben.

Alex had taken the map from the library. It would be a long-term borrow, as he didn't think he'd ever return it.

Mark peered over Ben's shoulder and said, 'That's an ordnance survey map. Quite detailed. I wonder what A and B means.'

Mark and Ben shared a look, and they both nodded with intrigue.

'I've read all the notes, I can't see any mention of what the map is for, but—'

Gavin interrupted. 'OK, yeah, righto. You expect us to believe this is the real deal? Um, no. Why are you such a massive bender, Clayton?'

The desire to punch Gavin on the nose, right there and then, almost overwhelmed Alex. The shrewd and suspicious creep had seen right through his plan.

'No wait… just wait a minute,' said Ben, his eyes wild with excitement. 'Wow, check this out.' He held up an open page. The page containing the family photo. 'It really is Freddy's.'

It took an hour of grovelling, but Alex convinced his nan to let him go camping for the night. She had even given him some money to go into town to buy a cheap tent and brought him plenty of snacks for the trip. He'd also been to the pharmacy with Leo and purchased some medical dressings and more cream for his wounds. They still hurt and he couldn't sit down for long periods. Plus, he could only sleep by laying on his front, and he'd frequently woken in the middle of the night in utter agony, after he'd spun over during his sleep. But the injuries were healing.

When Alex arrived, Mark and Ben were already at the barn waiting for him, with military-style Bergens at their feet. They looked bright-eyed, eager and jubilant. Alex felt bad that Mark was about to get dragged into the hoax, and he'd wanted to give him some warning about what they had planned, but Leo point-blank refused this request. If Mark blabbed to the gang or didn't play along convincingly, then everything they'd worked on would have been a total waste of time. It was too much of a risk.

Ben was gazing down the lane. 'Where is he?'

'Shall we just go without him?' suggested Mark.

'No!' said Alex, sounding far more concerned than he intended. Seeing the others share a puzzling glance, he said, 'If he doesn't come, he'll never stop going on about it.'

Just then, Gavin came strutting around the corner. And Alex felt a surge of dread. Gavin wasn't alone.

An hour later, Sheryl and Alex laughed as they watched Ben, Mark and Gavin roll aimlessly down the hillside, then disappear amongst the mass of bright yellow tansy ragwort weeds and wild purple oregano. Sheryl told Alex that the ragwort was poisonous and dangerous to livestock. It could even give a human liver failure, though only if a substantial amount was consumed. He considered it was strange that a pretty yellow plant could be so deadly.

'You don't fancy a crazy roll down the hill?' asked Sheryl.

Alex wanted to try it. He thought it looked like mad fun, but not with his injuries. 'I think it might hurt.'

'Ahh, yeah, course it would. Sorry.'

'Plus there will be adders. They bite if you disturb them.'

'Don't tell Gavin, he's terrified of snakes.'

'Can I ask you something, Sheryl?'

Sheryl nodded. 'If you like.'

'Why do you hang out with this lot? What's the deal with that?'

Sheryl gazed at him for several moments, then frowned, appearing puzzled by the question. 'They are my friends and they have always been there for me. They look out for me and helped me during a hard time in my life, when—'

'When your dad left?'

Sheryl nodded. 'Are you OK, Alex? What I went through isn't a patch on what you've had to deal with.'

'Yeah, I'm OK,' said Alex.

Alex did panic when he'd seen the girls arrive. He thought it was a disaster that Gavin had invited them behind their backs. Gavin just sneered at Alex when they'd turned up with all their camping gear. And nobody could say anything once the girls were standing there, and Gavin knew it.

But now, with Sheryl at his side, up on the hills in the bright sunshine, Alex was so glad she'd come. Ben had taken full control of the map, so he couldn't veer off course, but somehow, he'd need to sabotage the plans. Or try to find Leo and call it all off. He was up here somewhere, although Alex didn't expect to spot him. Well, not unless he wanted them to see him.

Thirty-four

'Jesus, I see your flat still looks like a show home, Nat,' said Hannah.

'Alex likes to keep things tidy and sparse,' said Natalie.

'Good thing he doesn't come to our hoose too often. He'd have a fricking meltdown, so he would.'

'At least it's a proper home. Lived in and lively.'

Hannah laughed. 'Well, aye, that's one way of putting it. I will have to remember that one.'

'Did you see the mirror?'

'I did.'

Natalie rummaged around in Alex's bedside cabinet. 'How can I kip under the same roof as someone capable of doing that in his sleep?'

'And he didnae remember a thing?'

'So he says.'

'Aye, that is strange, hen.'

Natalie pulled out a key-card and held it up. 'If there is anything to find, it will be in his office.'

'Is this a good idea, Nat?'

'I think so.'

'Where is he now? Are you sure talking about all this wouldn't be a better option?'

'He's in Kent. He has some *stuff* to sort out.'

'What stuff? … My word, you think it's about that girl, don't you?' asked Hannah.

'Yes.'

Natalie knew Alex had lied about his Dutch trip. She'd logged into his hotel booking app and confirmed the hotel he'd gone to was in Utrecht – not The Hague. She wondered if the trip was linked to everything else. Was that why he'd lied about it?

'Come on then, hen. We better have a good old snoop around your fella's office,' said Hannah.

Alex gazed across the dense woodland below, and out across to the mass of orange-brown leaves belonging to the vineyards that spread out for miles in the fields below. The vineyards hadn't been here last time he'd walked the route; it had all been farmers' fields back then. The landscape and vibrant colours were quite a spectacle. The South didn't quite have the epic and dramatic scenery of Scotland or Yorkshire, but it had its appeal.

'Kent is the garden of England, Alex,' he could hear his mum saying.

'Eight years,' said Janette, gazing down to the vineyard.

'Hey?' said Alex.

Janette pointed below. 'That's when those grapes will become wine. Chardonnay, to be precise.' With that, Janette continued along the woodland track, waving Alex to follow.

'How far back is he now?' Janette asked Gavin.

Gavin peered over his shoulder. He could see Alex and Mark a short distance behind, but there was no sign of Ben on the steep, snaking track. 'Can't see him.'

'If he moans about his blisters one more time, I might just leave him up here,' said Janette.

Gavin chuckled, thinking that she most likely wasn't joking.

'Is everything all hunky-dory with biker Brian?' asked Gavin.

'Yes, it's going very well with Will, thank you. And you? Anyone special in Gavin Gouch's life?'

'Nah, well, not anymore. There was someone, but it didn't work out so well,' said Gavin.

'That's a shame, Gav. The curse I take it?'

'What else?'

'What else,' she repeated.

'Oh, and Jan… I've missed you.'

Janette gave him a gentle shoulder barge. 'Shut up.'

Gavin tried to recall the last time he'd spent the night with Janette and guessed they must have been around twenty-six, perhaps younger. Their relationship had been a turbulent one, and they both knew, deep down, they were not destined to spend their life together. They were an unsuitable match. The sex had always been mind-blowing, experimental and rampant, but there was little else to their crazy union. Although somehow, after time spent apart, they'd always seem to find themselves back in each other's company. Gavin wondered if it was because of everything that happened. Maybe it was just their way of sharing the grief. He'd be fibbing if he said he still didn't have feelings for her, and he figured he would always love her in his own way. Zara's face flashed in his mind, and with it, a surge of guilt. He had ignored her since leaving Nottingham. She'd left voicemails the previous day and her voice had cracked as she had begged him to return to her, and then she broke into a sob that was agonising to listen to. But Gavin wasn't prepared to bend. Not yet. Not until he was certain that she'd stopped with the gear, and certain that she was ready to move on. If that day ever came.

'What do you make of all this, Jan? What do you make of him?'

'He seems genuine enough, but if I am honest... I don't know,' she said.

When Ben came into view, he had his hands on his hips and looked ready to drop.

Alex and Mark caught up, and they all watched Ben battle with the incline.

'This could take a while,' said Mark.

'So, what will be his excuse now? The dodgy ales last night, his twisted ankle, or the new boots?' asked Janette.

'I'm gonna go with boots,' said Gavin.

Mark took a drag from his vape. 'Yeah, the boots... no, the booze. And I vote Jan gives Ben a piggy-back.'

Gavin nodded. 'Second that.'

When Ben reached them, he looked spent. 'Aw, these damned boots are killing my feet.'

Gavin sniggered.

'Some would question why you thought brand new boots would be a sensible idea when tackling a three-hour hike,' said Mark.

'There must be a quicker route,' said Ben, ignoring Mark and speaking to Janette.

'Yes, there is a far quicker route. But that defeats the purpose,' said Janette. 'Being as though we are following the same route we all took.'

'Are you sure? I don't remember there being so many hills,' said Ben.

'It's the North Downs,' said Mark, 'there will be a hill or two, mate.'

'Well, they should call it the North Ups,' groaned Ben.

'The elevation is the same today, as it was back in eighty-eight. The difference is that now, you are unfit,' said Janette. She then turned and continued up the hill, taking big strides as she went.

'No, it's my boots, Jan,' protested Ben.

Gavin patted Ben on the shoulder and followed Janette. 'On your way, soldier. Or next time Jan will give you thirty burpees.'

'Yeah, she'll make a man of you yet, Napier,' said Mark, heading off with them.

Ben glared at Alex. 'Not joining in?'

'Nope,' said Alex, smirking as he followed the group.

Javon followed Timur into the spruce flat and nodded his approval. 'Yeah. Nice gaff, man.'

'Sken,' said Timur, speaking to a skinny man who was slouched on the sofa playing on a PlayStation. The man was wearing a red Adidas tracksuit top and blue joggers that clashed.

Javon viewed the huge TV. The man was playing a Call of Duty game, and Javon watched the gameplay in awe. It looked stunning on the giant 4K screen, and the volume was so loud, the room sounded like a war-zone, as gunfire and explosions boomed from the speakers.

'Skender!' shouted Timur.

Skender peered up at Timur and then gave Javon a sneering glance. He had a hideous wound on one side of his face, running from his eye down to his chin. A line of medical sutures looked as though they were holding his face together, and his swollen cheek carried an awful bruise around the injury. Javon guessed someone had taken a knife to the man. Or maybe a sword.

Skender turned down the volume. 'What did I say, Tim? Online orders only. I don't want anybody in my place.'

'He's not a buyer,' said Timur gruffly.

'What is he then, your new boyfriend?'

'Funny,' said Timur.

'I know Gavin Gouch,' said Javon, 'he owes me money. Rumours are floating around the city, that you are offering a reward for info on this bloke.'

Skender sniffed and tossed down the controller. 'OK.'

'He works with my uncle. At least, he did until recently. He brought my motor, but only paid me half the dough.'

Skender picked at his nose. 'So?'

'The car is still registered in my name. Kent Police contacted me about an incident involving the car,' said Javon.

'And that's not all, Sken,' said Timur, pushing Javon forward. 'Tell him.'

'Well?' asked Skender.

'I know where Gavin's flat is,' said Javon.

Alex followed Janette as they trudged up a hillside that had no actual pathway to follow. Even though all these years had passed, Alex still remembered the route, but he had expected Janette to take charge of things. He'd known she would have been first in line when he'd spoken about it in the pub. He'd been counting on it. When he scrutinised Janette's Strava account, he'd established that she undertook plenty of activities in this general area.

The group were in a staggered formation as they worked their way through the thorny bracken, dog rose and wild teasel, which was almost as tall as them. Ben was the furthest behind, a look of gritted determination on his face as he ascended.

Alex twisted his ankle after stepping into a rabbit's burrow. They were hard to notice, being buried under spongy, moss-like shrubs, so he shouted a warning to the others to watch out for the deep holes, but only received a grunt of acknowledgement from Mark in return for the heads-up.

Janette reached the hill's summit first, though Alex wasn't far behind her.

They both took in the view. The hazy autumn sunshine was low and bright, and there were shreds of misshapen clouds in the sky. Smoke flowed from a distant farm building and a biplane flew above them, its engine humming softly, and around half a mile away, a photographer stood on the hilltop, snapping photos of the scenery.

Alex studied the trail ahead, which would take them along a rising, dogleg shaped hillside, passing over the long chalk-split that stretched out a good forty feet. He recalled Leo calling that area the giant's teeth. He guessed they had just over an hour before sundown. The two trees were close by, in fact, they stood close to the area they'd first noticed: Killner's Land Rover.

Janette let out a long, exaggerated sigh. 'The state of Ben, you'd think we were attempting to conquer Everest.'

'I am wondering if we should have packed a couple of oxygen masks,' said Alex.

Janette gave Alex a thin smile and popped a sweet in her mouth. She didn't offer Alex one.

Mark and Gavin arrived at the top five minutes after them. A further five minutes and Ben had made it.

'What are these annoying things? They are like mini gonads made of bastard velcro,' said Ben, pulling off a handful of lesser burdock. Ben's boots and trousers were covered in the sticky balls. As Ben tossed them away, they re-stuck to his other trouser leg.

'Ready?' asked Janette curtly. Then she tossed an energy gel at Ben.

'What's this?' asked Ben, studying the packet and frowning.

Natalie and Hannah had spent fifteen minutes going through Alex's office. It wasn't very big, so the search was easy. One iMac was locked, and despite several attempts at cracking the login password, they had given up with that idea, and the second iMac didn't turn on and just froze on the Apple logo, so Natalie assumed it was faulty, and unplugged it. The two oak filing cabinets only contained work files and account information. There was also a tall white bookcase, which housed well-used photography books, a bunch of specialist photography magazines, and some newer books about analysing dreams and researching sleep deprivation. But the search had not been fruitless, as Hannah had located a tatty black address book in one of the desk drawers. It contained some work numbers and an Essex address that could prove useful – it was for Alex's Auntie Olivia.

As they headed up the wooden steps towards the two trees, Alex could almost feel their eyes burning into his back. He heard Ben swear, and he glanced back to see Mark helping him up from the ground. He assumed he'd slipped on the wet chalk patch that he perhaps should have warned them about.

As they reached the two large ash trees, the mood was solemn and expressions grim and sombre. They lingered there, scanning the area in wary silence. Not one of them spoke a word, and Alex did his best to avoid eye contact with everyone; instead, he focussed on a nearby paraglider.

Thirty-five

Kent, Summer 1988

Sheryl and Janette were sitting on a hillside that was teeming with daisies, cowslips and spotted orchids. The girls giggled as they ate their lunch and weaved flowers into each other's hair.

Ben, slouched against a fence, sitting topless, t-shirt draped over his head, and looking like some sort of chubby sheikh, was eating a complete Swiss roll to himself.

Gavin shamelessly gawped at Ben, licking his lips with every bite his friend took.

'Come off it, Ben, you have enough munch to feed an entire classroom,' said Gavin.

Ben stuffed the rest of the cake in and chewed uncouthly. 'Tough titties. You should have brought your own grub.'

Gavin stuck up his middle finger. 'You are one greedy fat shithead, Napier.'

Alex offered Gavin a sausage roll. 'Have this.'

Gavin looked at him with a suspicious expression, before snatching the offering and examining it. 'Any crisps to go with that?'

'Frazzles?'

'They'll do. And I need a drink.'

Alex rummaged in his rucksack and pulled out the crisps and a carton of juice. He passed them to Gavin, who grabbed them without a word of thanks.

'You're too kind, Clayton,' said Mark.

'Shut ya ugly face, Corkscrew,' said Gavin.

Mark nodded at the girls. 'And the plan was just us tonight, so why'd you blab to them?'

'Um, it just slipped out,' said Gavin, ripping open the Frazzles packet and jamming a handful of the crisps into his gob.

'I'm surprised you didn't invite Shane and Patrick too,' said Mark.

'I did. Patrick is playing soldiers with the cadets in Dungeness. And Shane said he was busy,' said Gavin with a smirk.

'My parents are away for the night, so my brother will be having a wankathon with the old-fella's porno collection,' said Ben.

'Who's having a wankathon?' asked Janette, striding over to the boys, her arm linked around Sheryl's.

'Oh, just Alex,' said Gavin nonchalantly.

Alex felt his cheeks redden. 'No… I'm not,' he stammered.

The girls chuckled. Both of them had decorated their hair with two big daisies.

'It's him. He's following us,' said Mark as he observed the Land Rover pull over in the lay-by below.

Alex joined him on the hilltop and glanced down. Sure enough, far in the distance, was a limestone-coloured Land Rover. Could that really be Freddy? The vehicle was too far away for any of them to be certain.

'How would Freddy even know we're up here?' said Ben. He was sitting behind them, trying to light a cigarette with a plastic lighter that wouldn't spark. Alex was glad Ben hadn't remembered to ask him about the zippo lighter he'd lost at the farm.

Janette glanced down the hill and blinked in the dazzling sunshine. 'He wants revenge. He's gonna hunt us down.'

Sheryl chuckled. 'You shouldn't have watched Lost Boys last night, Jan. I told you it would freak you out and mess with your head.'

'The Lost Boys film wasn't even scary,' said Mark.

'Er, yeah, it actually is, Corkscrew,' said Janette.

Gavin snatched the lighter from Ben, started shaking it, and got it to light. 'Yeah, righto, Corkscrew, I heard you couldn't sleep in your own bed for two weeks after watching Nightmare on Elm Street.'

Mark squirmed. 'That is not true. And I heard you sobbed like a newborn after watching Dumbo, Gav.'

Gavin shrugged. 'Yep, that is actually true.'

Ben puffed on the cigarette. 'It's just a farmer.'

'Some coincidence though,' said Mark.

The Land Rover pulled out of the lay-by and started crawling along the lane. From their viewpoint, they could follow the vehicle's progress as it drove along the country lane below them. It moved at a snail's pace and stopped after about a quarter of a mile, pulling into another lay-by that was partially covered by dense bushes.

'Maybe we should turn back,' suggested Janette.

Ben licked his front teeth. 'We keep going. If we spot it again, then we'll decide what to do.'

Alex knew the lane ran parallel to their planned route in the hills, so, in theory, they should easily spot the vehicle if it was trailing them. If it was Freddy, what was he intending to do? Was he tracking them down to teach them all a lesson? To take his retribution for what they did to his home. And to his dog. Alex had a terrible feeling that Janette was right. They should go back, because this wasn't part of the plan.

Alex focussed on the horizon as he urinated down the hillside. Earlier, he'd thought the sky, and the clouds appeared peculiar, but now, the sky looked like nothing he'd ever seen before. It was as though someone had taken a gigantic ruler and drawn a perfect line under the clouds, and that line stretched endlessly in each direction. The clouds were steely grey, and to Alex, they resembled a monstrous wave coming to swamp the land and engulf them in a dreadful, infinite darkness. He also noticed a flitting, bright flash of indigo, far in the distance. He looked up to the sky above him – still clear blue skies and dazzling sunshine. The sound of cracking twigs pulled his attention downwards, and he finished up.

'Psst, here,' said a voice.

Alex peered down the hillside. At first, he could see only bushes and thorny shrubs; then he spied a set of flinty eyes glaring at him from the undergrowth. Someone was laying in the bushes, close to where he'd been peeing.

'Leo? Is that you?' whispered Alex.

Leo pulled himself up into a crouching position. 'Yeah, buddy.'

He wore a full black ninja suit that was covered in a layer of foliage and lush green leaves.

'What is taking you so long?' asked Leo in an irate whisper.

'They keep stopping to eat and mess about,' said Alex.

'There is a storm coming, Alex.'

'Look, Leo, we should quit with this prank.'

Alex waited for the contemptuous reply he guessed he'd get from Leo.

'Why? Don't you dare tell me it's because that stupid girl has turned up? Don't you say that, Alex!'

'Don't call her stupid.'

'And you're *stupid* if you think she likes you. She'll never choose you over her proper friends. The sooner you get that into your dumb noggin, the better,' growled Leo.

'But—'

'But nothing. You know I'm right. *I'm* your true pal. Not them. You better keep going, Alex. I better not have wasted my time with you, because I thought we had a proper understanding,' said Leo.

'We do,' said Alex.

'So, now it's time to prove it.'

Alex nodded. 'OK, Leo.'

'Everything you've been through. All the injuries you've sustained. And for what? Her? You truly think she's worth all this?' asked Leo.

'Freddy Killner might be—'

'Alex… what are you doing?' asked Sheryl.

Alex spun around as Sheryl walked over to him.

'Huh, I was—'

'Your cheeks are cherry-red, Alex,' she said, flashing him a playful grin as she gazed down the hillside. 'Who were you just talking to?'

Alex followed that gaze. Leo had gone, though he couldn't work out if he'd somehow moved away, or was concealing himself right under their noses.

Sheryl crossed her arms and huffed. 'So, a little birdy said that you didn't want me to come on this crazy adventure.'

'Did that birdy have big ears? … And no. I didn't say that.'

'OK. If I'm not good enough. That's fine,' she said, sounding cross, though her eyes betrayed that she truly was.

'I was worried. I didn't want you to get hurt. Like I did. At the farm,' said Alex.

'I know that. I was teasing you.'

'Right, yeah, I knew that too,' then quickly added, 'it's because I care about you.' He felt his cheeks burning up now. He was astonished that those words had left his mouth.

Sheryl had on her usual denim skirt, and her favourite dye-pattern top, and with the flowers stuck in her hair, he considered she wouldn't have looked out of place in the sixties. His mum's favourite decade.

The clouds were shifting in closer now, and they grew darker and angrier. It was like the end of the world was edging in his direction. Alex decided the plan should go ahead. He'd look after Sheryl tonight, and he considered it might even bring them closer, but the others still needed to be taught a valuable lesson.

Sheryl twisted her hair with one finger and gave Alex an endearing smile.

'Shall we get back?' asked Alex.

'I like you too, Alex. I think you're cute. In a funny, nerdy way,' she said.

Alex couldn't believe his ears. Was he dreaming this? Was all this in his crazy imagination?

Sheryl chuckled. 'Sorry, I'm not *actually* calling you a nerd.'

'I don't mind.'

'Do you like ice skating? Perhaps we could go together sometime. If you wanted?'

'Just us?'

'Yes, Alex, just us.'

'Erm, well—'

'I can ask the others too if you'd prefer.'

'No… no, just us would be great,' he blurted.

Sheryl peered down the hill again. 'Come on then, let's go. Um, and stop talking to those squirrels, people will think you're a bit nuts.' She gave Alex a roguish smile. 'It was nice to see you getting on with Gavin.'

'I only gave him some lunch.'

'I reckon you two could be great mates. I know at times he acts like a moose, but he's not as bad as he likes to make out. He used to be like you.'

'How?'

'He got bullied at school, Alex. All the time. Kids used to call him the poison midget and the corgi.'

'Corgi?'

'They have huge ears and stumpy legs, Alex.'

Alex suppressed a grin. He sort of recalled a time when Gavin was picked on. Sort of.

'Ben took him under his wing and helped him. He was quiet and shy until Ben taught him how to stand up for himself. Don't you dare tell Gavin I told you this!'

Alex pretended to run a zip along his lips.

Sheryl popped a Juicy Fruit gum in her mouth and walked off, giving Alex a sassy grin as she went.

Alex didn't follow her straight away. Instead, he gazed back at those clouds. He was in a daze now, and he thought about everything he'd been through over the summer – the ordeals he'd endured. Was Sheryl enthralled with everything he'd done? Would she have still been interested in him if he hadn't climbed a crane, half-drowned himself and got his back slashed to ribbons, just to impress *her*? Or could he have just asked Sheryl outright for a date? If that's what this even was.

Ben's words echoed in his head. *'Sheryl's with us, Clayton.'*

Alex's initial elation was short-lived, and now he felt irritated, uncertain and addled. Yes, he was pleased, but he could not stop those niggling feelings creeping in. He knew he should stop being paranoid and overthinking it all. After all, he'd got what he wanted, and besides, Sheryl had tried to help him more than once. She wasn't like the rest of them; he knew that.

'See anything, Ben?' asked Janette.

'Nah, just a tractor carrying a steaming pile of crud,' said Ben.

'Why ask him? He has retarded eyesight,' said Gavin.

Ben flicked Gavin hard on his left ear.

'Ouch. Prat,' said Gavin, rubbing his ear.

'Where are your binos?' asked Mark.

Ben slapped his forehead. 'Ooh, yeah, top priority those, I can't believe I didn't pack them.'

Alex glanced at the sky again. Daylight was ebbing away and those dark clouds were now moving fast, blocking sunlight as they flashed by. Alex had expected the group to have made better progress.

The group spent twenty minutes trying to spot Freddy's vehicle, and no one seemed keen to head up to the two trees, fearing he was lying in wait.

'I'm going up,' said Alex. With that, he trudged on. He heard some bickering and moaning and knew they were all following him. Gavin and Ben's ego would get the better of them, as there was no way they would want to appear frightened, especially if he wasn't.

Sheeting rain was soaking them as he dug between the trees. Alex was using the collapsible shovel he'd used the first time he'd come to the spot with Leo. They'd concealed the hole well. Even he struggled to find the spot they'd marked with several white pebbles, which they had placed in a circle and buried in grass, twigs and weeds. Alex pretended not to notice them and let Ben take the glory, and he'd almost wet himself with joy after locating them.

All the boys took a turn to dig, whilst the girls kept a watchful eye on the lane below and surrounding hills and checked for any suspicious vehicles or signs of any shifty figures lurking around.

Ben passed the shovel to Gavin, who took his turn to dig, deliberately flinging mud into Alex's face as he did. Mark had a rubber torch and positioned it over the sludgy hole.

The wind started picking up, howling across the hill and shaking the trees.

They found something when it was Ben's turn to shovel – it was an item wrapped in a grease-stained cloth. Ben pulled off that cloth like an elated child unwrapping a Christmas present. 'It's a box!'

'What's that inscription say?' asked Mark.

Ben wiped the front. 'F... J... K.'

'Open it then,' said Gavin.

Ben prised the lid open, which took some effort, and, as if on cue when the lid popped, a rumble of distant thunder pierced the night.

Inside the box was a single key.

After spending ten minutes under the trees attempting to shield from the downpour and bickering about what they should do next, they decided to continue on the route and get to the next area on the map. Once nearby, they'd find a suitable, secluded place to camp, make a huge fire, and dry themselves out. Mark had protested that they should quit, go home, and suggested they venture to the second spot another day, but Ben was adamant it should be tonight, or the chance to discover what the key opened would be lost if Freddy had guessed their plans. The girls detested the idea of staying out all night in the hideous weather, but both had lied about their whereabouts – Janette was at a sleepover at Sheryl's and vice versa, so neither could return home now, or at least not without getting into trouble for lying. Alex stayed silent and let them debate amongst themselves. He knew Ben would get his way.

The rain eased off as they followed Mark's torchlight into the gloomy, wet evening. He'd had the foresight to pack extra batteries, though he'd already changed them once.

The mood was grim now, and nobody said a word as they headed up a steep, woody track, listening to the rain and occasional boom of thunder.

'Seems perfect. What do you think?' asked Alex.

Ben studied the area and nodded. 'Yeah, this is an ideal spot.'

Alex scanned the clearing at the foot of a high chalk face, which was a good forty feet wide and had a pathway to the left of it, although that path looked steep and dangerous; almost vertical. He'd slipped on the chalk path when he'd walked the route with Leo. It had been dry then too; so it would be hazardous in this weather. Thick, tall trees shrouded the rest of the clearing, and it was a suitable area to camp, as there was some respite from the rain. It also seemed secluded and safe. When Alex had been here previously, Leo had been convinced that the group would go for it.

'I say we split. Half of us make the camp and gather wood. The other half of us, follow the map,' proposed Gavin.

'Yeah, this bag is killing my shoulders,' said Janette.

'I think we should stay together,' said Sheryl.

Ben shoved the wet map to Alex. 'How far now, Clayton? I can't see shit, my specs are all steamed up.'

Mark provided the light as Alex pretended to read. 'Fifteen minutes. Maybe twenty.'

Ben seized the map. 'Stash up all our stuff under those trees. Then we'll all head off in one group.' With that, he yanked off his Bergan and placed it behind a tree. The others did the same.

Thirty-six

The climb up the steep chalk track had been slow and treacherous, but they all ascended with only the odd slip and skid. Alex had made sure he was last to climb, so he was at the rear of the group.

Fifteen minutes later, they stood on the summit of the highest point of their trek, and judging by all the piles of cow crap; it was a cattle field, though worryingly, they didn't notice any livestock, despite scanning the surrounding gloominess. They soon found more white pebbles that were placed next to a chunky concrete slab, and they started digging. The wind had got heavier, and the rain had started again, though just a drizzle, and the thunder sounded close now. Flashes of lightning snapped in vivid strikes across the distant land.

Soaked, silent and bone-weary, they all watched Alex dig.

Alex stuck the shovel in the ground and took a rasping breath. 'I've hit something.'

Ben shoved him out of the way. 'Let me look, Clayton!' He clawed the mud with his hands, pulling out an item wrapped in a tatty, striped tea-towel.

'Light, Corkscrew,' demanded Ben.

Mark complied, lighting up the item with the torch's beam.

Everyone was at his shoulder as he unwrapped the item. It was a steel lockbox.

Ben could not stand still as he fumbled to get the key in the lock. His lips pursed tight and his eyes were wide and ecstatic as he popped the lid. It contained a fat envelope, and Ben, apprehensive and eager, opened it. 'Oh… oh, my frigging, God. Ooh—' he babbled.

Gavin tried to grab it. 'What? What's in there? Ben?'

Ben fingered the notes inside. 'Only cash. Loads of bloody cash! Oh, man. Loads and loads. Yeah.'

Gasps of elated joy filled the air.

The girls had their hands over their mouths.

Ben bounced on the spot.

Mark danced in circles.

Gavin grabbed for the envelope again. 'Oi, let me look at it.'

Alex tried to appear happy as he took in the scene, but he felt terrible. Guilty didn't even cover it.

'How much?' asked Janette.

Ben tugged out a thick wedge of the notes and studied them.

'How much?' repeated Janette.

Then Ben's beaming smile faded, and he frowned in bafflement as he fingered the money. 'What sort of dosh is this?'

Gavin ripped a handful from his hand. 'Let me take a gander,' he said as he put the notes under the torch. 'It's Monopoly.'

Ben pulled a confused face. 'What is that like foreign cash?'

Janette let out an annoyed sigh. 'No, you utter dip-shit. Monopoly. The board game, you spaz.'

Ben looked as though he was on the verge of sobbing. 'So, we can't spend it?'

'No!' shouted Mark and Janette in unison.

Ben threw the money down. It blew all about the hilltop.

Sheryl pointed at a piece of paper still inside the box. 'What's that?' She picked it up and gestured for Mark to supply some light, as she read it aloud. *You burnt down my home. You killed my dog. I'm coming for all of you tonight. You'll all die up here.'*

Apart from the rain, it was silent. The group gazed at Sheryl for around twenty seconds.

Then it was chaos. Arguments erupted, and there was shouting, swearing and wailing.

Gavin yelled at Alex.

Janette screeched at Ben.

Mark was babbling.

Sheryl was trying to calm everyone down.

Alex knew there was no backing out now, he'd already laid the foundations, so he needed to finish what he'd started.

Janette pointed down the hill. 'There are lights. That's a village. I say we go down there now. Get help. And that might be a farm building along that lane.'

Mark put his arm around her. 'That's Hollingbourne, and it's further away than it looks, Jan.'

Gavin shook his head. 'We're not going to any weird farm, Jan!'

'We go back to the camp,' said Ben.

'This isn't some Goonies adventure, Ben. We're in real danger here,' said Janette. 'That nutter will kill us whilst we sleep.'

It surprised Alex that Janette, for all her tough exterior, had cracked so easily. Sheryl was calm and unshaken, or at least appeared as much, and this made Alex like her even more; she was a tough cookie.

'That stupid old fruitcake is trying to scare us. He won't dare try anything whilst we're all together,' said Ben.

Gavin shoved Alex. 'This is your fault, Clayton!'

'We need to get our gear. I'm not leaving it,' said Ben, 'my dad will go ape-shit if I lose my brother's new army Bergan. It cost loads.'

'We won't sleep. Just set a camp and guard the area,' said Mark, pulling Gavin away from Alex.

'I think we need to stay—' Sheryl's voice trailed off, and she stepped forward and pointed. 'Down there.'

In the distance, bright headlights were moving across the lane below.

'Turn off the light, Corkscrew,' said Sheryl.

Mark did as requested. They all stood in the darkness and watched as the vehicle slowed and stopped. It must have been a good mile and a half away.

'So, what? It could be anyone,' said Gavin.

'Why has it stopped in the middle of the lane?' asked Sheryl.

Ben stomped on a stray Monopoly note. 'We take a vote. Who votes that we head down to the lane, locate the nearest house and knock on some random's door, and ask for help?'

Janette and Gavin raised their hands.

'OK. And who votes we head back to our stuff and make a fire?' said Ben, his own hand raised. Sheryl and Mark raised their hands too.

Alex gazed in awe as a bent finger of silent, bright lightning struck far in the distance. He raised his hand.

The storm hit hard. The rain pounded. Thunder grumbled and lighting slashed in vivid bolts.

Mark led the group with his torch, its light fading with each step.

'Be careful, I can barely see the path now,' bellowed Mark over the rain. 'That chalk drop is close.'

'What is that?' shouted Janette. 'In the trees, over there.'

Deep in the trees, an orange light flashed, and the group stopped and focussed on it. Mark shone the light into the trees, but the stream had dulled to a thin, worthless glow. Alex felt someone touch his hand. It was Sheryl, her cold, wet hand gripping his. Alex could feel her trembling.

A sudden flash of lightning illuminated the woodland. In the passing bluish light stood an obscure, creepy figure in the trees. Hooded and statue still. Then pitch darkness enveloped them.

Sheryl's grip tightened as she screamed.

Janette let out a low, wailing cry.

'Get out of here!' yelled Gavin.

Alex tried to keep hold of Sheryl's hand as they all ran.

Mark's torch had given up, and they all sprinted in a blind panic.

They ran for several minutes, with rain slashing in their faces.

In the mayhem and confusion, Sheryl's hand slipped from Alex's grasp.

Someone skidded over. Gavin started cursing. Ben was shouting. It was frantic madness, and everything was a crazy blur of shapes. The rain thrashed down and Alex slipped and pitched forward. There were more screams and bellowing.

Alex placed his hands in the mud and grasped where he was – right by the edge of the chalk drop. Then a flash of lightning lit his world for a fleeting moment, and he stared down at the bottom and gasped at what looked like a shadowy shape sprawled on the ground. Alex rubbed the rain from his face and peered again. But there was only darkness now. Then a loud boom of thunder rolled out, and a harsh terror gripped him. 'Sheryl! Sheryl, where are you?' cried Alex. He peered over again and strained his eyes to get a second glimpse. Then another slam of lightning hit, and this time, he could see nothing below.

Janette sat in front of a fire with a sleeping bag draped over her shoulders. The group had erected two tents in the clearing, both appeared soaked and unstable. The fire had taken over two hours to get going, but Gavin had been determined to set one, after promising Janette he could do it despite the wet conditions.

Gavin had used some flint as a part of the edging, which they had soon learnt explodes and spits in the air when it gets hot. A piece had flung up and burnt Gavin's eyelid, and one tent had now acquired several air holes.

They'd searched for Sheryl into the night and early hours, scouring the direct area and shouting for her, but none of them ventured too far from the clearing, fearing what was lurking out there, although none of them admitted as much. Ben strutted around the campsite like he was on sentry patrol, brandishing a sharpened stick. Janette had fallen over during the chalk descent, cracked her knee and could not put any weight on her left leg.

The rain had changed to a faint drizzle and it wouldn't be long before dawn would start breaking. Rainwater poured down the tree trunks of the surrounding trees. No one had slept, and Alex considered that the group now resembled a shattered and bedraggled bunch of homeless kids.

'She wouldn't have just gone off like that, Ben. You know it,' said Janette. She shivered and sobbed.

'Sheryl must have just got lost, Jan,' said Gavin.

Mark nodded in agreement. 'Gav's right. I bet she got split from the group and couldn't find the rest of us.'

Janette shuddered. 'No, she would have come back here.'

'I reckon Sheryl's already home, laughing about us morons stuck up here like drowned rats,' said Ben.

Janette fixed her eyes on Alex. 'And what about what *he* saw?'

Ben rested the stick on his shoulder and said, 'That div doesn't know what he saw.'

'I know I saw something down here,' said Alex sombrely.

Ben glowered at Alex. 'Well, I'm quite sure if she'd fallen from the top, we would have found her here.'

Janette snivelled. 'But, what if she fell, and she's hurt?'

Ben rounded on Alex. 'Did you actually see her fall or not, Clayton?'

Alex shook his head.

Mark rubbed Janette's shoulder. 'Nah, she didn't fall, Jan. Clayton can't possibly be sure what he saw. It was way too dark, and the rain was belting down.'

'And what the hell was in those trees?' asked Janette through gritted teeth.

'I didn't see bugger all,' said Mark, 'just a flashing light. And I only ran because you lot all legged it.'

'I thought I spotted the outline of a person. But my glasses were all smeary,' said Ben.

'Well, I spotted somebody out there,' said Janette.

'Me too. I was certain I got a glimpse of a man out there. He looked like he was hanging by the neck,' said Gavin.

'Lightning screws up your vision and you see plenty of weird stuff. We all need to stop freaking out. Sheryl's fine,' said Ben in a reassuring voice.

The rain stopped, and the sun made an appearance. Birds were chirping, and it was as though last night's events had been nothing but a nightmare.

Alex, huddled by the waning fire, arms wrapped around his knees, eyed the smouldering, white logs. Clothes were drying on makeshift stands, made of branches that the group had positioned about the fire. Alex observed as Ben quietly packed up his belongings. Janette and Mark were curled up in sleeping bags at the entrance to one of the tents. They lay still and Alex couldn't tell if they were asleep or not. Gavin lay in the second tent, his legs half hanging out. He was sure Gavin had dozed off, judging by the occasional snore and grunt coming from inside.

As Ben looked his way, Alex pretended to be asleep.

'Wake up. Clayton?' whispered Ben.

Alex half-opened his eyes. 'Where are you going?'

'We'll walk back now. Find out if Sheryl made it home. And I'll get someone to collect Janette.'

Ben kicked Gavin's leg. 'Gav, you coming or staying?'

'I'm not going yet,' came Gavin's sleepy groan.

Ben walked to the other tent and gently shook Mark. 'Corkscrew,' he whispered, 'look after Jan. I'm going with Clayton.'

'Any sign of her?' asked Mark in a drowsy croak.

'No,' said Ben.

The top of Mark's head popped out from the sleeping bag. 'What now?'

'Make your way to that village at lunchtime. Find the post office. Wait there for a pickup,' said Ben.

'Call my dad. He'll come and get us.'

Ben rested the stick against the tent. 'Jan can use this to help her walk. Keep your eyes peeled.'

Mark nodded. 'Yeah, OK. You too, compadre.'

Alex and Ben walked in grim silence. They headed down a steep byway, with loose rocks underfoot and rainwater rushing down the deep ruts that ran along it. Alex slipped and grabbed Ben's Bergan to steady himself, but before Alex knew it, Ben slammed him onto his back, climbed on top of him, and put his hands around Alex's throat.

'What are you doing?' shouted Alex, as pain tore through his back – Ben's weight pushing down on his injuries caused him to cry out in agony.

Ben came nose to nose with Alex. 'If I find out you set us up… I promise you'll regret it. And if she's hurt—'

Alex could only whimper in response.

'Don't follow me. Go home on your own,' snarled Ben. With that, he got up and kicked Alex hard in the ribs.

Alex held his side and groaned as Ben ambled down the byway, skidding and stumbling as he went.

Alex sat up and rubbed his sore ribs. He ached all over, and the thought of walking home was a depressing one.

Alex put his hand in the pocket of his wet shorts, pulling out the crumpled daisy he'd found in the clearing. He held it in his palm and stared at it. What had he done?

Thirty-seven

Kent, Autumn 2019

Janette slid in some sludgy leaves, pitched forward and landed on a stile, which broke and sent her plummeting shoulder first into the dirt.

Ben glanced down at her. 'Whoops, Jan. Clumsy.' He tried to help her up, but she pushed his hand away and lifted herself using part of the broken stile.

'I'm fine. It's not a proper hike unless you stack it at least once.' She dusted herself off, cheeks rosy from embarrassment, adjusted her bag straps and continued on her way.

With Janette's quick pace, they arrived at the clearing just before sundown.

Janette aside, Alex guessed that none of the others had returned here since '88. Alex walked to the chalk face and ran his hand over the craggy, crumbling stone as he gazed upwards, and he estimated the height was at least thirty feet. The ground underfoot was hard, with broken chalk pieces and rock debris scattered about. Alex pictured Sheryl falling from the top – her body connecting with the ground with a sickening thud. He pulled a large chunk of chalk from the wall, and more lumps fell away and broke up. When Alex turned around, the others were huddled into a group, and were gazing into the trees. He raced over to join them and froze when he caught sight of what everyone's attention was focussed on. It was a child's swing, attached to a wide branch, and sat upon its wooden seat, was a bear, with its arms cable tied to the rope.

Ben broke the silence. 'It's just someone's sick idea of a joke.'

Janette stepped towards the swing and touched the pink bear. It had a rainbow emblem on its stomach.

'It's a Care Bear… Cheer Bear, to be precise,' she said.

Gavin glared at Alex as he said, 'Maybe somebody is trying to prank us again.

Screwing with our heads.'

'It's working,' said Mark.

Alex walked over and squeezed the bear's head. It was damp.

'When did you last come here, Jan?' asked Alex.

Janette shrugged. 'This actual spot, dunno, two years ago. This wasn't here then.'

'It's almost as though somebody knew we would come out here,' said Gavin tartly.

Janette stared at the bear with a vacant expression. 'It's hers.'

'Nah, it can't be Sheryl's bear,' said Ben.

Janette touched the bear again. 'She loved this bear. Her dad gave it to her. The year before he… left.'

Mark sucked hard on his vape. 'Is anyone else seriously creeped out by this? This is so messed up.'

'That would mean someone took it from Eileen's,' said Ben, 'seems unlikely.'

'And have you been to see Sheryl's mum, Clayton?' asked Gavin.

Alex knew from Gavin's accusatory tone, he was blaming him, and he knew it was pointless to defend himself, so he just ignored the question and headed for the chalk path.

They all watched the sun drop on the horizon, as it became an alluring orange smudge amongst the tattered clouds. Alex flicked on the light to his portable lantern. For its size, it was bright, so he dimmed the setting, then removed five coloured glass jars from his rucksack and handed them out to each of them.

With Janette going first, they each took turns to walk to the edge of the chalk drop, place their jar and light each candle nestled inside.

After all the jars were lit, Janette placed a photo of Sheryl against each jar, using chalk pieces to secure them. All the photos were of Sheryl smiling brightly, and one of them was of Janette and Sheryl hugging. Alex was glad Janette hadn't opted for the notorious tabloid photo that he'd seen so often in his dreams. The one on all those posters. They had been everywhere.

The five of them stood in silence, surrounded by the calm glow of the lantern. Gavin and Ben had their heads bowed. Mark had his hands behind his back as he rocked on his heels. Janette gazed at the dipping sun, lost in her thoughts.

The temperature was dropping and Alex's breath plumed in front of him, as he took in large nostrils of air and exhaled.

Once they'd all had their moment to reflect, he'd tell them a secret that he knew they needed to hear. He dreaded what their reactions would be.

As Timur brought the black Golf GTI to a stop, Javon knew he'd made a serious error coming to Skender about Gavin Gouch.

Javon peered out of the steamy back window. 'What are we doing here?'

Skender turned in his seat. He was wearing a thick Parka jacket with a fur-trimmed hood. 'Quick house call.'

'My uncle told me Gouch hasn't been back to work. He won't be at the flat, they don't think he's back in the city,' said Javon.

Skender gestured under the seat. 'So, we'll leave him a present. Use that.'

Javon sighed and took a look. There were two plastic bottles of liquid. He snatched one up and scanned the label – a cheap shop-brand lemonade – though he didn't need to open the bottle to confirm that it wasn't a fizzy drink inside, because he'd got a faint whiff of petrol when he'd first sat in the car.

Javon put the bottle down. 'Nah, man. No way.'

Skender gave him a brooding stare. 'Come on, it won't take long.'

Javon shook his head. 'Nah, man, I'm not up for this. I've already been here, and the neighbour is a right nosy tosser. I bet he's already clocked us sitting here.'

Timur turned in his seat and laughed. 'So, do *his* place too.'

'We need to send a message here, Javon. This can be like your… initiation trial, if you like,' said Skender.

'Nah, I just wanted my wedge back. This… this is some next-level shit. What if someone is in there?' asked Javon.

'We can all see the place is in darkness. Stop being such a baby,' said Timur.

Javon, about to tell the big man to do it himself, froze when Skender held up his phone and he saw the photo on the screen – a young black girl with braided hair in a big top knot, beaming and waving.

'What are you doing?' asked Javon. 'My sister is seventeen, man.'

Skender started scrolling through more photos, tongue clenched between his teeth as he leered at the shots.

Skender grinned. 'I've just messaged her, told her I'm your new friend. I've asked if she wants to meet up sometime.'

Javon zipped up his hoody. 'Don't *do* that.' With that, he yanked his hood over his cap, snatched up a bottle and stepped out of the car.

He closed the door and fast-walked across the car park, tilting his cap over his face and hiding the bottle under his arm. In the window of the bottom flat, Javon could see into the kitchen, and the elderly fella with the fat nose was busy making a cup of tea. Javon jogged past his window and made his way to the building's entrance, then glanced back at the Golf, seeing the shadowy figures watching. He shot the pair a look of contempt and slipped into the entrance.

'Well, his sister would defend him,' said Janette.

'I'm not saying it is the truth, but she genuinely believed it, Jan,' said Mark.

'It's true,' confirmed Alex, 'she seemed candid to me.'

'The guy was a demented psychopath,' said Janette.

Alex sighed. 'She admitted he was violent and unpredictable. But the guy was a grieving widower. And he lost his two daughters.'

'And we antagonised him,' Mark put in.

'We all saw his Land Rover that day,' muttered Ben, studying the candle.

Janette laughed without humour. 'So, you plan to rock up and blatantly ask him if he's now prepared to chat about this. What's your thinking here? That he wants to get all this off his chest? That now he'll suddenly have a conscience? Good luck with that.'

Mark pulled the wax jacket about him and shivered. 'Did we see him, though? The police found no evidence.'

'Jesus, what is this, the new Freddy Killner fan club?' said Ben.

'I know everyone always believed he was involved, but perhaps there was no proof because he didn't do anything,' said Alex.

Gavin, who'd been standing away from the group, hands stuck deep in his pockets, stepped forward. 'Have you got anything else to tell us, Clayton?'

Alex took a deep breath and ignored Gavin's question. 'Look, I know what happened was on me. I've had to live with that. I've blamed myself every day.'

Gavin clenched both fists and Mark stepped in front of him and said, 'Let's just talk, Gav. If we're honest, are any of us blameless? I mean, technically, Sheryl wouldn't have even been up here if you hadn't—'

'Stop there. You can fuck right off, Corkscrew!' said Gavin.

'God, stop calling me that, my name is Mark.'

'No, he's right, Gavin,' said Janette, 'Sheryl didn't even want to go that day. She said to leave you boys to it. Yet I convinced her. I told her it would be a right laugh... so, there... I'm guilty too. Her mum even blamed me.'

'No, she didn't, Jan,' said Ben, softly, 'plus it was my idea to go back to the camp. I insisted.'

'We voted, Ben,' said Gavin.

'Not to mention we should have gone for help the very moment we lost her,' said Janette.

Gavin shook his head and prodded an aggressive finger at Alex. 'No, he is the one that should feel guilty. Not me. Not you, Jan. Not any of us.'

'Even so, I do,' said Janette.

Javon scanned the hallway for signs of life or signs of any CCTV. Even the doorbells had cameras built in these days. You had to keep your wits about you. As he reached Gavin's flat, he peered inside the letterbox. A sudden thought occurred to him – what if he'd come back from Kent? What if he was home? Setting the place ablaze was one thing, but if he was inside – that changed everything. That wasn't a path he intended to go down. He gave it a few seconds. It was quiet inside the flat and dark, too. He took one last check around him, undid the lid and started pouring the liquid into the letterbox, squeezing the bottle as he did. Javon left enough to dribble a decent amount down the inside of the door and around the letterbox, then he used his plastic lighter with the cannabis leaf emblem to set the blaze. A whoosh of flames jetted up from inside and he felt an instant heat blast from the fire. Then he ran.

Gavin stood statue-still as he listened to Alex explain everything about his reoccurring memory dreams, that he claimed had been ruining his life, and destroying his marriage, and how he'd become too anxious to sleep, fearing these realistic dreams that were haunting his mind. He could no longer bear revisiting the events from '88.

It amazed Gavin at how long he was able to hold back his laughter. Did Clayton think he was the only one having bad dreams? *Join the club, you dozy wanker.*

Gavin threw back his head and laughed. 'Right, this all makes perfect sense now. This selfish prick is only back for himself. This has nothing to do with Sheryl or any of us. So, Clayton, is this your therapist's idea or something? Do you need some closure so you can get a lovely night's sleep?'

Alex stiffened and held his head up. 'I don't have a therapist.'

Gavin snorted. 'Well, you need one. We all will at this rate.'

'I'm back here for Sheryl. For all of us,' said Alex, in a matter-of-fact tone.

'You're thirty years too late,' said Gavin, his tone condescending.

Alex turned away from Gavin and focussed on Janette. 'I have something that I need to share with you all.'

'Are you gonna admit that you pushed her?' asked Gavin.

'Just shut up, Gavin,' said Janette.

'It's about the other boy that helped me,' said Alex.

Zara flicked her eyes open and blearily gazed about the gloomy living room. The first thing she did was check her phone to see if Gavin had been in touch, and her heart sunk when she saw he hadn't. She couldn't blame him, of course, he'd warned her enough times, and she'd let him down every single time. This time would be different though. She had pined for Gavin and wanted him back with her.

The last of Zara's gear lay on the table. One last hit tonight, then after that, she'd be heading back to the rehabilitation centre faster than you could yell, 'Cold chuffing turkey.' She closed her eyes and drifted away again, but just before the darkness took her, she thought she could smell something burning.

After Alex told the group about Leo's involvement in the setup, there was a moment of silence whilst they processed the information.

Mark sucked on his vape, frowning.

Ben appeared puzzled.

Janette gazed at him, expressionless.

Gavin threw him a poisonous glare.

Alex lowered his head. 'I should have told the police about him. I know that now.'

'And why didn't you?' asked Janette.

Alex rubbed the back of his neck. 'Leo was older than me. He convinced me not to tell anybody. He said I'd get him into trouble.'

'Where is he now?' asked Mark.

'I don't know. But I think I've found his twin, in Dorset... but Leo never met Sheryl, I can't understand why he would have—' Alex left the sentence unfinished and frowned, remembering his conversation with Leo on that hill slope. Did he dislike Sheryl that much? Enough to do something stupid? He always seemed more... sinister, in his dreams than he was in Alex's memory. Had he been so seduced by the older boy back then that he was blind to the nasty individual he really was? It had been a constant thought in his mind of late. Well, ever since those dreams started. It was one of the reasons that had forced him to return to Kent and face all of this.

'Is there a chance that Leo knows something? Perhaps he saw Killner that day?' asked Mark.

Gavin stepped towards Alex, shaking his head and smiling darkly. His lunge was lightning fast – he grabbed Alex by the jacket and shoved him backwards until he was leaning over the edge of the chalk drop. Alex's boot hit a jar, and he heard the faint smash of glass as it landed below. Alex peered into the murkiness behind him, and then, in an unshaken and deliberate manner, he turned his attention back to Gavin. He left his arms at his side, and somehow he kept composed. In fact, he wasn't in the least bit afraid.

'I should drop you over the side and we can see if *you* survive. Shall we put that to the test?'

Mark and Ben flanked Gavin; approaching as though attempting to calm an escaped, wild animal.

'Gav, don't be stupid,' said Ben.

'Don't be a dickhead,' added Mark.

Alex could feel the chalk crumbling under his boots and hear it tumbling down into the gloom. 'Only one way to find out. Just let go, Gavin.'

'Don't you dare!' hollered Janette.

Alex fixed his eyes on Gavin's, and his anger shifted to a look of bewilderment. Gavin hadn't expected Alex to show such resilience to his threat. And Alex believed it was just that – a threat.

Ben edged closer and risked placing a gentle hand on Gavin's shoulder. 'This isn't the way. Come on, Gav, mate.'

'Was that boy involved?' growled Gavin.

'I don't know... but Leo had no reason to hurt her. He never even met her,' said Alex.

Gavin shoved harder. 'We can't believe anything you say, Clayton.'

Janette, her voice stern and sharp, said, 'If you drop him, Gavin Gouch, I will throw you over the side with him.'

Gavin gritted his teeth. 'Why are you sticking up for him? You of all people, Jan.'

'You're standing on her photo. Get off it. Now!' she said.

Gavin's face dropped, and he peered down to see his trainer was right on Sheryl's face. He gasped and stepped back, as though he'd just established that he was standing on a sacred burial ground. Ben and Mark grabbed at the pair and dragged them away from the edge.

Janette snatched up the photo and wiped the trainer tread from it. 'We're leaving.'

Thirty-eight

Timur gunned the Golf. Javon noticed the pair had been rubbing their noses and judging by the way they were fidgeting and energised, he assumed that whilst he was setting the fire, they had been on the sniff. *Tight, sneaky goons,* he thought. They hadn't even offered him a quick cheeky bang to motivate him.

Javon gazed outside and could make out they were speeding down Middleton Boulevard. 'Can you drop me somewhere near Bulwell?'

'Is that where your sister is?' asked Skender.

Javon chewed his lower lip. 'Look, I need to get home and change. You should slow down, man.'

Skender grinned. 'Yeah, you should. We have a potential murderer in the back, Tim.'

Timur cackled. 'Good point.' Though he increased the car's speed.

Javon didn't speak, he just gawped at Skender in disbelief.

'Did I forget to mention that Gavin's girlfriend lived there? Junkie slut. Was she home, by the way?' asked Skender.

Javon's head became woozy. His chest tightened, and he struggled to breathe. Was Skender winding him up?

Skender was laughing like a maniac. 'I bet the silly bitch was blitzed. I doubt she even noticed the inferno surrounding her until her skin started peeling off.' Skender stopped laughing, pulled a face as though in pain, and placed a hand on his injury. 'Ow, balls.'

Javon knew Skender wasn't lying. He'd done him over, and there was no way he was taking this. He didn't care who these dick-heads thought they were – they were in for a shock.

Skender's phone beeped, and he read his message with an eager grin. 'You'll have to put in a kind word for me, Jav. Little sis is playing hard to get. She doesn't believe we're friends. Would you text her? Tell her I'm your new pal. Hey, can we take a photo together? We'll have to capture my good side, though.'

Anger rose inside Javon as he'd never experienced before, and he was almost shaking with rage. What was wrong with this crackpot? They were fleeing a crime at top speed, and this wacko was trying to hit it off with his kid sister.

'We can pick her up. I'll take you all out for some nice food. What do you say, Jav?'

Javon didn't reply. His sister meant the world to him; he would rather die than let these sickos even look at her, let alone try it on with her.

Skender winked at Javon. 'Does she like Caribbean chicken? I know a wicked little place, that does the best chicken in the city. You have to taste it to believe it.'

'What?' said Javon, incredulously.

'I'll ask her,' said Skender.

Before he even knew what he was doing, Javon unscrewed the lid to the second bottle of petrol and pushed it under Skender's seat.

Both men in the front sniffed the air.

'Eh, is that petrol?' asked Timur.

Javon used his foot to nudge the bottle further under. 'I already said, I need to change my gear.'

'Check that bottle isn't leaking over the floor,' asked Skender, too busy texting away to pay much heed.

Timur hit the brakes and waved his fist at another driver, shouted abuse in his native language, before racing off again.

Javon used the distraction to slip out his lighter. He could hear Skender sniffing in the darkness, though he couldn't tell if it was because of the drugs or the heavy petrol stench that was acrid in the air.

'It stinks,' complained Skender, 'it must be leaking from somewhere.'

Timur nodded in agreement. 'Let's check. I'll pull over up here.'

Javon checked his seatbelt and took a deep breath. He'd only get one chance at this. Neither Skender nor Timur were wearing their seatbelts.

Skender's face lit up with amusement. 'Yeah. Laughing emoji. I think she likes me,' he sang.

Javon reached down, flicked on the flame and ignited the fuel.

Everything that followed played out in surreal slow motion. Skender screamed as a surge of flames shot up from underneath his seat, and he went berserk, bouncing around the seat like a madman. His trainers were also alight.

Timur turned and watched in wide-eyed astonishment, his mouth fixed in a big O shape. Then the car started spinning and Javon sat rigid as he anticipated the impact.

The collision jarred and rocked him; glass showered him.

Javon blinked, wondering if he'd been knocked unconscious for a short time. He wasn't in any pain, but his vision swam in a psychedelic whirl of glaring colours.

Skender's body was halfway through the smashed windscreen, and the front half of him lay across the bonnet, leaving his twisted legs dangling over the dashboard. Timur was bleeding from a horrendous head wound, and the impact had crushed him against the steering wheel. Javon then realised that some of Timur's ribs were protruding from his side – poking right through his padded leather jacket.

Javon dived for the door behind the driver's seat – but it didn't budge. He then comprehended that the car was wedged against a wall, so he shuffled across the seat to the other door.

Timur awoke, screeched in pain, thrashed about, and no longer sounded like an intimidating beast of a man. He sounded like a scared child.

Javon got out of the Golf and sprinted out from under the bridge where the car had ended its final journey.

Javon knew he'd need to leave the city tonight.

When they reached the village of Hollingbourne, Mark turned his phone's silent mode off and the screen sprung to life. Ten missed calls, all from Daan. He groaned.

Janette turned off the light she'd had strapped to her head and placed it in her rucksack.

Ben pointed to a pub across the road. 'Do we have time, Jan?'

Janette checked the time. 'No, he'll be here soon.'

Mark called Daan back. As he did, he watched as Alex paced along the path. He was acting oddly and was muttering to himself.

'Marko, thank God,' came Daan's voice.

'Are you OK? What's the drama?' asked Mark.

Daan snivelled. 'It's over. She's had me, Marko. She's—' He didn't finish. Mark could hear him sobbing.

Gavin leaned against a van and was reading something on his phone, a frown creasing his forehead.

'The bitch somehow cleaned me out. Took my life savings. I'm ruined,' said Daan.

'Daan, calm down, we'll sort this,' said Mark, in a placating tone.

'She left me a note, saying she knows I'm a cheat and a liar. She's taken two hundred thousand euros, Marko. Disappeared with some American arsehole called Laurence,' gabbled Daan.

Mark was about to respond when he noticed Alex fast walking towards Gavin – then, to the surprise of all present, he lunged at him with such a sudden burst of violent anger, that Mark nearly dropped his phone.

Alex wedged his forearm against Gavin's neck. 'Just for your information, Gavin. I never forgot. I never gave up looking. Just because I wasn't here.'

Mark saw the whites of Gavin's eyes and he was staring at Alex as though seeing him for the first time. Mark had to admit, the rage emanating from Alex was nerve-wracking. Daan cried and mumbled in French, but he was intent on hearing Alex's words, so blocked his manager's voice out.

Alex applied more pressure. 'My nan forced me to flee town after she found out what you lot did to me in Gallows Hill Woods. I had no choice.'

'Marko, are you there?' called Daan.

Mark, like all of them, was now transfixed on the scene in front of them.

'Get off me,' growled Gavin.

'What have *you* done, Gavin?' Alex glanced at Janette. 'What have any of you done to help find her? Because I can guarantee you this – not nearly as much as I have!' he shouted. 'You have no idea. None.' With that, Alex let go of Gavin and turned on Ben and gave him a challenging stare. Ben shrunk away from the smaller man, unable to even meet his gaze.

Alex took a deep breath, adjusted his jacket and relaxed. 'I think this is all the therapy I need. To face my demons.'

'So, showing your true colours at last,' muttered Gavin.

Alex shot Gavin a curious grin, turned on his heels and trudged over the road, and towards the pub.

'He's nuts,' spat Gavin.

Mark put his phone back to his ear. 'I'll call you back in ten, Daan.' His manager protested, but Mark switched him off.

Gavin looked startled and embarrassed, and Mark was certain he wouldn't be able to stand for that degree of humiliation. He half expected Gavin to race into the pub and start throwing punches. But he didn't.

'Um, the taxi is here,' said Janette.

Mark thought about joining Alex, but considered he needed time to calm down.

Gavin sat in the back of the people carrier. There was space in the middle, but he'd opted to sit away from everyone. He was so annoyed with himself. How could he have let Clayton mug him off like that? He felt a total prize prat, though he had to admit to himself, Clayton's rage had caught him off guard. But it wouldn't happen next time. When they next met, he'd show that muppet who he was dealing with. He would pay. Now he was more convinced than ever – Alex Clayton was somehow involved in Sheryl's disappearance. The bloke was a maniac.

Gavin's phone rang, and he guessed it would be Zara calling yet again. Roland's landline flashed up and Gavin's heart skipped a beat. A nasty sensation, like a twisting pain, hit his stomach as he answered. 'Hi, Roland, what's up?'

Roland didn't speak straight away. He was breathing heavily. Gavin heard him swallow hard. 'I'm glad you picked up, lad.'

Gavin could tell by his neighbour's cracked voice it would not be good news. 'Is… everything, OK, Roland?'

'I'm so sorry, lad. It's awful news. Someone started a fire… and… I'm sorry. I don't know what to—' Roland's voice faded.

Tears were streaming down Gavin's face. 'No, please no. Don't say it… please. No.'

'The firefighters arrived fast. They did everything they could… but she'd taken in lots of smoke. I'm so sorry. She's gone, lad. They couldn't bring her back.'

Gavin let the phone fall from his hand. 'Stop the car! Stop. Now.'

The taxi came to a sudden halt and Gavin leapt from the vehicle. He screamed as he sprinted up the lane. 'What did I do?' he bellowed, over and over, then dropped to his knees and pounded the road with his fists. He didn't stop punching until Ben and Janette pulled him up from the road and embraced him.

Thirty-nine

Kayla passed Ben two steaming mugs of tea. 'What's going on?'

'Gavin's staying here tonight. Something happened earlier and I'm not leaving him alone.'

Ben assumed Kayla would object, but she'd perhaps grasped something bad had happened, because she looked more concerned than annoyed. 'Let me know if he needs anything. I'll make up the guest bed.'

Ben kissed her on the forehead. 'Thanks, hun.'

'Is this about… Sheryl?'

'I'm not sure what's going on.'

Gavin was sitting on a low wall that was positioned under two Japanese maple trees. He was holding one of the red leaves in his hand, studying it.

'Here, Gav. Nice warm cuppa. You left your phone in the cab. It's in the kitchen,' said Ben.

Gavin took the mug and smiled his thanks. 'Nice garden lights.'

Ben smiled. 'Cheers. Installed them all myself.'

'This garden is impressive.'

'I need to pick up some leaves. Though I don't mind the maples floating about.' Ben sipped his tea. 'So, want to tell me what that call was about?'

Gavin gazed into his cup. It was a good two minutes before he responded. 'A year ago, I had it all. I was so happy. Then just like that… it all turned to crap. In an instant.'

Ben put a hand on Gavin's shoulder.

'She was six months old when we got together. Isabella… Zara's daughter. She even called me Daddy, Ben. I was like her real dad. I treated her like she was my own.' Gavin wiped his eyes, but more tears came. 'The night it happened, Zara's shift had been a nightmare. She was a nurse, I'm not sure if I told you that? Anyway, she came back from work and the babysitter, Trish, left. Zara only drank a couple of glasses of wine, but she was so shattered; she drifted off for a moment.' Gavin sipped his tea and began coughing. 'Before she zoned out, Zara said Isabella had wanted to go outside to play ball. The baby gate wasn't closed properly, and she'd recently worked out how to flip the latch if it wasn't clipped down properly. So she went outside to the front garden to find her ball, and it rolled away from her. It bounced out through the gate and into the road—' Gavin started sobbing.

Ben slapped his hand over his mouth. 'Gav, no.'

'The driver was just a factory worker returning home from his shift. He didn't have a chance of stopping. A neighbour said she just stepped straight—' Gavin wept. 'Just three. It's not fair, Ben. How is that fair?'

Ben put his arm around Gavin and pulled him into a firm embrace. 'Why didn't you tell me?'

Gavin sniffed and wiped his nose. 'I came here to get away, and to find something else to focus on. I tried, Ben. I tried so hard to fix her... but she always started again.'

'Started?'

'Booze, ketamine and prescription drugs at first. But then she met that scumbag... and he introduced her to smack.'

'The Skender guy?'

Gavin nodded and grunted.

'That's why you ripped him off. It was about revenge.'

'It was the ultimate escape for her, and it became all she lived for. All she cared about.'

Ben shook his head. 'God, I'm so sorry. I had no idea.'

'She's dead, Ben. They fire-bombed my flat last night.'

Ben stood up and dropped his mug; it smashed amongst the maple leaves.

'And it's all my fault. I left her there alone and now she's dead.'

Ben tried to speak but fumbled to find any words in response.

'But if I'm honest, Zara died the day her daughter walked in front of that car. She would never have forgiven herself.'

'I'll get us a proper drink,' were all the words Ben could manage.

When Ben nipped inside to retrieve the Jack Daniel's and two tumblers, Kayla gave him a quizzical and concerned look. 'You look rather peaky, Ben. What's wrong?'

Ben told his wife about Zara and the fire. For obvious reasons, he neglected to tell her about the part involving the drug dealers, who had most likely set the blaze in retaliation for Gavin's foolish undertakings. Ben knew with absolute certainty that men prepared to take such actions wouldn't stop there. Gavin had to go.

Janette and Peanuts sat in the back of Alex's Jeep. She had phoned in sick this morning, as she felt she needed to be part of this. She'd expected Alex to apologise for his actions the previous night, but he'd yet to bring it up. He probably thought his behaviour was justified, and maybe it was. Mark, slouched in the passenger seat, had been chatting about how he'd been talking to his manager until the early hours, doing his best to convince him not to kill himself. Apparently, the man had serious sex and drug addictions, and his hot French wife had taken flight with all his money. Not the usual Monday morning chit-chat Janette was accustomed to. 'Some greedy-guts ate all the Hobnobs,' was about as scandalous as it got in the office. Her co-workers were about as interesting as watching a fat cat snooze after its breakfast.

'So, any news on Gavin, Jan?' asked Mark.

'No, he went home with Ben.'

Mark scratched his stubble. 'Must have been pretty serious.'

'Alex, can I ask you something?' said Janette.

Alex nodded.

'Last night, those things you said when you were angry. What did you mean?'

Alex cleared his throat. 'I made a lot of enquiries, and I spent years searching social media for clues. Plus news reports, forums, and newspapers. I also hired a detective agency to search for Adrian Denton too.'

'You did?' asked Janette, unable to keep the surprise from her voice.

'They thought they had tracked him to an address in Glasgow, but it turned out to be a false lead.'

Janette hadn't expected to learn that Alex had carried out his own investigations. Eileen had hired people too; the police had searched far and wide; but yet, Sheryl's estranged father was never located. He was like a ghost. They had been confident that Adrian Denton would have come forward in the early days, but he didn't.

Janette could see Alex's eyes in the interior mirror, and he focussed on her.

'Gavin made it sound like I'd just run away and forgot, and that isn't what happened. I can promise you that,' said Alex.

Mark sighed. 'We all had to move on, but that doesn't mean any of us stopped caring.'

Alex nodded, then spoke in an upbeat voice. 'But my search for answers led me back to Scotland, and that's where I met my wife and found my new life. Funny how things turn out.'

They drove in silence for a while, then Janette spoke. 'Do you really believe Adrian Denton was involved, Alex?'

'I read an article in a local paper, that an elderly resident reported seeing a beige Austin Allegro in Hollingbourne. The day before Sheryl went missing.'

'I didn't read that,' said Janette.

'So?' asked Mark.

'That was the crappy car Sheryl's dad drove,' said Janette.

'I know, it could just be a coincidence, but the same resident confirmed that they'd not seen that car in the village before, and a middle-aged man was sitting inside for some time,' said Alex.

Janette pondered on this information. How was she just hearing this for the first time? She wondered if Eileen knew.

'And there was something else I read that stuck in my mind,' said Alex.

'Go on,' said Janette.

'In the mid-eighties, Adrian was a regular at Killner's cider shed. They knew each other,' said Alex.

'A lot of people's dads were regulars there,' said Janette.

'The newspaper's source was a police officer who frequented the shop, and he was under the impression that Adrian and Killner were pals. He spent a fair bit of time in the shack, sampling the wares and chewing the fat with Killner.'

Ben watched from the doorway as Gavin and his son laughed together. To his astonishment, Gavin seemed in a buoyant mood, plus he'd also shaved and tidied up his hair.

Gavin whispered something to Ryan that had him sniggering.

'More coffee, Gavin?' asked Kayla, coffee pot already poised.

Gavin lifted his cup. 'Mmm, please. This omelette is the best, Kayla. Seriously, it's ace.'

Kayla poured the coffee. 'That's nice of you to say. Now, are you certain you don't need some cream on those grazes?'

Gavin examined his knuckles. 'Well, I guess it wouldn't hurt. Cheers.'

Ryan stuffed in a mouthful of food. 'You should hear some of Gav's stories, Mum. About what he got up to with Dad.'

'I'm not sure I want to know,' said Kayla.

Ryan laughed. 'They did a quality prank with one lad at school, where they would swap all his clothes during P.E. Replacing them all with exact replicas from lost property.'

Kayla held up her hand. 'Yep, your father has told me. Several times. Clothes several sizes too small.'

'His face was always a picture. Silly sod never did cotton on to what was going on,' chuckled Gavin.

'So funny,' said Ryan.

'Yeah,' said Ben, crossing his arms.

Ryan sniggered. 'And the time you two jumped into the ice-cream van, and Gavin climbed under the pump.'

Ben smiled thinly. 'Yeah, I remember that too.'

Ryan chewed on a slice of toast. 'The ice-cream hadn't set, Mum, and it exploded over Gavin's face!'

Gavin grinned. 'Face? I got covered in the milk-like goo! We were on a lunch break, so I had to return to school in that sticky state.'

Ben sighed. He'd already told his son both stories, though he'd barely listened. Though coming from Gavin, it was clearly hilarious. Ben felt privileged to get a hello out of his son, let alone a full-on belly laugh. Although Gavin had the same mental age as Ryan, so he knew he shouldn't feel too narked by it. The ice-cream incident had been hilarious though; Gavin's wide-eyed, shocked expression when that liquid blasted into his face, wasn't something he'd ever forget.

Ben walked into the dining room and kissed Kayla.

'Morning Foxy-Mister,' she whispered.

'You ready to get a wiggle on, Gav. I've got to get to work. I'll drop you at your mum's place,' said Ben.

'I can take him if you don't have time,' suggested Kayla.

'No!' said Ben, much more urgently than he intended. 'I mean, it's fine. I'm heading that way,' lied Ben. He hadn't slept a wink last night. He'd checked the CCTV several times during the early hours. The sooner Gouch was out of his family's orbit, the better.

A care worker, a short lady, with a high forehead and wearing a pair of thick-lensed glasses, led Janette, Mark and Alex around to the rear of the huge residential complex. They walked across a grassy garden area, set out with picnic-style tables and potted bay trees. The building itself was a modern, two-storey development that had small balconies on each dwelling.

Janette felt her whole body quiver; her throat became dry and her heart was fluttering frantically.

'This way,' said the care worker, 'Fredrick likes to spend the majority of his time down here. He's not had any visitors for such a long time.'

They followed the lady to a low fence where a man sat in a wheelchair, facing out to the sea.

'Morning Fredrick, you have visitors,' she said, in an over-the-top, chirpy tone. There was no response. The care worker peered down to Peanuts, then up to Janette. 'Please keep the dog on a lead,' then turning to Alex said, 'good luck.' With that, she tottered off to deal with an elderly lady who was gazing aimlessly around the garden with a puzzled smile.

The trio stared at the back of Fredrick's head for several moments before Alex and Janette stepped forward so they were visible to him. Fredrick didn't seem to notice them. Instead, he stared, dead-eyed, at the serene sea view.

Janette guessed he was in his late seventies; he had a thick mass of wild, white hair, and his stony face was heavily lined and wrinkled, but despite his age, he was still an intimidating figure. He had on a threadbare green cardigan, and Janette could make out some nasty scarring on his right hand.

Alex cleared his throat. 'You don't know me, but you will remember me. For what I did on your farm. For setting the fire… and what happened with your dog.'

Janette shook her head in annoyance. No response, not even a flicker or twitch.

Seagulls squalled, and the waves washed against the shingle beach.

Alex kept trying. 'First, I want to apologise for what I did. And I'd like to say how truly sorry I am about your family. That was a terrible thing to have to deal with.'

Janette stepped forward. 'And we want to ask you straight out to your face. Do you know what happened to Sheryl Denton?'

Still not even a glimmer of acknowledgement from the man.

'Forget it, Alex,' Janette tapped her temple, 'nobody is home.'

Alex sighed and placed his business card on Fredrick's lap.

Janette let out an impatient snort. 'This is your chance, Mr Killner. The chance to tell the truth at long last.'

Fredrick's arm fell to the side of the wheelchair, Peanuts sniffed his hand. To Janette's surprise, Fredrick reached over to the dog and rubbed her ear. Janette curled her lip in anger and yanked her dog back by her collar. She could tell the action annoyed Alex, but she couldn't care less, because this prick wasn't prepared to give them anything. She hated him, and if there'd been no fence, she would have been quite happy to push the ugly shit-stain onto the beach and leave him down there for the tide to claim him. As far as she was concerned, he was still prime suspect number one, and if he hadn't been involved, why did he go into hiding and abandon his farm?

Janette glanced at Mark, who was standing back from them, hands in his pockets and watching them. His shoulders slumped, and he appeared crestfallen.

Alex leant on the fence and looked out to sea. 'This is a pleasant spot. I can see why you spend your time here. We spoke to your sister, Veronica. She's a nice lady. It's a gorgeous house they've built there.'

Janette noticed the tiniest twitch on Fredrick's cracked lips at the mention of his sister, and for a moment she pondered on Alex's words – was there a disguised threat in those words? No, unlikely.

Alex sighed again. 'Well, you have my card. I've said what I came to say.'

Alex nodded at Janette, and they turned to leave.

'You deserved everything you got! I should have killed you,' said Fredrick, with a deep, gruff voice.

Janette froze, her blood ran ice cold.

They got no further response from Fredrick Killner that day.

Forty

Gavin finished up in the toilet and studied the family photos in the hallway. Ben and Kayla on their wedding day, a canvas print of the pair with their children; baby portraits, family days out; and a decorative heart-shaped wooden plaque marked with the words: *And they all lived happily ever after.* Gavin couldn't help but feel envious of his friend. He had it all. Good kids, stunning home and a decent wife. His own life was a total shambles in comparison. He was a middle-aged man whose life had no direction or stability, and he didn't have anything or anyone. His life was just filled with loss, regret and hatred.

Janette threw a handful of pebbles into the sea. Peanuts, now off the lead, was running along the beach like a lunatic, and barking at fat seagulls. She'd plunged in the sea several times and Janette hoped, for his sake, that Alex had some towels in his car. Alex and Mark were sitting on the pebbles eating cod and chips. Janette had declined lunch, because she wasn't much of a chip lover and couldn't face food after the encounter with that vile pig. She'd been praying they'd find some answers today, but if she was truly honest with herself, she knew the visit would be unsuccessful and disturbing.

'I got you a coffee, Jan,' said Alex.

Janette sat next to them and took the coffee, smiling her thanks. She glanced at Mark, who was picking at the food like he was being forced to eat fox crap. Peanuts came skidding over, spotted the food, sat down and started whimpering.

Janette pinched one of Mark's chips and tossed it to her dog. 'Sorry, she's a greedy beast, this one.'

Mark let out a long, heavy sigh. 'Can I tell you two something? It's important.'

Alex squeezed a sachet of brown sauce onto his chips and nodded.

The seagulls tried to return, but were soon chased away by the dog.

Janette frowned and nodded. 'What?'

'The Doberman on the farm. It wasn't Gavin that killed it. It was me.'

There was a moment of tense silence before Mark continued. 'Gavin froze when the dog caught up with us. He dropped the pitchfork, and the dog locked onto his arm. I picked it up.' Mark tossed Peanuts a generous chunk of fish. 'I hit her in the face and she let go of Gavin. Then it was all a bit of a blur… but the dog ended up yelping on the floor. It was horrific. I've never forgotten it.'

'OK,' said Janette. She didn't know what else to say.

'I think Gavin could tell I was mortified by what I had done. When we caught up with Ben, he made out he'd done the deed, and it was an unspoken secret. We both never mentioned it again. I'll say this for Gouch, he's loyal.'

Janette had given Gavin some major shit over that dog's death, and even years later, when they'd been going out, she'd brought it up several times, yet he'd never told her the truth. Not even hinted at it. He'd held that secret back, despite how bad it made him look.

'We shouldn't have even been on his land,' said Mark.

Janette shook her head. 'No.'

Mark laughed, but there was no humour in it. 'My kids have been desperate to get a dog, and I've had it in the neck so many times, but I've always firmly refused. I even had to lie and say I'm allergic. Every time I glance at a dog, any dog, I think of that day, and hear that Doberman's cries of pain.'

'You panicked, Mark. You were protecting yourself,' said Alex.

Mark's face darkened. 'So, what, you think I'm being ridiculous? Still fretting over this all these years later?'

'No,' said Janette, her voice flat and stern. 'It's not ridiculous. Not in the slightest.'

Mark focussed on Alex. 'I won't deny it, your visit kinda blew my world apart. I mean, I tried to appear unfazed when we met, but it brought all these messed-up memories flooding right back with real intensity. I always felt responsible for what happened. That somehow, by killing his dog, I started the chain of events that led to that mad arsehole coming after us… led to Sheryl… I guess that's why I'm keen to know if Killner is innocent. At least if he is, I might stop kicking myself over all this.'

Alex screwed up his chip paper and his shoulders slumped. 'Yeah, well, I was the one that let go of her hand.' With that, he got up and threw his chips in a nearby bin.

'This was the place,' said Ben.

'Thanks for the lift, and for last night,' said Gavin. He opened the car's door, then hesitated. 'What do you make of his story about the Canadian boy?'

Ben shrugged. 'Seems weird he's only just mentioned it.'

'I think it's total crap.'

'Why would he make that up?'

Gavin's eyes narrowed. 'I dunno, but he's hiding something, and I'll find out. Even if I have to beat the truth out of him. I know he's involved. Somehow.'

Gavin got out. Ben watched Gavin climb the gate and head into Colt Wood, taking the same route they had the night the police chased them. Just seeing Gavin disappear into the trees was a relief. His old friend was a ticking time bomb, and when Gavin exploded, he was going to make one hell of a mess, and Ben had no intention of being hit by the shrapnel.

Natalie had told her partner she was taking some time off, so she could recharge her batteries and recover from a stomach upset. Rhona had told her to enjoy a couple of days off to relax, since she'd earned it, telling her she'd hold the fort and would only contact her if she deemed it essential. The real reason was so Natalie could visit Olivia in Essex. She just hoped Olivia was still living at the address they'd found. Natalie had tried to obtain her number, but she was listed ex-directory, which at least indicated Alex's aunt was still associated with the address. Hannah had insisted she borrow their car, rather than taking the train. Natalie had little need for a car, as most of her business was conducted in Edinburgh and she was happy to use public transport. Plus, Alex always drove everywhere else.

Hannah gave her the keys to the white BMW Gran Coupé that sat on their gravel driveway. The vehicle was freshly polished, and Natalie accepted the keys with a nervous grin.

'Evan's golf clubs are in the boot, you can drop those fricking things off on your travels. Or use one to knock some ruddy sense into your fella's heid.'

Natalie grinned. 'Aye, I might just do that. Are you sure Evan's OK with me taking it?'

'Aye, of course, he is. And it would be tough shite if he wisnae OK with it. It's my car too, hen.'

Natalie hugged her sister. 'Thanks, Hannah.'

'Drive safe.'

After dropping Janette back home, Mark had persuaded Alex into making a detour on his way to Dorset, so he could drop him at his parents' place in Hampshire. Mark had ignored Alex for most of the trip, as he'd been glued to his phone until they stopped at Fleet services, on the M3, for a quick cappuccino and a slice of cake, pit-stop. When they hit the motorway once again, Mark turned in his seat. 'What happened in Gallows Hill Wood?'

'You seriously don't know?' asked Alex.

'None of them spoke about what happened. But the rumours were that's where that creepy psychopath, Patrick, had his accident. The rest is an untold mystery.'

Alex felt his chest tighten, and he clasped the steering wheel. 'Well, they were going to kill me.'

Forty-one

Kent, Summer 1988

Alex's nan was calling him, and he contemplated hiding in the shed. He guessed *they* had arrived, and he didn't want to face them.

'Hey, over here,' said a voice.

Alex walked to the fence. He could see a set of eyes peering through a zigzagged crack.

'The police are here, Leo,' said Alex.

Leo's eyes blinked. 'You won't mention that I was there, will you?'

'Why?'

'I'm older than you. That means I'll take all the blame.'

'Leo, she's still missing, and it's all our fault,' said Alex.

'No, buddy, don't say that. We were just having a bit of a laugh. We can't blame ourselves.'

'What happened? Where did she go, Leo?'

Alex's nan appeared at the doorway, waving him in.

'Please don't tell,' pleaded Leo.

Alex followed his nan into the lounge. Two police officers sat on the sofa, drinking tea. One was female, young and pretty with ginger hair tied back in a bun, and the other a thin-lipped man with a dodgy comb-over haircut.

The female officer stood and flashed Alex a friendly grin. 'Hello, Alex. I'm PC Tefler. And this is Sergeant Gray. We need to talk to you about your friend, Sheryl Denton.'

The sergeant gave Alex a tight smile. 'Take a seat, lad.'

Alex sat down, gave the officers a timorous smile and instantly cracked. He sobbed as he told the officers everything. About the Monopoly money; the roadwork light that he stole and planted in the woods; and the spooky scarecrow he'd made in the days leading up to the hoax.

The officers nodded and took notes as he blubbered out his confession. Alex knew the search party must have found the light and the creepy figure he'd tied to the tree, so it was best to come clean. He'd stolen some clothes from a neighbour's garden to create the figure and stuffed twigs and foliage inside it to bulk it out. He'd also borrowed one of Eduardo's ninja hoods to make the head. In the light of day, the thing looked like a real mess, but at night, it was very frightening. When the gang had passed the spot, Alex had switched on the light and hurled it into the trees. Then he unhooked the rope to drop his dummy from its hiding place in the tree, so it was hanging by the neck, awaiting the group's return. But Alex hadn't accounted for the awful weather, or Freddy Killner being out stalking them for real.

'It was meant to be a joke,' said Alex. 'And now she's vanished!'

With Tefler taking the lead, the officers took turns to gun questions at him.

Did he actually see Mr Killner?

Why did they think Mr Killner was after them?

Did he see Sheryl fall from the chalk drop?

Did he see anyone else lurking about?

Was he certain he didn't tell anybody else about their trip?

By the time they'd finished with him, Alex was drained of energy. Sheryl was missing, and he was to blame.

Penny shot him a solemn and disappointed expression, and Alex sat slumped in the chair as the officers walked to the door. He knew he should inform them about Leo's part in this and almost did, but stopped himself.

Three days after Sheryl's disappearance, Alex's nan finally let him out of her sight, and he slipped out of the bungalow and made his way to the Brookacre estate. His heart sank when he saw the police roadblock and the cars queuing, as officers walked along with clipboards knocking on windows. One officer held up a poster. Alex couldn't see it, but knew it was Sheryl's face on that paper.

When he reached the post office, he froze and gawped at the window. They had removed the cats' posters and replaced them with a big missing person's notice – Sheryl's face gazed back at him. In the photo, she smiled – a carefree smile he'd seen so many times. Alex couldn't pull his gaze from it. He stood there a long time.

The tap on his shoulder made him jump, and he turned to find Ben standing there, shoulders slumped and eyeballs red, bloodshot, and wet with tears.

'Clayton,' said Ben.

'Ben,' said Alex.

'You coming to join the search party?'

Alex was reluctant to go anywhere with Ben, but nodded and followed him. How could he say no to that request?

Ben had been in a strange and morose mood as they headed into the woods. Alex didn't have a clue where they were going and when he'd questioned Ben, he'd told Alex that they were heading to a secret camp that Sheryl liked to hide in. When upset, she'd often hide out there, and she'd spent several days hanging around the den during the time her dad had gone away. But none of it rang true with Alex – why would she be hiding now? It made little sense.

They came to a metal gate with a large *'keep out'* sign on the front, and the pair climbed over it and headed into the dense woodland.

They'd walked for ten minutes when Alex felt a terrible worrying doubt that he shouldn't be here. That he should run whilst he had the chance, but like an obedient child, he followed Ben.

They reached a dilapidated tractor that had a web of vines around it. The roof was entangled with a layer of thick, dark-green ivy, and at the rear of the tractor, was a discarded trailer, its wooden planks black with damp-rot, moss and fungi.

Alex was studying the machinery when he realised he was alone. He scanned the surrounding trees, but Ben had gone.

He heard a thump – like wood hitting metal. Then he noticed Gavin, standing on the tractor's roof.

Gavin shot Alex a look of pure loathing.

'Hey, Gavin, what's up?' said Alex, stammering out the words.

Gavin jumped from the tractor, ran at Alex, and punched him in the stomach. Alex stumbled back, the wind taken out of him.

'You're dead, you shithead,' said Gavin, stepping forward. But he'd not expected the kick Alex spun at him, catching him in the shins. Gavin squealed and lunged at him. The pair started fighting. They traded aimless, weak punches and kicks, and Alex decided that Gavin was more useless at fighting than he was.

Gavin, apprehensive now, backed away. He'd not expected Alex to put up a fight.

Alex tried to kick him again and Gavin stepped away, his face pinched and angry. Then something wrapped around Alex's neck and he was dragged backwards and someone tried to strangle him.

Ben and Patrick emerged from the trees.

Alex clawed at whatever was around his neck, it was cutting into his skin and choking him.

Gavin stepped forward, now emboldened by the arrival of his backup. Ben was carrying a lump of wood. Patrick was brandishing a cut-throat style razor.

For a moment, Alex thought he was going to pass out – but his attacker shoved him to the ground and Alex gasped and gulped desperately for air. Alex rubbed his sore neck and glared at his assailant.

Shane gave him a wicked sneer, as he draped the rope over his shoulders, and picked up a curved woodsmen's axe which was stuck in the earth.

'Careful, he thinks he's the Karate Kid today,' said Gavin, waving his hands and chopping the air. 'Kii-ya!'

Alex's legs turned to jelly. 'What do you want?'

'Payback,' said Gavin, as a grin, full of threat, spread across his face.

Alex caught Ben's eye; unlike the rest of them, he appeared distraught and irresolute. He wasn't relishing in the scene like the other sickos, who watched Alex, smiling and silent now. Alex could hear his furious breathing as he stared icily at Shane, who nonchalantly swung the axe at his side whilst whistling.

Gavin wiped his nose and a tiny trickle of blood slid from one of his nostrils. 'They used to bring killers and paedos here, Clayton. In the old days, if a criminal escaped justice, the locals would march the culprit here, and hang them themselves. That's where the name Gallows comes from.'

Shane laughed. 'I've made you a special noose.'

'I haven't done anything,' cried Alex.

Gavin squared up to Alex. 'Time for your last test, Clayton. We'll give you one minute. Then we're coming for you. If you escape the woods, you pass. If we catch you, then—' Gavin pulled an imaginary rope about his neck and feigned choking.

Shane fingered the rope and grinned. 'You swing until you die.'

'And you'll join the rest of the lost souls that walk these woods,' said Gavin.

Alex turned to Ben, eyes pleading for help – but Ben averted his gaze, his expression despondent. Alex then realised something – Ben no longer called the shots.

'Tick Tock. We're already counting,' said Gavin, in a sing-song voice.

Alex sprinted into the trees.

Forty-two

Alex ran like crazy through the undergrowth. Stinging nettles attacked him, thorns slashed his legs; he snapped branches that blocked his way, jumped logs and fallen trees. He ran until his lungs were burning and shoved himself up against a tree to gather his thoughts and steady his breathing. The boys screamed, howled, cackled and shouted boisterously. The sounds seemed to come from every direction, and he felt surrounded.

Then the noises ceased and an eerie silence followed that was far worse than the rowdy outcries. Alex, lost now, had no clue which way to run. He took a few calming breaths and considered hiding. Maybe up a tall tree? Or perhaps he could burrow deep in some bushes, inside a hollow stump, or down a hole? But how long would they spend searching for him? They'd not give up that easily. If he made a dash for it, he might at least have a chance of reaching the exit. But would he be able to make it out? Unlikely, he thought… Gavin snatched away his option to hide as he appeared behind him. Alex bolted into the trees.

Alex skidded downward into a steep decline and grabbed at a couple of spindly trees to stop him from tumbling right down the slope. He stayed still and silent, and watched, praying that Gavin hadn't seen him hurry down here.

Gavin slowly peeked from the top and laughed, his face red and sweaty from exertion. He continued the pursuit.

Alex crouched down and fumbled at the base of a tree, placing his hand on a chalky rock the size of a tennis ball. As Gavin came for him, Alex launched the rock, and it bounced off Gavin's chest with a dull clomp. The impact did little in stopping Gavin; it just enraged him.

Gavin roared as he began running, desperate for revenge. He gained so much speed, it became impossible to control his descent. It was almost comical to watch, as Gavin sprinted, then fell, flipped over backwards, rolled twice, and still ended up back on his feet, as he continued at a wild pace downwards. Unable to stop himself now, Gavin careered straight past Alex in a kaleidoscopic twirl of limbs and ended his run by colliding with a fat tree stump. Gavin doubled over and let out a low, wailing cry. He fell sideways and a wet patch crept across the front of Gavin's beige cargo shorts.

At first, Alex assumed Gavin had wet himself on impact, but he was rolling around in sheer agony, teeth gritted. Gavin slid one hand down his shorts, and as he carefully removed that hand, he expelled a high-pitched scream, because his hand was slick with bright blood. Alex squirmed at the sight, and he gaped at the tree stump that had several severed, pointy shards protruding from it. Gavin must have impaled himself on one.

Gavin rolled around, kicking his legs. 'Aw. My balls! My fucking balls have exploded! Ahhh!'

Alex tried to block the image of Gavin's ruptured testicles, as he used some sprouting tree roots to haul himself from the ditch. He needed to move fast, as Gavin's screams of pain would soon attract the rest of the gang in this direction.

'You're dead, Clayton,' came Gavin's yell from below. 'I'll rip out your eyes!'

Alex pulled himself out of the ditch and spotted Shane making his way through the trees. Shane caught sight of Alex and momentarily stopped, gave a toothy grin, before thrusting the axe in the air. 'I've got him, lads! Over here. Quickly.' Shane pointed the axe towards Alex, as though he were leading a war charge. 'He's here. Hurry!' he thundered.

Alex made a break for it. The trees and bushes blurred as he raced deeper into the woodland. Shane's footsteps stomped behind as he gave chase. Alex tripped on a rock, lost his balance as he staggered forward. Another figure moved through the brush ahead of him, so he veered his direction away.

Alex felt queasy, sapped of energy, and his chest was burning, but he didn't stop pushing on; knew he couldn't quit. They wanted to kill him, he was sure of that much.

The terrain became rocky underfoot, and the land grew steeper with every step. He dared a glance behind, seeing Shane struggling to keep up now, his bulk slowing him. Alex spurred himself, his thighs and calf muscles working as er had to ever before. There were chalk-covered hills up in the

'd heard about the haunted quarry in Gallows and guessed that's

what he could see.

Alex found himself on a proper track – a byway wide enough for a vehicle. He wondered if he should head up or down. He headed up. His thinking that Shane would bust his gut getting up there and give him some advantage. He dropped his pace to a fast walk as he tried to get his rasping breathing back under control. The route kept climbing, and he lost sight of Shane.

Up he trudged, until the byway narrowed down to a skinny path, coiled in densely packed trees, towering nettles, and tangled vegetation. Then he sighted Ben making his way down the hill, so Alex made to turn and head back the other way – but that was no longer possible – because Patrick was standing there, silent and menacing.

Shane bellowed something nearby.

They'd trapped him, and the only possible escape route was through the tangly undergrowth.

Alex leapt into the unknown – brambles ripped at his face, arms and legs; nettles stung every inch of his body. He started falling and crashed aimlessly through the thicket and branches; he flapped his arms as he plummeted. The fall didn't take him far, and he landed at the base of a huge, overturned tree. Alex ignored the endless stings, scratches and bumps, and searched the surroundings in a mad panic. He stood in a rocky aperture, and Alex assumed it was the area where the tree once stood before strong winds must have toppled it. It most likely went over during the great storm the previous year. A mass of thickset bracken and overgrown shrubs loomed over him. The brambles looked impenetrable, but it sounded like one of the boys had started hacking through them. Climbing out of the hole would be a task in itself, let alone having the energy to battle through the deep, spiky shrubbery beyond. He heard voices and rustling. They were coming, and he was so weary he just wanted to drop to his knees and beg them to stop. Beg them not to hang him. He'd had enough, he couldn't take any more.

Patrick was first to emerge through the coarse nettles. Alex sobbed and edged backwards against the bulky tree base, its huge roots hovering over him like a giant witch's gnarled fingers.

Patrick moved in, emotionless.

Alex grabbed at a root – then turned and started climbing in a frantic, panicked scramble. More shouts filled the air, as he grabbed and pulled at those roots with every fibre of energy that remained. Mud was crumbling from the base; roots were ripping from the mud. There was a searing pain in his ankle; he glanced down and caught sight of Patrick, razor in hand, readying another swipe – not prepared to let him get another hit, Alex pulled his leg up and felt the swish of air, as the blade whizzed by, mere inches from his calf.

Alex hauled himself up, kicking down mud and showering it onto his pursuer. He made it to the top and climbed over and dropped onto the oak's trunk. Blood was pouring from a deep gash on his ankle and soaking into his sock and trainer. If he'd had any hopes about his survival, that lunatic had just quashed them, because he wasn't messing about.

Alex gazed across the length of the bulky oak. It was a monster. It had fallen into a mass of densely compacted trees. It was a long way to traverse, but it was the only route. If he could reach the grouped trees, he would have a chance of climbing to safety.

Alex held out his hands for balance and started to gingerly move along. After the first ten feet, there were branches to grab hold of. This would be the worst bit to tackle, he knew. He tried not to think about who was coming up behind him, and he tried to block out the pain seeping from every part of his body.

The bushes below gave way to a sloping, boulder-filled clearing. There was at least a twenty-foot drop under him. He grabbed for the first branch and held on. Underfoot there was ivy and creeping vines, twisting and knotted about the trunk. Then he checked on Patrick's progress, and to Alex's dismay, he was already walking along the trunk with zero fear. He held that razor at his side.

Ben appeared then, a panting, clumsy mess, as he dragged himself over the tree's base.

Alex knew he'd unlikely outrun Patrick, so considered dropping below, but if he landed wrong, it would be game over. Up here he had a chance. Then he remembered what he had in his pocket.

Alex reached in his shorts for the pouch, relieved when his fingers touched it. He removed the shuriken and poised it. Patrick stopped, tilted his head, and gave Alex a curious look. Then, to Alex's astonishment, offered him a sneer and kept coming for him.

'I will throw it,' shouted Alex.

Patrick, still sneering, still came.

Alex, jaw clenched, threw that star as hard as he could. He watched, utterly gripped, as it whirled towards Patrick, whizzed right past his face, and spun off.

Patrick observed, mesmerised by the action, and his eyes followed the star's path until it embedded itself deep into a tree trunk. His gaze returned to Alex. He flashed a malevolent grin, and then, almost in slow motion, Patrick lost his balance and fell. He landed with a dull thud.

Alex and Ben shared a perplexing look – then simultaneously, they dared to peek downwards.

Patrick stumbled to his feet, his mouth gaping open. He started making strange, monkey-like grunts, as he fumbled to pick up his cut-throat razor. It was at that point when Patrick, Ben and Alex all shrieked in unison. Patrick could not pick up the razor, because his fingertips were missing. They were, in fact, scattered about the blade which must have closed itself on impact with the ground. Patrick recoiled at the sight, clutching his bloodied hand against his chest. Patrick went sickly white and floundered about the slope, falling to his knees as he made a bizarre, throaty growl. His mouth was wide open and spittle rolled down his chin. He looked up to Alex and let out the most blood-curdling scream Alex could ever imagine a human being making.

Alex took one final look at Ben – then hurried along the trunk. His legs almost fell from under him, and the sight of Patrick's injury was making him feel light-headed. He reached the tangle of trees and half climbed, half fell, into the mass of leaves and branches.

Alex landed on his back with a thud and had the breath knocked out of him, but he pulled himself to his feet and limped away.

Alex's nan was a tough lady; he hadn't seen her cry before; Penny didn't even cry at his mum's funeral. She'd been tearful, but she hadn't sobbed like she had when she'd seen Alex's injuries. After Alex returned from Gallows Hill Wood, he knew there was no point in attempting to hide his wounds. He'd looked in a car mirror and saw the mess he was in, and could think of no sensible explanation for the multitude of nasty scratches and slices covering his face, deep slash on his ankle, and red, raised rope burn on his neck. From the lacerations on his face, you'd think he'd got into a fight with Freddy Krueger.

So Alex had told his nan all about the tests.

Within a week, they were preparing to leave town. His nan was adamant that after everything that had transpired, Alex wouldn't be safe staying in the area.

It didn't dawn on Alex until weeks later that he'd managed to pass all the tests. It disturbed him that he cared – but in a way, he was quite pleased with himself.

Forty-three

He connected his telescopic lens to his Nikon's camera housing, attached the camera to the tripod he'd already set up at the rear of his Jeep, then flipped the viewing screen and adjusted the camera's position. Happy he had it set accurately, Alex unfolded his camping chair, opened a cold coffee, sat and waited.

Alex sipped his drink; he'd been waiting less than twenty minutes when something caught his attention. Alex watched the screen as a blue Ford Transit van came into focus, its roof loaded with kayaks. A man stepped out, olive-skinned, well-muscled, with receding hair set in a widow's peak, and despite the fresh morning chill, the man was wearing a tight t-shirt and swimming shorts. Alex zoomed in and snapped several shots of the man's face, then zoomed back out. Alex used the camera to track the man's steps, as he removed a set of keys from his shorts and approached a wooden hut. A sign on the front of the building said: *'Jurassic Coast Adventures – Guided Tours and Equipment Hire.'*

Alex scanned back to the close-up. Despite the dark, bushy beard, Alex was certain the man was Eduardo.

Natalie approached a tall end-of-terrace property. The Victorian building was decorated in a bright, bone-white colour, and Natalie noticed it was the only house on the entire street that wasn't the standard dull-orange brick colour. There was no doorbell, so she used the brass butterfly door knocker. The door opened, and a heavyset lady gazed out at Natalie.

Natalie smiled politely. 'Olivia?'

Olivia was a short lady, somewhere in her late sixties, with light-grey hair, in a messy, pixie-cut style. Her eyebrows looked as though she had drawn them on with a permanent marker pen, and Natalie had to stifle a laugh when she caught sight of them. They looked awful, making the woman appear a bit like a cartoon character.

'I'm Natalie. Alex's wife. I know we haven't met.'

'You have green eyes,' said Olivia, in an almost accusatory tone.

'Hmm, aye.'

Olivia fixed her with a strange stare. Natalie, uncomfortable now, shuffled on the spot, and then she remembered the bottle of wine she was holding and offered it to Olivia. 'Hope you like Rioja.'

Olivia accepted. 'So, you've driven down from Edinburgh?' she said, her tone now cheery, and her smile bright. 'Come on inside, my love, come on in.'

Natalie followed her inside. 'I stopped over at a friend's place near Leeds, so I broke up the journey.'

'I do love Edinburgh, such a marvellous city. And the Old Town is absolutely stunning. I have told Alex, on many an occasion, that I'd love to come and visit you guys.'

'He's never said.'

Olivia pursed her lips and led Natalie into a large open-plan dining room. 'Now, I'll make us a pot of tea. A tad bit early for wine. Make yourself comfy, deary. I have heard so much about you and your family, it is so wonderful to meet you at long last, my love.'

Natalie took in the spotlessly clean room. It had a square sofa that wouldn't have looked out of place in a modern office; a brilliant white dining table, with two chrome chairs, and a tall bookcase that took up an entire wall. Natalie gazed at the books – there were hundreds of them, and from what she could see, they were books about the royal family, travel guides, and romantic fiction.

Olivia coughed. 'Kettle is on. Quite the collection, wouldn't you say? My three loves, the monarchy, European travel and romance.'

Natalie spotted two framed photos that sat side by side: one of Princess Diana, and one of Olivia, dressed identical to Diana, with hair styled similarly. Alex had told her frequently that his aunt was eccentric and delusional. She could see where he was coming from. Apparently, when Diana had passed away, she went into mourning for an entire month and wore black. Alex had been adamant he didn't want his aunt to attend their wedding. He'd been keen to keep the event a very private, intimate affair. His nan, Penny, had been the only relative to attend on Alex's side. The only relative Natalie had ever met until today.

'I take it you're here for answers,' said Olivia. 'I'm guessing that Alex is acting strange, and you have no clue what to do about it.'

'Um, well, I have some concerns.'

'I'll get that tea, my love.'

Alex watched through the camera screen as Eduardo spoke with a tall, middle-aged lady. He handed her a flyer with a flirtatious smile and was chatting away, as he gestured to the row of paddle-boards he'd lined up outside earlier that morning. When the woman headed for her car, Alex packed up his equipment and drove down to the kayak shack. It was time to talk to Leo's brother.

Natalie sipped her tea. It was weak and tepid, and she now wished she'd opened the wine.

Olivia sat next to her on the sofa. 'Alex phoned me a few days ago, asking if I had his father's address.'

'He did? And do you?' asked Natalie.

'Yes, despite our loathing for one and other, we hooked up via social media many years back. We've had some quite pleasant chats over the years.'

'Does Alex want to speak with him?'

'Alex said he would be visiting his friends, and was considering dropping in on him, yes.'

'Alex told me he had no interest in speaking with his father,' said Natalie, struggling to keep the irritation out of her voice.

'Ian isn't the man he was, Natalie. I always detested the man, but he is genuinely sorry about the way he treated my sister. It's hard not to feel sorry for the man.'

'I see.'

'Ian tried to love Alex, but even as a toddler he never accepted him. He had a bond with his mother. A special, I don't know… bubble, I guess, that Ian wasn't part of. His frustration eventually led him to resent the boy. Disliking him even.'

'Sounds like they need to talk.'

'But, I'm assuming you want to talk about the girl. Sheryl.'

Olivia's words stunned Natalie. Hearing that name caused her heart to pound. 'Yes. Alex has been having terrible dreams.'

'And what did Alex tell you about her?'

'That she was a childhood friend. But he won't explain why he screams her name. And he's been acting weird. Out of character. Sometimes I don't know who he is anymore.'

Olivia sighed sadly. 'Oh, dear. I'm going to get some of my mum's stuff that I kept. I'll also pour you a glass of that wine, as I feel you'll going to need it, my sweet.'

As Olivia left the room, goosebumps prickled Natalie's skin, and she shuddered.

Alex walked into the kayak shack.

Eduardo was busy behind the counter. 'Two ticks and I'll be right with you.'

The shack was stacked with kayaks, surfboards and buoyancy aids. Alex noticed a framed photo behind the counter of Eduardo and three young children, two boys and a girl.

'If it's rentals you're after, I'm afraid the sea is way too choppy for that today. This weather wasn't predicted either. Wind has picked up out of nowhere. Tomorrow should be better,' said Eduardo, appearing from the counter.

'I'm here to talk to you. You're Eduardo Moreno, right?' asked Alex.

'Um, yeah. No one calls me that. I'm Ed,' said Eduardo.

'You probably won't remember me, but I used to live near your grandparents. Near Maidstone in Kent. We didn't know each other that well.'

Eduardo hadn't been taking much notice of Alex, but now he studied him, and his eyes hardened and his body stiffened. 'No, I remember you. How did you find me?'

'Your Facebook business page,' said Alex. He guessed what Eduardo meant, was how did he know his surname. Alex had remembered seeing Eduardo's surname on a label stitched onto his equipment bag. Although he hadn't exactly recalled what that name was, and so spent ages searching through Spanish surname databases. He guessed that once he saw it, he'd remember it, and *Moreno* had jumped off the screen.

Eduardo gave him a long, scrutinising stare. 'You stole from me.'

'I'd say more borrowed. But I apologise.'

'Right, I *see* you were just borrowing.'

'We gave everything back. Apart from that star. You have a long memory, Ed.'

'Yes, I do. How could I forget the creepy little kid that liked to ask too many questions? The boy that was always sneaking about spying on me. The boy who was mixed up in the disappearance of that girl. Who they *never* found,' said Eduardo in an accusing tone.

Alex, shocked by Eduardo's attitude, stepped back from him. He hadn't quite expected such a frosty reception from the man. 'Sheryl… that's why I'm here. It's Leo I'm trying to get in touch with.'

Eduardo drew back his head and gave Alex a puzzled look. 'Huh?'

'I need a chat with him. It's important.'

Eduardo gave Alex an incredulous look and said, 'What is this? Are you on some sort of wind-up?' Eduardo reached under the counter, pulled out a rounders bat and placed it down in front of him. 'What's this *really* about? Stop bullshitting me.'

Alex held up his hands. 'Easy, Ed. I'm not here to make trouble. And I don't mean Leo any harm.'

Olivia placed a shoebox onto the dining table, along with the wine and two large glasses. She popped the cork and poured two sizeable measures. 'My mum became obsessed with the case.'

Natalie sat at the table and popped the lid. She almost considered shutting it back up and running from the house. She was shaking as she removed the bundle of crumpled newspaper clippings:

The search for the local missing girl, Sheryl Denton, continues – Local man, Fredrick Killner, again held for questioning – Hunt for the missing girl, Sheryl Denton, sparks a new search for her father, also missing – After ten years, a mother pleads for new information on her missing daughter.

Natalie scanned the heading of each crumpled page, and focussed on a grainy image of Sheryl, her eyes filling with tears as she took in the girl's face.

'There is a coloured image too,' said Olivia. 'I'm so sorry, my sweet.'

When Natalie viewed the full coloured photo she gasped, held her hand over her mouth, made her way outside, and vomited in the street.

'I have *no* brother. How many ways can I say that? Get that into your head.' He spoke calmly, but Eduardo scowled and placed his hand on the bat.

Alex didn't continue to argue. He knew there was no point, as he was certain by Eduardo's muddled and bitter expression that he was telling the truth.

'I don't know what sick game you're playing, but I want you out of here, right now! Or I'll smash out your front teeth, you total nut-job.'

Olivia handed Natalie a tissue. 'It's a lot to take in, my love.'

Natalie sniffed. 'Why did his gran not say anything? We met plenty of times, and she never said a fecking word.'

'She never told me either. For the same reason, Alex kept me away from you. He knew I'd have said something. Simple as that. My mother always vehemently protected that boy; it turned her life upside down.'

Natalie gazed at Sheryl again, blinking away the tears. There wasn't just a slight resemblance – it was almost as though Natalie was staring at a photo of herself. The same eyes, same hair colour, same splash of freckles and the same heart-shaped face. Even their hairstyles had been similar at that age.

'There's something else,' said Olivia, reaching into the box and removing a Dictaphone.

Alex sat on the empty beach and watched the heavy waves smash onto the shore.

'Fancy a swim?' said a familiar voice.

Alex glanced to his right. Bassem was sitting next to him. He had a concerned smile on his face.

'You must have had some clue, Alex. It's not as though it hasn't happened before.'

'It's how I remembered everything. It was real to me.'

'Perhaps you didn't tell anyone about Leo, for the same reason you haven't told anyone about me.'

Alex flinched as though in pain. 'I don't know what to do, Baz.'

'Find out the truth. Just like you set out to do, Alex,' said Bassem.

'And what if the truth is—'

Bassem interrupted him. 'You need to do this, Alex. You know you have to.'

'Am I mad, Bassem?' asked Alex.

Bassem smiled. 'Well, yeah, a bit, mate. But *I've* never held that against you.'

Olivia pressed the Dictaphone. 'The man in the audio is my late father's friend, David Proctor, a psychiatrist, and a good one, in his day. My mother recorded their conversation. This was back in the early nineties.'

There was an annoying fuzz in the background of the recording – then a man's deep, well-spoken voice became audible. 'When did Susanna first get diagnosed with breast cancer?'

'In '84, when Alex was ten,' replied Penny. 'Although he wasn't told until much later, Alex sensed something was wrong.'

'And that's when it started?'

'He'd suffered from night terrors, memory blackouts and sleep deprivation in the past, but the really peculiar behaviour started when she became sick.'

'Can you give me some examples?' asked David.

'Alex constantly spoke about his friend, Harry, the boy with curly, jet-black hair and light blue eyes. Sometimes Harry would shake him awake at night, or, he'd awaken and find him sitting at the end of his bed, or peering through his window. Sometimes they'd play in the garden.'

'I see. What did Susanna make of Harry?'

'In the early stages, she played along with the game, and would set Harry a place at dinner, make him bedtime hot chocolate and silly stuff like that. It drove Ian insane.'

There was a pause.

Natalie was staring at the Dictaphone and willing it to continue, and for a moment she assumed the tape was stuck, but then it made a cracking sound, and she heard a faint cough.

'Susanna found glass fragments in Ian's dinner,' came Penny's voice. 'When she asked Alex about it, he said that Harry did it. And Harry also killed Alex's pet hamster. Alex sobbed when he told her that he'd begged Harry not to hurt it.'

'What did he do to it?' asked David.

'He… he put it in the oven. Well, the grill. On another occasion, Harry turned up in the early hours and woke Alex up by blowing on his face… then told Alex he would tape a plastic bag over his head if he fell back to sleep. Alex didn't sleep properly for over two weeks because of that.'

The Dictaphone made a shrill buzzing sound, and the voices sounded alien-like for a few moments; then David's voice improved. 'If there is a severe psychological disorder, the person can most definitely believe that there is an imaginary companion or friend present. Not that Harry sounded like much of a friend.'

Natalie drank her wine in one gulp. Her cheeks became hot and her mouth dry.

'And yes, they can believe this person is real,' continued David.

'But… I can't understand how,' said Penny.

'It is very hard to comprehend, Penny. But Alex may genuinely not be able to differentiate from what is real – and what is imagined or created in his mind.'

'Are you saying my grandson has a serious disorder? Is he some sort of schizophrenic?' she asked.

'It might be a coping mechanism for the trauma he's suffered. If he was that close with his mother, it may have triggered something. First, I'd need to see him—'

'No!' interrupted Penny. 'I'm just getting the facts, David.'

'Penny, without a proper diagnosis, Alex won't be able to get the medication needed to—' The tape made a shrill, scratchy noise.

Olivia switched it off. 'That's the end, love.'

Natalie sat in shocked silence for several minutes, whilst she processed what she'd just heard. The end of what? Her marriage? Her sanity? She felt enraged, betrayed and hurt.

'Olivia, did Penny believe he had something to do with Sheryl's disappearance?'

Olivia placed her hands on Natalie's. 'She had some concerns, yes. But that's all. Most people were convinced that monster Fred Killner abducted her. They just never proved it.'

'God.'

'There was another… friend if you like. Lee, or Leo. My mum would hear him playing with this boy in the garden. It was that same summer. He taught Alex kung-fu or something.'

Natalie stood up, paced the room with her hand clasped over her mouth. How could she have been so blind? How could she have not seen this man for what he was? Was she that ingenuous? Had she been so utterly wrapped up in her own hectic lifestyle? How ridiculous did she look now? She wanted to scream, because she'd come here for answers, but would leave with more questions. And those questions could only be answered by one person – her husband.

Forty-four

He didn't think he was insane. He'd always known Bassem wasn't real. Or at least, not to outsiders. But he was real enough to Alex, and it wasn't as though Alex could ever control him. Bassem spoke his mind and did what he wanted. Sometimes he was just there, often when Alex needed him, and occasionally when he didn't.

Alex learnt a long time ago how different he was, and that his imagination sometimes got a little... out of control. He wasn't sure how it happened, or why, just that he'd learnt to accept it as part of his life, and even implement it sometimes, and treat it as a gift. Unfortunately, he hadn't always understood how things worked, and the confusion when he'd been growing up often overwhelmed him. His mum had been the one person who understood. She once spoke to him about his feelings towards his childhood friend, Harry, and she told him not to be ashamed. She even made it sound like he possessed a talent, and he wasn't like other kids, because he had special abilities, a bit like a superhero. Alex often wondered if things would have been different if she'd got him some professional help all those years ago. Treatment to stop his mind from playing the games they did. And treatment to stop the faces he'd see in the darkness when he closed his eyes at night. Sometimes they would terrify him. Alex often saw odd people, or things, monsters even, that weren't there. He remembered his mum smiling at him as she told him it was amazing that he'd created another person – with their own characteristics and personality – even their own flaws, and God knows, Harry had those in abundance. Harry had a very playful sense of humour, which would sometimes manifest into pure wickedness. But she always told Alex he wasn't to blame for Harry's horrid actions. When Alex was in his mid-twenties, he went to the cinema to watch the movie Fight Club. He'd guessed the plot twist well before the end, and he left the cinema that day with the biggest smile on his face. The movie did make him feel less of a freak, made him feel that there must be more people out there like him, and he'd sympathised with the main character. He enjoyed it, but he never watched it again. Had Harry and Leo been his own alter egos? That made sense; they certainly held traits Alex didn't possess – but Bassem? What did he bring to the table? Perhaps the voice of reason, or was he merely someone to unload his problems to?

Did he know back then about Leo? Was that the real reason he never told the police or any of the others about his involvement? Alex didn't remember it that way. He'd eventually learnt the truth about Harry, even as a kid, but in his memory, Leo had been as real and alive as Gavin, Mark or Janette. He could even recall the smell of Leo's cigarettes and the Hai Karate deodorant spray that Leo always wore. But then he would often get a waft of the food Bassem was eating too.

Alex thought about his wife. He loved Natalie so much, and he hated himself for all the lies and deceit. But it had only been to protect her – hadn't it? That's why he'd gone for the vasectomy in his late twenties. He'd been too young to have the snip through the NHS, so he instructed a private clinic to do it. He didn't want to risk passing, whatever *this* was, onto his children, because that wasn't fair. More lies, he thought.

He sat for several hours just thinking, and the hazy flashbacks came – Alex pictured himself burning pages; visualised himself creating that diary, though he did not know where he'd been at the time – he'd most definitely been alone. His nan's shed, perhaps? Alex even remembered the smell of the burning paper and recalled the sticky PVA glue between his fingers. He'd taken his time with it, he knew that much. He pictured himself stealing the underwear from a washing line – sneaking into the pub to buy condoms from the toilet vending machine – though he had no recollection of planting the items in his dad's house.

A sudden dreadful realisation hit him like a kick in the teeth: If Leo was indeed a figment of his imagination, and his memories were full of large blank holes – what else had he done that he'd wiped from his memory?

Forty-five

'Smells like feet and onions in your van,' said Janette.

Ben sniffed the air. 'Smells OK to me.'

Janette and Ben had agreed to meet after work and visit Eileen together. Janette had jumped into Ben's van to discuss tactics.

'Who's going to search her room?' asked Ben.

'Me. You can keep her chatting. You know how she loves you, Ben.'

'And do we tell her about the weekend's events?'

Janette shook her head.

'What about Clayton? Do we mention him coming back?' asked Ben.

'No, best not. We'll just claim we popped in for a cuppa.'

'And what's your thoughts on Clayton? All this stuff about that Leo lad.'

'Maybe we should speak to the police. Technically, he is also another suspect.'

'We can't do that, Jan, what exactly would we say?'

Janette shrugged. 'It would sound crazy.'

'Do you think he came here?' asked Ben.

'You mean, do I think Alex took her bear?'

'Do you?'

Janette sighed. 'If I'm honest, I just can't see what his angle is. He seems like he's genuine and he is trying to help, but I just dunno.'

'Gavin reckons his story is bollocks,' said Ben. 'He's going to do something stupid, Jan.'

'Of course, he is. What else would you expect? And speaking of Gavin, what was Sunday all about?'

Ben puffed his cheeks. 'It's messed up, Jan.'

Eileen put the kettle on. 'I've got a lemon drizzle cake. Would you like a slice, Ben?'

'Yum, yeah, lovely,' said Ben, looking at Janette and gesturing the door with his eyes.

'Can I use the bathroom, Eileen?' asked Janette.

'Of course, you know where it is, Jan.'

Janette smiled and left.

'You look well, Ben, have you been working out? You remind me of a butch rugby player with those shoulders,' said Eileen, using a knife to cut up the cake.

'Jan's the fitness freak. I'm too busy with work for all that malarkey,' said Ben.

'Business still good? How many employees do you have now?'

'Four lads. Plus the subcontractors. It's been a decent couple of years for the company.'

'You did a fantastic job on my neighbour's extension. Do you remember him? His name's Michael Finley.'

'Of course, smashing bloke,' said Ben, thinking what an absolute pain in the arse Finley had been. The intrusive tosser was always checking every tiny detail on the project. His employees would have happily buried the man under the foundations.

'What about Gavin? Have you seen much of him?' she asked.

Ben wondered if he should even mention seeing Gavin. He shook his head.

'Such a cheeky monkey, that one,' she said.

Ben gazed at Eileen and his heart sank. The poor woman's life had been a train wreck, and taking into consideration all she'd been through, she looked well. Certainly younger than she was, which he guessed was mid-sixties. He'd remembered seeing something in a newspaper about her being thirty-four at the time, and Sheryl often bragged about how cool it was to have a young mother. She'd had Sheryl before she was even twenty. Gavin and Ben both had secret crushes on Eileen when they were younger. Now, instead of the long, sweeping blonde locks, she had short hair, dyed toffee blonde, but the charming smile was still there and she'd kept her figure in great shape. Regular yoga sessions and years of swimming had no doubt helped.

'What about Mark Corkscrew? How's his music career?' she asked in a bubbly tone.

'He's good. Loaded. But a tight sod,' said Ben with a wry grin.

Eileen offered Ben some cake. 'I listened to one of his fast music sets during a Zumba class. It was all a bit too frantic and intense for an oldie like me,' she laughed. 'But I can see the appeal.'

Ben sniggered. He couldn't.

Walking into Sheryl's bedroom was like stepping back in time, and Janette had to bite her bottom lip as the nostalgic memories came over her in a deep flood of overwhelming emotions. Her cheeks were wet from tears and she had to hold on to the doorframe because she felt giddy. She gazed around, absorbing every item. Eileen once told Janette that she'd never change Sheryl's bedroom, and it would stay this way all the time there was a glimmer of hope – that one day, somehow, Sheryl would find her way back home, and on that day, she'd see her daughter's sweet smile again, and they'd bury the darkness from the past. Whatever happened – they'd get through it. No matter how bad, no matter how traumatic and upsetting – they'd survive and move on.

For years, Janette believed there was a chance she'd see her best friend again, but not anymore, because she knew in her heart that Sheryl was gone, forever.

Janette took a deep breath and steadied herself as she scanned the photos on the cork-board. Some of herself, some of Ben and the boys, but most of them were of Sheryl and Eileen on fun days out together. She studied the wall of posters: The Cure Boys Don't Cry; the bandana-wearing Axel Rose and Aerosmith's lead singer mounted on a motorbike, all plastered the wall. Janette used to hate all those rock and head-banging songs, and she had attempted to get Sheryl into groups like Bros and other popular stuff, but Sheryl had been obsessed with rock music. Sheryl was always the individual and liked what she liked. It was ironic, because Janette now shared a similar taste in music, thanks to Will's influence in her life; once, being a member of an '80s style band himself. Janette remembered picking up the Appetite for Destruction cassette in this very room and arguing with Sheryl about Guns N' Roses and told her the band would never be a huge success. Sheryl had grinned and said, 'Well, we'll see.'

Now, every time she heard the song *Sweet Child O' Mine*, Janette would break down and sob. The song had hit the UK charts the year after Sheryl's disappearance, but it had featured on that cassette, and Sheryl had played it a hundred times in this room, despite Janette's protests. It once played in a pub during a night out with her work colleagues, and she ended up dashing into a toilet cubicle where she lost it and cried for a good thirty minutes straight. When her work colleagues came searching for her, she pretended to be throwing up, claiming she'd drunk too much wine.

In contrast to the rock wall, the bedside area was much more girly. A bed cover with a cartoon dog, pink fluffy pillows and various animal cuddly toys – a giraffe, a hedgehog, and tatty panda with an eye missing, all strategically placed. Janette walked to the shelves on the far wall. One containing dusty books, and the other housing Sheryl's beloved items: A Teddy Ruxpin. A Paddington, Rupert Bear, and five Care Bears. When Janette noticed the gap where a fifth bear had once sat, a cold shiver surged through her veins.

She considered what her options were. Tell Eileen and upset her, without all the facts? Speak to the police? She wouldn't have a clue where to start there, and what would she tell them, anyway? There was hardly enough new information for them to reopen a thirty-year-old cold case. She'd wager they wouldn't even take any action in the matter.

Forty-six

The two police constables were on a routine patrol when they'd taken a call notifying them they'd been assigned to sound out a rural area at their earliest convenience. Ordinarily, follow-ups relating to a historic, missing person case would be a very low priority, but the media had also obtained some information on the case, so they'd been advised to act urgently on this. An anonymous email had been received, containing a grid reference; for a location where vital fresh evidence pertaining to a missing person case would be found. The constables, both under twenty-five, had never heard of the name, Sheryl Denton, who'd been missing for over three decades.

The officers complained it was most likely a hoax, or some time-waster sending them on a wild goose chase, as they parked up the patrol car in the narrow dead-end lane. Both officers headed into an overgrown wooded area, using a map on one of their phones, to follow the GPS coordinates. The pair spent ages walking through the dense undergrowth, and they were soon caked in wet mud and tangly weeds.

When they reached the location, the officers scoured the little enclosed lake that was buried in a thick layer of brown leaves. They took great care where they stood.

The shorter constable held up his hand to stop his colleague. 'We need some tape, ASAP. And cordon off the area by the road. No one comes through these woods. Get this entire area sectioned off,' he ordered.

'What is it?' asked the taller constable.

The shorter constable looked drained of colour as he pointed ahead. Then the taller officer glimpsed what his colleague was showing him – a rotten rowing boat, half-submerged at the water's edge – or more accurately, what was inside that boat.

The shorter constable swallowed hard and fumbled for his phone. 'I'll stay and act as scene guard,' he stammered, 'and I'll let the Sarge know.'

On Wednesday morning, after breakfast, Fredrick saw the image of Sheryl Denton on the huge TV in the communal room, and he spun his wheelchair around to get a proper view. A white-haired lady with a Zimmer frame stopped right in front of the screen and blocked his view, and she gawped at the TV with a gormless frown.

'Fucking move, Ethel, you dopey old cunt!' growled Fredrick.

Ethel gave him an indigent look, scrunched her lips and shuffled on. There was no sound on the screen, but a stout, balding man, tagged Detective Chief Inspector Reynolds, was being interviewed.

Fredrick sighed, knowing it wouldn't be long before he'd get dragged back into the mix.

Three times those hard-faced detectives questioned him in the eighties, and on each occasion, he'd sat there and said nothing. Not one word. He would not be duped into tripping himself up. They'd tried everything – the softly-softly approach, intimidation, and they even used his dead daughters as leverage. That somehow, he'd snapped and taken the girl in some twisted, warped fantasy, or bizarre breakdown. But Fredrick never cracked – never said a single word, and just glared at those suited arseholes in detached and controlled defiance. Oh, they hated him. They'd wanted to pin it on him so badly they couldn't bear it. One detective, a bony-faced man called Jim Brogden, with breath so foetid it could have laid out a Tyrannosaurus Rex, kept whispering in his ear, saying that he'd pay, and one day they'd make him regret his actions.

The Coldred campsite had been notorious in the '90s for its drug connections, family feuds, and a ton of other unscrupulous goings-on. Gavin's mate, Max Robins, had been held captive here for two days, whilst his brothers spent a frantic weekend trying to gather the cash he owed to one of the families here. Max told Gavin that they kept him in the dog compound and promised they'd break his arms and legs and bury him alive if the cash didn't materialise.

Now, though, the place resembled a quiet Butlins holiday camp. There were less dodgy-looking caravans, and more static mobile homes, with picket fences and well-kept gardens.

Gavin got out of Patrick's Hilux with his filthy rucksack. He'd got lucky on his third search of the damn place and located the bag.

Gavin followed Patrick into one of the mobile homes. Inside he met with a short, stocky man in his late sixties, that Patrick introduced as his Uncle Jonah. He had a craggy face, small, bright eyes and a crooked smile. He gave Gavin a firm handshake, with a calloused hand that was covered in chunky gold rings. Although he wasn't a large, or even intimidating figure, he had the aura of a man that you wouldn't dare to cross.

On the day Fredrick found that note on his Land Rover's windshield, he'd been quite perplexed by the find. He wondered if it was some sort of trick to lure him out into the open. The note confirmed the time and place where he'd find the trespassing troublemakers. He couldn't believe one of those boys had the audacity to return. Brash little bastard. He was certain only one boy came as he inspected the ground, finding a single pair of size five trainer tracks.

When he'd arrived and seen those lads preparing for a camping trip, he started planning his revenge. He planned to wait for the wretches to set up camp, then set fire to their tents, whilst the disrespectful sods were fast asleep. He thought that would be apt. After the two girls showed up with the skinny boy, he changed his mind. There was no reason to hurt those young girls. OK, he followed them for a bit, keeping them in his sights, and making sure they would notice his motor on the lane below. But he only intended to put the wind up them.

He didn't know that one of those girls had been Adrian Denton's daughter. That news he later learnt from the papers. That was a blast from his past.

It was the evening before he was due to leave for France with his wife and daughters when Adrian showed up at the farm on that late spring afternoon in '85. He was a regular at the shop; one of his best customers. They'd often spend hours chewing the fat and drinking glasses of Killner's Triple Vision, straight from the vats. He sort of considered the man a friend, even though he was a social worker. How wrong had he been? The dirty git was only screwing some

Glaswegian girl that was half his age. She'd been mixed up in a case Adrian had worked on the previous year in Medway. Fredrick later learnt her name was Tiffany Bains, a troubled girl from a tough Scottish family who lived in The Gorbals, and she'd moved to Rochester to stay with her brother, because of some abuse in the family home.

Adrian came to Fredrick's home, asking for money because he'd left his wife and was low on funds. Adrian knew full well he kept a decent sum in the cider shack's safe. The little shop made a tidy tax-free packet. When Fredrick refused to loan him any, Adrian threatened blackmail – saying he'd put him out of business by telling the police about his illegal cider business. Fredrick laughed in his face and told him to try it. So, when that idea failed, the crazy idiot tried to rob him. The pair ended up having a vicious scrap, and when Adrian snatched up a claw hammer and attacked Fredrick with it, Fredrick disarmed him and beat the foolish man about the head with it. The mess was unreal. He must have clumped Adrian with it twenty-odd times.

When Fredrick stepped outside for air, he found Adrian's young girlfriend sitting in the passenger seat of his beige Austin Allegro, with bags piled high in the rear seats. Fredrick couldn't believe it. His wife and kids were due back at any moment, and he was splattered with claret, had a dead social worker in his shack, and the man's bit of fluff parked out in the courtyard. Panicking, he'd grabbed his hunting shotgun and marched up to the car. The girl didn't even clock him approaching, as she'd been too busy reading a copy of Just Seventeen and chomping on gum. He had no clue how he managed to undertake the ungodly deed, but he unloaded both rounds into her pretty head.

Fredrick moved the car behind the barn, covered it with some blue tarpaulin, locked his cider shack and showered. When his wife and daughters returned from shopping, he'd told them he could no longer join them in France. Furious, she'd left for that trip without even saying goodbye. He never saw his wife or daughters again. Whilst they went away on a trip that claimed their lives, Fredrick spent the weekend using his chainsaw to dismember the two bodies, so he could dispose of them in several woodland graves fifty-odd miles away. He'd stuffed their corpses in the big outside chest freezer the night before and never used the appliance again. He also burnt the car and buried its shell in a deep hole he dug in one of his paddocks and cleaned the farm of evidence.

Fredrick had killed Adrian and managed to get away with it, only to get accused of abducting his daughter all those years later. Something he'd had no hand in. He couldn't believe the cruel irony of the situation. During the Denton investigation, he'd been worried sick the police might find the buried car, but, to this day, that car remains hidden. Fredrick did have a little chuckle to himself when someone reported seeing Adrian's car in Hollingbourne in '88. Not likely.

'Did you dig up someone's stash?' asked Jonah, referring to the muddy rucksack and silver packets scattered on the table.

'Something like that,' said Gavin.

Jonah studied the packets. 'What's with all this weird packaging?'

'They were for online orders.'

'Um, is that the… black-net?' asked Jonah.

Gavin nodded.

Jonah examined the powder. 'That you stole?'

Gavin nodded again.

'Locally?'

'No. The Midlands,' said Gavin.

Jonah scratched his chin and pondered for a moment. 'I dunno, my lads don't deal in smack. If you had a decent bit of weed or ching, then we'd have been on a winner, pal.'

Patrick picked up a packet and flicked it with one of his stumps. 'You must know somebody, Jonah?'

Jonah pursed his lips. 'Perhaps. Depends on what sort of money we're talking about.'

'I'd estimate the value at twelve hundred,' said Gavin.

Jonah laughed and tossed down the packet. 'I wouldn't be interested at that price, fella.'

'I don't want money,' said Gavin.

Jonah raised his eyebrows and glanced at Patrick. The pair shared a confused look.

'I need a gun,' said Gavin, candidly.

Jonah screwed up his lips, puzzled by Gavin's request. He scratched his chin again and observed Gavin as though weighing him up. Then he held out his hand. 'OK, deal. I'll take this off your hands, in exchange for a clean shooter.'

Gavin took his hand. 'And rounds?'

'Of course with rounds,' said Jonah, with a gruff laugh.

They shook on it.

Fredrick couldn't recall where he put the photographer guy's card, but he remembered him as a boy and he didn't regret stripping the skin from the lad's back. Those unruly kids had no business being on his property. Although, he'd be the first to admit that perhaps he took things a step too far during his endeavour to dish out a suitable and unforgettable form of vengeance.

His dog, Delila, was a ferocious bitch, but she adored Fredrick and shadowed his every movement on the farm. She was a working guard dog, but he still considered her as *his* pet. He'd snuggle that pooch to bed at night like she was a child. During winter nights, he'd hear Delila whine when her blanket had slipped down, and Fredrick would have to drag his tired ass out of bed and cover her back up. God, how he regretted letting her endure more pain just so he could frighten the daylights out of that horrible kid. If anything, he scarred himself just as much. He'd never shaken the last look Delila gave him. If he could replay that day, he'd have ended Delila's suffering the instant he'd found her. And the boy would have been left broken on the railway tracks.

If this Clayton bloke wanted information, he'd give him some. Anything to stop the police and media spotlight beaming back over his head again.

It was like her world suddenly ended. When the plain-clothed family liaison officer had turned up on her doorstep last night, Eileen broke down. The female constable had been professional, calm, empathetic and level-headed. She'd sat Eileen down and gone through the details as sensitively as was humanly possible. After receiving an anonymous email, police were notified of a location where they would find evidence relating to her daughter's case. Uniformed officers attended the scene and discovered the historic remains of a body, believed to be female. It was also apparent that someone had removed the body from the lake, prior to the officers attending the scene. There was a chance this would prove useful, as forensic experts may now gleam current evidence from the scene, relating to the person, or persons, who had visited the scene to move the body. Forensic teams and divers were now searching the entire area. Whoever notified the police had also notified the media; and the papers and online news feeds had already begun running with the story that – although it was not yet officially confirmed, the body found was most likely that of Sheryl Denton, missing since late August '88. It was too late to contain the story, as the media frenzy had been whipped up by the late afternoon. The morning papers, which Eileen had not read, and breakfast TV news, which she'd stringently avoided watching, had all centred around the case. Eileen's street was a hub of activity, as reporters, journalists, and nosy residents were waiting out there to get morbid gawp. It seemed whoever moved the body had been keen for officers to locate it quickly.

Gavin waited outside whilst Patrick walked off with his uncle, presumably to collect the firearm. Gavin could hear a creaking noise and noticed a young girl, around eight years old, playing alone on a swing in an enclosed play area. The girl swung back and forth, her sharp eyes fixed on him. Gavin stepped towards the play area. The floor was covered in wood chipping, contained a slide, a wooden sheep on a spring, and a swing set. One swing, he realised, was missing.

Gavin waved at the girl. 'Hey, how long has this swing been missing?'

The girl blew him a raspberry, jumped from the swing, and strutted from the play area, scowling at Gavin as she passed him.

Patrick and Jonah now stood talking by the Hilux. Jonah spoke to Patrick in an angry whisper, jabbing a finger at his chest. Patrick accepted a box from his uncle, nodding sternly as he did.

Gavin looked back at the swing and shook his head. He was seeing conspiracy everywhere now. It was ridiculous. A missing swing in a traveller's encampment – get a grip. For a moment he could see Sheryl sitting on the swing, a smile plastered on her face as she flew higher and faster. He remembered the gaping hole she left in his life that day she disappeared. Gavin was positive that the hole had never been filled, and he doubted it ever would.

A part of him had also been taken away that summer's night.

Then Gavin pictured Isabella sitting on the wooden sheep, giggling and waving to him. He could see her dark, wavy hair and cheeky smile as she sprung from side to side.

Patrick called him over and snapped him out of his daze.

Mark was eating breakfast at Heathrow Airport when he'd read the newsfeed on his phone. He'd choked on his coffee when he'd seen Sheryl's image flash up. He left his breakfast and abandoned his flight to Milan without a second's thought.

'Shouldn't you be at college?'

Ryan cracked open a can of Pepsi. 'What's up with Dad? He was in the playroom, bawling his eyes out. It freaked Molly out. I've downloaded Paw Patrol on my console to cheer her up. She can't use the controller though, but it is keeping her entertained.'

'He's upset,' said Kayla.

'Are you leaving him, Mum?'

'No. The girl on the local news. Have you seen it?'

Ryan nodded. 'Who hasn't? It's all over social media. They reckon she's been in that lake for over thirty years!' Ryan's mouth dropped open. 'Did Dad know her?'

Kayla nodded. 'He was with her the night she disappeared. They'd been on a camping trip.'

'No way!'

'The media has gone crazy over this. Don't speak to anybody, OK, Ryan?'

Ryan nodded.

'I mean it, your dad's in bits over this. This has haunted him for years.'

'Who killed her, do you think?'

'They questioned a guy they suspected back in the '80s, but they never found evidence to charge him at the time. That might change now, of course. Plus, Sheryl's father hasn't been seen since the mid-eighties. So lots of unanswered questions there too,' said Kayla.

'Wow, that's crazy.'

'Then there's Alex Clayton. The boy that moved away,' said Kayla.

'Moved away?' asked Ryan.

'He returned to town the other day. And not long after he returns—'

'The body shows up,' he finished for his mother.

'You can't go and see her, Jan.'

'She'll be in bits,' said Janette, pacing the room. She'd been pacing back and forth across the lounge for ages. Will had turned off the TV and taken away the iPad, refusing to let her watch, or read, anything else.

'How can they report all this stuff? They don't even know if it's her,' asked Janette.

'It's a historic case. It was bound to cause a stir. This is a thirty-year-old mystery,' said Will.

'It's disrespectful.'

'It might help them gather information, Jan.'

'I need to call them again. The detectives need to know about everything that's been going on.'

'Jan, listen to me. Calm down and breathe. They will come and speak to you. And you'll get your say. But take some time to process this,' he said tenderly.

Janette nodded. 'OK.' She stopped pacing and plonked down on the arm of the chair. 'I can't believe this is happening.'

'Do you really believe this Alex fella is responsible, Jan?'

Janette shrugged.

'Why would he come back though? When he could have just tipped off the police from Scotland.'

'Maybe he was trying to mess with us all.'

'Do you actually believe that, Jan?'

'I'm taking the mountain bike out. I need to clear my head.'

Will looked as though he was going to argue, but gave her a hard nod and said, 'Take it easy, please, Jan.'

Not one for being constantly attached to his mobile phone, or interested in checking updates every ten seconds, Gavin had only just seen the news, after his mum messaged him asking if he knew what was going on.

Patrick, driving, with a roll-up hanging from his lips, said, 'You OK, Gav?'

'How many rounds did I get?' asked Gavin.

Forty-seven

'Don't, Marko. Don't joke with me, my man,' said Daan.

The Uber driver sighed. 'M25 is backing up, boss.'

Mark gave his driver the thumbs-up. 'I'm sorry Daan, what else can I say?'

Daan muttered swear words in French; he'd momentarily disappeared from Mark's phone screen.

'Trent can handle my spot, he knows my style better than anyone,' said Mark.

'They didn't book DJ fucking Trent, they booked DJ Corker. Are you trying to ruin my reputation? Now of all times! There is some serious buzz and anticipation for your set, Marko-man, and after Utrecht, you've sold out the event. Even prices on Ticket-Swap are almost tripling.'

'I'm not coming, Daan. If you don't trust Trent, then what about your girl, Annie Flex?'

'She's in California… getting married,' barked Daan, 'and her flavour is nothing like yours, she's more minimal and tech-house, so she couldn't take the prime slot you're booked for. They are expecting to be elevated into another galaxy! Jesus, have you seen the competing line-up in the Blackout area?'

'Trent's your guy,' said Mark.

Daan slapped the top of his head. 'Nobody knows him. It will be a disaster and your roadie will end up playing to an empty room!'

'He hates being called that, Daan,' said Mark.

'Um, guys, I am part of this call,' said Trent, in a huffy voice. Trent's annoyed face popped up onto the screen.

'No offence, Trent,' said Daan.

Trent rolled his eyes theatrically. 'Right.'

Mark ran a hand through his hair. 'I dunno what else I can say.'

Daan's nostrils flared. 'So that's it? You are bailing on me?'

'An hour before the set, I'll post on social media that I've been involved in some sort of accident, and Trent will step in. I guarantee he'll blow that venue's roof off.'

'He better!' spat Daan. With that, he cut off the call.

Trent puffed out his cheeks. 'No pressure then.'

'Try not to think about how huge the crowd is and pretend you're in that crazy little basement club in Bristol that you used to be a resident in.'

Trent sniggered. 'Let's hope most of the crowd will be too wankered to suss it isn't you up there.'

'You'll enjoy it.' Mark ended the call and looked out of the window at the solid traffic surrounding him. He considered calling Ida; he'd barely spoken to her in two weeks. They were so used to being apart, it was the norm for them. Not that she cared. He'd realised a long time ago that Ida didn't love him. His Swedish wife had been extraordinarily stunning when they'd first met, and their relationship had been electrifying and thrilling. A whirlwind romance that resulted in them marrying within a year, but once he purchased their grand house and they'd had the children, she'd changed. She let herself go and stopped trying – in all departments. Mark felt like he was just a cash-cow now. She was so cold towards him these days. He could be gone for weeks, and he'd step into that house, with a broad smile, only to be met with a thin smirk, a peck on the cheek, and a bunch of demands. Take, take, take, and his boys weren't much different. Right now, he was putting his family far from his thoughts; along with Milan, his career, and his despondent manager, because his old friends needed him, so he was going home.

'Here, get that down ya.'

Gavin accepted the large glass of whiskey from Patrick.

As soon as they'd heard the awful news, Patrick suggested that they stop at the nearest boozer to process everything.

'Thanks, Pat,' said Gavin, sipping the drink. All he could visualise was Alex Clayton, on his knees in the mud, pleading for his life. Gavin got the gun to take back to Nottingham, as he'd planned to locate Skender and put six bullets in the fucker. He already had Sammy on the case, and the Liverpudlian promised to do some digging for him. But that could wait for now. He had business here first.

He'd be using some of those bullets to destroy Alex Clayton.

Alex wasn't sure how long he'd been sitting outside the block of ivory-coloured maisonette flats, or why he'd come here in the first place. He had nowhere else to turn. He got out of his car and started towards the building, but stopped and hesitated.

'Alex? Alex, is that you?' said a polite voice from behind him.

Alex turned around. Ian Clayton was standing there, gazing at him with an astonished grin.

The sat-nav said there was another twenty-five minutes before she reached her destination. Natalie floored the accelerator on the BMW. Olivia had given her Ian's address, and that's where she was heading. If Alex had asked for his father's address, there'd be a chance Ian would have at least seen her husband. She wouldn't be going home until she'd found him. Natalie had watched in shocked awe when Olivia switched on the morning's news and they been greeted with the unsettling sight of Sheryl Denton's photo. Someone had unearthed the poor girl's body, and that someone wanted everyone to know it.

'Well, look again,' said Fredrick.

The care worker frowned. 'If you needed the card, why did you bin it, Fredrick?' she said, her tone amiable, though her eyes were hard.

'Just find it. It's important,' he spat.

'What was the name on the card? Perhaps I can search on the internet?'

'Alex Clayton Photography.'

'I'll check. But I'm not warning you again, Fredrick. Stop using the C-word with the other residents. You've upset Ethel again.'

Fredrick was about to tell the ugly blob of a woman that she could go screw herself up her fat ass with a sharpened broom handle, but stopped himself and instead gave her a smarmy smirk.

'It was whilst on a camping trip with friends, during the late summer of '88 when Sheryl Denton vanished in a remote area of the North Downs near—'

The TV went quiet and Alex watched as the female newsreader spoke. Alex realised Ian had muted the TV.

Images of the North Downs came into view and the camera panned along the undulating hills, past the chalk-split, the two ash trees and beyond; then the screen cut to footage of the kidney-shaped lake where forensic teams worked the scene. The secret lake – the place Alex had never spoken of or shown to anyone. Where he spent those warm afternoons chatting with Leo. He grimaced at that grim thought. It appeared different from how he remembered. So desolate, dingy and haunted. A pain seared through his skull as he tried so hard to awaken those memories that had somehow strayed into oblivion. The lake was four miles from the last place they'd all seen Sheryl, thought Alex. *Four miles.* How did she get that far away?

'Tea, Alex?' asked Ian.

Alex shook his head, stared at his father, and was stunned at how well he looked. Ian was lean, clean-shaven, and his grey hair was smartly cut. He wore well-ironed trousers, a crisp white shirt and had on a pair of round spectacles. Alex thought he had the air of a mature and efficient lawyer.

Then Alex wondered if this really was Ian Clayton. How could he be certain what was real and what was imagined anymore? His mind was a complete crazy mess.

'Olivia said you'd recently been in touch with her,' said Ian. 'It's so good to see you again, son.'

'What happened to Kay?' asked Alex.

'She moved away. I heard she's married with several kids now.'

Alex scanned the living room – sparse, clean and modern.

Ian let out a long, sad sigh. 'I'm sorry, Alex. More sorry than you will ever know.'

Alex nodded, eyes fixed on the TV – the lunchtime weather report now – light showers.

'I just wanted to get that out there. So now, I've said it,' said Ian, forcing a smile. 'I turned my back on you… when you needed me the most. I didn't know how to deal with you. Not like Susanna did.'

Alex froze when he saw the row of framed photos on a bright white, Ikea-style sideboard. Among them, his mother, giving the camera a sassy smile, and another of himself aged around three, holding a bucket and spade at Camber Sands. Alex picked up the most intriguing photo of all and studied it.

'You look happy there, Alex. Olivia gave it to me. You must be what, twenty-five?'

Alex placed the photo of himself, leaning on a Lion at Trafalgar Square, back down and picked up the one of Susanna. 'Twenty-eight.'

'That's a nice photo of your mum. Would you like a copy?'

Alex nodded as he struggled to avert his gaze from the photo. She looked so happy and alive.

'Sometimes, Alex, I feel her love for you clouded everything else… she just wouldn't—' Ian's voice lowered. 'It was a sick love, and she smothered you. She treated you like you'd break if—'

'Don't!' interrupted Alex. 'You don't get to bad mouth her. Not you.'

'OK, calm down. I don't want to bicker, but I'm just saying, I don't know who had more loose screws… you, or her,' said Ian quietly.

'And there *he* is,' muttered Alex.

'You don't know everything.'

'I should leave.'

'Alex, wait. We need to talk about this. About what you did!' exclaimed Ian.

'What I did?' asked Alex.

'Alex, I'll go with you. We can explain about… all your issues. Back in those days, mental illness wasn't such a big thing. Kids were just branded weird at school, they didn't diagnose problems as they do now. Christ, there were kids at my school that would have been sectioned these days.'

'Well, you did always call me weird,' said Alex, 'and soft.'

'I'll take my share of responsibility. I should have got you some professional help back then, and we can tell them all this. Explain the situation and make them understand.'

'You want to hand me over to the police?'

Ian shook his head. 'No, no. Not hand you over… just talk to them.'

Alex laughed. 'Wow, a great time to play the role of concerned daddy.'

'Surely this is why you have returned, Alex?'

Alex rubbed both his temples. 'Well, I came here to say sorry, for ruining your relationship.'

'I don't care about all that. You had every right to be pissed off with me, Alex. I was an arsehole, and things would have never worked out with her, she was too young.'

Alex shrugged. 'But I still owe you an apology.'

A long pause followed.

Ian looked down at the floor. 'Look, I had my concerns back then. I think Penny did too.'

'So, you both thought that I—' Alex couldn't bring himself to finish the sentence.

'I will help you deal with all the fallout from this. I owe you that much, Alex.'

Alex's phone rang. He stared at the screen and didn't recognise the number, but something inside of him told him it was essential that he answered that call.

Forty-eight

Fredrick finished the phone call and gazed out to sea. Alex had called him a selfish monster for withholding the information all this time. As he had every right to.

Fredrick thought about his wife and two daughters, and he pictured them so vividly. Both his daughters would be grown up now, but he only ever envisaged them as young girls that were innocent, carefree and adoring. They'd have children of their own by now, and he would be a grandparent. God, how his wife would have revelled in that. He often wondered about the life he should have had. Fredrick cried then. Cried for his lost family, and for the couple he'd killed on his farm, and for the poor girl that had spent thirty years lost to the world; lost to her mother. He was going straight to hell for the vile things he'd done.

'Who was on the phone?' asked Ian. 'Whatever they said clearly shocked you. What's going on?'

Alex fast-walked to his car. 'I need to see somebody. I have to go.'

'But we need—' Ian didn't get to finish.

Alex was in his Jeep and speeding off down the road.

Natalie couldn't believe her eyes when she spotted the Jeep Cherokee go speeding past her in the opposite direction. She was certain it had been Alex's. Slamming the brakes on, she reversed the car, turned it around, and gave chase.

Alex flicked through the Snapchat group and selected Gavin's profile. A horn sounded, and he snatched the wheel, stopping his car from veering into an oncoming bus. He knew the way to deal with Gavin would be face to face, and preferably alone. He'd speak to the others too, but, as strange as it seemed, it was Gavin he wanted to speak to the most, and the one he was most desperate to divulge the information to. The one who, perhaps, needed to hear it the most.

Gavin was on his fourth beer and chaser when he received an audio call via the Snapchat app. It was the last person he'd ever expected to contact him today.

'What?' said Gavin, struggling to keep the anger seething from his voice.

'I need to meet you. As soon as you can,' came Alex's urgent voice. 'Where are you?'

Gavin considered his answer for a moment whilst he sipped his beer.

'Gavin, are you still there?' asked Alex.

He cleared his throat. 'I was actually about to take a stroll. To clear my head. Join me?'

'Where?'

'I dunno, I was thinking, Gallows Hill Wood. What do you think?'

'I'll be there in ten minutes. By the old gate. I need to tell you something.'

Gavin ended the call, walked to the bar area and gave Patrick a confused smile. 'Well, I dunno about you, but I fancy a bit of target practice.'

'Who was that?' asked Patrick.

'I'm taking a slash, then I'm off to Gallows Hill. I've got a date with my old mate, Clayton. He wants to tell me something.'

Patrick watched Gavin go and pulled out his mobile phone.

Natalie's heart was racing. She'd jumped a red light, failed to stop at a pedestrian crossing, and almost lost control of the car twice, in her race to keep up with Alex. She could still see the Jeep in the far distance, but at the rate she was going, she'd kill someone – or herself. Natalie decided to try to call her husband again and try to speak to him. She needed to tell him to stop his damn car and speak to her.

Alex saw Natalie's number flash up on his screen. He wanted more than anything to speak with his wife and explain everything, and say how much he missed her and desired to come home. But now was not the time. Right now he had to focus on his encounter with Gavin.

Alex assumed Gavin intended to hurt him, or worse, so it was a massive risk meeting him alone out in such a rural place, but he was going regardless, because this encounter with Gavin was unavoidable. With just the two of them present, Gavin would have to listen, and, if necessary, Alex would force him to hear his news. He suspected Gavin would bring a weapon to their rendezvous; but Alex wasn't afraid of him, armed or unarmed. He'd taken self-defence lessons and felt he could defend himself if need be. Yes, it had been over a decade ago, but he still remembered how to takedown an armed assailant. He was adamant Gavin would want to hear the information Fredrick had divulged to him.

'What?' asked Ben.

'I'm going to finish what we started,' said Gavin.

Ben screamed inside. Why did Gavin always have to mess things up? Ben held his phone so tightly he thought he might break his screen again. 'The police will deal with Clayton. Don't you dare do anything stupid, Gav.'

'Kinda guessed you wouldn't have the bottle to do what's needed. Your brother is coming.'

'He is?'

'No chances this time. He's not leaving Gallows today. So come... don't come... the outcome will be the same. See ya.'

Ben cursed. This was getting out of hand. He had to stop those idiots, and fast. He grabbed his coat and keys, left the house via the back door, and called Janette as he headed for his car. Ben couldn't think of anyone else who was capable of stopping this madness, because the last thing he wanted was Gavin and his brother going down for murder.

Janette had her phone cradled on her handlebars and she answered via her headphone set. 'Hey, Ben, how you holding up?' she said, out of breath from the last hill climb.

'Gavin's on the rampage, he's going after Clayton,' said Ben.

'Is Alex even in town?' she asked.

'All Gav said, is that Clayton won't be leaving Gallows. I have no clue if that means Clayton's willingly meeting him, or if he's planning to kidnap him or something!'

'Jesus. I can be there in fifteen minutes. Meet me there.'

Ben opened the Range Rover's door, and he was about to get in as his brother's red VW Transporter came speeding up the drive. Shane gazed at him through the windscreen. He looked absolutely fuming.

'What are you nosing at?' asked Kayla.

Ryan was peeking through the lounge blind. He looked at his mum, a perplexed expression on his face. 'Dad has been having a barney with Uncle Shane.'

'What? Is he still out there?'

'No. Shane was shouting right in Dad's face, and it looked like he was going to punch him one, but they both drove away in Shane's van.'

Janette was pedalling like a lunatic. She'd tried to phone Alex, but he wouldn't answer, and she'd left a frantic voicemail pleading with him to stay away from Gavin, explaining that the man was not in the right emotional state and would do something foolish.

Janette considered calling the police, but she was confident that she could handle Gavin herself. She was the one person who could talk him out of taking this mindless action. Even if Alex possibly deserved what was coming. This wasn't the way. Gavin was a massive pain in the arse, but she cared for him more than she liked to admit.

'Pull over here and get it. I need to load and prepare it,' said Gavin.

Patrick shook his head. 'I'm not driving about with you waving a shooter about.'

'I'm starting to question if your uncle even gave it to you.'

Patrick smirked. 'It's in a hidden compartment in the back. Besides, think about it… a gun? You don't need that.'

'Why wouldn't I?' asked Gavin.

'Perhaps we had it right the first time, Gav.'

'What, we should hang him?'

'Maybe he was feeling a little suicidal after finally letting out the truth,' said Patrick.

'We still don't even know the truth, Pat.'

'Whatever bullshit he wants to spin, I say we don't give him a chance. We grab him, noose him and hang that prick from the nearest tree,' said Patrick.

Gavin scratched his chin and nodded. 'Agreed. Do we have anything to use?'

Patrick smiled. 'Got three metres of tow rope.'

'That might work,' said Gavin.

Gavin glanced at Patrick, noticing how much he was sweating. It was cold today, and the heaters were only on a fraction. The man had been acting strange since they'd left his uncle's caravan. Patrick was always so composed and calm, and he never appeared agitated under any circumstances. He guessed Patrick was super keen to take his revenge, but yet again, Gavin thought back to that missing swing, and he couldn't shake the image which was irritating him. Christ, he needed to get a grip.

Since he'd sped along a quiet country lane, Natalie had lost sight of Alex's Jeep, and not helping was a low mist that had layered the area, making visibility poor. She'd passed three different turnoffs, so had no clue if she was even following the correct route anymore. Natalie was so engrossed in searching for Alex's Jeep, she almost didn't notice the cyclist shoot out from a concealed turning. Natalie slammed on the brakes and stiffened as she brought the car to a skidded stop. The mountain bike ended up coming to a halt on a grass verge, and the rider toppled off and landed in a bush.

Natalie sprung out of the car to check on the rider. 'Are you hurt? I'm so sorry. Ah dinnae know these roads.' She considered she wasn't technically at fault, but the stern-faced woman looked riled as she pulled herself up, so decided it was best to pacify her. As Natalie approached, palms held up, the woman's mouth dropped open, and she stared at Natalie with a look of consternation, and it suddenly dawned on Natalie that she hadn't contemplated the ramifications of her visit to the area. She'd not even considered the consequences of running into someone that would mistake her for Sheryl Denton. The girl whose face was today plastered all over the television and social media.

'I'm looking for a grey Jeep Cherokee. Don't suppose you've seen it, hen?' asked Natalie in the chirpiest tone she could muster.

Forty-nine

He brought his Jeep to a stop and got out in front of the main gate. The thin track leading to Gallows Hill Wood was a squelchy mess of sodden and churned sludge. The iron gate had, at some point, been rammed at the bottom, and was twisted and bent out of shape. Two huge tractor tyres lay in front of it. Alex made his way through the boggy mud, opened the boot and removed his walking boots from the boot bag. No sooner than he'd changed his footwear, he heard a diesel engine fast approaching. Alex gazed along the track, seeing a black mud-splashed Hilux racing towards him. He slammed the Jeep's boot down and tried to recall where he'd seen this vehicle before – he was certain he had. He couldn't see the driver as the windows were dark and tinted. It was going so fast it aquaplaned to a stop, blocking the route back out. Two men got out. The passenger was Gavin, wearing a black beanie and leather gloves. The driver wore jeans, and a faded black leather jacket, over a grey hoody, with the hood up. Alex only needed a fleeting glance at that face to perceive it was Patrick Lynch standing there. The expression on Patrick's face said it all. It said, *'You're utterly fucked, pal.'* And Alex knew there was now just one option available. He half ran, half slid towards the gate, clicking his Jeep shut as he went. He cursed when he remembered his phone was still charging on the dashboard and there was no chance of getting to it.

Alex quick glanced over his shoulder, seeing both men struggling and skidding in the mud in their bid to reach him. He jumped onto one of the tyres and vaulted over the gate.

Alex raced into the trees and once again, he found himself running for his life in Gallows Hill Wood.

'Where is Gavin?' asked Ben, peering out of the van's window and gazing at the quarry entrance. This place creeped him out. He always remembered those ghost stories about the skateboarding kid that got sliced in half during a storm. Shane got out of the van, his face like thunder. They'd got into a major slanging match on the brief journey here, almost resulting in Shane pulling the van over and the brothers having a dust-up. Now Shane was ignoring him, his expression that of a sulky child who'd been told by his mother that he wasn't getting any sweets for the foreseeable future. Shane slammed the van's door and started making his way into the misty trees, stomping as he went.

Ben got out, stepping around a pile of abandoned wood, as he followed his brother into the trees. He guessed Gavin had gone in via the top of the byway, or maybe he'd used the gated entrance. He just hoped he wasn't too late to stop his bullheaded friend from making a huge mistake.

A fox cub darted in front of Alex as he made his way through the squelchy mess. Even wearing decent boots, the going was tough. He turned to see Patrick struggling in the sodden mud behind him; he caught Alex's eye and shot him a hateful glare. There was no sign of Gavin.

Janette had removed her bike's tyres and placed her bike across the backseats of the BMW. As they travelled, she just couldn't stop gawping at Natalie. It was so surreal to be sitting next to her.

'Must be weird, hey,' said Natalie, guessing what Janette was thinking.

Janette gave her an uncertain look. 'How long have you been married to him?'

'Eleven years.'

Janette couldn't comprehend any of this. Scottish accent aside, she was sitting next to an adult version of Sheryl. She'd put Sheryl's photos through plenty of ageing apps, and the result was the exact face she was staring at now.

'You've just found out?' asked Janette.

'I have,' said Natalie.

'Jesus, Alex has some serious explaining to do.'

'I'm sorry about your friend. That poor wee lass. I can't even begin to imagine.'

Janette didn't reply, instead she sent Alex a message via Snapchat telling him she'd just run into his wife and they were both searching for him.

Gavin had never been much of a runner, but nowadays anything more vigorous than a brisk walk resulted in severe sciatic pain that darted from his lower back to his ankle. He was now furious with Patrick; he'd totally screwed up the plan they'd agreed on. Gavin was supposed to approach in a calm and friendly manner, start chatting with Alex, and then unexpectedly charge him to the ground. Only then was Patrick meant to appear and wrap the rope about his neck. Instead, the moron had raced up the lane, leapt straight out, and sent Clayton bolting off into the wilderness. Then Patrick had raced after him like a possessed lunatic.

Gavin's trainer got sucked into the gummy mud and he groaned. The place resembled a swamp.

A group of mean-looking crows watched him from their perch on a skeletal tree, as Alex took stock of where he was. The mist sat thicker in the deeper part of the woods, which in a way was comforting, as it meant he'd be harder to locate. There was no point attempting to reason with Gavin now. His plan had gone out of the window when he'd shown up with Patrick, and it was evident by the belligerent expression on Patrick's face that he hadn't come along for a little chit-chat or to reminisce about bygone days. Alex decided his best course of action would be to discuss the new developments with Janette and approach the police with the new information; though God knows if they'd act on it. Patrick showing up hadn't been something Alex had even considered. Had Patrick somehow predicted what he'd planned to tell Gavin and wanted to silence him?

Alex thought back to Fredrick's phone call and what the old-timer had told him as he spoke in that harsh, throaty grumble.

Fredrick had stubbornly refused to speak to the police back in '88, and Alex knew why he hadn't mentioned the information he'd furnished him with today, because, by admitting what he'd seen, he was inadvertently confirming that he *had* been present on that tragic day. Once he'd confirmed that, the police would have never stopped their dogged investigation until they'd buried him. From what he'd heard, they'd already been unrelenting in their quest to incriminate him.

Alex's heart was thudding as the memory of his previous encounter here came flooding back. He could almost hear the shouts and curses coming from the boys as they hunted him that grim day. The terror had been overwhelming. But he'd not succumbed to them, and he'd fought back and escaped, and he'd do whatever was required to repeat that scenario.

He stood in the circle of dead trees. It was a chilly day, but even colder air lingered in this unsettling place. Just as it always had done. The location always evoked images of a secret ritual circle. The sort of macabre place an eerie cult would sacrifice a victim and spray fountains of their blood across the age-old, gnarly trees. Patrick remembered all the depraved things he'd done here all those years back. Not that he necessarily regretted everything, but, no matter how sick and atrocious, they were still a part of his character. Though his ethos may have altered as he matured, the urges diminished, and his hunger for slaughtering contained – his passion to kill, or inflict pain, was still a constant one. He had one regret, though. One major regret. Sheryl Denton. The way things panned out that stormy summer's night on those hills… Patrick hadn't wanted that.

He'd liked and admired Sheryl, and it was a rarity for him to feel anything for another person. Empathy was one of the many emotions he wasn't accustomed to feeling.

He'd been hiding down in their camping area when he saw her hit the ground. She'd landed with a stomach-turning smack, just a few metres from where he'd been crouching. And he couldn't believe it when she pulled herself straight up and started ambling away into the trees. The shock from the impact, he guessed. Her right arm appeared bent out of shape, and she looked in a bad way. Her forehead carried a deep, five-inch gash. Sheryl hadn't got far when her legs buckled and she collapsed to the ground. Patrick run to her, gently scooped her up, hoisted her over his shoulder and carried her away. He recalled how light she was. How broken she felt. When he found himself on a chalky pathway, with knotted tree roots splitting up through the ground, she started to recover consciousness. He placed her down into the mud. Then Sheryl saw him, and her eyes had opened impossibly wide, and she freaked out when she'd caught sight of his face. Patrick tried to calm her, spoke in a soothing tone and tried to reassure her he was going to help her. He wanted to save her. But she screamed then and fought, scratching and slapping at him with her unbroken arm. So he was forced to clamp a hand down over her mouth. Then what played out in the moments that followed was completely out of his control.

Alex used his Garmin watch to find the nearest thing to a road and set a path to follow it. He found himself at a sloping, leafy pathway that was littered with discarded tyres, bags of rubbish and smashed up bathroom parts. He started climbing up through the abandoned junk. A vehicle must have been used to ditch the stuff, which meant that some sort of road must be near. He glanced behind – nothing but misty trees surrounded him.

Alex froze and listened, hearing a faint sound of voices ahead of him. One he was certain belonged to Ben. The voices drifted away, and he continued the climb. He considered the second voice could be Shane, in which case all the guys had turned up to the party.

Janette and Natalie left the car and continued on foot, knowing the mud was too deep for the BMW to handle.

'There's Alex's Jeep,' gasped Natalie, 'what about the black truck?'

Janette stared at the Hilux. 'No idea.' She knew it didn't belong to Gavin. Unless he'd pinched it.

Natalie peered into Alex's car and tried the door. 'He left his phone in there.'

Janette assumed that was a bad sign, but didn't say as much.

'What will that man do?' asked Natalie.

'I'll deal with him. He's my ex. And he listens to me.'

The pair stared at the entrance to the woods. Janette considered the place would be a perfect setting for a sinister scary movie where two dippy females trudge into the misty trees, never to return.

'After you,' said Janette.

Gavin opened up the floodgates and sighed with relief. He could piss like an elephant, especially when he'd necked a couple of sherbets. As he urinated at the base of a withering tree, he gazed around the shadowy woods and felt a stabbing pain in his testicles. He received regular pains down below. Ever since he ripped his nut-sack open during his last visit here. Gavin was certain that's why he had never fathered his own children. He was shaking himself off when he heard deep voices. He zipped up and pressed himself against the tree and crouched on his haunches.

'I'm not going to keep debating this. We need to find out exactly what Clayton wanted to tell Gavin,' said the irate voice. Gavin knew it belonged to Ben.

'I don't care! You promised you'd take the secret to the grave, Ben. You swore on it. We're family,' boomed the other voice. Gavin recognised that unmistakable voice. It belonged to Shane Napier.

'Keep your voice down, Shane!'

Shane grunted a response that Gavin couldn't hear.

'And what about Sheryl's mother, Shane? You don't think that poor woman wants closure?'

Shane let out a long sigh. 'You'll regret this, Ben. They'll find something… The DNA profiling and all that clever forensic stuff they can do is insane.'

'They *won't* find anything,' said Ben. 'I was so careful. Believe me.'

'Mate, I get it. I do. With Clayton back in town, it probably seemed like the ideal time, but it was stupid. You should have let this be,' said Shane.

'I can't handle this anymore. Every time I look at Molly, it breaks my heart to think of the awful pain Eileen has suffered. All those years of not knowing… of holding onto a tiny shred of hope that—' His voice faded and became inaudible.

Gavin peered around the tree and watched the two bulky shapes vanish into the mist. Gavin gripped the tree so hard, the bark tore away in his hands. He tried to process what he'd just overheard. He felt so repulsed and outraged that his legs became weak and he almost crumpled to the ground.

Patrick stood on the byway and lit up a roll-up. The lane was set in a tunnel of coiled and disfigured trees and the ground had two large, water-filled tyre scars running through it. He leant against an abandoned fridge freezer and scanned the mess. Rows of appliances, bags of rubble and bricks were strewn all over the place. This lane was a well-known dumping zone, and the authorities had surrendered their effort to stamp it out. He was quite certain Alex would end up coming out this way, so he reckoned that to stay put was the sensible option. The lane winded downward to the quarry entrance, and from there it was a short trek to a quiet country road. Heading up the byway also led straight out of the woods, though it was a harder, hillier route, and had been the direction Clayton opted for on their last unforgettable encounter here.

Patrick, thrilled at the prospect of their one-on-one showdown, moved his head from side to side, clicking his neck. For all these years, he'd visualised the pain he would like to inflict upon Alex Clayton. He had ruined his dream of joining the Marine Corps. That idea flew out of the window the day he'd lost his bastard fingers. No special operations force accepted disabled people. His love of stealth, intrigue with killing, and thirst for action would have been catered for in that profession.

Patrick had been so obsessed with stealth as a boy, and he wondered if it was because he was so unsightly that he preferred to stay hidden from the prying eyes and mocking stares. He spent entire days keeping to the shadows and following people around. He'd followed the little weirdo Clayton too. Patrick knew he had issues himself – but that nutter, wow, he was in a league of his own. He once tailed Clayton through the woods and watched, mesmerised by the boy's baffling behaviour. Patrick spied from behind bulky trees, spiky bushes and lichen-covered logs, as Clayton trekked through the woodland and chatted away to his *special* friend like he truly believed he was there. Patrick trailed him to the secret fishing lake, watching in awe as he spent the afternoon gabbling away to himself animatedly. It had done Patrick's head in, and he wouldn't have believed it, not in a million years, had he not witnessed it with his own keen eyes. Patrick didn't even know about that lake. God knows how Clayton had happened across it.

Patrick flicked the roll-up away.

After around two minutes, Alex stepped through the mist.

'And they all lived happily ever after,' came a low growling voice. Ben and Shane stopped, gazed at one and another, before turning around. Ben sighed in relief when he saw Gavin standing there. But that relief soon dissolved when he noticed the mean, twisted look on his friend's face. Then his heart thudded in his chest as he considered what those words meant.

Gavin glared, his face reddened, and the veins in his temples bulged.

'Gav,' was all Ben could muster in a meek voice.

Fifty

In a slow, calm movement, Patrick removed his knife from the inside pocket of his jacket. He popped the button on the tanned leather sheath and slipped out the blade, all the time keeping his stare fixed on Alex. The black, six-and-a-half-inch blade was super sharp, and it had a serrated back edge. The weapon was an Ontario Mark III, and a standard-issue knife for the US Navy Seals and Patrick carried it everywhere.

Alex took a step back, his eyes flicking around the rubbish heap, keen to locate a weapon of his own no doubt.

'What happened last time you came at me with a blade, Patrick?' asked Alex.

Patrick merely sniggered at this.

'So, what was it you were so keen to tell Gouchy boy?' asked Patrick, keeping his tone friendly.

'Fredrick Killner called me earlier. He told me he saw you following us that day.'

Patrick shrugged. 'What *day* do you mean?'

'He said he watched you hide your BMX in the bushes. He mentioned the bike was sprayed chrome. He was quite specific about that.'

'Nope, not me, I was out of town,' said Patrick, amiably.

'I dunno, Patrick. "He was wearing army gear. And he was an ugly lad with nasty skin. Very spotty," were Killner's exact words.'

Gavin felt so betrayed, his heart physically hurt. It was as though an invisible beast was shredding the organ with its razor-sharp talons. He pressed a hand on his chest and prayed this wasn't the onset of a heart attack.

Ben stared at him with a sad and regretful expression plastered over his chunky, pathetic face.

Shane was scowling at him, fists bunched like he was going to throw a punch at one of them. Gavin was sure if that gun were in his grasp, he would have shot Shane straight in the bollocks, there and then, and smiled whilst doing it.

'No wonder you lot were so keen to go after Clayton. Makes sense now,' said Gavin, glaring at Shane as he spoke.

What a total idiot he'd been, thought Gavin. They had fed him crap, and he'd gobbled it up without question. How could he have been so blind and stupid? If they'd hung Clayton like they'd all planned to, everyone would have assumed the lad took his own life because of guilt and remorse.

Patrick laughed. He couldn't believe that mad pensioner even remembered him. Yes, he'd seen Killner's Land Rover parked up in a lay-by that afternoon, though he wasn't aware that he had noticed him because he'd been too busy trying to observe the group's movements. As a kid he considered Killner to be a total legend. He didn't take any shit and Patrick respected him for that.

Patrick smiled at Clayton. What did this ponce think was going to happen here? Did he think he'd just break down and confess to everything because he had stumbled upon a clue? Did Clayton think he was in an episode of Scooby Doo? When Patrick finished up here, he'd be leaving town for the foreseeable. He'd move to his cousin's place – a sprawling traveller's encampment near Cardiff – and he'd drop off the grid and hide out for a year, or at least until all the madness with the media and police died down. Not that he expected the police to find any firm evidence to connect him to Sheryl. And Shane wouldn't talk. Ben was, and always had been, the weak link in their group, but Patrick would never admit to anything. So let the fat wanker blubber like a big baby, because he would only end up incriminating himself. Patrick knew he'd been the one that had cracked and unearthed her body. He couldn't believe he'd held out for so many years.

Patrick ruminated about how things had played out after Sheryl's death. There'd been a palpable sense of relief when he found that phone-box in Hollingbourne village and knew he could rely on Shane to help him; the boy was thick as hippo crap, but stupidly loyal to him, believing they had some sort of bond. His parents had left their car at home that night, as they'd gone to an anniversary party, so Shane took it, along with a length of chain from the shed, some plastic, and some weight plates from his bedroom. Shane didn't even ask Patrick why he needed his help and what the stuff was for, he just came to his aid with the items that Patrick requested. In an unfortunate twist of fate, they'd gone and run into Shane's dozy-arse brother trudging down that lane, and things got complicated.

Patrick delivered his best sinister smile. 'I was on a night exercise with the cadets. Evade and capture. I remember it well because a thunder flash exploded right by my hiding spot. Maybe they have historic records that can be checked. Maybe they don't.'

Janette and Natalie found themselves lost in the wood proper. The mist was denser, and after several attempts at phoning Gavin, they'd decided it would be best to find their way out of this grim, maze-like place.

'So, do you have kids, Janette?' asked Natalie.

'No… no, I don't. I always wanted a daughter, but it never happened… I miscarried a girl once. When I was in my early twenties.' It baffled Janette that those words had slipped out. She'd told nobody about that baby. Not even Will.

'Aww no, so sorry to hear that. How far gone were you?' asked Natalie.

'Five and a half months. Technically, it was a stillbirth. I never even told the father. I didn't see the point. We weren't together at the time, anyway.'

Janette knew she should have told Gavin about the baby. He would have blamed the Gouchy curse, of course. Gavin and that stupid curse. Sometimes even *she* thought it existed – bad luck did seem to follow that man.

Natalie gave her a sad smile, and Janette couldn't help but see Sheryl standing there. Was that why she was being so open with this woman? Was she secretly acting out a scene she'd dreamt about all these years? Where she spoke to her oldest friend as though she was still here and alive today. Still her best mate and the person she would turn to when life got too much to cope with, or when she desperately needed a sympathetic shoulder to cry on, or someone to waffle nonsense to when she needed to let off some steam, moan about her drab job or complain about her fella's incessant snoring. She'd never found another friend like Sheryl. Not a proper best friend.

Janette wiped the tears that were pricking the corners of her eyes.

'And I'm so sorry about your friend, hen,' cooed Natalie, 'I truly am.'

Natalie hugged her then, and Janette embraced her back.

Janette considered this was possibly the most surreal moment of her life, but for just a fleeting moment, this Scottish stranger with a calm and endearing voice, made her feel closer to Sheryl than anything, or anyone else had done, since the day she disappeared.

Natalie stepped back from the hug, now confused by her aberrant display of sensitivity that, for those brief seconds, had completely overcome her.

Alex took several steps back, his gaze flicking from the knife to Patrick's face, waiting for any indication of his advance. He hadn't prepared himself for this confrontation. Gavin, he could handle. He wasn't afraid of him – but Patrick terrified him; he always had. Gavin had a temper and was quick to lash out, but Patrick Lynch was capable of anything. Alex crouched and made a grab for a piece of broken roof tile, and as he snatched it up, Patrick sprung forward, and Alex propelled the tile; it hit Patrick's jaw with a thwack, causing his head to snap back.

'You've got this all wrong, Gouchy boy,' said Shane, trying to sound jocular.

Gavin shot Shane a look of contempt. 'I can see by the look on Ben's face you're talking total bollocks, Shane. So just button it, you silly fat cunt.'

Shane shrugged, crossed his arms and offered Gavin a disdainful sneer. 'And who will listen to anything a loser like you has to say?'

'Don't you worry, I'll make them listen,' said Gavin.

Shane moved towards Gavin, a sly grin etched on his face. 'Yeah, we'll see, mate.'

Ben shoved Shane in the chest. 'Enough!' he bellowed.

After she heard a shout that sounded like it had come from Ben, Janette raced off in the direction of the noise. 'Come on, this way.'

Natalie attempted to chase after Janette, but her flat shoes were caked in so much mud, she struggled to walk, let alone run. She had no chance of keeping up.

The injury sent Patrick into a raging frenzy and he steamed towards Alex like a demented beast. The knife caught Alex across the face and he felt a seething pain in his cheek. He stepped away and held a hand against the gash, as thick, warm blood seeped through his fingers. He found himself backed up against a row of festering fridges. Patrick was grinning psychotically now, his teeth red with blood and tiny lumps of flesh. A deep wound was gaping open on his jaw, but he seemed not to notice, or care. He came at Alex again with the knife. Alex grabbed for Patrick's knife hand, but his palm was slick with blood and he struggled to grip his wrist. The pair grappled and fought and Alex found himself down in the wet mud, with Patrick atop of him, as they wrestled on the ground for the weapon. Then Patrick's fist hammered into the side of Alex's head with such force, it was akin to being walloped with a hefty wrench. Alex battled to stay conscious, but his vision swam and he knew he was in serious trouble.

Fifty-one

Natalie wondered how her life had taken such a bizarre turn. Not so long ago, she was married to a man she loved and admired, ran a thriving business, and was content with her life. Now, she was at the other end of Britain, lost in a spine-chilling forest that wouldn't have looked out of place in a hammer-horror movie, and wondering if her husband was some sort of mental case and if life would ever be the same again. To top it off, she had to deliberate on the hideous thought that her husband had come back home to remove his childhood girlfriend from the lake he'd concealed her in thirty-odd years ago. Not to mention she was practically the dead girl's doppelgänger. Her resemblance so uncanny, the girl's poor best pal had used her as some sort of conduit to connect with her lost friend. Though she understood. Of course she did. But this was a lot to digest, and just thinking about it all made her mind spin and her head hurt. Natalie couldn't recall a time where she'd ever felt so alone and afraid, and she wanted nothing more than to be back home in Scotland. To be with her sister and parents, where she'd be safe. But her husband owed her some explanations, and she wasn't leaving without getting them.

As Janette approached the three men, they all went silent. Ben avoided her gaze and looked as though he was on the verge of crying.

Shane just glowered at her.

Gavin met her eyes and there was a deep sadness in them. She could see his chest heaving and his hands were shaking at his sides. Janette could read Gavin. She always could, and the look of utter betrayal was clear on his face. Janette stepped towards Ben. He gazed at her for mere seconds and broke down. Ben trembled as he sobbed. 'I'm so sorry, Jan. Ah, God, I'm so, so sorry.'

Patrick booted Alex in the side of the head several times. He was out for the count now, and he'd rolled sideways into a watery tyre rut. Patrick thought about leaving him there to drown. But he didn't. Instead, he pulled him out and kicked him a couple more times; this time on the other side of the head, just to even out the damage. He wanted him alive. At least for a while, so he could take his revenge. He stood over Alex and smiled at the state of his head. It had ballooned up nicely and his eyes were bulging like two purplish golf balls.

Ben saw the murderous glare his brother was giving him, but that wouldn't stop him. It was way too late now. Through the sobs and snivels, he tried to explain what had happened. That shortly after he'd left the camping area, he'd stared in confusion at his dad's blue Ford Orion as it came bumping up and down that craggy byway. How he'd been so pleased his dad had somehow found him out there. How he hadn't expected Shane to be driving. And when he'd spotted Patrick in the passenger seat, a surge of dread washed over him.

Mark's taxi was out of the traffic and was twenty minutes from Maidstone. He'd left Janette a message, saying he was on his way to find her and that he was so sorry about the news. Mark knew she would be in bits and would be desperate for a friendly shoulder to cry on. He also tried Ben, Alex and even Gavin, but everyone was either going straight to voicemail or wasn't answering. Then he considered all those times his manager had tracked him down. For weeks Daan was secretly following his movements using the Snapchat app. So he opened the app and clicked on the recent group chat Janette had created under the name - *The Brookacre Pack*. He selected Janette's profile.

As she watched the snivelling wreck in front of her, Janette wondered if she was fast asleep and trapped in some sort of bizarre nightmare.

'I didn't know what happened, I swear it. I didn't have a clue. All I did was sit in the back of my dad's car like a scared pussy as we all drove in silence.'

Janette wanted to say something – anything – but her mouth became so dry she couldn't swallow and her throat felt like it was on fire.

Patrick put a knee on Alex's right forearm, pinning it down. Alex whimpered and moved his head to the side. Patrick slapped him about the face. 'Oi, wake up, Clayton. You don't want to miss the best bit now.'

Ben felt like a scolded schoolboy confessing, with snot, tears and dribble smeared on his face. He wiped the back of his hand across his nose and sniffed. The hatred poured from Janette and Gavin. Their expressions contorted into speechless grimaces.

So he tried to make them understand why he'd stayed silent. 'When they got out, I sat in the car with my eyes shut. I knew what they were doing. But I was so scared I couldn't move from that seat.'

'You stupid idiot, Ben,' groaned Shane.

Ben scowled at his brother but ignored him. 'When they finally came out of the woods, Patrick got in the back with me. He was wet and smothered in mud. He stared at me the entire journey. Fixed me with a nasty glare, whilst holding his razor. We dropped him back to find his bike, and we never spoke about what they'd done.' Ben eyeballed his brother as he said, 'We referred to it as "the forever secret." I couldn't stand seeing that car on the driveway, knowing she'd been in the—'

Ben moved his gaze to Gavin, and to his surprise, he didn't look angry now - he looked deflated and broken-hearted. Ben knew how deep this betrayal would have cut Gavin. The years of sharing their grief. The rage, the tears, the finger-pointing. But they'd been brothers-in-arms, and they'd always watched each other's backs. Them against the world. Yet he'd kept this wicked secret from him all these years, and that would be a bitter pill to swallow.

'I needed you there, Gavin. For all my bullshit posturing, I was nothing but a fraud. A chicken,' said Ben. 'You'd have stood up to Patrick and tried to stop him. Even if it meant you joining her in that lake. You would never just sat there like a helpless... pussy! You would have done something, I know you would. Because you were the fearless one.'

Ben sat down, head in his hands, and wailed in rasping sobs, mucus hanging from his nose. Even Clayton would have put up a fight, thought Ben. If only Ben hadn't ordered him away, at least he wouldn't have faced that horrid moment alone.

'It was months later when I plucked up the courage to go into those woods. When I found that lake, I knew it was the right place. For years I visited… I'd talk to her and say how sorry I was that I left her there. Sorry for being such a spineless mug. Knowing she was alone… it was unbearable. Sometimes I'd stay down there for hours, talking about those long summer days and letting her know she'd not been forgotten.'

Patrick placed the knife across Alex's ring and baby finger. Alex looked up at him, though he couldn't open his eyes fully now. That was a real shame because Patrick would have liked him to watch. But you couldn't always have everything.

Janette leaned against a tree to steady herself. She stared at the pathetic man crying on the floor and could find no words in response to what he'd said. A pain stabbed her stomach, and she heaved. Then she comprehended Gavin was shaking her and saying something.

'Jan, Jan… listen to me,' said Gavin, his face a mask of concern. 'Patrick is here. He came with me.'

Patrick pushed down the blade. He knew the blade was sharp, but it still surprised him how effortlessly it severed those two fingertips. The delayed scream Alex let out was ludicrous, loud and high pitched. It reminded Patrick of that unforgettable day he'd removed half of that teacher's face. The scream had been very similar and made Patrick feel somewhat nostalgic. He smiled, proud of his work.

'Jesus,' exclaimed Janette, 'what was that?'

Gavin was already racing off.

Janette gave Ben one final icy glare and sprinted after Gavin.

Patrick used one hand to muffle Alex's cries of agony as he placed the knife across Alex's middle and index finger.

Alex tried to move his hand, but it was a feeble attempt. This time Patrick used the serrated edge. He started sawing.

Natalie heard the ghastly screaming and followed those grave cries. Her blood ran cold as she emerged onto a byway strewn with discarded junk. Amongst the rubbish heap was a sight that would haunt her for the rest of her life – a grotesque man with a blood-smeared knife, pinning down her husband and hacking away at his bloodied hand. The man froze, mid slice, as he gaped at her with massive bulging eyes and blood oozing from his jaw. He then pitched backwards, as though he'd seen a ghost, and scrambled down the byway away from her.

'You stupid prick,' mumbled Shane.

'And where are you going?' asked Ben, following his brother.

'To pack. I'm off. Tonight. I'll go to Tony's place in Lisbon. You have fun mopping up all this shit.'

'You don't get to just go. No way, Shane. You can face the fallout with me.'

Shane spun and rounded on his brother. 'Do you think you'll come out of this with any sort of life? Do you think Kayla will forgive you? You've ruined everything, Ben. Why couldn't you just leave things be?' With that, he started marching away. Then he broke into a jog.

Patrick hadn't hallucinated before, or not without a serious amount of drugs, anyway. It was this place. It was fogging his mind and toying with his head. He didn't believe in all that ghostly afterlife nonsense, no more than he'd believed all those silly stories about the boy that died in the nearby quarry. He needed a stiff drink. That's all. Then he'd jump in his truck and be on his merry way to Wales by this evening.

Alex groaned in pain as he caught sight of the obscure face gazing down at him. For a moment he thought it was his wife, but dismissed that notion. That wasn't possible.

'Alex, we need to get you out of here,' said the blurry face. It sounded like Natalie, but he was sure he must be imagining things. That was until she took hold of his butchered hand, and he yelled in agony.

Shane got to the van and wrenched open the door. Ben grabbed his arm, yanking him back. 'I need you to back me up on this. Please, Shane. It's time for us to face the music.'

Shane looked past him, his brow furrowed in confusion. Ben followed his brother's gaze. Patrick was standing there. He held a blood-covered knife at his side, his arm was drenched in gore, and his jaw was smashed open.

Looking at Shane, Patrick said, 'I need a lift back to my motor. If you wouldn't mind. It's parked on the other side of the woods.'

Ben puffed out his chest and stared defiantly at Patrick. 'Put the knife away, Pat. Come on. It's over.'

Patrick turned to Ben, delivering him a venomous sneer. 'If you say so, hero.'

'Where now?' asked Janette.

Gavin spun on the spot, trying to gauge the correct direction.

'This place is a damn labyrinth... I think up there,' said Gavin, heading under a colossal oak tree, its long branches resembling huge, outstretched, octopus-like arms.

Natalie put her two leather gloves over Alex's hand and tied one of her jacket toggles around them. Blood was already seeping through, and she knew he'd lost a lot of blood. She helped him to his feet. 'You need to walk, Alex.'

'Are you my wife or an angel?' muttered Alex.

'Both,' she said, 'now move your dopey wee arse.'

Natalie guided her husband in the opposite direction to which the vile man fled.

Patrick saw the murderous glare on Shane's face and guessed he was no longer part of the Patrick Lynch fan club. 'Come on, Shane. In the van now.'

Apprehensive, Shane gazed at Ben, then back to Patrick, unsure what to do.

'Don't make me ask again, Shane.' said Patrick. Then, out of the corner of his eye, he saw Gavin charging at him, and the wind was wiped out of his lungs as he thudded onto the ground.

Mark looked at his phone. To his annoyance, Janette's Snapchat icon hadn't moved from the lane close to Gallows Hill Wood. He worried something bad had happened to her. He'd tried her mobile several times, and it just kept going to voicemail.

'Gavin!' yelled Janette.

Patrick and Gavin rolled around, arms and legs thrashing about as they grappled in the mud.

Janette searched a nearby rubbish heap for something to use as a weapon. On offer was a mouldy armchair, rotten wood planks and a Calor gas cylinder.

Patrick spun Gavin over onto his back. A fierce struggle for the knife broke out. Blood gushed from Gavin's lip. His hand was sliced and slick with claret. The pair grunted and hissed, kicked out and punched. Gavin snatched a handful of Patrick's hair and jerked his head downwards. With the other hand, Gavin held Patrick's knife arm, stopping him from stabbing at him.

Janette went to grab the cylinder, then saw a mass of broken concrete hidden under a swath of thick, hair-like moss and greenery. She snatched up a jagged piece with both hands.

Patrick grabbed Gavin around the throat, pulled his knife arm free. He prepared to plunge the blade down.

Ben leapt forward and clasped Patrick's knife arm, then brought his knee into Patrick's chest. It connected with a clomp but did little to stop the man.

Patrick turned the attack on Ben, sending him whirling back as he dodged the blade's threatening arc.

Ben skidded and fell backwards, smacking down with a heavy thud.

Shane watched all this with a dumbstruck expression, as though he wasn't quite certain which side to assist in the fracas. Then he shouted, 'Stop... Patri—' He didn't get to finish his sentence, because Janette let out a shrill cry that rang through that place like a chilling, barbaric battle cry, as she slammed the concrete down across the back of Patrick's head. It hit with a sickening crunch. The blow felled the man, and he landed sideways with a dull thud. Not giving Patrick a chance to react, Janette raised the concrete high, and brought it down once more, pounding Patrick's temple with a loud, grisly smack.

Janette pitched forward and crashed down onto her knees, her breathing raging.

Patrick's legs twitched for several moments. His body spasmed. Then he was motionless.

Fifty-two

'Pull over,' shouted Mark.

'What's wrong, boss?' asked the driver, bringing the car to a stop. Mark jumped out of the taxi and stared in utter disbelief at the pair ambling along towards him. Alex looked like he'd been run over by a herd of stampeding rhinos, and was being propped up by an attractive woman, who was trying to tap on her mobile phone. And he would swear that woman was the absolute spit of Sheryl Denton; well, an adult version of her, anyway. He did a double-take at her. What the actual fuck was going on here? Had he fallen asleep and woken up in the frigging twilight zone?

'We need help,' said the blonde, speaking in a Scottish accent, 'I've just called an ambulance, but—'

'Quick, get him in the cab,' said Mark, helping the woman.

Jesus, he'd need to ping the Uber driver a major tip after this.

Rain pounded down and Ben could not move his gaze away from Patrick's body. The smell of blood and putrid crap filled his nostrils, and he put his hand over his mouth to stifle the stench. Janette was on her knees, shaking and staring into the trees. Gavin crouched down next to her, put his arm around her, and pulled her close, whispering in her ear. 'You don't need to see this, Jan. Just keep your eyes closed.'

Shane was frozen to the spot and gawped at Patrick with a stupefied expression.

Ben felt this turnout could work out for the best, because somehow he'd calmed himself, and he was thinking clearer now. He'd quit with the self-pity bollocks and started thinking about his survival, and about keeping his family, his life, and his freedom.

'Calm down, Jan. It will be OK,' said Gavin.

Ben tried to stop gazing at the grisly wounds on Patrick's head and so stepped past him. 'We can sort this, Jan.'

'We need to call somebody,' said Janette. She stood up and stepped to where Patrick lay. 'Is he dead?' she asked, her tone cold as she eyeballed the crumpled mess at her feet.

'Yes, Jan,' said Ben.

Janette wiped her tears and stared emotionlessly at Ben. 'I'm not sorry.' She took out her phone and started punching in numbers, but Ben stopped her.

'Get the hell off me!' she shouted, shoving him away. 'Don't come near me. Don't you *ever* come near me again, Napier.'

Ben held up his hands. 'Jan, this is, at the very least, manslaughter. You could go down for this.'

'It was self-defence,' she said.

Ben hovered a hand over Patrick. 'Jan, don't you get this? Look at the state of his head. And his face. You stove his skull in.'

Gavin glared at Ben with an expression of pure malice and shook his head in disgust. Ben was certain Gavin had guessed his plan, but Gavin would do anything for Janette; because deep down he still loved her, and he always had. And being as though Patrick's head appeared as though someone had squashed it in a vice, their options were limited.

Gavin prised the concrete from Janette's tight grip. 'He's right, Jan.'

Janette shook her head and backed away. 'Gavin, no… no, we can't do this. It's—'

'What? Immoral?' said Gavin.

'Open the van doors, Shane,' demanded Ben.

'No. Screw this, Ben. We're not going down that road.'

'You did it for Patrick, and now you can damn well do it for Jan!' Ben spoke through gritted teeth and glared at his brother. He didn't stop until Shane finally understood what he was doing here. He was trying to save their arses and trying to wrap the four of them in a new shared secret that would bind them all to silence. Then he heard footsteps and the four of them spun to face the new arrival heading down the hill.

Mark Corker's face was a mask of pure shock when he took in the grim scene in front of him. 'Um, I'm guessing I missed the pa—' He didn't finish the sentence, he turned away and leant against the van's bonnet, his mouth dropped open and he grabbed for his vape. He sucked on it so vigorously, you'd have thought his life depended on it.

Janette held out the palms of her hands, letting the powerful rain cleanse the blood from them. Then she screamed.

Fifty-three

Twenty minutes after dropping off Mark and a subdued Janette back to civilisation, he took the Hilux back to Patrick's caravan. He was glad the vehicle had the tinted windows, as he knew any cameras that captured its movements, wouldn't have identified him as the driver. Gavin cleaned away all trace of himself, then took the muddy riverside pathway route away from the industrial area. He kept his hat on, his head down, and luckily, didn't spot anybody during the drop-off. He crossed over the river and met Ben and Shane. The pair had been shopping at Wickes for some clean-up equipment.

The three of them travelled in a nail-biting silence to Shane's lock-up on the outskirts of Chatham. Gavin had to admit that Shane's storage area was impressive. It was huge. The size of a barn. He had his KTM dirt bike in there, plus his jet-ski, mountain bikes, golf clubs, fishing gear and several wetsuits. Together with a ton of various sporting equipment and random junk. Ben often said his brother had fleeting obsessions, spent a fortune on the kit, then only used the stuff on the odd occasion. Seeing this place, he wasn't wrong. Even his girlfriend didn't come here and did not know the amount he squandered on his so-called hobbies. Shane worked in sales and marketing in central London and made some serious dough. Gavin would have been surprised if Shane could sell a perfect vision package to a blind lottery winner, but what did he know?

Shane started rummaging for items as Gavin checked out the rigid inflatable boat that was perched on a trailer. The outboard for it sat on a tubular sack barrow that had a ratchet strap keeping it fixed in place. It had been Ben's brainwave to use the RIB. They'd zip out to sea in the early hours, under the guise of a fishing trip, and dump Patrick in the ocean. They'd bleach the van within an inch of its life, burn all their clothes, and never speak of the incident again.

Shane tossed several chunky padlocks to the ground, then speaking to his brother, said, 'Take that plastic off my son's kayak, that's like a giant bag. And we can slide some weight plates in there with him.'

'Good idea,' said Ben, doing his brother's bidding.

'Six hundred quid and the ungrateful arsehole ain't even used it yet,' complained Shane, as he struggled with two sixteen kilogram kettlebells, which he placed by the entrance. Rolls of industrial tape, weights and chains joined the equipment pile. Shane had everything required here to get the job done.

Ben tugged the thick plastic off the kayak.

'Gouch, gather up the fishing gear. And grab us some buoyancy aids,' said Shane, as he wheeled over the sack-barrow.

Gavin stayed in the lock-up whilst the brothers lumbered out to the van with the gear. As Gavin gathered up the rods and jackets, he heard Ben dry heaving more than once.

Gavin stripped off his clothes and tugged on a wetsuit that was hanging on the wall. It was a tight fit, so he assumed it must have belonged to one of Shane's sons, as there was no way that fat bell-end could fit in this himself. As he re-dressed, he could hear chains being dragged, metal clanking on the tarmac, and Shane snapping at his brother.

'Will you answer her!' said Shane.

'Stop bitching at me, Shane. I'll call her later, I'm hardly going to chat to my missus now,' said Ben.

Ten minutes later, Gavin walked outside to see Shane scrubbing the inside of the van, and the smell of strong bleach stung his throat. Then he saw the package sitting atop the red sack barrow, now laid down at the rear of the vehicle. The brothers had bound Patrick's body in plastic, taped it, coiled two metres of the chain right around the bundle, and for good measure, used an industrial ratchet strap to finish the job. He had to admit, he was impressed with their efficiency. They were professionals at this. Ben looked chalk white, though, and his eyes were wide and bloodshot.

It was still dark when they reached Sandwich Bay. Fog hovered low on the water, and it was a chilly morning. It didn't take long to get the RIB down to the water's edge as it was high tide. Gavin was happy he had on the wetsuit, despite it making him move like a defective robot. There wasn't a soul in sight as they loaded Patrick and the fishing gear onto the craft. When they returned the trailer to the van, Shane suggested Gavin stay with the motor, but he told him he wanted to see that scumbag sink. Plus, it would have been strange if one of their fishing party stayed behind. He was going with them. End of story.

Ben struggled to pull on a tight wetsuit jacket and said, 'Well, shall we get out there and do this?'

The craft glided through the morning waves. The wind was low, and the sea calm as they zipped along. They cruised a good five miles out until the land behind them was nothing but a fuzzy smudge of lights. Gavin guessed they reached about twenty miles per hour, and he was looking forward to having a go on the outboard himself. Gavin picked up the concrete he'd taken from the quarry entrance and propelled it out into the sea. Then he threw Patrick's knife. After another five minutes, Shane slowed the boat and cut the engine, letting them drift.

'Let's get this over with,' said Shane.

Ben grabbed the handles to the sack-barrow. 'OK, I'll take this end.'

Shane set the two kettle balls on top of the bundle, and using the padlocks, secured them to the thick chain. He then picked up the footplate end. 'Right, go.'

Gavin didn't help them lift. He observed the pair struggling to heave up the bulk, veins bulging in their necks as they grunted from the effort. They dropped the barrow over with a satisfying plop, and Patrick sank into the blackness.

As the pair leaned over and watched, Gavin stepped forward and booted Shane hard in the back, sending him hurtling overboard with a huge splash.

Ben spun around. 'What the—'

'You can join that fat wanker,' said Gavin.

Ben nervously eyed the black revolver pointing his way. He put his palms up. 'Gav, please. No, mate. Don't do this.'

Gavin wiggled the weapon. 'You can drop in with a bullet in your flabby guts if you'd prefer. But you are going in there.'

'Who gave *you* that thing, Gavin?' asked Ben, his voice filled with apprehension.

Gavin snorted. 'That is the least of your concerns right now.'

'Think of my kids. My daughter. Please. I'm begging you. I'll do anything,' pleaded Ben.

Shane swam over to the boat, and he reached up to the side and started to pull himself up. Gavin kicked him square on the nose, and he plunged back in.

'Get in, Napier!' spat Gavin. His words came out with such aggression, Ben recoiled and nearly fell over the side.

'I was just a stupid kid when this happened, Gav. This is madness,' said Ben.

'I thought we'd always be friends, Ben. And I trusted you like a brother.'

'I'm sorry. You have to believe that.'

'In!' said Gavin.

Gavin thought he'd need to fire off a round or two to get Ben to comply, but after a few more aggressive waves of the gun, Ben obediently slid over the side.

As he watched them struggling in the freezing water, Gavin started to wonder if the gun worked. He mulled over shooting a few rounds, then decided it wouldn't be a good idea to attract attention. Not that he could see any signs of activity out here.

Gavin moved to the rear of the boat and placed his hand on the outboard.

Ben was crying and pleading for help. 'My kids. Think about my kids!'

Shane, to his credit, was being more stoic and was glaring with hard eyes and cursing, albeit with his teeth chattering together. A nasty cut had swelled on the ridge of his nose.

Yes, Gavin felt bad for all their kids. It wasn't fair to Ben's little girl. But he'd made a solemn promise. To himself, to Sheryl's mum, and Sheryl. Should he ever learn for certain that anyone had hurt or killed her – he'd somehow take revenge. And that was that. He'd never forgotten. Thirty years later or not, it made no difference. The two men bobbing about in the water also knew this, because he explained this to them often enough during the years they hung out together. Maybe they presumed he was beer talking. Just silly Gouchy boy being full of bullshit, as usual. Gavin wondered if they'd been laughing about it behind his back, sharing secret looks and taking him for a complete mug. He envisioned all these things and more. He'd been powerless to take action for all these years because he hadn't known the truth, but now he did.

Ben struggled to stop his jacket from going over his head. 'I was a boy,

Gav… I was just a frightened boy. Not a single day has passed by when I haven't regretted what I did.'

'I think it's more what you *didn't* do,' said Gavin.

Ben blinked and choked on a wave that slapped him in the face.

'Patrick may have killed her, but you chose to lie to us for all this time, Ben. You let her rot down there whilst you carried on with life as normal. So, you don't get to carry on. That can't happen.'

'It wasn't like that, Gav… please let me explain. We can talk about this.'

'You only came clean now, because you knew we'd all blame Clayton. Admit it.'

'I'm your best mate,' said Ben.

Gavin sighed theatrically. 'If you say so. Oh, and Shane, if you're secretly thinking that those flares might get you out of this pickle… think again. Because I removed them from your jackets at the lock-up.'

Earlier Gavin had watched the pair tuck their phones away in the dry-bag, along with the yellow PLB rescue unit that Shane told them could send out an SAS signal and trigger a rescue alert. That would come in handy now, thought Gavin. They should count their lucky stars that he'd let them keep their buoyancy aids on. He'd at least given them a chance of survival. Admittedly, it wasn't much of one. He was freezing his nuts off and he was nice and dry.

'Wait, wait. Gavin, just listen and wait… please,' said Ben. 'Ten grand. It's yours. Today. No, twenty. I can get you twenty.'

'Twenty?' asked Gavin.

'I swear on my children. I won't go back on my word.'

Gavin nodded and pretended to muse on this offer. His best chum didn't know him at all.

'Hey, I have an idea,' said Gavin, 'pretend this is like one of your tests. If you can survive, say… I dunno, two hours. I'll come back and rescue you. If you are still alive… I'll pull you out, and you pass the test. Deal?'

'You're twisted,' spat Ben. 'You keep going on about the Gouchy curse, but I think it's *you* that's cursed. You're like a disease, and you infect everyone who comes into your life.'

'I guess you're right,' said Gavin thoughtfully.

Gavin recalled his first test. Ben and Shane captured an adder from Colt Wood and placed it in a hollowed-out tree stump. Gavin was told to take off his t-shirt and to hold his hand deep in the dark hole for five minutes, during which Shane and Ben dumped hundreds of red ants all over his naked torso. The snake which he later identified as a large grass snake, not an adder, hadn't chomped down on his hand, though the ants had had a great time biting the crap out of him. Why? Simply because Ben knew Gavin hated snakes. Gavin was also terribly claustrophobic, and another test resulted in him being placed inside an oil drum, stuck in the ground and being covered in rocks and soil. They fed a hosepipe inside so he could use it to breathe, but Shane thought it would be funny to pour water inside. He'd been half-submerged in dirty water by the time they'd let him out. Ben told Gavin it was all about overcoming his fears, but in reality, he summarised that Ben just got a kick out of making people suffer. Alex's tests had been far worse, though.

'Well, good luck then, lads,' said Gavin.

'Gavin, I know you're messed up because of what happened to Zara... and Isabella, but—'

'Shut up, Ben! You can't talk your way out of this.'

'Is ripping my family apart really the answer?'

'Bye, Ben.'

'No, Gavin... please. No, don't—'

Gavin pulled the cord to start the outboard. Ben was calling out and made a feeble attempt to re-board, but Gavin twisted the tiller and sped up the boat with a jerk, sending Ben reeling back into the sea.

The RIB cruised away.

Gavin had been tempted to steal Shane's van but perceived it would be a foolish move. Instead, he headed in the general direction of the launch point and barrelled along the coastline toward Ramsgate. He planned to abandon the craft near Pegwell Bay and plod into Ramsgate on foot. En route, he would pop their phones into a bin, and get a train to Canterbury. There, he would have a nice fried breakfast before making his way to Maidstone.

He started thinking about his retribution on that arsehole Skender. He'd taken revenge for Sheryl; now he made a silent oath that he intended to do the same for Zara.

Gavin gazed out to sea and couldn't help but feel an immense surge of remorse. He wouldn't have been able to pull that trigger on Ben, not in a million years, but justice needed serving, and they'd wrangled out of any chance of being implicated legally.

Ben *had* been his best friend since they were snotty-nosed brats, they'd been through so much together over the years, and he was a huge part of Gavin's life. Tears streamed now, blurring his vision, and it took all his willpower not to spin around and bolt back to save him.

Ben was blowing his whistle like a madman.

Daylight began creeping in, but he kept focusing on the moon that was high above him and kept telling himself he wouldn't die out here. A part of him hoped Gavin would return for them, and that this was just some sick and twisted payback he'd concocted, but, ultimately, he was just messing with him. Though deep down, he knew that was nonsense. He'd almost pissed his pants when he'd spotted that gun. What idiot would put a shooter in that man's hands?

He let the whistle drop from his mouth. 'Shane… talk to me. Shane!'

His brother didn't respond. He felt guilty he was now wearing his brother's wetsuit jacket. Even if he was glad of the extra layer. But his legs, face and hands were numb beyond belief. He swam over to Shane. 'Stay with me. Do you want to try swimming?'

'I can't… move,' said Shane, his voice quiet and peculiar. His face carried a bluish tinge to it, and Ben knew his brother couldn't hold out much longer. He was also adamant that neither of them could swim the length of the average swimming pool, so there was no point attempting to swim to safety. They'd never make it to the shore if it were a fraction of the distance.

Shane stopped shaking and was staring at him with wide, unblinking eyes. Ben felt his brother had already given up. He contemplated if the early stages of hypothermia had set in. He was doubtful he would survive another hour out here. Ben saw the first glimpse of the fuzzy sunrise edging up on the horizon, and under different circumstances, it would have been a beautiful sight. It reminded him of his recent early morning visit to the secret lake. He'd gone just before sunup. It had taken a while to pluck up the courage to start the grim task of searching the water, and he must have looked like a right lunatic, wearing his fishing waders, two pairs of rubber gloves and Ryan's swimming cap and goggles. The water was past his neck when the long pole he was using to dredge the lake hit on something significant. He sank under and fumbled to grab hold of something he could yank on. It was harder than he had expected. On the third attempt, he pulled the bundle by a piece of chain. He didn't once look back, but something fell away as he dragged Sheryl's remains to that decaying rowboat.

The sea splashed over his face and his vision swam. His contacts were ruined now. That's all he needed.

'It wasn't even him,' mumbled Shane.

'What?' asked Ben, assuming his brother was just ranting nonsense now. Then Ben's jaw locked up, and he was worried he'd no longer be able to speak.

Shane's breathing was shallow and his eyes looked like they belonged to a frantic animal. 'Pat… trick… told me… he didn't kill her.'

Ben stared at his brother and wanted to drown the dense idiot himself. Why hadn't he told Gavin this? That information could have been the ultimate bargaining chip. 'Wh… what did… you keep from me… Shane?' he sputtered.

Fifty-four

He'd been awake for a while, though couldn't bring himself to open his eyes to the world. Feeling an overwhelming sense of failure and sadness, he considered it might be best if he didn't wake up. He heard the nurses chatting earlier, and he had been semi-awake when the police officers visited, but he pretended to be out cold. One of the staff explained to those officers in no uncertain terms that this patient wasn't up to talking, and they should return tomorrow at the earliest.

Alex felt like he'd messed up in a spectacular fashion. Patrick would be long gone by now, and he was no closer to ending this. How would he ever prove Patrick's guilt?

The familiar voices in the room jarred him from his gloomy thoughts. It sounded like Mark and Janette.

'That nurse has arse cheeks that could crack a walnut,' he heard Mark say.

Alex opened his eyes. 'Shouldn't you be in Milan, Corkscrew?'

'Hey, he rises,' said Mark. 'They predicted rain for Milan, so—'

'Where's my wife?' asked Alex, his voice sounding hoarse.

'Gone outside to call her sister,' said Mark.

Mark seemed on edge. Then he considered how rough Janette looked; she appeared as though she carried the weight of the world on her shoulders, although he guessed he didn't look a million dollars himself.

Alex winced as he sat up, moving the drip tube, and elbowed the pillow in a vain attempt to get comfy. He owed them an explanation. Of course he did. He opened his mouth to speak, but upon spotting Gavin standing in the corner, he almost fell out of bed in disbelief.

Gavin sat down on a chair, crossed his legs, and smiled cordially. 'How are you getting on, Clayton?'

Gavin had a fat, cut lip and his hands were both bandaged.

Janette tapped Mark on the shoulder and motioned for the door, and said, 'We'll let you two have a chat.'

With that, they left.

Alex wondered if he should buzz for the nurse.

'I'm glad they could save some of your fingers,' said Gavin.

Alex examined Gavin's face, assuming that he'd spot a hint of loathing or mockery, but there was none. He looked genuine and sounded it too.

'We need to speak about Patrick,' said Gavin, then got up, reached for a jug of water and poured some into a plastic cup. 'Here, take a drink.'

Alex went to accept with his bandaged hand, frowned and received it with his left. 'Thanks,' said Alex, taking a sip and wondering if he was dreaming. When Gavin reached into his pocket and took out what looked remarkably like his mum's brooch, and held it in his splayed hand, Alex thought he must be.

'I found this bit of junk in my old bedroom. I stashed it in my Paul Daniels magic kit.'

Alex put down the cup, gingerly accepted the jewellery piece and stared at it, wary and confused.

Gavin sat back down and grinned. 'I did a sneaky little magic trick of my own, and I swapped it over with a chunk of rock. I wanted to be a magician so badly when I was a kid, but I kept that a secret of course, otherwise the nicknames would have driven me bonkers.'

Alex traced his fingers over the item. It was in perfect condition. He gave Gavin a cynical look.

'I always intended to give it back. I was waiting for you to finish your tests, and, well... stuff happened.'

'Yeah, stuff happened,' repeated Alex, not taking his eyes from the brooch.

'Perhaps by giving it back I'll break my family's curse.'

'Curse?'

'Doesn't matter, it's all a load of horseshit, anyway. Right, so, I know we're never gonna be best friends or anything, Clayton.'

'No, that would just be weird.'

'But, I dunno, maybe not enemies,' said Gavin.

Alex nodded. 'OK. Agreed.'

Gavin stood up and winced in pain.

'Are you hurt bad?' asked Alex.

Gavin smiled. 'Yeah, I've been in the wars a bit, though I can hardly complain about my injuries, can I? I mean, you look like you've been used as a plaything in the gorillas' enclosure at Howletts.'

Alex grinned. 'They might have gone easier on me.'

Gavin cleared his throat. 'OK, we need to get our stories straight.'

'Sorry?'

'About what happened in Gallows Hill Wood,' said Gavin.

After they finished their discussion, Alex's head was hurting, so he pressed the button on the handset to administer himself some medication. It was a relief to learn that the group knew Patrick was the guilty party, but everything else was quite inconceivable. He didn't know if he should be chuffed that Gavin and the others felt they could trust him enough to bring him into the fold, or concerned about the secrets they now expected him to keep. God knows there'd been too many of those already, but knowing that justice had been done, albeit unethically, was some consolation.

The pair sat in reflective silence for ages. It was Alex who broke it when he chuckled and said, 'Sheryl would have been pleased about one thing.'

'What's that?' asked Gavin.

'That the two of us are finally… well, seeing eye to eye, if you like.'

Gavin gave him a broad grin. 'Yep, she was on my back all the time about giving you a break. Sheryl liked you, Clayton. God knows why.'

'It's a mystery.'

'I'll be honest, Clayton, I gave you a hard time because I… I guess I was jealous of you. I kinda had a thing for Sheryl. A mad crush, if you like, and then you turned up—'

And for the first time in Alex's life, he gave Gavin an unadulterated smile and the deep hatred he held for his rival began to fade. Because there was something they'd both had in common all along, though neither of them had realised it, he considered. They had both adored Sheryl, and they had both been so deeply affected by what happened that late summer's night, that it had changed their lives forever.

Mark watched the footage Daan sent him on his iPhone. The music venue was buzzing and Trent was annihilating the place. His roadie appeared to be revelling in the limelight, as he pumped his fists and cracked out some intense, banging beats. Trent's set had been astounding and was receiving rave reviews all over social media. Trent told Mark that his shredded nerves faded the moment he'd seen his name rolling across the enormous screen above the DJ's booth, in vivid, bold letters – *DJ Trent R King.*

With his manager placated, that was at least one less thing to worry about, although he was loath to ask about how the situation regarding his stolen bank funds was going. He caught Janette's eye as she ordered coffee at the busy hospital canteen. The last few days had taken a toll on the poor woman, and it showed. She gave him a lazy smile as she paid for the drinks. Finding out what happened to Sheryl should have brought her some sort of peace and delivered a conclusion to this terrible situation, but the secrets unearthed and the events that unravelled, meant more torment, more worry, and ultimately more heartache. Life wouldn't be the same for Janette again, nor would it be for any of them; himself included. She had been against telling Alex everything that had transpired, and, surprisingly, it was Gavin who insisted that Alex be brought into the mix. For two reasons. The first being that having everyone on the same page would lower the risk of conflicting stories. And the second was that he reckoned Alex had every right to know the truth, after everything he'd been through, both back in '88 and in recent days. This then raised the debate that they should also give Eileen the full story, but both Mark and Gavin had disagreed, saying that this would be too risky in case she notified the police who were a constant presence at her residence since the case reopened. Though Mark had a sneaky suspicion that once everything started calming down, Janette would somehow tell the grieved woman the truth. If he knew Janette, he was almost certain that she would, and he wouldn't blame her. After all, Eileen needed and deserved to learn the truth more than anyone.

Fifty-five

They travelled in silence for over an hour and were just leaving the M25 when Natalie switched off the radio. 'What happens when we get home?'

'I think you should get Evan's car valeted. It's filthy, and the back seats are covered in mud,' said Alex.

'Don't insult me.'

'Sorry, Nat. I'm sorry about everything.'

Alex thought back to the day he met Natalie. He'd done some detective work and a day or two of surveillance to prepare for what he'd planned – a subtly plotted chance encounter at a café. It took him a while to pluck up the courage to ask her for directions and engage her in conversation. It had been far easier than he'd expected, and it was soon apparent that, although Natalie was the very image of Sheryl, she was in fact Scottish born, Natalie McCloud. She wasn't, nor ever had been, Sheryl Denton. Alex's theory that somehow Sheryl's father was involved in her abduction and moved Sheryl to Scotland, was soon quashed. But something unexpected happened during their encounter. Something he hadn't planned on. They hit it off, and they liked each other. No, more than that – there had been an instant and intense attraction. Fate seemed to be the only way to rationalise it, and as things progressed and a steady relationship flourished, how could he have confessed?

At the time he thought it was romantic. It seemed like a genuine love story, because they'd lived at each end of the United Kingdom, yet been brought together by these incredible circumstances. All because of a single childhood photo that Natalie shared on social media. The photo that Alex had seen on someone else's Facebook feed. The photo which had triggered another search in Scotland and changed his life. He'd deliberated the circumstances from Natalie's point of view and knew his actions could be perceived as deceitful and even a tad creepy, but when exactly would have been a good time to pop that into a conversation? *By the way, Nat, now, you're gonna laugh when I tell you this. It's quite a story. It's about how we first met—'*

Alex had confided to his nan about the situation with his new girlfriend, and she'd told him to do what *he* deemed right and sensible. She also confirmed that she would not interfere in the matter.

When he'd explained this to the others, Janette said she wouldn't have been impressed, and placing herself in Natalie's shoes, she'd consider divorcing him. Mark didn't comment, but he'd been enthralled by the story, and Gavin, well, he'd just nodded thoughtfully and said he understood why he'd stayed quiet.

Alex tried to find some profound words for his wife. Words that would communicate this unambiguously. But they didn't come, or perhaps they didn't exist. Sometimes words were not enough, he considered.

'I fell for you, Natalie,' he said.

'What we had, was all a lie, Alex.'

Alex shook his head. 'No. I swear, what we had is real. What we *have* is real. It always will be.'

It was a while before she responded, and when she did, she spoke in a sad, broken voice. 'I'm gonna need time… to process all this. You have to understand that?'

Alex nodded. Of course, he understood. He had plenty to process himself.

'What do you mean? Who did them in?' asked Gavin.

He'd phoned Sammy as soon as the train left St Pancras International Station. He sat alone, supping on a can of lukewarm Heineken.

'Word is, after they set that fire, they crashed their motor at speed. CCTV footage placed a third man at the scene, and the bizzies reckon it was some internal beef, though the third guy hasn't been identified,' said Sammy. 'Sorry about your girl, man. That was a sick, twisted and cowardly move.'

'Dead? Both of them?'

'The huge fella died in the ambulance, and that Skender lad is messed up bad. Major head trauma and he's still in a coma. Fingers crossed he croaks it,' said Sammy.

'Thanks for digging into this. I owe you,' said Gavin.

'The boys have all been asking where you're at, Slash. They miss getting bladdered with you. And miss all your crazy shenanigans, bro. Are you coming back?' asked Sammy.

Gavin smiled, pleased to hear his work pals were asking after him. He looked outside as outer London flashed by and he processed Sammy's news. He'd be lying if he said he hadn't felt an immense surge of relief – because the prospect of going after those men by himself was a grim and scary one. If Skender recovered, Gavin pledged to return to the city, but for now, he would hide the revolver in his dad's shed.

'You still there, bro?' asked Sammy.

'Tell the guys I'll catch up soon. But I won't be coming back for the foreseeable,' said Gavin.

He intended to jump off the train when it stopped at Luton and get the first available one back. After everything that had happened, he knew Janette would need him back home, and he didn't intend to bail out on her again.

Natalie woke with a start. Her hair was drenched in sweat and her heart palpitated. She turned to Alex, finding him fast asleep on his back with his bandaged hand laid across his chest. Natalie sat up and recalled the dream. She'd been back in that awful place – Gallows Hill Wood. She'd been alone and sprinting barefoot through that byway lined with rows of deformed, dead trees. Her feet and hands were bleeding from a mass of deep slashes. She'd actually felt the pain in the soles of her feet as she ran; each step worse than the next. She stopped and checked the wounds, lifted her feet in turn to examine the deep gashes. And then Natalie realised *he* was shadowing her, sneering, eyes blazing and bloodied combat knife in hand. Turning to run, Natalie saw the girl from North Berwick, dripping wet, face mangled and teeth broken. She started laughing at Natalie. When she'd gazed back down the lane, Natalie cried out… because that creepy man held his blade to Sheryl Denton's neck, who was now on her knees in front of him, pleading for Natalie to rescue her. He smiled as he began slicing her throat.

Natalie snapped out of the dream before he killed Sheryl. Now, though, she considered that perhaps the girl hadn't been Sheryl, because she wore a light blue, vintage check dress. A dress that belonged to Hannah, and that Natalie had been fond of borrowing.

She slipped out of bed and padded across to her husband's bedside cabinet. Alex didn't stir as she rummaged inside and snatched out his sleeping pills. There was half a glass of water he'd used to take his painkillers, and she picked it up. Alex let out a gentle snoring grunt and Natalie was so tempted to empty the drink straight over his head. Even the thought generated a chuckle as she necked two pills and sipped the water. Her husband's face looked a mess, though strange as it was, he also seemed at peace in that moment.

Natalie grabbed the fluffy throw from the bottom of the bed, stuck two pillows under her arm, and headed to the lounge. She'd watch TV until the pills took hold and sent her off again.

Fifty-six

Janette paused her watch timer and tugged her water bottle from the front pouch of her running vest. She took a deep swig, gazed around the byway and wondered why she'd ended up here. It hadn't been her intention to come this way. She crouched down to the spot where Patrick died and shuddered. What happened still didn't seem real. None of it did. Speaking to the police was hard, but she stayed calm, focussed and kept it together. Well, she hoped she had.

Janette walked over to a log, slung off her running vest, and sat down. Peanuts came over and sniffed the log. Janette gave her two biscuits and considered that this seemed as good a place as any to have a proper think on what she needed to say. She considered writing everything down, rehearsing it and then burning the notes, but decided against that ridiculous idea. The right words would soon come to her once she was with Eileen.

After Sheryl's funeral, Janette would sit Eileen down, pour her a stiff drink and tell her about Patrick. There was a risk involved, of course, but she'd take that risk because there was no other option. Eileen had suffered enough. She needed closure, and Janette would give it to her and suffer any consequences that followed.

After twenty minutes, Janette put on her running vest, and took a final scan of the area. Then she pictured Alex running past, not even fifteen years old, and being forced to run for his life, as Ben and the gang chased him with weapons. He had told Mark that the gang were going to hang him from a tree. This thought made her shiver, and she was surprised that Alex had ever been able to muster the courage to return to his hometown; she wondered if Ben would have ever let out his secret, had Alex not come back.

Janette called Peanuts over and they set off. She didn't intend to return to this place again.

Alex sat back in his chair and gazed around his office. He was glad to be back, though he had no idea when he'd be ready to return to business as usual. It had been nine days since his encounter with Patrick.

Alex placed his hand on the desk and attempted to visualise what it would look like once they removed the dressing. Adjusting how he used his cameras and equipment would be a challenge for starters. He stared over to the spare office chair and half expected to see Bassem sitting there, slurping on a cold cappuccino, or chomping on a chocolate bar. He wondered if he'd ever see him again. It was quiet in here without him. Alex tried to use his imagination to make him materialise and chuckled to himself. It didn't work that way. He couldn't control Bassem. But it would have been nice to speak to him about everything that happened and hear his crap jokes regarding his missing digits. He wouldn't have abstained from bombarding him with silly wisecracks. Perhaps he'd see Bassem again… perhaps.

He should ditch that broken iMac, he thought.

The police had yet to release Sheryl's remains, so they'd set no funeral date as yet. He'd agreed to accompany Mark, Janette and Gavin to the service, once a date was set, so they could all finally say their goodbyes to their childhood friend.

In a way, the four of them were now bound to one another by the lies they'd paved. That thought worried Alex, but perhaps not as much as it should, considering the repercussions should one of them slip up.

Like Alex, Gavin had given a false statement to the police, just as they'd agreed. Gavin confirmed he was present at Gallows Hill Wood, saying that he'd agreed to meet Alex after they spoke on the phone. He'd been in the pub with Patrick when he received that call, and witnesses could clarify that. On the journey there, Patrick confessed to Gavin that he'd been involved in Sheryl's murder, the concealing of her body, and that he planned to hang Alex to make it appear that he was indeed the guilty party. When Gavin refused to help, Patrick went for him with the knife. They fought and Patrick stormed off after Alex alone, vowing to kill them both. By the time Gavin caught up, something he'd struggled to do because of his bad back, Patrick had beaten Alex half to death and fled.

Alex corroborated Gavin's story, adding the part that he'd received the information about Patrick from Fredrick's phone-call, and that he'd already visited him in Herne Bay to speak to him in person. Alex knew there'd be records for both. The police didn't question Natalie over the attack, which may have complicated matters. When the officers arrived at the hospital, she'd just left with Janette to collect Evan's car and his Jeep, which Janette then parked on her driveway, where it could stay until he returned to Kent to collect it.

Ben and Shane's fate remained a mystery to Alex, and the part they played in helping Patrick was, as far as he was aware, not divulged to the police. What Gavin had done to the pair was chillingly calculated, and when Gavin had said, 'They wanted to stay and keep Patrick company,' none of them could quite believe what they were hearing. Nevertheless, Alex found it difficult to find any sympathy for the brothers. They'd carried on their lives as normal for all these years, withholding that awful secret that had affected the lives of so many others. It was hard to comprehend how Ben kept that under wraps, especially as he was a father himself. A brother's bond, he summarised. Simple as that. It also made what they did to him unforgivable, and even more heinous. When he thought about Ben leading him to the premeditated ambush the boys had orchestrated, made his blood run ice cold. The weird thing was, that part seemed even more deplorable than the events that unfolded afterwards.

For once, it was Ben who took the brunt of Gavin's wild and unpredictable nature. Quite fitting, he thought. After all, hadn't he helped to create Gavin's unpredictable persona, anyway?

Alex checked the recent news reports and hadn't yet stumbled across a story about two middle-aged anglers falling overboard on that stretch of Kent coast, or anywhere along the English Channel. He even phoned the listed number for Napier Renovations, but the line rang out with nobody answering the call.

In the days since returning to Edinburgh, Alex slept better than he had in months. It was as though he'd found an off switch, and the dreams no longer plagued his nights. Things were still strange with his wife, which was to be expected, but he vowed never to give up on their relationship. Natalie staying at the flat came with one non-negotiable condition – Alex must be evaluated by a psychiatrist of her choosing, and she'd already booked his first appointment with a Dr Kapadia, a specialist in psychiatric and personality disorders; and according to his wife, one of the most qualified in the city. He considered it a good thing. He didn't want those memory blackouts to return.

Alex reached into his pocket and pulled out the brooch. He studied it for a brief moment and placed it in his desk drawer. He'd linked up with his dad on social media and swapped a few photos. Alex had contemplated on the idea of popping in to see him on his next visit. He'd yet to decide if he would.

It would be a lie to say he wasn't suffering any trauma after what happened to him. On several occasions, he'd been gazing at his reflection in the mirror, examining the state of his new, deep facial scar, only to see Patrick standing behind him, with a predatory grin, and murder in his bulging eyes. Alex could even smell the musty tobacco and ripe stink of stale alcohol on him. But, after a few blinks, the sinister manifestation would vanish, and he would just remind himself he was gone forever.

Fifty-seven

Eduardo's mind swam with scenarios. Did Alex Clayton know the truth, and he'd just been playing mind games with him? What was all that weird talk about him having a twin brother? It was all driving him insane with worry. He glanced at the photo of his family and bit his lower lip in frustration. Alex Clayton turning up freaked him out, but the news reports about that girl, just the very next day, had shocked him to the core. He felt like he was suffocating and it was like life as he knew it would soon come crashing down as his murky past reared its ugly head.

Now it was official. It took over a week, but the media finally reported that the girl's remains had indeed been that of the missing girl, Sheryl Denton. The police issued a statement confirming that they were searching for a man wanted in question with the case. The photo of Patrick Lynch wasn't the most flattering, and he appeared every bit the demented killer. Eduardo had shuddered and almost chucked up when he caught sight of Patrick's mugshot on the news.

Eduardo cast his mind back to when everything started. That day when everything changed. The day he'd come across the spotty boy in an army surplus shop in Maidstone, the year before the girl's death. He'd never seen such a funny-looking individual. The boy, oozing attitude, followed him outside and offered to take him on. If he didn't accept, he told Eduardo he'd shoot him in the jaw with his new catapult.

Eduardo, happy to oblige, followed the boy in silence to a derelict garage forecourt. Then the pair went at it like a couple of wild animals. Eduardo beat him, but it hadn't been an easy scrap. Patrick just didn't quite possess the skills to defeat him. His style had been more akin to street fighting, with the odd karate move thrown in; whereas Eduardo had been trained in Ninjitsu and Jujitsu.

That fight was the first of numerous frenzied encounters. They'd meet in secret, mostly in the woods, though sometimes in empty playgrounds, and battle it out with knives, nunchucks, and often recreate fight scenes from their favourite martial arts and ninja movies; something they both had a fondness and deep obsession for. Often they'd need medical care after their brutal contests. They both loved the bouts, and it wasn't about proving to anyone else who was the best. They never fought for an audience. It was just about them. A weird bond soon grew - a deep and toxic friendship that was always going to end in disaster. They started moving their twisted friendship to the next level, discussing other depraved fantasies they shared. Patrick told him about the tests his friends from the Brookacre carried out, so Eduardo suggested a new version; a more egregious version that would put everything to the test. *A real manhunt.* Eduardo wanted to go after the thieving little nerd, Alex Clayton, and Patrick's target had been the lanky arsehole, Mark Corkscrew, or whatever they called him. Patrick hated him with a vengeance. Eduardo told Patrick that this was for real and they'd race to get the job completed. This wasn't birds, dogs or cats – this was serious stuff. When night fell, they'd go after them.

When that Sheryl girl fell during the storm, their plans changed. Though as far as Eduardo had been concerned, another opportunity had presented itself.

When Patrick crouched down beside the girl, Eduardo whispered in Patrick's ear. 'Do it. I dare you. Just do it. She thinks you're a freak! Slice her neck open.'

Patrick placed his straight razor blade to her throat. He wanted to do it. Had it been one of the other kids laying in that muddy puddle, Eduardo was adamant he would have done the deed, but it wasn't – it was Sheryl. So Patrick could not follow it through. The more Eduardo considered things, the more he believed Patrick intended to rescue her.

Eduardo pushed him aside, put his hands about her skinny neck, and throttled her. It took longer than he thought it would.

Afterwards, he remembered laughing nastily at Patrick. He called him a total pussy and said it was his mess to clean up. It was only fair. His part was done. At first, he thought Patrick was going to lunge at him, but instead, he gave him a meek nod and scooped up the girl's body. And Eduardo watched as he trudged off into the rain-soaked night, cradling her limp body in his arms.

One week later, Eduardo returned to Alberta in Canada, and he didn't come back to England for another three years.

Eduardo poured himself a large, neat vodka and took a tiny sip. It was such a curious thing, but when he recalled that day, which he often did, it always evoked that smell – that aroma of fruity chewing gum, that had emanated from the girl's mouth during her last breaths. It was always so potent; a hundred times stronger than it had been on the actual day. Then his vodka smelt of it, causing him to shove it away.

He'd once again shut himself in his kayak cabin whilst he gathered his thoughts. There was no way his family could ever learn about his past. It would destroy them.

Eduardo couldn't eat or sleep, or even look at his children without feeling an unrelenting surge of panic, guilt and remorse. He stared at the door fearfully, as though at any moment it would burst open and the police would crash in to arrest him. He knew he'd have to find out if his secret was safe and do whatever was necessary to keep it that way.

ABOUT THE AUTHOR

I was born in 1979 and live in Kent with my wife, children and Dalmatian, Dexter.

I ran a private investigation agency for over fifteen years; dealing in cases that involved breach of contract claims, commercial debt recovery, and process serving. My agency also specialised in people tracing, so much of my work revolved around tracking down debtors, dealing in adoption matters and locating missing persons.

Since 2014, I have worked self-employed in the pet care industry, and I am a keen trail runner, mountain biker and kayaker.

I've had a huge passion for screenwriting for many years and started writing novels during the first lockdown. My first novel, *The Tests*, published on Amazon in 2021, was based on a spec screenplay that I originally wrote back in 2009.

My second novel, *The Feud on Dead Lane*, a dark gritty crime thriller, will be available in early 2022.

If you would like to be informed about my new book releases, don't forget to subscribe to the newsletter @ robertkirby.co.uk/subscribe.

Printed in Great Britain
by Amazon